T I E R R A

TIERRA

Contemporary Short Fiction of New Mexico

✣ Edited by
Rudolfo A. Anaya

Cinco Puntos Press El Paso, Texas

 For information call or write Cinco Puntos Press, 2709 Louisville, El Paso, Texas, 79930, (915) 566-9072

SECOND PRINTING 1990

Manufactured in the United States of America.

ISBN 0-938317-09-1
Library of Congress Catalog Card Number: 89-091054

Cinco Puntos Press would like to thank Bruce Lowney for permission to use his lithograph "The Last Hill" for the cover of Tierra.

Book design by Vicki Trego Hill of El Paso, Texas.

Typeface is Goudy Old Style and is set by TypeGraphics of Tyler, Texas

Many thanks to Elizabeth Sinkovitz for data entry and her writer's ear.

Printed on acid free paper by McNaughton & Gunn, Inc. of Saline, Michigan.

El Paso • Texas

CONTENTS

ACKNOWLEDGEMENTS

Many thanks are due to the following authors, publishers, and publications for permission to use the material indicated:

"Iliana of the Pleasure Dreams" by Rudolfo A. Anaya first appeared in *Zyzzyva*, Winter 1985 (Volume 1, Number 4). Copyright © 1985 by Rudolfo A. Anaya and is reprinted with his permission.

"Alba in Directed Light" by Terry Boren. Copyright © 1989 Terry Boren and is printed with her permission.

"Hang Gliders and Onions" by Eduardo Chavez. Copyright © 1989 by Eduardo Chavez and is printed with his permission.

"Blizzard" by Max Evans was originally published in an anthology entitled *Southwest Wind* from Naylor Company, 1958 (San Antonio, Texas). Copyright © 1958 (subsequently renewed) by Max Evans and is reprinted with his permission.

"The Best Looking Boy" by Nancy Gage was first published in *Story Quarterly*, Number 23, 1987. Copyright © 1987 by Nancy Gage and is reprinted with her permission.

"My Apples" by Robert Granat was orignally published in *New World Writing*, Number 10 (1956) by New American Library. Copyright © 1956 (subsequently renewed) by Robert Granat and is reprinted with his permission.

"Bandido" by Drummond Hadley. Copyright © 1989 by Drummond Hadley and is printed with his permission.

"Replacement" by Tony Hillerman. Copyright © 1989 by Tony Hillerman and is printed with his permission.

"Edna's Pie Town" by Debra Hughes-Blanks. Copyright © 1989 by Debra Hughes-Blanks and is printed with her permission.

"The Day It Rained Blood" by Tim MacCurdy first appeared in *La Confluencia, A Magazine for the Southwest*, Volume 3, Numbers 3 and 4, February 1980. Copyright © 1980 by Tim MacCurdy and is reprinted with his permission.

"T. Bob in The Yard" by Robert Masterson. Copyright © 1989 by Robert Masterson and is printed with his permission.

"The Complete History of New Mexico" by Kevin McIlvoy first appeared in *Indiana Review*, Volume 9, Number 1, 1986. Copyright © 1986 by Kevin McIlvoy and is reprinted with his permission.

"The Scars of Old Sabers" by Gabriel Meléndez was first published in *Writers' Forum*, September 1985. Copyright © 1985 by Gabriel Meléndez and is reprinted with his permission.

"The Revolt of Eddie Starner" by John Nichols. Copyright © 1989 by John Nichols and is printed with his permission.

"Men on the Moon" by Simon J. Ortiz was published in his collection *Fightin'* from Thunder's Mouth Press. Copyright © 1969 (subsequently renewed) by Simon J. Ortiz and is reprinted with his permission.

(Continued on page 272)

PREFACE

The vast space of earth and sky in New Mexico is its most imposing feature. This space of earth and sky dictates the rhythm of *la gente* of New Mexico; it is also an ingredient which dictates the natural pace of the stories in this collection. That space, which I call *tierra*, nourishes our creativity.

Each one of us has a favorite place in New Mexico where we feel a special relationship with the land. I have a cabin in the Jemez Mountains that is such a place; there I often contemplate the red cliffs that rise from the valley floor, and I am inspired and healed by their beauty. I have seen other mountains—the Alps and the icy grandeur of the Jungfrau, the majestic Tetons in Wyoming, the slopes of Machu Picchu in Peru—but for me there are no more inspiring mountains on earth than the red cliffs of the Jemez.

Small spaces confine us; the writers in this collection are inspired by the larger landscape and that landscape is, often, a rural one. For some the setting is the desert, for others the inspiration is the Sangre de Cristos of northern New Mexico. Some use the llano of the east side, others are attached to the Rio Grande flowing past our pueblos and fields, while others explore the unique border life we share with Mexico. These writers agree that there is a compelling power in this earth we inhabit. It inspires the content of our stories, our aesthetic, and the slow, natural rhythm of our storytelling.

You, the reader, will find reflections of our love for *la tierra* in these stories. I believe you will also find here a unique New Mexican point of view, a reflection of the diverse cultures of our state. The talent of these writers provides some of the flavor, *un sabor*, of the richness of our lives in *la tierra*.

Rudolfo A. Anaya

CREASE

Lisa Sandlin

SIX months or so ago, about the time Ray and I split up, Livvy sent me to a palm reader. She was not in the least exotic. A bit overweight, with straight brown hair, she was as ordinary as a houseshoe. Her apartment was filled with plants and as she grasped my hand, a quiet current passed. She said, "When people like you come, I tell my plants…" here her voice piped up to falsetto and she confided to a shefflera, "…don't worry, she'll be gone in an hour." I wasn't insulted. I once boarded my plants with a friend who commented, "You should run a plant concentration camp." So she was right on, just with a handshake.

She made all sorts of positive predictions, although it's difficult to remember them precisely. Things like—"You will live in the country," "You will meet your mate in three years time," "It is possible that he will have money."

She gave me practical advice. Sleep with my head pointing east. Eat more protein. The absence of moons in my fingernails proved I should eat more protein; she pointed out only one, mostly submerged moon. Actually only the halo of one submerged moon. Anyway… (now I sound like Ray) she did tell me some good things. But what I remember best are the bad ones.

The first thing that made me feel bad was when she found Ray in my right palm. He was a crease about 3/8 of an inch long, so faint that if I tilted my palm toward her candle, he disappeared. The palm reader was disturbed—at a remove, of course; her voice registered the kind of irritable disbelief people express when they say "What *will* she do next?"

"You married him?" she asked me. I didn't say anything. I had already told her I married him. "You married him?" she insisted. "You weren't supposed to marry him."

Well, I did. But the thing that shook me the most was when she inspected my left palm. That one, she informed me, mapped out the history of my past lives.

"Will you look at that?" she said. "You've never been old."

The dangling lines, the isolated x's, the dead ends in my left palm upset me more than Ray's invisibility. I could have taken it, I suppose, this way: I've had a natural taste for blazes of glory. For lifetimes, I've left a good-looking corpse. But that's not how I took it, concerned, as I am, with the task of the life at hand.

As a child, I dogged my grandfather, Daddy Arthur. I puzzled over his stories, his skills, his tricks, and poked at the mysterious caving in of his body. Daddy Arthur could shuffle and deal with one hand; he could make the cards stream like water or sift out onto the table like cake flour drifting into a bowl. Daddy Arthur knew things. He knew why hell was hot—not naturally, no, hell is naturally cold. But every Friday, the jaybirds dip their beaks into steaming sand and carry the sand down to hell, scattering it all around. His mouth would work in and out, in and out, until it was loose enough to smile, and he would croak out a secret laugh. Daddy Arthur's shoulders got thinner and thinner; my teeth fell out and grew in, but I was still his shade: I was like having a shadow that bumped into you when you stopped. It was because I felt he knew something he would never tell me.

So when the palm reader said to me "You've never been old," how I took it was as a handicap: Here I am, yet again, without the stored wisdom that will allow me now and then to intuit either disaster or a lucky break. She was telling me mine was a raw soul. And why I felt so bad was that the second she said it, something shifted in my chest, and I knew it was absolutely true.

RECENTLY, as she tapped a cigarette on the table, Livvy asked me, "Why Ray? I don't mean to say 'How could you take it all those years?,' but why Ray?"

But that was what she meant to say and all I could think of was that by the time I couldn't take it anymore, Ray was home. I am a rooted woman. I can make homes out of motels and sleeping bags; they assume, in an hour, the sentimental aura of my territory. Livvy said, did I know the story of the Archangel Gabriel collecting everyone's troubles and dumping them in sacks? He lined up all the sacks on a fencepost and told everybody to run get one. And they all raced as fast as they could to snatch their own troubles back. Was that what I meant?

That's one way of looking at it, I said.

I was new to Santa Fe when I met Ray. Out job-hunting, the last place I tried was a small bar with a giant harlequin snake painted directly onto the wall. Purposeful as a divining rod, its thick tongue forked toward a row of glittering bottles. It was 11:30 in the morning, and there were only the bartender, one customer and me. Prying the completed application form from the sticky rings on the small table, I began to half-listen to the story the bartender was telling his only customer. The customer was half-listening, too, while he tossed cherries in the air and tried to spear them with a tiny plastic sword.

"...so I asked him to move his chair. He won't. He's a young guy, a real hard case Chicano, got the bandanna, got Guadalupe on a chain. Got the red ass in general for the whole Anglo world. Anyway, he puts his feet up on the table, won't let me by. He's staring out the door like I'm the Invisible Man. Hey, scout, I tell him again, I gotta get by here. He's looking at me, you know, but he's not seeing me.

"So I'm standing there getting mad enough to dump the whole tray on his bandanna when Benny Duran comes over. You know Benny? Works downtown at Kraft's selling shoes."

The customer said, "Guy with one shoulder lower than the—"

"Yeah, that's Benny. He's not Superman, know what I mean? Anyway, right away I see this is a scene. Benny's walking Pachuco-style, kinda loose and swinging, like he's got an hour or two to cover the five feet up to the guy's chair. He gets there, he just stands there. Both of them, not seeing the other.

"Everybody gets real quiet. I known Benny fifteen years, he always comes to hear me play the guitar. But even I'm looking at him, wondering what's up."

"Benny Duran, got one shoulder lower....Hey, all right!" the customer lurched forward, a cherry stuck on his sword.

"Madre de Dios, some people's kids....Anyway, Benny kind of straightens up, gets both shoulders real even like they're carrying something. Then he bends down. He grabs the arms of the chair and picks the guy up...picks up the whole goddamn chair and sets it down out of the aisle. Makes a big thump. The guy's looking at him now, and I guarantee you, he's seeing him.

"So Benny leans over and in this real quiet voice, he introduces himself, he says 'Capitan Benjamin Eduardo Antonio Duran y Salazar, a su servicio.' I'm thinking, Benny where the hell you getting this rank, but mostly I'm thinking Benny my man you are gonna get your throat jumped. But the guy sweeps off the bandanna like it's some kind of cap and says 'Tenente Juan Diego Vigil y Romero, a sus ordenes.' They look at each other for a minute and nod. Then Benny walks off. Mr. Pachuco again. Guy was polite as hell for the rest of the night."

"Give me another Manhattan, over easy," the customer said. He wasn't impressed.

But I was. Maybe lots of people could fail to be charmed by a story like that, but not me. I love seeing people swell into themselves. I watch for it.

I handed the bartender my sticky application form. By then he had a toothpick in his mouth. He took it out. "Hi, I'm Ray," he said.

RAY IS A LITTLE MAN with beautiful hands and tiny terrier eyes. His being little never bothered me. I could put my arm right around his shoulder and look straight into his eyes. In our moments of harmony, we could walk the earth that way, two little people locked at the shoulders striding down the street on a snowy day.

Just today I remembered a conversation that took place years ago. It was with a vacuum cleaner repairman who assured me that my husband had a heavy burden to bear in this society. The vacuum cleaner repairman was from Oklahoma, and little. He let me know he earned $50,000 a year, enough to support two ex-wives and a penchant for gambling. He stared at me hungrily when I told him that size didn't mean anything.

"Don't you never believe it," he warned, pointing a miniature screwdriver at my young face. "He's on the lookout all the time. He's gotta be." Well, I don't know, but the man fixed the vacuum cleaner in five minutes flat. He made me think.

How Ray expanded himself was by talking. Early on he told me, with the sort of odd, downcast pride you might feel if you discovered your backbone was double-jointed, "I can sit down at a table and within 10 minutes I can dominate any conversation." Ray told stories, segueing one into the next, to the bar at large. The painted snake behind him was a fitting decoration. There was Ray, there were the customers: charmer and snakes.

On a Saturday night, still jobless, I took the last seat at the bar without one intuitive twinge that this was the evening that would etch Ray faintly into my palm. As I sat down, Ray dropped a glass. Two minutes later he served a Bud Light to a regular whose drink was scotch and milk. Red-faced, he apologized and gave the guy a Bloody Mary. The people at the bar all knew Ray, and they were getting a big kick out of his being so flustered.

Finally he came over to me. He wiped his hands on a bar towel and took one of my hands in his. "I'm glad you came in tonight," he said, and paused, looking back over his shoulder to the row of heads turned toward us. He started to say something else, but he was interrupted by a commotion at the back table.

Two drunks were pouring beer on each other, trying to fill up the pockets of their denim shirts before the beer seeped out. Angry, Ray walked up and jerked his thumb like an umpire. "You're eight-sixed, both of you! Useless as balls on a priest!"

They snuck around to the back. Ray knew they were coming. They were stumbling around out there, knocking over empties. Just as they kicked the back door open, I saw Ray do something that made me fall in love with him. Very carefully, gently, he removed his glasses and laid them on the bar. They were big guys and Ray is a little man. The moment seemed infinite to me—the back door flying open and Ray, with exquisite resignation, setting his glasses on the bar. Then he was sitting on top of one guy with his thumbs on the guy's eyes and the other one had tripped over a chair and was moaning on the floor, his hand to his stomach.

I saw reluctance in Ray's gesture with the glasses; I saw willingness, too. The look in his bare eyes went past the calm of a man preparing himself to...the deepest understanding, the kind of understanding that means forgiveness. He forgave them, he forgave himself; he owned the moment absolutely. Unhampered by even a feather's weight of premonition, my soul welled up: I saw a man who knew something.

"So why don't you come over and bring your guitar after work?" I asked him. Ray wiped his glasses and put them back on. "Okay," he said.

We built a big piñon fire. Ray unsnapped the case, lifted the guitar, and set a chair out of range of the flying sparks. He tuned, patiently. Then he played, not a slow, warm-up piece, but a surging, hundred-mile-an-hour rhythm. The guitar and the leaping fire filled the room with motion. I felt I was watching the rhythm, like a train with glinting windows, rush by. The flamenco music was terrible and wonderful and despairing and joyous. That's all I could make of it, all those contradictions.

"Do they sing to this?" I asked.

"Oh yeah," Ray said, "it all comes from the *cante*, the singing. A guy out plowing his field and singing. Beating an anvil with a hammer and singing. Listen." He sang a verse. It sounded drawn out and chopped up and very sad.

"That says something like 'For every step forward, I take two steps back.' And this one, I love this one. Listen now." Since I couldn't understand the words, I followed his hands. His long elegant fingers had a life of their own. He never attended to them. They flew gracefully, from fret to fret, as he sang.

"That one says, 'My mouth hurts me, gypsy girl, from asking you if you love me.'" We looked at each other for a while. "I love that one," Ray said, finally.

So I began to learn flamenco when I moved in with him, into his one room with the painted iron bed and the tv set that had to be turned upside down two or three times to get the sound to work. Ray sat in a wooden chair and played the fast rhythm—*bulerías*—while I danced a series of short steps that joined each other in a circle. My teacher had taught me these steps so that we could practice without stopping, on and on in novice infinity until Ray got tired of playing. Around and around I went, passing myself briefly in a Woolworth mirror we had hung on the wall. When I faced the mirror, my arms arced out of its borders. Ray played, resting his cheek on the guitar. When he was tired, or I had got it right enough times in a row, he nested the guitar in its case and snapped the locks. His terrier eyes lit up. I was very happy, I was. With my arm about his shoulder, we walked downtown to get a coffee.

I see what I'm doing—explaining to Livvy and the palm reader that faint crease that should have been outside my destiny. Now that I put it down, I see Livvy still tapping her cigarette. Here in my room, I tilt my palm under the 25 watt bulb and find only a patch of unmarked skin. I wasn't supposed to marry him? Well, I did.

IT IS BECAUSE OF RAY that last night I dressed in a long ruffled skirt and a fringed shawl and went off to dance at the Sheraton. Livvy came over, too, to dress, and to warm up before another night of hometown flamenco. We performed, enacting the torture of human misfortune, while the Jaycees ate and drank and slid their arms around giggling wives. It went okay, mostly, but it doesn't always. Inappropriate things happen. We take them in stride, that being the one condition of continuing to do jobs like these.

One night, as Livvy intoned the notes of the tientos, pulling the audience by the hair into the mood of the song, a waitress walked by her shouldering a tray of food. She stopped to ask Livvy if she knew which was table fourteen. Another time an old man whipped out a violin and fiddled along with our guitars. In between numbers, he jumped in with ancient jokes. We've danced on stages like trampolines, under latticework that snared the fringes of our shawls, on particle board set on a slope so that we had to dance uphill, heaving like wrestlers with the effort.

But Ray and I had a dream. We would live in Spain for a year so I could study there. I would learn to dance with all the *gracia* of the village flirt, the girl by the fountain with eyes like honey and a soul as deep as a well. Then what? He would play and I would dance. It didn't go any farther than that, but it was a dream of remarkable buoyancy. It lasted well into the years when we only remembered what the dream was, and not how it felt. Misfortunes intervened, of course; they ravaged our savings like bears at a campsite: an emergency appendectomy, a car, unemployment. I haven't been old. I wasn't prepared for the way our dream broke up, in big bits, in little bits. I think now that that was one of the ingredients of Daddy Arthur's secret croak. He'd sift out the cards and grab me by the waist and laugh, a rooster in a pen, cackling at the inedible feed he knew was coming.

I ENVY LIVVY not because she has the rugged gold look of a lioness but because she remembers past lives and so cannot be as unequipped as I am. When she was little, she said, she drew pictures of elevators. Not plain boxes ascending in larger boxes, but lacy, wrought iron cages with attendants in uniform. She was an old lady in Paris and the wrought iron elevator went up to her penthouse apartment.

"What did you do up there?" I wanted to know.

"Oh, I think I watched people. I spent a lot of time watching people on the boulevard and in the park. I was very old. My family and friends were gone, so I adopted strange faces from my window." I was afraid she was downplaying it for my sake, but just then, with all the voluptuousness of a woman slipping a silk strap from her shoulder, she opened a fresh pack of cigarettes.

"I dipped snuff, too. From tiny lacquer boxes." After Livvy brought an imaginary pinch of snuff to her nose, she tapped a cigarette on the table and pursed her lips lovingly to receive it.

Her other drawings were a source of consternation to her parents. They were of breasts. They came from her life as an African bushman, a hunter who fed his family with a spear.

"So why didn't you draw lions or gazelles or spears?" I pursued.

Livvy flicked her lighter; the flame hissed between us. "They were my wife's breasts. I can see them—they hung low on her chest with nipples like black beans. I must have loved her very much."

Now maybe breasts and elevators don't add up to a big advantage in life, but I'm not so sure. I think of what Livvy's bushman knew of love, and what her old lady made of the faces performing daily under her patient gaze. And that is much more than I can claim—a virgin in a hand-planed coffin, her lily eyes directed only to heaven.

WE TOOK THE TV and the painted iron bed and moved to a bigger place, a house on Cold Water Street with startling floral linoleum. On the way, our car stuffed with boxes, Ray decided that this move was so official we might as well get married. We were at a stoplight. His eyes were very bright and he shot me a look, sideways. He slipped his hands in his pockets.

"What do you think?"

"Ray, you're driving," I reminded him, thinking that when we drove on he would say something more.

"Oh yeah," he said.

"It's a green light."

He grinned. "I'm glad you feel that way."

We got married at the courthouse. Judge Archuleta asked me did I take this man Ramon to be my wedded husband. He should have said Raymond, but I stared into Ray's bright eyes and took him. My mother sent a silver heirloom, Daddy Arthur's pocket watch, as a symbol that I was now bound into the generations. Its small oval case sparkled. But the fat Roman numerals which had taught me time had faded to the breadth of eyelashes, as though in a decade without Daddy Arthur, someone else's anxious glances had worn them thin. For weeks I wore it on a ribbon around my neck, until Ray convinced me to stash it in a drawer and not ding it up.

There on Cold Water Street, on the tappy, rosy linoleum, two other kinds of practices developed besides the one which ended in a stroll downtown for coffee: bad and solo.

I am stepping and clapping on our red floor with its pattern of massive yellow roses. I'm barefoot, in a limp polyester nightgown that has worn clear in patches, like panes of glass. One step, then a clap, step, clap, over and over until some semblance of a counter-time emerges. My heavy hands are cold and they sting, the cold linoleum burns my feet. I have one good long run before I mess up—ticka-ticka-ticka-ticka.

"That's it," Ray says, clapping out the *palmas* and using his tongue to sound the clicks in a syncopated roll. "Only fifty times faster."

Ray loves to coach; he's too into it to stop and get dressed. He's hunched on the edge of the couch wearing only the holey t-shirt he sleeps in. When he coaches, Ray is the bad cop. He rattles me. I step again.

"Jesus, you're not gonna break," he barks. Part of me escapes out the window, out to where snow is falling from a white sky, where trees and powerlines are traced white.

"Play," I urge him. "I do better with the music."

"Look, I know it's not your culture. The Spanish learn it as babies. Hell, the kids count eggs to *bulerías* rhythm. Listen, now. Uno dos *tres*...cuatro cinco *seis*...siete ocho nueve *diez*....Don't fling yourself around like that!"

Half-naked, he hops over the freezing yellow roses to tuck his feet into the rungs of the kitchen chair next to the heater. He grabs the guitar, rubbing his hands, talking, talking. Like toffee between my teeth, Ray's voice is pulling at me.

"Listen now...uno dos *tres*...."

The solo practice is very different. Ray's at the bar. I am watching a late movie and dancing around the living room during the commercials. As soon as Robert Mitchum and Susan Hayward fade away in their sportscar, I bang the tv and flip on the record player. A fast *bulerías* charges the room. I dance with a Goodwill lamp as though it were my iron-spined partner. Often, carried away, I dance through whole sections of movies. Something—some heavy, wild sediment—is being stirred up from the bottom of me. The lamp and I forget the late show. We cast passionate, bobbing shadows, shadows that inhabit the room as satisfactorily as company.

Then I hear Ray coming. The dogs start up. The one at the corner barks and, like a song sung in rounds, the next dog takes it up and the next one. When Ray is far enough past the corner, the first dog drops out, then the second one, until they are all quiet. There is a jingling, and

Ray's key turns in the lock. He hangs his cap on the nail and is filling me in on his shift before his bomber jacket has quite slipped off his shoulders.

"What a night. You should of been there. This nut with a blond wig came in. Guy must have been 6'4"and the wig is supposed to make him into a girl. He went into the ladies john and when I went in to get him, he's combing his pubic hair. *Madre de Dios*, maybe I could join the civil service."

In between sips of tea, he lays out the rest of the night. After a while, I interrupt to trot out my inarticulate evening. "Ray, let me tell you. I danced all around the living room. Watch this step." I show him.

"Oh, good one," he says, nodding. "Anyway...." He presents me with the information he collected from various customers. This information could be anything—the derivations of words, civil war strategy—but tonight it's about remittance men and Elvis Presley. I'd like to talk about something else, something silly and important, but we don't. Ray preferred to leave those subjects alone when they applied to the two of us, untouched, stashed—like Daddy Arthur's wedding-silver watch, too rare to use everyday.

THESE DAYS, with Ray gone, I walk through the house as though through water, cutting a temporary wake that seals behind me as I pass from the room. When Ray was not practicing, bent over the guitar in the kitchen, he kept the house filled up with theories, opinions, jokes, stories.

"Do you realize," I asked him when we'd been married a while, "that you talk like an essay?"

Ray leveled his eyes with mine. "Hey, I'm sharing things. Things that mean something to me because they're weird or enlightening or just go to show how stupid people are. Stuff like that's as good as a ten dollar bill to me. Remember the guy I told you about the other night? The one who wanted to axe his sister-in-law because she had a nervous breakdown? He didn't believe it was real. She's an actress, he said; everybody's got problems. God only gives you more than you can handle, *once*, he said. Now that's worth talking about. He stiffed me, the bastard, but he dropped that little insight on the bar. So I brought it home to you. Anyway...you're certainly welcome to join in. A conversation implies two people. Is it so hard for you to say something at the end of the sentence?"

But by then I was inalterably in receiver mode. "At the end of the paragraph, Ray," I replied.

The semantic problem there is "sharing." Ray was giving. He brought information back to me like a retriever—gossip, obscure facts about Sicilian bandits, the workings of cranberry bogs. Sharing, no; Ray never left a space for me to share back. He finished a story with "Anyway…," flinging out that stopgap word like a portable bridge, clicking his teeth to reserve the next block of time while he organized his thoughts to fill it.

The change that came was like the stretching of children's bones—as an event in time, inevitable and common, but in itself, rather magical. He wasn't at all ready for it. Ray wanted to go on and on, me and him and the Woolworth mirror.

ONE AUGUST EVENING we performed for a fiesta on the Santa Fe Plaza—Ray and I; Frank, the second guitar; Cynthia, a dancer; and Livvy, our singer, in a long black shawl. It was a lovely mountain night, starry, with a light wind carrying the tang of two seasons.

Ray played the slow, compelling introduction to the *soléa.* Frank joined in. Scanning the ring of upturned faces, I lost them. I saw only the late summer night with its air of a last invitation. As Livvy sang the first sad notes, I rose from the chair as though lifted. I turned toward her, but she disappeared. Only the night was there. I let it in—the stage was gone, my feet and my twisting hands were gone. For all I knew, I was still sitting in the chair, a faint, awkward ghost waiting for the summer night to return my borrowed body. Livvy told me later that, when I'd finished, the audience was silent for seconds before they began to applaud. I don't know. I didn't hear anything until I was off the stage.

Ray was waving his hand. "Christ, I broke a nail! I didn't know what the hell you were gonna do next!"

A woman from the crowd pushed past him. "That was wonderful!" she said to me. "It was incredible what you did."

When, from surprise, I didn't respond, she was confused. Looking me up and down, she suddenly smiled. "Oh, you're from Spain, aren't you? *¿Habla ingles?*"

Ray stared at me, too, like I was something new.

A month later, it happened again. I danced at an exhibit of Spanish pictures, across a polished gallery floor lit with strips of late afternoon sun. The only real thing to me then was what was inside—some part of me that knew something—and it wanted to get out.

We had a turning point. It was invisible then, but now, looking backward, I can see it, insignificant but rebelliously upright, like one of those roadside crosses the Spanish people here use to mark a violent death.

We were dancing in a bar. After the show, a drunken Englishman bought a round of drinks for the whole troupe. He caught me before I could disappear into the dressing room, a dusty storeroom at the back of the bar. "I bought them for you, actually," the Englishman said, his eyes luminous. "You've got such sorrow in your face."

When he walked away, rather unsteadily, Ray grimaced. "What a bozo," he said. It was that, as much as anything, that set the end in motion: that Ray had to refuse me such a small moment of distinction.

Now I wanted to talk back to Ray when he came home, I wanted to share. Ray listened, but he walked around while I talked, polishing the telephone with a dishrag. I followed him around the kitchen with new thoughts.

"Uh huh, uh huh," he muttered, chipping black off the burners with his fingernails. Then he put his hands on my shoulders and seated me gently at the table. I liked his hands there; they made me feel warm. He sat me down like I was a guitar, and breakable. He had something curious to say. From habit I listened.

I began to have black and white dreams of laundromats. I was forced to do endless loads of laundry for unnamed persons. The dreams altered my dancing schedule. I danced during *Hawaii 5-0*, and on into *Quincy*. By the time the late movie came on, I was tired, and went to bed. Ray complained about coming home to a dark house, but I couldn't seem to help myself; I was overcome by sleepiness. It relaxed my knees, closed my eyes by 10 p.m. Ray shook me awake to tell me about the evolution of hardshell beetles or how the median IQ of licensed drivers in Boston is 80, but I drifted off between sentences.

His voice rolled into my dreams as a soundtrack. I was alone in a nightlit laundromat in New Orleans, stuffing wet sheets into an oversize dryer. Suddenly his voice ran along the edge of the dream like a banner of words at the bottom of the television screen.

"This guy told me hardshell beetles have come a long way," I heard. "Did you know they started out with really flimsy coverings? Thin, like negligees." Pulling out a load of billowy sheets, I was horrified to see beetles marching up them, an invasion of hardshell beetles. "Call them back, Ray!" I yelled from the dream, but probably I was only shaping the words with my lips.

One night I was shaken awake to find the light on and a suitcase by the bed.

"I'm moving out," Ray said. "But I want you to know that I know you moved out first." He jerked the quilt I was folded up in and I tumbled onto the floor. I sat in the corner, watching him dismantle the iron bed with a hammer.

"There was love here," he said between blows.

I was pinching the skin of my forehead. "Could you please just say that another way?"

Ray took off his glasses and wiped them with his shirttail. I couldn't read his eyes; he kept them closed. He threw back his head and sang a flamenco verse, beating the iron with his hammer. Halfway through, I recognized the words: *My mouth hurts me, gypsy girl, from asking you if you love me*. He carried out all the bed pieces and the suitcase. When I got up a couple of hours later, I found he had taken his tv, too. It was a pain, that tv with its tiresome ways, but when you get used to something, you miss it when it's gone.

Sometimes, now, I talk to Ray, to the kitchen chair where he would be running down his scales. Ray, I say, I bought a dress today. It's the color of a winter sunset on the Sangre de Cristos; it's the color of blood. Ray, I saw Benny Duran today. "*¿Come te ha ido?*" he greeted me. "Do you know why Española is covered with shards of glass?" No, Benny, why? "It's for the Penitente break dancers, man." We laugh like crazy, Ray, and you are with us, a white, peeling, live roadside cross.

LIVVY SHOWED UP LAST NIGHT looking like the mindful Russian peasant she is. She wore a long Russian blouse over a taggy print skirt and her sharp face stood out in gold relief from her tangled golden hair. "So what'll happen to us tonight? We'll fall off the stage? Frank'll miss all the chord changes? What?" Lifting the print skirt, she did a flourishing *remate* step. She was in a good mood.

"Frank's done mostly okay without Ray. It's hard to just jump in there as first guitar. It's been hard...."

Livvy shut me up with a look. I ironed our shawls while she transformed herself before the bathroom mirror. She hummed in her throat. In half an hour, the lioness was hidden. Blue-lidded, black-lashed, fuchsia-cheeked, she had a luscious red mouth and a red dot at the corner of each Tartar eye ." '*Amanos, chica*," she said, snaking a black and green polka dot dress up her hips. She winked at me, her painted face merry as a carnival.

We met Frank and Cynthia at the Sheraton. Frank wandered over to the bar. We headed upstairs so Cynthia could wipe the lipstick off her teeth. Livvy stood at the door to the ladies' lounge, absorbing the gestures of a short, handsome Jaycee in a white suit.

"Think you could stretch it out a little?" he gazed nervously up to Livvy.

"Uh oh, we'll do what we can, but stretch it out how long?"

"Say 20 minutes, something like that."

"Uh oh," Livvy was shaking her head as though some unfortunate mistake had been made, but certainly not by her. "I think you should have paid us more."

"We've got a delay," she told me. "They've bungled their guest speakers. Naturally. The committee chairman says he can't speak after the Archbishop; he'll stutter or something. I'm going to check out the mikes."

I sank into a fat armchair and drew the shawl over me like a sheet. Cynthia was busy at the mirror with a Kleenex. Slipping out my right palm, I examined it in the dim light. It was wet. Sweat sparkled in the creases. I didn't look for Ray; instead, I followed my lifelines. That was another thing the palm reader showed me. I have two lifelines; they run in unbroken parallel from the veins of my wrist to the base of my middle finger. "Well, what does that mean?" I asked her. She smiled, getting up to move an African violet further away from me, to a bookshelf.

"It means in this life you'll live to be old. It means there's a hell of a lot going on there." Bending over, she whispered something to the violet. She shrugged, such an easy shrug, but then it was me and not her with these endless lines. She sat down again, her brown eyes inert as buttons. "It means you're learning, dear."

"Thirty more minutes, *chicas*!" Livvy strode into the lounge. "Definitely time for a cigarette. The Archbishop is warming up." Carefully, to avoid smudging her gorgeous mouth, Livvy inserted a cigarette, puffing with puckered lips.

I hauled myself out of the armchair and walked into the bathroom. I began to do footwork patterns on the black and white tile. Though I was not dancing lightly, the sounds were sharp, weightless. I went on and on, doing step after step from my *soléa*. Ray has an original Queen of the Gypsies album, the one on which Carmen Amaya recorded her inhuman *alegrías*, rolling rhythm after crushing rhythm, counter matched by counter-rhythm to the sole accompaniment of clapping hands. No guitar, no song, just the steady palms and an occasional shout of encouragement. Carmen Amaya danced the *silencio* for an eternity of fourteen minutes. I stopped to take a very deep breath. Then, gathering the skirt to my side, I cradled the ruffles and started the footwork again. I was realizing that, while she danced it, it must have felt to Carmen that that *silencio* could go on forever.

All in all, it was a fairly good night. Frank caught the chord changes. Cynthia and I didn't mess up. The Archbishop thanked us himself; that was nice. But near the end a mike gave out, and Livvy had to climb off the stage and circle the room as she sang, in order to be heard. The handsome little Jaycee, motivated by taste or by pique, leveled his spotlight on the dancers' chests, abandoning our sorrowful faces to the dark.

BLIZZARD

Max Evans

IT was at least an hour before sundown when the coyote howled from the rolling hills north of the house. A little farther on another answered and another and another. The way it sounded to me, every coyote in the world was having a say about things. I knew what that meant—blue norther. Besides, the leg I'd cracked up in the Cheyenne rodeo back in my better days was stiffening up. That was a sure sign.

Well, I had it coming, I reckon. I'd been down here on the lower camp for three winters, up until now the quietest winters a man could ask for. There were times when I began doubting how much longer I could hold out.

I remember when I'd first asked old Joe Rivers for the job. He'd said, "Mr. Manners, I've been running this outfit for over twenty- five years."

I interrupted. "Dave. Just call me Dave."

"All right, Dave. As I was sayin'. Twenty-five years of hiring men to work the lower camp has made me just a wee bit leery about the matter. Some make it through the winter and pull out in the spring, but most leave in the late fall when we need 'em the worst. Always throws us in a tight. Have to hire some no-good and give him double pay to sit down there and roast his shins while the cows shift for themselves. I suppose a man gets lonesome thirty miles from the nearest living soul. I'll hire you if you'll stick out the winter."

"You've got a hand," I said. And he did have.

They'd furnished me good horses and fair grub, and that grub was what I was thinking about when I saw Sandy Malone riding up. Although he was a quarter of a mile away, I knew it was Sandy by the way he sat in the saddle. Besides, he nearly always rode the bald-faced sorrel he was on now. I rolled a smoke and waited there by the corral gate.

As he pulled up, he let out a war whoop that to my mind must have answered all the howling coyotes at once, and then some. "Howdy, Dave, you old worn-out, soul-seeking hermit. How about some frijoles?"

"Just took the thought out of my mind, Sandy. Turn your horse loose and we'll see what we can do about the hollow place in your belly. How are things at headquarters?"

"Fine," answered Sandy. "The old man sent me down to check on you before snow flies."

"You're too late, Sandy. She'll hit in the next twenty-four hours."

"Aw come on, Dave. You know better than to predict the weather in this country."

"You'll see, Sandy, my boy. You'll see."

Sandy had put his horse in a barn stall and pitched him a little hay and corn. We headed for the house. The sun was doing its last do over in the southwest where it went to sleep this time of year. I put the beans on the pot-bellied heater as soon as I had a fire blazing. I fetched a chunk of venison from the only other room in the lower camp house that I used for storing things.

"I've got to go over north and get another deer right away," I mentioned, as I dropped slices of the dark meat in the skillet. I had a little two-hole iron wood stove that I did most of my cooking on. It had a reservoir on the side that kept hot water whenever I remembered to keep water in it. The venison was juicy, tender, the beans just right. We washed it down with hot black coffee, and settled back for a smoke.

That's when it hit.

It got a little hard to breathe all of a sudden, as if all the air had been knocked out of the house. A window rattled warningly. Then, wham! It was upon us. Sandy got up and went over to the window to look out.

"Looks like you've got company for a while, Mr. Weather-Prophet," he said. "The old man will be worried silly, but from the looks of things, I can't do much about it." Sandy was right as rain.

By morning, everything was white—the ground, the air, the whole world, it seemed. The wind was getting stronger and stronger. I went out to let the horses into a hay stack. I was covered with the white powdery stuff when I got back to the house.

"Perty rough," I told Sandy. "I reckon the cows will drift down to the brush country east of here."

"Yeah, they'll make it all right, if it doesn't last too long," Sandy said encouragingly.

Sandy was a good-natured boy and laughed a lot. The two of us usually made payday in town together. That wasn't often, three or four times a year.

We passed the day off talking and eating. There's something about northers that makes a man hungry as a starved grizzly. Sandy was saying, "Remember the time we got in that fracas over at Santa Fe? That hombre thought you were trying to horn in on his gal because you said 'Excuse me' when you brushed her elbow, and took a sock at you."

"I'll never forget it," I said. "He missed me a mile and knocked his Suzy as cold as a judge's voice."

We got on stuff like that and talked for hours. And ranching, too—just about everything in the game. It was warm inside, our bellies were full and there was plenty of black coffee. With the resulting comfort, many memories came back—some sad, some so funny we'd laugh like idiots. Finally, way in the night, we played out.

The trouble that was going on outside had taken voice now. We could hear it howling like some lost animal.

I pulled out a folding cot and made it up for Sandy. Then I set out my own bed roll. I was sitting on the edge of it, pulling off a boot, when I heard a mouse gnawing in a little cupboard off the kitchen. I went over to the shelves where I kept my few eating utensils. On top, I found a couple of mouse traps. I set 'em, using a bean for bait, and went off to sleep in a hurry.

I've been in the habit for years of getting up with the sun. There wasn't any sun this morning, just greyness. I lay in bed for a couple of extra hours.

The wind was playing a tune to my memories. Neither the tune nor the memories were pleasant. I remembered the blizzard of my childhood. My father, mother and myself were traveling across country in a covered wagon. The blizzard had struck with terrible force. Father had tried to pitch camp, hobble the horses and gather firewood. The horses had become lost in the storm. The snow had driven so fast and hard, Father couldn't see to hunt for firewood. The three of us had huddled almost freezing in the wagon. The second day, Father had tried to go for help. He had frozen to death less than a hundred steps from the wagon. Mother had covered me with her coat. The storm finally played out. Some trappers found us almost frozen and starved to death. Mother died a few hours later. I knew I wouldn't be here listening to the wailing wind now if she hadn't given me her coat.

I dreaded to get up. The room was cold. I could hear Sandy snoring away. Well, it had to be done. I raised myself to a sitting position, when I saw a mouse over there in the cupboard doorway. It was a big mouse, bigger than I'd seen since camping down here. Lighter in color, too. I had set the traps up against each side of the doorway. The mouse was standing there looking at me, eyes crystal-black and cunning. He was quivering all over, twitching his nose now and then like a rabbit. I wondered why he wasn't in one of those traps. Maybe he doesn't like beans, I thought. This irritated me a little because I've eaten more beans in my time than I've breathed fresh air. When I reached for my pants, the little dickens scooted back out of sight somewhere into the cupboard. I got up and shivering plenty had trouble getting my boots on.

Sandy woke up, yawning. "It's too cold for a fire to burn, Dave. Better get back in the sack."

"It's not polite to sleep when you've got company," I replied. "Besides, I don't want you to lay there and starve. Ground is frozen too hard to dig a grave. You're not the only company we had last night," I added.

"What do you mean?" asked Sandy.

"There's been a mouse moved in with us."

"Well, he's not getting my bed, even if he thinks I'm not polite to company. He can sleep on the floor or crawl in the bed with you, Dave."

I finally got the fire started. Slowly at first, then faster. It was really melting wood by the time Sandy got up. I told him I was gonna try to make it out to the barn and corrals to check on the horses. So maybe he could mix up a few biscuits and slice off some venison. Sandy agreed.

I put on a heavy sheeplined coat and tied on a bandana around my face; then with another I tied my hat on. I put it over my hat and under my chin. I'd lost good hats in this kind of weather before. When I opened the door, the storm didn't wait for me to ask it in. The icy blast nearly knocked me down and I could barely pull the door shut behind me. I thought I'd never make it to the barn. The air was made of ice with a million flailing arms to drive its coldness through a man. Here and there I could tell I was on a spot where the ground was swept bare by the whirling wind. Then I'd hit a drift waist deep. Once I fell, numbed…and it suddenly seemed warm and almost safe down in the snow. That's when I knew it was bad. It must have happened to my father that way. The memory flashed through my mind. I shivered, the cold rushing back into my body.

I made it all right out to the horses. They were bunched upon the south side of the haystack, heads down and painted white with snow. I managed somehow to get them into the barn. I paused for a moment's rest. When I had gotten my breath back, I started for the house.

The return trip wasn't so bad. I guess maybe because I knew there was a fire and warmth at the end of it. Sandy had venison on the table and was just putting the biscuits into the oven.

"Have a cup of coffee, Dave, and thaw out your clinking old bones."

"Man!" was all I could say as I took off the frozen coat. The coffee worked wonders, and Sandy's bread wasn't bad, although I thought I could've made better. We enjoyed the meal and were talking about the possibilities of the cows making it through the storm when the mouse made a dash across the cupboard and into the "junk" room. The crack under the door looked too small for him to crawl through, but he made it.

"That baby's too smart for my traps, but I'll get him tonight," I told Sandy. I got up from the table right then and set a different kind of trap. I got a bucket and melted snow until it was about half full. I then laid a piece of firewood so that it sloped from the door right out over the middle of the bucket. I took thin splinters of wood and laid them at the end of the firewood. I tied this down with a worn piece of string. On one end of the splinter I stuck a piece of venison. That was sure to get the little dickens. He'd smell the venison, climb the firewood, then crawl out to get the meat. The string would break and he'd take a dive into the bucket. I set the new trap right in the center of the doorway to the cupboard where he'd been standing. I could see where he had gnawed a hole in the floor. I wondered what kind of nest he had down there.

The day passed quickly. The wind had settled down to a steady roar now. Once in a while it hesitated, then blasted forth as before. The old wooden frame house was shaking a bit now and then. We didn't talk as much as before. We'd sorta talked ourselves out the past night. I got to sitting there waiting and watching for that little mouse. He showed up a couple of times all right. I wondered when he had crossed over again from the "junk" room to the cupboard. He ran right under the piece of wood on the trap and peeked at me from the side of the bucket. The little devil was ignoring the trap. This riled me a little, especially when Sandy said, "You've got to be smarter than a mouse to catch one."

Darkness had now spread its dim blanket. I moved my chair over by the cupboard. I held a stove poker in my hand, determined to bash in the mouse's brains if he took another peek at me from the cupboard. I waited and waited, getting stiff and uncomfortable sitting there. Sandy had gone to bed. I was about to give up, when I saw those dark, gleaming, beady eyes fastened on me. This paralyzed me for a moment. Then I let fly with the poker. There was a loud ringing noise, and Sandy jumped up like he'd had a rattlesnake for a bed partner. The mouse was gone. I'd knocked over the bucket and spilled the water. The ricochetting poker had sprung one of the traps I'd first set. I felt like an idiot about it all. I suppose from the way Sandy stared at me, I looked like one, too.

Sandy crawled back in bed and didn't say a word. I went to bed too, but I was a little shaky and lay there looking at the ceiling and listening to the song of the wind. I don't know what made me do it, but I got up and took my old 30-30 off the hooks above the door and laid it by the bed roll within easy reach.

I was just dozing off, when I felt something run across my chest. I bolted upright in bed and grabbed the gun. At that instant, Sandy said, "What in the world is the matter, Dave? That mouse get in bed with you?"

I cut him short angrily, then felt sorry about it. I realized too late that I needed someone to talk to. I didn't sleep a wink the rest of the night. I kept thinking I could feel that mouse scratching my head or crawling down my back. Part of the time I lay there with sweat breaking out all over me. I was afraid to move, even to breathe.

I rose before daylight the next morning, taking all the nerve I could gather together to do so. When Sandy woke up, I was sitting over by the stove drinking coffee and smoking cigarettes about as fast as I could roll them.

I was thinking about what the boys at headquarters had told me less than a year ago. Another man like myself, except that he had a wife, had been trapped here at lower camp. Their food ran low; then there was none. They'd been so hungry, he had finally dashed out into the blizzard carrying his rifle, screaming repeatedly to his wife that he'd get food. The boys found him sometime later with his hands frozen to a barbwire fence. His gun was lost.

The memory depressed me. I didn't see why exactly, except that I began to have a sort of dread about being here alone most of the time. I suppose I didn't feel too kindly toward Sandy either when I thought he would skip out as soon as he could. Well, damn him, let him. As for grub, I certainly wasn't worried even if we did have to make it for a while on beans.

By the time Sandy got up, it was daylight, and I felt better for a while. I even began wondering at myself for going off the deep end. But when I saw Sandy looking over at the 30-30 by my bed roll, and then looking at me on the sly, I got into a rage inside of me.

The mouse made several trips back and forth from the cupboard to the "junk" room. I sat down on the bed roll, picking up the rifle. I'd wait. My head began to pound. I thought I could hear the mouse laughing at me in a screeching voice that seemed to keep time with the wind outside. I don't know how long he'd been standing there in the middle of the floor when I saw him. I jerked the trigger of the 30-30, working the lever feverishly. The noise sounded like a thousand sticks of dynamite going off at once. I stopped after the hammer clicked empty several times. I'd had genuine buck fever over a mouse.

I was standing now in the middle of the room, with nothing to show for my outburst except some holes in the floor and a loss of breath. I looked foolishly around at Sandy. He was standing over there by the cot with his forty-five in his hand. I knew that a moment before it had been pointing right at my back. His gun belt was hung across a corner of the cot. It hadn't been there the last time I looked that way.

I hunted up some shells and reloaded the 30-30. I also got my forty-five and stuck it in the waist of my pants. Sandy was lying on his side on the cot making out like he was asleep; but I knew he was awake and was watching me through the slits of his eyelids. I thought the storm had got him—driven him out of his senses. I figured he was planning to kill me.

The day went slowly. By nightfall, I was shaking inside and out. I didn't eat another bite, just sat and stared at the cupboard door. I even forgot Sandy. When darkness did come, I was afraid to go to sleep. I kept thinking things were crawling on me. Once in a while I'd think something was slipping up behind. It didn't matter which way I sat. I was scared silly. I kept the fire going and it cast funny lights about the room where it shone through the vent in the front of the stove door. It had been hours and hours since I'd slept. Finally, against my will and from sheer exhaustion, I dozed off.

I dreamed that my arm was hanging off the bed roll and the mouse was eating my fingers. I struggled and strained with all my might: I couldn't move my arm. He ate my fingers, my hand, my arm. His belly was getting bigger and bigger. I kept looking for it to burst. The little devil had started talking to me now. He said I'd been mean and tried to trap him, tried to drown him, tried to shoot him. He said he was going to eat my arm off and then go get a hundred more mice and let them have the rest of me.

I woke up screaming at the top of my voice. The mouse was crouching there in the flickering light. I hurled the covers back and dived at him with all my might. The world turned into flashing lights—all of them red, some in circles and some in straight lines that went off into space out of sight. Then it was soft purple and hard black and that was all.

THE LIGHT WAS IN MY EYES. It would have been sunlight except that sunlight couldn't get through the windows for the frozen snow. I was covered up in bed. My head was heavy and when I raised myself, pains shot all through my body. I struggled to a sitting position. I felt my head. It was swollen on top and there was a little dried blood.

Sandy's cot was empty. There was a note lying on it. I could tell by the broad line that he'd written it with the lead of a bullet. Guess he couldn't find a pencil. It said that he was going to try to make it in, as the old man would sure be needing him. I'd bumped my head and he'd dragged me back to bed. There was something else, but he'd scratched it out. Well, anyway, I wasn't scared any more. Maybe I was too sore and too cold to be.

As quickly as I could, I got myself into the rest of my clothes and stepped out into the world of glaring white light. It was still and quiet. I saddled a horse and rode down east to check the cattle. They were all right, browsing about in the brush in search of food. I felt good, not having any losses. Soon the horse was tired from moving about in the deep snow, and I headed back for the lower camp house to get another.

As I unsaddled, I realized how long it had been since I had eaten, and how hungry I was. I built a fire in the cook stove and put the last of the venison on. Now I set about stacking the few plates on the table, getting the crumbs together. I reached for the half-biscuit left over on the bread plate, intending to finish it, when it fell from my fingers and rolled to the wall just by the door to the cold room. Suddenly I knew that's where I wanted it to be. "That's your grub, little feller," I said half aloud.

I thought I might as well get some beans to soak for future meals. They were in a hundred pound sack in the "junk" room. I took a pan with me and stepped into the icy place. There in the middle of the barren floor was the little mouse. I could tell by the stiffness of him that he was dead. He looked a lot smaller than before, there by himself.

Even with the fire going and the venison sizzling, the house seemed unaccountably cold.

WITCHERIES OR TOMFOOLERIES?

Sabine R. Ulibarrí

IT was a land of witches. It was a time of witches. I don't know which.

Witches, ghosts, evil spirits and elves colonized the countryside, ran up and down the streets and inhabited the homesites. There wasn't anyone who didn't have direct or indirect experience with these people beyond the pale. Difficult people to identify because they often took the form of an animal: a dog, a cat, a pig, an owl.

Naturally, there were some witches we knew. Matilde from Ensenada, for example. Everybody knew she was a witch. And she had her clientele. No one like her for the evil eye. She had powders, herbs, ointments, bones, scorpions, toads, amulets of all kinds for every illness and every goodness. It was to her that the old maids looking for a husband went, the poor who couldn't afford a doctor, the sick without a cure. She attended them with her extraordinary medications. She must have been very successful in order to gain the popularity she had. Most of the people stayed away from her.

I caught up with her on the road one day. From the moment I saw her I felt like turning back or circling around her to avoid her. But since I am quite a man, and always have been, I swallowed hard and went on to pick her up.

She was very fat, and from behind, beneath the voluminous shawl she wore, full of mysterious bundles, and her long, black skirt, she looked like an amorphous pyramid. Her walk made you laugh. Because it wasn't a walk; it was a rock. She rocked from one side to the other, from one foot to the other. That is how she moved forward. Nobody knew how.

I prayed that the witch wouldn't identify me as one of the boys who shouted to her from a distance: "Witch! Whore! Bitch!"

My courtesy, my manliness, spoke for me. It certainly wasn't me. I offered her a ride, not for valor's sake but for other reasons.

"Good morning, doña Matilde, let me offer you a ride."

"May God give you a good day, my son. Thank you very much. This damn heat. I can't take it any more. May God bless you."

She started to pass on to me bundles, sacks, boxes, baubles and all sorts of ratty things. Her darn bosom was the horn of plenty vomiting filth without end. I sweated whey to get her in the wagon. Balls and rolls and waves of rotten flesh that shifted, swayed and tumbled in every direction in the giddiest way. Between nauseas and aversions I managed to situate the monster by my side.

I slid as far as I could to the opposite end of the seat. In fact, one of my buttocks was hanging over the side, hanging in the air, in awe and in vain. She smelled bad. From top to bottom and in between. Everytime her clothes touched me I got goose pimples and chills up and down my body. I was tighter and whiter than a bone in the desert.

"How is your mama? That one is the goodest and the bestest in Tierra Amarilla (my mother didn't even know her). And your papa? That one is a sanavagan. That's the way I like men, with them well-placed and well-hung. If you ever get to be half as much a man as your papa is, you'll be a real *pinche*." (I think that in her vocabulary "pinche" meant something like "a somebody.")

She kept on in the same vein, and she never stopped. A monologue without end. Everything between son and bitch. The old hag had a poisoned tongue. Everything about her was bad. For modesty's sake I don't repeat it. I didn't say a word—because I didn't want to, and because I couldn't.

In this way we drove into town. Everyone saw us from the windows and the porches. Then came the grief of unloading her. Moans, groans and grunts, and bad words. I suspect that somebody died of laughter, even though it wasn't announced in mass. The word got around (those things are important out there) that I had guts. This didn't do my chances with the girls any harm. The palms of my hands were sweating, and so were my armpits; I could feel the cold sweat running down my side. I think even my feet were sweating. Naturally, I kept all of this to myself. When one has talent, one knows when to take advantage of a situation.

This was one of my direct contacts with witchery. There are more.

One day I was returning from the mountains, leading a string of mules. I had delivered groceries, block salt for the stock and other necessities to the sheep camps. It got dark on me. The animals had to feel their way because the path was craggy, steep and dangerous.

It was one of those tumultuous and violent nights, mysterious and complex. You carried the clouds on the top of your head. You were the target of a thousand bolts of lightning, fired at you from every direction. Lightning that caught fire and remained floating in the air, licking the fuzz on your face and the hair on your legs, right through your trousers. The illumination hovered long after the lightning had disappeared. Thunder. Thunder that exploded and rolled over and under the clouds and remained trembling as it died on the ground beneath your feet.

They say animals can see the devil, or feel his presence, when we cannot.

My horse was trembling from head to foot. He snorted. He squirmed. And squirmed again. Wanting to soothe him I stroked his neck. A living flame of light would sprout from my hand. I felt sharp electrical stabs over my entire body. My two dogs, so very brave before, were now cowards. They huddled, they crouched, underneath my horse. They whined. Sudden dashes. Abrupt and frightened barking. The mules, strung out in a chain behind me and lost in the blackness, were scared. The lead rope would tighten. They would shake me up and frighten me over and over again. According to tradition, the devil was riding along with me and amusing himself at my expense. The animals knew it. I did not disbelieve it.

Nothing happened. But a great deal of discernment, philosophy and understanding is required in order not to believe in another world of figures and characters, of forces and authorities that are not of this world.

I read books, I was intelligent. I didn't believe in such things. I didn't believe without ever ceasing to believe.

I said that everyone, in one way or another, was touched by the superstition that was in the air, in the land and in all things.

One of my uncles, a university man who had been around, returned to the roundup campfire. He told us how a ball of fire followed him around. That it jumped from hilltop to hilltop all around him. Not a single cowboy laughed. I laughed at my uncle in silence—and I didn't, also in silence.

Another uncle, also a university man, was a cripple, first in bed and later in a wheelchair, for seventeen years, until he died.

It appears that he went to a dance in Canjilón some ten miles from Las Nutrias and the hacienda of my grandmother. On his return in the wee hours of the morning he got caught in one of those fabulous rainstorms left over from the Deluge. He got home wetter than water. Next morning he couldn't get up. His cold became pneumonia. The pneumonia became something else. Now they call it poliomyelitis. In those days we hadn't ever heard the name.

He went to many hospitals. He was operated on many times. Nothing worked. Then my uncles investigated. They discovered that the night of the dance a certain Guadalupe Ríos had offered my uncle Prudencio some chocolates. He was tall, blond and handsome. He had blue eyes. Besides, he was an Ulibarrí. Enough said.

The uncles concluded that my uncle was bewitched. As is well known, if the witch is caught in time, she can be forced to cure the sick one, with the threat of death, naturally. My uncles kidnapped Lupe. Took her out into the country. Put a rope around her neck. Threatened to hang her if she didn't confess. She confessed. But she said that it was too late to cure my uncle. They brought her to our house anyway.

She gave my uncle water to drink with her mouth and did other equally nonsensical things. With no effect whatsoever, as was to be expected. It occurred to me then that under the same circumstances I would have confessed to the murder of Lincoln.

For some unexplainable reason a veritable plague of owls descended on the ranch house. They surrounded the house at night. Their constant "who-who" had all the women scared. Rosaries, novenas, Holy water. Palms from Palm Sunday in the fire. I was a child who observed all of this without understanding it, but the fact that I can remember all this, after such a long time, shows how impressive it must have been.

Since my uncle did not improve, every night my father, my uncles and the hired men went out to shoot owls. As everyone knows, owls are witches, vile vermin at the service of the devil. First, it was necessary to carve a cross with a knife on each bullet. Second, it was necessary to wear your shirt inside out. Everyone would kneel and my grandmother would give them her blessing. Then they went out into the night.

Inside, we heard shooting all over the place. My little brothers and I with eyes as large as plates and with our hearts turned to pudding. We heard many shots and many stories, but we never saw a dead owl. Evidently owls do not die when they should, but only when they want to.

People were talking all over New Mexico in those days about the

Sanador (healer). He was supposed to make miraculous cures. Although nobody there had ever seen him, they said he dressed like Christ, spoke like Christ, and looked like Christ.

It was decided in the family to go find the Sanador for my uncle. So the brothers set out to look for the man of the miracles. They ran into an unexpected problem. The man was impossible to catch. Everywhere they asked about him. "He has just left." They drove and he walked (because he refused to ride), and they couldn't catch up with him. It was supernatural the way the man could mobilize himself.

The brothers became more and more excited because they themselves were witnessing the extraordinary powers of this man. They said that when he was asked where he was from, he would answer, "Heaven." Where he was going, "Heaven." This, the way he dressed, his physical similarity to Christ, the fabulous cures, his unheard of appearances and disappearances, had converted the man into something superhuman, into a saint, perhaps into Christ himself.

They finally caught up with him in an arroyo near Las Vegas, on his knees, praying. They approached him with misgivings, perhaps reverence, so imposing was his look, his figure, his fame.

They explained their mission, stuttering, awkward. The Sanador agreed to visit my uncle, with a gentleness and a sweetness that shook up the brothers religiously or superstitiously. He refused to accompany them. He told them that on such a day at such an hour he would be there.

As they said goodbye, the Sanador approached my father, removed his glasses and smashed them on a rock. My father was left mute and confused. They all left without a word. A miracle. Who knows. The fact is that my father never again wore glasses for the rest of his life.

On the day of the arrival of the Sanador the whole ranch was excited. Movement everywhere. Preparations. There was an atmosphere everywhere of high hopes, confused feelings, religious or superstitious emotions on fire. It seemed that the solitude and the silence of the ranch, the very air that surrounded us, had been humanized. It seemed that they were an extension of our own incensed sensibilities. The silence, the solitude and the air throbbed and trembled along with us.

My grandmother's house was situated on a knoll in the center of a wide valley. It was surrounded by gardens, pastures and fields of grain. There was a sparkling stream that ran along one end of the valley. There was also a pond alongside the corrals to water the stock.

In the distance there was a pine grove, which in a very large measure was the end of the world for us. A narrow road came out of the pine grove, almost always dusty, sometimes covered with snow, sometimes muddy, depending on circumstances, and came as far as the house.

That grove and that road were tremendously significant to me. All good things came from the grove: the few visits that animated our tranquil life and broke the eternal routine, the candy and the goodies to flatter the palate of children, letters, books and the "Denver Post" with its funny papers. I remember it all now with emotion and tenderness.

Lonely and isolated people live in a constant state of expectation. They search every horizon for any movement that will announce a tiny surcease from the weariness of custom.

If the pine grove had always been the Mecca of our looks of longing, today it was truly a cynosure, a target where our eyes were fixed since early morning.

We saw him come out of the pine grove about two o'clock. Someone shouted, "There he comes!" Everyone came out on the porch. There was something like a murmur that started, undulated and terminated. What remained was an intense and conscious silence.

Down the solitary road the Sanador walked alone. From afar we could see his golden hair and beard shine in the afternoon sun. His steps measured. His body erect.

As he approached we could see that his eyes were densely blue and his look was incisive as metal. His expression, benevolent and compassionate. He wore a tunic that reached to his feet and over it a blue robe. Sandals on his feet. For me, and I believe for everyone else, he was Christ himself.

Without preambles, and before anyone said anything, he asked, "Where is the sick one?" His voice was as sweet, and smooth, and rich as the rest of his person. There was an aura of light, well-being and confidence that irradiated from this man that convinced and converted the most incredulous.

He was taken to the room of my uncle Prudencio. He walked directly to the bed, took his hand in both of his, and looked deeply into his eyes. Then he walked to the opposite extreme of the room, and extended his two arms toward my uncle. He said to him, "Rise and walk." His imperious voice was the voice of God. My uncle, who had spent years in bed, almost completely paralyzed, sat up in bed. He placed his feet on the floor. He stood up. He tottered a little. He straightened up. Took a step. Then another. He walked to the Sanador. And returned to the bed. The Sanador blessed him.

I saw all of this through the windows. Exactly as I tell it. With my own eyes I saw it, and now I tell it. And I don't lie.

Someone tried to kiss his cloak. He didn't allow it. The women were crying. Some of the men too. Everyone with the awareness that they were in the presence of the miracle and holiness. The saint counselled us to be good, to love our neighbor. He blessed us and left. Alone as he came. We saw him climb the hill to the pine grove. He disappeared as he had appeared.

I don't know if they gave him money or not. I am afraid they did, but I want to believe they didn't. I didn't see it, and I am not going to find out.

Magician, charlatan, hypnotizer, saint? How can I tell? I only know what I saw, and no one can take that away from me. The fact is that my uncle perked up quite a bit, maybe his attitude improved, but as for the rest he remained the same. He never left his bed again. Shortly after the Sanador disappeared entirely, and no one ever saw him again.

Another mysterious figure that appears from time to time in the villages of the north to give people something to talk about is La Llorona. She is a traditional and folkloric personage.

I don't know the real history of this unreal woman. I only know that she is a nebulous figure that appears at night and wails like a lost soul. Naturally everyone is afraid of her because she brings with her all of the terror that lies beyond the grave.

I am going to tell you of a real experience I had with this nocturnal lady. It seems that La Llorona appears only in the summer. One summer her lament was heard. Every night in a different place. Some people even saw her in the distance, but they didn't dare get near. They said she was dressed in white.

The whole town was upset. People didn't talk about anything else. They were afraid to go out at night. Any little sound produced a deafening silence in the house. Everyone stopped breathing. Everyone expecting to hear the lingering lament of a soul in pain.

My house was some distance from the town. Every evening I joined the kids in the church yard to play hide-and-go-seek and baseball. My two German shepherds always went with me.

This particular evening my mother instructed me severely to come home before sunset. But, as frequently happens with young boys, time slipped up on me. It got dark on me before I realized it.

So I was returning home alone in the dark. I was scared. Walking fast. Looking all around. Wetting my lips with the tip of my tongue. A cold sweat in my armpits.

First I heard her. Then I saw her. I stopped. I stiffened. I froze. It seemed that long and twisted roots had grown out of the soles of my feet and penetrated deep into the earth. My blood flowed out of my body through my feet into the earth. I was as pale as a peeled potato. I was nailed. My throat was closed. Run? No chance. Shout? No way.

Like a conscious corpse, stiff and straight, I could see and hear and nothing else. I have known fear other times in my life. On occasion fear has filtered to the very marrow of my bones. But never a fear as total and as mortal as the fear of that night.

I listened fascinated. Without breathing. It was a lament of another world. A lament that flowed out of the earth, undulated in the air, wrapped itself up the pine trees, and climbed up stairways of its own to the very portals of the moon. It descended, dragged itself over the ground, climbed up your legs and flowed into your pores.

It was a theatrical lament. A corrosive chant. It seemed to have echoes and resonances in very ancient times, in very distant places. It seemed that I was familiar with all of this. That in another life, in another time, in another place I had heard this same lament. That this lament was part of my subconscious history, something unknown that I carried in my blood.

Without knowing how, instinctively, all of my body, my mind and my feelings became attuned with this harmony that innundated the wind among the pines in a unique, vital and oneiric atavism. I breathed and palpitated to the rhythm of the melodic spirals and arabesques that rose and fell, that sometimes pierced the heavens, sometimes the earth. Now with joy, now with delirium, now with grief.

The lament was a chant. Studied, disciplined, orchestrated. The measures were punctuated with fleecy sobs and metalic tears. The rhythm, rhapsodic and hysterical, kept pure with the guitar of the diaphragm. Every note was a spasm. Every pause a wound. Trills in the throat that were gasps of agony. If this event had taken place in an opera house it would have been the success of the century.

In the distance she was white, slender and tall. So white, she seemed to be foam, or cloud, or mist. She appeared to float, to swing and undulate in the breeze and in the light of the moon. So slender and so tall that at moments she seemed to stretch out as far as the very portals of the moon, swaying to the rhythm of her song, floating over the waves of her musical wail. Suddenly, she, woman of mystery, and her magical and mystical music became one. They became a real fantasy that filled the night and the world with life, and love, and fear.

I don't know when I realized that all that miracle was over. Everything had changed. The crying continued but now it was a carnal cry. Desperate screams of a woman of flesh and bone. Barking. Snarling. It was difficult for me to analyze what was going on. It was difficult for me to return from where I'd been lost.

My dogs had attacked La Llorona and were killing her. I ran to her. I took the dogs away from her. There on the ground, wrapped in sheets, she whimpered in the basest way, she moaned in the most ordinary manner and covered her face. I ripped the sheet off. It was Atanacia. What a horrible disappointment!

Atanacia was mentally retarded. She was the wife of Casiano. Everyone knew that Casiano was a drunk, a woman-chaser and a poker fiend. A street-fighter and something of a thief. He would disappear for long periods to work elsewhere. He would return with money and new clothes.

He would then proceed to give himself a ball in the cantina, the dances and other places he alone knew. Atanacia lived alone when he was away, and she lived alone when he was home. People said he beat her. Once in a while when they were seen together, he walked in front, she behind, following him like a dog, adoring him like a dog.

Her despair, rage and frustration reached such a point that she got it into her head to straighten him out, frighten him to death or poison his blood. She got the idea of La Llorona.

At night, as he followed his roads of love, she followed him. Since there were no motels or houses of assignation, that is, commercial nests of love, anyone who had nocturnal tastes outside the confines of matrimony had to slip out to the woods, scurry behind a barn, hide in the fields or blend with the shadows. That is why La Llorona appeared in so many places. When word of my discovery got around, Casiano disappeared.

I was never the same again. Through the years I've tried to explain to myself what happened to me that night. There is no doubt, I was transported to another life, to another existence. Maybe to another dimension of this life. My memory recalled things never seen, never heard. My intelligence recognized segments of the unknown. My body, my blood and my nerves harmonized with echoes and resonances of a past beyond my own. On revealing a petty and puny mystery, I found myself with a major and ferocious mystery.

How could the poor idiot Atanacia awaken in me, perhaps in others, such strange feelings and reactions? I never tried to explain to anyone what I couldn't explain to myself. Is it that there is a heritage, an intrahistory, that has nothing to do with biology or with intelligence, that flows unknown from generation to generation? Something that one carries in his blood?

Well, amigos, I could tell you more witcheries, but let's leave them for another time. But I want to tell you that what I have told you happened exactly as I have narrated it, as I saw it and understood it in those years and in that place, Tierra Amarilla.

THE REVOLT OF EDDIE STARNER

John Nichols

AROUND ten o'clock every morning, if it was sunny, an old man, Eddie Starner, settled into a rusty, wrought-iron lawn chair on the ten-foot-square patch of Bermuda grass fronting his three room bungalow, and basked for hours in the bright warmth, reading the morning paper for a while, then watching the street life, then daydreaming. His working days were long over. Three years ago Effie had died, and their two children had become strangers in faraway places. For a time, after Effie's death, Eddie tried living with dogs. But Blackie was a chicken-killer—and had been shot. Toughy never did cotton to house-breaking, so Eddie returned him to the fate he had saved him from at the pound. Then Joe, the Collie, was hit by one of those ass-end high, wide-wheeled cars the teenagers constantly raced up and down the washboard dirt street despite a sign ordering them to Beware of Children. All those canine deaths miffed Eddie, finally, and he threw in the towel. He had his newspaper—it was delivered every morning at six; and he liked to watch TV. Eddie lived off Social Security; his aches and pains were paid by Medicare.

In the past, Eddie had often puttered slowly along the festering irrigation ditch near his house to the bus stop on Central, traveling thence to the main branch of the Public Library where he passed many a pleasant hour browsing among the books, magazines, and national newspapers. But the days of that freedom were over. He'd had a colostomy; his heart had developed a dangerous murmur; there were varicose veins and hardened arteries galore; a broken bone in his left foot had never properly healed; and cataracts in both eyes were just starting to reduce his vision. Therefore, any voyage much beyond the confines of his tiny lawn was strictly taboo. A neighbor did his minimal shopping. Eddie had no phone—who would call? The mailbox, the TV, the newspaper and the streetlife were his connections to the outside world.

Eddie had known for a long time he was waiting to die; even before Effie's heart attack—years before that. They had bought this house right after the war and had spent twenty years paying it off in tiny monthly installments, knowing it would be their only security. Effie, all her life, had been a maid, a laundress, a menial servant. Eddie, the handyman, quietly and efficiently (but never with much imagination) had handled any job from gardening to pumping gas. He had washed dishes, been a grade school janitor, worked for a tree surgeon, and managed a car wash. His best job, for several years, had been as an apprentice to a plumber. His worst jobs had been menial unloading tasks in warehouse districts. Eddie never joined a union—commitments had always made him nervous. He disliked meetings, had never played politics, always followed whoever were the leaders, and kept his own counsel. As a result, his career had proceeded uneventfully along on the margins.

In school, Eddie had barely made it through seventh grade. He was no athlete and had never won a prize. His ambition had never focused on anything more powerful than a desire to finish the day, have a beer with his supper, and then listen to the radio or (later in his life) watch TV. Eddie laughed easily, liking the comic programs, but when television began tracking the Sixties, the violence left him puzzled and uncomfortable. Eddie could not remember ever having to fight, for he threatened no one. He had gotten along well with black people. And, although this dusty street of side-by-side cube houses was mostly Chicano, there had never been tension. For years neighbors had waved and talked about the weather. Although he had developed no true friends, as such, still, his neighbors were mostly non-committal in a good way. Keeping safely to himself, Eddie's life had had an uneventful routine, an impoverished security that was nevertheless a security many people lacked. Thrifty, prudent, and never ones for flash, Eddie and Effie had avoided financial overextension. And even if he and Effie hadn't talked much for thirty-five years, there had existed between them an uneventful understanding and love that had been strong and enduring. Now, seventy-eight years after it all began, Eddie was neither particularly dissatisfied nor uncomfortably curious. Life, which he had never challenged, had forged no bitterness in his heart. Accepting the way one day followed another, bored and lonely but experiencing little agony, Eddie had never wanted anything more than he had gotten; thus he felt little disappointment at the outcome.

So he sat in the sun reading his paper or listening to the radio at his feet, or watching automobiles rumble dustily by. He waved when the people inside the cars waved. He watched the kids playing baseball or football in the road, or congregating nervously and loudly in groups before this house or that one. And one day continued to run quietly into the next one.

Neighborhood people called him Eddie, but almost nobody knew his last name. They regarded him as a neutral old man entirely incidental to the local squabbles, triumphs, or tribulations. This was a street where very poor people paid exorbitant rents for tiny houses, and most of the men were unemployed, and the young girls were beautiful and always laughing too shrilly. Kids spent most of their waking hours in the street; a lot of dope circulated; stolen goods were constantly being purchased at back doors; many of the men and a few of the women were ex-cons; and almost every miniscule back yard had a chicken coop, or a rabbit hutch…and there were goats, sheep, cows, and a few horses, also.

One day in late September, when the desert city was beginning to cool and faint white powder delineated the hefty ridgeline of nearby mountains, something happened to Eddie Starner. He had spent almost the entire afternoon in his chair with the radio tuned low to a music station. Now, as dusk gathered, a light-brown mist, raised by automobiles returning from work, hung over the street and over the box-shaped houses. Because it was Friday afternoon, an end-of-the-week excitement sent a quiver through the dusty atmosphere. Autumn itself, and that new snow powdering the mountaintops, had added to the evening's ante. Captured by the moment, Eddie dawdled a bit past that time when he should have shuffled inside to prepare supper.

Suddenly, his chest was almost cleaved open by the sight of a girl across the street. She merely walked out the front door of her parents' bungalow as he had seen her do a million times before. But for some reason—the street being clear of traffic for a second, and everybody else momentarily indoors—she appeared as a unique, almost miraculous vision. He had heard her called Brenda; he guessed she was about seventeen. Long black hair framed her beautifully big-eyed and cheerful Chicana face. Her breasts were lovely, etched prominently against the soft fabric of a green, V-necked sweater. Tight, powderblue bellbottoms completed the outfit, a standard one for the street. Yet when she emerged into the soft beige atmosphere heading for a parked automobile, something in Eddie burst, and a startling, stifled cry sprang from his lips. Brenda slipped behind the wheel, turned on the radio before starting the car, and disappeared down the street, leaving behind traces of a lilac perfume on the moats of dust circulating passively around Eddie's buzzing, astonished head.

Moments later, while sitting in his chair gazing down the street toward where her car had gone, Eddie began quietly to weep.

That night sleep was impossible. His loneliness had been multiplied a thousand times. Perhaps once every half hour he got up to go to the john.

Around dawn, Eddie finally dozed for a while, emerging into the sunshine well after eleven. But he could not sit still. He puttered around the lawn, raking a few leaves which had fallen from a neighbor's trees, and then burned the leaves. The smoke in his nostrils conjured up a nostalgia that caused his body to twitch from hurt. Going inside, he brewed coffee, then returned to his lawn and stood beside his chair gazing confoundedly at the neighborhood. A hawk slammed into a tree, scaring some English sparrows. His hearing seemed to have sharpened tenfold, and he was aware of myriad radio and television programs. He was also picking up interesting snatches of personal conversations. Chickens, too, after laying eggs, cackled. In fact, the whole neighborhood seemed to resound with a virtual *chorus* of clucking that he had never heard before. And when a car door slammed far down the street, his body ached with a concentrated longing.

That afternoon, by accident, the postman misplaced a letter for the woman next door in Eddie's mailbox. The old man should have conveyed it immediately to the rightful owner. Instead, hunching over the letter like a thief, he rushed into the house, and, seated at his kitchen table, opened the envelope with trembling fingers. It had been mailed from El Paso, and contained nothing special. The writer, a relative, gave one sentence sketches of about a half dozen family members, the marriage of one, the death of another—a good rosary was had by all. By the time he finished reading, however, Eddie was crying again. He read the letter a dozen times, and forgot to fix dinner before going to bed.

Come morning, it seemed as if the chemistry of his body had undergone a radical change. He was so alert he felt crazy. The buzzing of flies became terribly distracting, and, rolling up a newspaper, he tried awkwardly to kill them. The aroma of his morning coffee seemed to almost hum with titillating richness; the taste was damn near sexy it was so pleasant.

Frightened, Eddie stumbled outdoors, his fragile heart racing. The day was a bit breezy and very clear. A kingfisher, perched on a telephone wire over the murky irrigation ditch, waited to spear the minnows which flourished in the scummy drainage littered with tin cans and trashed shopping carts from the nearby K-Mart over on Central. Opening his gate, Eddie ventured into the street. A car beeped goodnaturedly, veering to avoid bumping him. Watching it rattle down the street, Eddie had a fierce urge to travel.

Back inside he fished several dollars out of a tin can, then hit the road. Shuffling along the high ditch bank, his clouding eyes (which focused with unnatural perception) skipped over the water, prodding the murky liquid for a tinsel flash of minnows. A muskrat—he had never seen a muskrat in that inhospitable water—stopped eating something and looked up.

Eddie halted several times, catching his breath. Enormous black crows strutted among the garbage and prickly tumbleweeds of a vacant lot. Eddie observed them for so long, and with such intense curiosity, that eventually, growing nervous, they took off. And Eddie resumed his voyage, arriving soon at the outer limits of the crowded parking lot which lay two hundred yards from his home.

For over a year Eddie had not journeyed so far. Cautiously, he crept between rows of dazzling automobiles. Then he limped inside the crowded grocery section of the enormous store.

Bewildered, Eddie merely wandered, unable to think of what to buy. At a paperback book rack he gazed transfixed at a thousand exciting novel covers. Nearby a few girls and an elderly lech were leafing through magazines like *Playboy*, *Oui*, and *Viva*. Huge pink limbs and other female accessories jumped loudly in Eddie's direction—the girls were giggling.

It was all so strange. Baffled, tingling, squeezed and choked-up and scared, Eddie meandered among the abundant merchandise. So much of everything existed; the colors were incredibly bright and nearly sizzled. Raucous kids dodged among the shoppers. Lush girls sauntered by, flaunting their bodies. Ugly women with their hair trapped in curlers had lips frozen into snarls. Indians wore black cowboy hats; and Chicano youths—hip, mustachio'd, their costumes on fire—boasted loudly through this mundane business of grabbing the groceries. The cheese bins had a smell, as did the bread counters. And the coffee counters sang of coffee, the meat cases yodled about fresh meat. The air was chilly over the ice cream freezers; Eddie shivered. An odor of summer hovered above the fresh fruits and vegetables. Gingerly, picking up apples, Eddie revolved them slowly in his hands; cautiously, he fingered waxy cucumbers. Next, he lifted a grapefruit to his nose, sniffing. But he could think of nothing to buy, having no idea what it was he wanted.

Then Eddie was exhausted. His legs, trembling, buckled. Frightened, he made his way out of the chattering supermarket. Cars glared hotly in the parking lot; a police siren went off; people scrambled everywhere, as if for shelter.

For a moment, turning in circles, Eddie lost his bearings. A ragamuffin carting a small, greasy box asked if he wanted to buy a tamale; Eddie shook his head and pushed off into the parking lot. The sky was changing a little, a misty gray color giving it a kind of frown. Eddie found his way to the ditch, almost tripped on a concrete border, and, albeit at a snail's pace, hurried home.

Although he should have collapsed, a terrible need to answer the bustle gathering in his head with corresponding physical activity kept him moving. Eddie scouted his kitchen for edibles, put together the sort of meal he had not fashioned in ages—fried potatoes, two eggs, green peas, toast—and hunched at his kitchen table ravenously eating, washing the meal down with a last can of beer which had been in the refrigerator for months.

His teeth were chattering when he lunged outside and seated himself in the lawn chair. The day was still warm, if overcast. The sky, hard blue beyond the mountains, was misty directly above. Then the air went off with a sharp prickling *bang!* and tree leaves, reacting to nervous currents, uplifted silver'd stormy edges. All dust settled, and Eddie beheld his immediate neighborhood with a clarity that defied understanding.

Rain, at first an almost imperceptible drizzle, began to fall. And Eddie sat there, growing damp and crying again for perhaps five minutes, until, with an abrupt, passionate shout, half lifting out of his chair, he shook a fist defiantly at the sky like a man accusing God for giving birds, instead of men, wings.

THE DAY IT RAINED BLOOD

Tim MacCurdy

MOST residents of Albuquerque know how the Sandia Mountains, which form the eastern rampart of the city, got their name. Minutes before sunset the slanting rays begin to play a game of magic colors on the western slope of the mountains, bathing them in ever-changing hues of green, gold, rose, red, and purple. And finally the mountains take on tones of dark gray, almost of funereal black, as if they were mourning the death of the sun.

In this mutation of colors there is a moment, a precise and fleeting moment, when the reddish tints call to the mind of some observers the color of an opened, well-ripened watermelon. For this reason, it is said, when the Spanish explorers passed through the central Rio Grande Valley in search of the golden cities of Cibola, they tried to capture and eternalize that fleeting moment—that elusive color—by naming the mountains the Sandias.

The Watermelon Mountains? I have no reason to doubt the authenticity of this tradition, but for me those haunting shades of red never coalesce into the red of a watermelon. Rather, they approximate the vivid crimson of the Sangre de Cristo range whose color captures the awesomeness of the Passion. But there is an unmistakable difference: the Sangre de Cristo's red remains bright, arterial, until it simply fades away; the Sandias' luminous red changes instantly to the color of venous blood, darkening before the viewer's eyes into the imminence of death.

I was always intrigued by that difference; then by chance, by sheer accident, I discovered the secret of the Sandias' uncanny red.

During the summer session, as I had done many times before, I took my anthropology class to examine Sandia Cave in Las Huertas Canyon toward the northern end of the mountain. After we inspected the cave we gathered on the flats above it for a picnic supper; then, as twilight began to descend, most of the students wandered off to explore the area before darkness set in. I remained behind, leaning against a boulder and musing upon the centuries of life—of birth and death—to which the cave had been both theater and spectator.

Suddenly my attention was arrested by a sharp object that protruded two or three inches above the surface of a shallow gully. At first I thought it was a sharp-pointed rock that remained half buried, but after digging around it with a stick, I saw it was the prong of an antler. I went to the edge of the cliff and called to a student to bring a shovel. By the time he made his way up to the flats it was almost dark, but we dug away until a set of antlers was faintly visible. Because of the growing darkness I suggested that we cover the antlers and return the following day to continue with the excavation.

I cannot expect anyone except those who were present—I didn't find it credible myself—to believe what we unearthed the next day. There were two deer skulls, those of a large buck and a doe, but there were also two human skeletons. It is not unusual, of course, to find human and animal bones in the same grave, but what was remarkable was that we found no skeletal remains corresponding to the animal skulls, nor did we find human skulls pertaining to their skeletons. Baffled by this circumstance, we submitted the bones to laboratory tests which led to only one possible conclusion, one we were reluctant to accept though we had no alternative: the vertebrae of the spines and necks clearly joined the skulls, so the animal skulls belonged to—indeed were part of—the human skeletons.

It was a simple matter to date the remains by additional laboratory tests; both skulls and skeletons had met "their" deaths in the sixteenth century. There was another curious bit of evidence that intrigued me: lodged in the chest cavity of each of the skeletons, in the exact location formerly occupied by the heart, was a large flint spearhead. The spearheads, however, were quite different. One seemed to be of the design used by the hunters of Retama Pueblo, twenty-five miles north of Albuquerque, from the twelfth to the seventeenth century; the other, quite distinct in its greater length and narrowness, appeared to have been fashioned by hunters of Marana Pueblo, nineteen miles south of the city.

Anxious to verify my identification of the spearheads, I went to see Pablo Jaramillo of Retama Pueblo who had been my student many years before. Now a councilman of the pueblo, Jaramillo had immersed himself in the history and traditions of all the Tiguex pueblos and had become an authority on their artifacts. He listened intently to my story, but he could shed no light on the inexplicable mixture of human and animal remains. However, he confirmed the identity of the spearheads, though he remained puzzled by the fact that spears of Retama and Marana pueblos should claim victims in the same hunt.

Jaramillo repeated what had long been accepted as fact by anthropologists and historians of the pueblos: the people of Retama and Marana had been bitter enemies long before the Pueblo Revolt of 1680 and the abandonment of the pueblos following De Vargas' reconquest in 1692. It was therefore unlikely that they should join in the same hunting party in the sixteenth century, unless the hunt had something to do with the curse of Fray Ramón.

"The curse of Fray Ramón?" I asked. "What was the curse of Fray Ramón?"

Jaramillo lowered his head and stroked his chin, as if he were trying to recover an elusive fact from the deep well of memory. After a few moments he said that he had forgotten many of the details concerning the curse of Fray Ramón but that he would try to arrange for me to meet a man who could tell me about the curse.

Two days later Jaramillo telephoned me to come to Retama. When I arrived he said he wanted me to talk to a man named Mohol, the oldest inhabitant of the pueblo. He led me beyond the pueblo to a small adobe house on a knoll near the cemetery. He knocked on the door, entered without waiting for a reply, and returned to motion for me to come in. There, sitting in a chair with his head thrown back, was a white-haired man whose eyes were fixed on the ceiling. Flies buzzed about his head and occasionally landed on his face, but he did not flinch nor did his eyes leave the ceiling. I assumed he was blind.

Jaramillo said something to Mohol in Tiwa which I did not understand, but for a minute or two the old man did not reply, continuing to stare upward. Then, without moving his head, he asked me in Spanish if I spoke the language. After I answered I did, he said Jaramillo had told him about my discovery in the flats above Sandia Cave. He offered no explanation of the mixed human and animal remains, but he said he could tell me something about another occasion when Retama and

Marana spearheads were found in the same victim, a victim who was close to Fray Ramón.

"But who was Fray Ramón?" I asked.

For the first time Mohol changed his position, letting his chin drop to his chest before answering. Fray Ramón, he said, was a Franciscan friar who had accompanied Coronado on his expedition to New Mexico. When Coronado returned to Mexico (which I remembered was in 1542), he left several Franciscan friars behind to live and work among the Indians. Two of the Franciscans, Fray Juan and Fray Ramón, remained in the Tiguex pueblos. Though respected by most of the Indians, Fray Juan was later killed by *indios bárbaros* while making his missionary rounds in Santa Barbara Pueblo.

Fray Ramón, a young man, lived in Retama Pueblo where he became "one of us." He learned the language, the customs, the traditions. He joined in hunting parties; he participated in the dances and other rituals. He rejoiced when the harvests were good, but suffered when times were bad. So anxious was he to help our people that he persuaded the medicine man to share his secrets with him. But Fray Ramón never forgot his Christian duties. He started to build a church, but work on it was interrupted when the Maranas staged a raid on Retama, killing several people and taking one captive, a young man.

"But what caused the enmity between the two pueblos?" I interrupted.

"Once we were friends," Mohol replied. "We spoke the same language; our people used to marry their people. But later when the Maranas sided with our enemies, the Pihucas, the bad blood began. They raided us and we raided them. Our fathers warned our young people that if they married Maranas they would bring a blight on our pueblo and the guilty parties would be punished by being transformed into animals."

"What do you mean they would be transformed into animals?" I asked.

The old man shrugged his shoulders and continued. Fray Ramón urged his people not to take revenge on the Maranas for the raid, saying he wanted to go live a while in Marana Pueblo and teach them the ways of peace. The Retamas were unhappy to see him go, but when he assured them his absence would not be long, they promised to continue work on the church dedicated to the Christian God.

But Fray Ramón stayed away for a long time, and when he returned he seemed to be a changed man. He showed little interest in the church which was nearing completion, and he brought with him a Marana woman "with whom he joined." At first the Retamas were reluctant to accept the woman in their midst, but Fray Ramón told them her presence would insure peace between the two pueblos. Gradually she was accepted, and the two of them—Fray Ramón and the woman—often visited Marana Pueblo as messengers of peace.

Mohol again tilted his head back, fixed his eyes on the ceiling, and let out a guttural moan. Then, he said, the bad years began. Many moons without a drop of rain. The springs and arroyos dried up, the fields became arid, the maize and the beans withered, the winds buried many houses in drifts of sand and dust. The Retamas began to perform rain dances almost daily, but when the rains refused to come they called on Fray Ramón to intercede with the Christian God. Fray Ramón shook his head sadly and told them to have faith in their shaman and their dances, and often he would lead the dances himself, yelling strange words and throwing himself on the ground.

Then one day the murder happened. The Marana woman was found tied to a tree on the knoll with Retama and Marana spears piercing her heart.

"Retama and Marana spears?" I exclaimed. "Then who killed her?"

Mohol continued as if he had not heard me. The Retamas thought Fray Ramón would be very sad when he learned of the woman's death, but he said only, "Now the bad days will end. The curse will be lifted."

But the bad days didn't end. For several moons no rains came and the fields lay wasted. Fray Ramón kept to himself, in this very house where we sit, but one day he appeared before the council and said, "I promise that tomorrow the rains will come."

Early the next day the people gathered in the plaza but Fray Ramón did not appear. When they looked for him in the church and at his house, they could not find him or his horse. Late in the afternoon, as the sun began to sink, clouds started to build up over the mountains and suddenly it began to rain. It rained and rained—but blood, not water. Torrents of blood ran down the arroyos on the western slope, and a single cloud drifted over Retama Pueblo and drenched it with blood. Our fathers called it The Day It Rained Blood.

I looked at Mohol in disbelief. "But what about Fray Ramón?" I asked. "Did he ever return?"

"He's buried out on the knoll, next to the Marana woman."

"What do you mean?" I asked.

Mohol didn't answer me but said something to Jaramillo in Tiwa.

My friend took me by the arm and led me outside. He took me to the top of the knoll and pointed to a gnarled old cedar. He said, "This is the tree the Marana woman was tied to when they found her murdered. Just before sunset the tree casts a shadow that points towards the Sandias. The woman and Fray Ramón are buried in that shadow."

I walked over to the shadow that was beginning to lengthen as the sun was sinking in the west. Just beyond the shadow, in the direction of the Sandias, was a small spring that oozed clear water. But as I watched it, every few moments it would spurt out a deep red liquid.

"That," said Jaramillo, "is the blood of Fray Ramón. That's why we call the spring *el Ojo de la Sangre de Fray Ramón.*"

Sunset cast its golden rays on the western slope of the Sandias. The gold began to change to rose. I glanced at the spring and its clear water suddenly changed to dark red. I looked back at the mountains whose rosy hue gave way, at that very instant, to the color of venous blood.

WHEN I RETURNED HOME I was intrigued but confused by Mohol's story. I had never heard of Fray Ramón before, and I didn't understand what his curse was supposed to mean. A curse upon him? A curse on the pueblo for which he was responsible? Or was it just a baseless Indian legend?

I went to the library and dug out the writings of the early Franciscan chroniclers of New Mexico. All speak specifically of three Franciscan friars whom Coronado left behind to continue their missionary work among the Indians: Luis de Escalona who was later killed by Indians at Cicuyé (Pecos), Juan de Padilla who was martyred at Quivira (Kansas), and Juan de la Cruz who met his death in the Tiguex pueblos. Fray Juan de la Cruz would correspond, of course, to the Fray Juan whom Mohol said was murdered by *indios bárbaros* in Santa Barbara Pueblo.

None of the chroniclers mentions a Fray Ramón nor a fourth Franciscan by any other name. Was Fray Ramón a fictitious being created by the Indians, or was he a real person whom the historians, for some obscure reason, chose to bury in oblivion?

I was also perplexed by the striking similarity in the circumstances of the murder of the Marana woman, as related by Mohol, and the death of the creatures whose remains I had found in the flats above Sandia Cave. Was it significant that the instruments of death in both cases were spearheads of the inimical Retamas and Maranas?

My curiosity—my eagerness to know—permitted me no rest. Early the next morning I called Pablo Jaramillo to see if he could arrange for me to speak to Mohol again. Jaramillo told me to come to Retama and he would try to arrange a meeting. Again we climbed up to Mohol's hut on the knoll near the cemetery. Again Jaramillo knocked on the door, entered, and returned to usher me in. Mohol was in the same position as I had first seen him the day before; he was sitting in the same chair, his head thrown back, his eyes fixed on the ceiling. I greeted him, but he said nothing.

Jaramillo gestured with his hand for me to proceed with my questions. I told Mohol as tactfully as I could that I didn't doubt his story but that the Franciscan chroniclers didn't mention a Fray Ramón. Could it be possible that his forefathers had confused Fray Ramón with Fray Juan de la Cruz who, the chroniclers agreed, was killed in one of the Tiguex pueblos?

For minutes Mohol remained silent, impassive. Then suddenly the furrows in his face deepened, his lips trembled, and he began to speak: "Before I die I want my people to know the truth. Fray Ramón did live among us; he is buried beside the Marana woman in the shadow of the cedar. We have his rosary and prayer book. I have never seen them, nobody has ever seen them, but they are buried below his feet just above the spring."

Jaramillo was as impatient as I to excavate the graves, but he said the entire council must give its approval before the excavation could begin. Days passed, weeks went by, but nothing happened. My impatience grew until, one morning, Jaramillo called to say the pueblo council had given its permission. Late that afternoon, when the cedar's shadow almost reached the spring—*el Ojo de la Sangre de Fray Ramón*—we began to dig. Three feet, six feet—nothing.

Wearied from their work, the diggers wanted to give up the task but Jaramillo and I urged them on. Then, at the depth of eight feet, they struck the first bone. In my excitement I grabbed a shovel and unearthed the remains of two bodies, a man and a woman. Lodged in the chest cavity of the female were two spearheads, one from Retama Pueblo, the other from Marana.

I dug cautiously below the feet of the male skeleton and struck a hard object. A rock? After we succeeded in removing it, we scraped away the caliche that clung to it. It was a large earthen pot. Inside it, covered with sand, were a rosary and a breviary.

A typical sixteenth-century breviary, its Latin text was printed in

Gothic letters on parchment folios. Inserted through the breviary at irregular intervals were several loose parchment leaves, apparently torn from another religious book. They bore printed Latin text on one side, and on the back, in cursive handwriting, were passages written in Spanish. The first such passage was clearly legible, though many of the later leaves were blemished and blotted. The handwriting also became jerky and erratic, as if the writer had been hurried or extremely tense.

At the top of the first entry were three crosses, underneath which appeared the words, "Jesús, María y José." In the following text the writer speaks of the blessing granted by God in allowing him to remain among the savages to win souls for the Savior. He goes on to speak of his desire to build a church for which he had already selected a name, *Nuestra Señora de Atocha.*

The second leaf, inserted several pages further on in the breviary, reflects the writer's enthusiasm over the success of his mission. He had made numerous converts and had started construction on the church with the help of local artisans. Moreover, he had begun to take an interest in the rituals and ceremonies of the pueblo, for even though they were fraught with ungodly paganism and superstition, he could better carry out his work if he understood them.

The third entry, apparently written months later, mentions that work on the church had progressed well, but what intrigued me most was a reference to a raid made by the Maranas on the Retamas in which several people were killed and a Retama youth named Miguel was taken captive. It was the first time that a specific detail contained in the handwritten entries coincided with an incident related by Mohol.

I was then ready to admit that Fray Ramón was a real person and the loose leaves inserted in his breviary constituted a kind of journal, for even though they were not dated they were spaced in chronological order. Furthermore, in addition to the mention of the raid, the texts conformed in a general sense to the story Mohol had learned through the oral traditions of his people, although there were a few discrepancies.

The next insertion was obviously written after Fray Ramón had been in Marana Pueblo for a long period, since he notes that he was beginning to enjoy the confidence "of my new children" and he was assisted in the mass by "my beloved Miguel," the Retama youth captured by the Maranas.

One morning after mass Miguel confided to Fray Ramón that he was in love with María, a recent Marana convert, but he was unable to marry her publicly because of the enmity of the two pueblos. Sympathetic to the young couple, Fray Ramón thought that their marriage, once celebrated, might be the very means by which peace could be brought to their peoples, so he decided to marry them secretly on the occasion of the forthcoming deer-dance when the Maranas would be occupied with their festivities.

On the appointed day, after having performed the ceremony, Fray Ramón went to the plaza to watch the dance which went on until the late hours of the night. Suddenly an old woman appeared in the midst of the crowd and began yelling that the Retama youth and María were lying together in a field behind the pueblo. Enraged, the people hurried to the field, but the couple managed to escape in the darkness.

This long entry closes with a single sentence of self-condemnation. "Because of my fear of alienating the Maranas I did not tell the people I had married them."

The next few inserts were so erratically written that I could decipher only a few isolated sentences. Most of the sentences appear on different parchment leaves, an indication they were written at various times, but when one reads them sequentially, they form a startling and, paradoxically, a predictable pattern. In view of what Mohol had said about Fray Ramón's Marana woman, I should have been prepared for the revelations contained in these brief sentences, but on reading them in the priest's own frenzied handwriting, I was shocked. I transcribe them in the order in which they occur:

Lent, penance, mortification. Love God.
I shall scourge myself of lust.
I fear I shall lose my soul for the body of a woman. God keep me from despair!
And if thy hand offend thee, cut it off——

Then comes the final entry among these spaced insertions, the last one written in Marana Pueblo. Hand-printed in block letters are words taken from the Lord's Prayer. "THY WILL BE DONE," but these words are negated by that wrenching utterance spoken by Christ on the Cross, "MY GOD, MY GOD, WHY HAST THOU FORSAKEN ME?"

There is a long interval in the breviary before the next insert which was written after Fray Ramón's return to Retama Pueblo with the Marana woman. He speaks of having spent the night enroute at Nafait (now Sandia Pueblo) where the hunters told him that on several occasions they saw two deer, a buck and a doe, in the brush on the cliff above a canyon. Every time they closed in on the deer they disappeared into thin air (in Fray Ramón's own words, *como por magia*).

I can only assume that Fray Ramón's heart told him the deer were Miguel and María, for without any transition whatsoever, he goes on to say he spent two days searching the area described by the Nafait hunters, and suddenly the couple appeared before him. Miguel told him that whenever they were seen by hunters, they would climb over the edge of the cliff to seek refuge in a cave whose mouth was concealed from the canyon below and from the flats above by dense brush.

Sandia Cave, of course, I said to myself. Then I remembered Mohol said Fray Ramón and the Marana woman made several trips to her pueblo "as messengers of peace," but I became convinced that the trips were pretexts to take provisions to Miguel and María.

Only four parchment leaves remained inserted in the breviary. Although the annotations on them were written on different occasions, perhaps days or even weeks apart, all seem to point to an inexorable conclusion. The first of the four is significant because it contradicts what Mohol had said about the Retamas' acceptance of the Marana woman. It reads, "They vilify the woman but they should vilify me, for I who preached purity and chastity to my people continue to commit an abomination in the sight of God."

There is, however, a confirmation of part of Mohol's story in the next entry. After describing the drought that blighted the fields of Retama Pueblo, Fray Ramón notes that his parishioners pled with him to invoke the intercession of the Christian God, but he urged them to trust in their rain dances. When the drought continued, the shaman summoned the people, telling them that in the past a prolonged drought was caused by the violation of a taboo: the cohabitation of a Retama and a Marana. The drought could be ended only if the offenders were identified and slain with Retama and Marana spearheads, one of each for the two "animals."

Then, in this same written entry, Fray Ramón shifts from the shaman's words to his own. "I have violated the taboo. My sin has brought this curse upon my people. I must sacrifice the woman. When I bind her to the cedar, may God deliver her as he delivered Isaac from the sword of Abraham!"

Even though I was now convinced of Fray Ramón's complete

derangement, I was not prepared for the chilling words written on the last two parchment leaves. The next to last reads, "My sacrifice of the woman has not found favor with the Lord. The drought continues because of them. I must go to the cave and slay them both, for they are animals, accursed animals!"

I could hardly control the shaking of my hands when I removed the last insert from the breviary. Its words haunt me yet. "'Tis done! The blood, the blood! The blood will wash away the drought and let me sleep in the shade of the cedar."

When the last rays of the setting sun strike the western slope of the Sandias I do not see the red of an opened watermelon. I do not see the arterial red of the Blood of Christ. I see venous blood cascading down the mountains until it disappears underground and seeps out again in *el Ojo de la Sangre de Fray Ramón.*

THE SWING

Michael A. Thomas

WHEN they arrived, Plutarco was sick with diarrhea and fatigue. He'd come to help Alberto if he could. They had worked together on a job. Plutarco did finish carpentry and Alberto worked for the roofers. They were laid off and no work would turn up for a while. Alberto decided to use the time to see about the trouble his wife had mentioned in a letter. He was worried. His wife had written that someone had bought their village and everyone had to move. She was staying with an aunt in Oaxaca City, miles from the small village. Alberto couldn't believe what he read. He had to see for himself. Plutarco went along. They'd travelled deep into Mexico, through the desert, into the highlands, and down, down, a long valley to Oaxaca. It seemed as far from Deming as the moon.

The aunt lived far from the center of Oaxaca City in a poor colonia, *El Arco Iris*, the rainbow. The corrugated cardboard house was in the midst of other poor houses near the river. The yard was full of children, chickens, and flowers potted in coffee cans. Alberto's wife welcomed Plutarco formally. She had the weirdest accent in Spanish he'd ever heard. Everything was aspirated and she talked very slowly. She got a straight-backed wooden chair from the kitchen and placed it in the center of the yard. Plutarco sat down. Alberto sent his little girl to get another chair and began to play with his little boy. When the girl finally brought the chair, he took it and immediately ordered her off to get beer. He gave her money, told her to take a bucket, and admonished her to be careful. He then turned his attention briefly to his wife, telling her that their guest was hungry and in need, as well, of medicine for his diarrhea. The woman hopped to, began making tortillas and fixing a meal. Maria Equibel Zot P. could speak very little Spanish. Alberto claimed to be "breaking her to the language" by refusing to speak the Indian dialect. Mostly he just gave orders.

It was the darndest thing Plutarco had ever seen. Five days they were there, and Alberto didn't really converse with his wife. It was difficult to understand. In his family the men and women liked nothing better than sitting around the kitchen table jabbering for hours and drinking beer or coffee. Alberto was more like a boss in the house, odd and aloof with his wife and children.

The house belonged to Maria's Aunt Serafina Crisostomo, who lived in a house that shared the south wall. Serafina was in her sixties and greatly different from her niece in temperament and demeanor. She was small in stature but powerful in her presence. Plutarco could see that Serafina was the kind of person who made a little money on everything she did. She sold textiles on the sidewalks in Oaxaca City. Some of these she made and some she bought from other women, women even poorer than herself. She invested the money she made in pigs. These she fed with scraps she collected in buckets each morning at 5:30 when the marketeers in the Oaxaca vegetable market prepared the day's wares. She lent small sums of money at interest and, for a good price on finished products, provided sewing materials to women too poor to buy their own. When she slaughtered a pig she sold the cracklings and expanded the meat, making a seemingly infinite number of tamales. Boys sold the tamales on a commission basis. She organized her kin and her *comadres* to do the work. Along these paths a portion of the tiny amount available in the *colonia* seemed to find its way to her. She had, as she said, no husband to drink it up, so she was able to build at least three houses. Plutarco suspected that the compassion she'd shown her niece was related to the fact that Maria had a "mite" from Alberto she could use as rent.

Serafina had the one bed in the neighborhood, a twin-sized bed that consisted of a frame and springs. On top she put her straw *petate*. Everyone else slept on *petates* on the hard clay floor. At night it rained and got hot. It was hard to sleep. Given Plutarco's weakened condition, it was agreed that he should take Serafina's bed during the day while Alberto found out what he could about the land. Serafina was around the house all day—sewing, buying textiles from women who waited respectfully at the gate, and caring for her pigs. She talked to Plutarco at length, and he enjoyed it. She spoke Spanish very well, while Maria barely spoke it at all. When Plutarco mentioned this, the old lady replied.

"She's a country girl, just like the country mouse. I was like her at that age. She has not learned yet that to be an Indian is to be lower than a dog. Alberto is a man who knows; he is handling her the way she's got to be handled. I tell her she's got to forget that Mixtec funny business, even though the sounds of that tongue still bring tears to my eyes. Her mother, my older sister—more a mother to me—spoke no Spanish. 'Look at you,' she told me. 'Start speaking that hwadadadada, and then you start cheating people.' They call Spanish 'hwadadadada' to mock it. But you live on the backs of others unless you're an Indian. Then everyone else lives on your back. This old girl will take the hwadadadada." She called Plutarco "The Black Gringo" and laughed. He tried with very limited success to explain that there were quite a few people of Spanish ancestry in the U.S. This made her laugh even more. "Spanish?" she said, "Pure Castilian too, I'll bet—you look like your Granny was an Indian, your Grandpa, too, for that matter. *Puro Castillano.*" Here she laughed for some time. "That's an Indian with his first pair of shoes he's cut with holes to ease the bunions from his huaraches—*puro Castillano.*"

Plutarco got mad, and slept for a while. She brought him tea a little later. After drinking the tea, he asked her how the people of Alberto's village had lost their land.

"Just like it always happens," she said. "The strong prey upon the weak. It happens all the time. Where do you think the people in this place come from if not the sticks? They leave. They get kicked out. They lose water rights. The big boys take them over. They get drunk and sell. Their mother dies, and they mortgage everything for the funeral. Nobody helps each other in the countryside any more. It used to be that when a man was in a jam he could call on his compadres...'*eh, compadre*,' he'd say, 'lend me, for the love of God, an oxen or 50 pesos for seed or whatever.' Now a man's *compadres* are scattered all over the world, and for many there's no recourse. The banks eat people alive. I lend people money. If they get into a scrape I say 'Just pay the interest till you get on your feet.' The banks come in and take all that a person has."

Plutarco was interested in the details in the case of Alberto's village. He pressed her.

"It boils down to this, my little black gringo: The rich and powerful take by force from the poor and weak. You still don't understand that's the way of this world. This place here should be called the *colonia* of the losers. Every day they arrive. They seem to drop from the very skies with nothing but the clothes they wear, an appetite, and fingers quick to steal.

"Before I was born, there was a war in the mountains. One day soldiers with funny hats came to my grandparents' little cabin. They raped my mother all morning and shot her older brother when he tried to stop them. Finally they left and took the pig and all the chickens. Two days later, soldiers in grey shirts showed up. When they found no livestock, they said my grandparents were helping the enemy. They shot my mother's other brothers and spent another half day raping her. My half-brother, may he rest in peace, was the issue of the rapings. That's how Alberto lost his land. Those with the wherewithal took what they wanted, making no apologies. It's the way of this world, my little black gringo."

The day passed with alternating intervals of rest, medicinal teas, and conversation. The teas worked pretty well. Alberto spent the day here and there in Oaxaca City, trying to get information about his village and his land. By the time he returned, Plutarco was feeling almost normal. His bowels, though still a little tender, were neither painful nor cramping uncontrollably. The day had not been particularly fruitful for Alberto. He'd found one *compadre* who knew little about the land situation in the hills. He'd decided that the only way to learn about the land would be to make a trip to the village. He had relatives, godparents, and *compadres* in nearby villages.

The next morning, Alberto woke Plutarco in the magical stillness of predawn. In the poor light of a candle augmenting a nail-paring moon, Maria prepared a meal of tortillas, beans, and the sugared coffee Plutarco had learned to loathe. They ate quickly and left in the darkness. They took 20 or 30 tortillas and a little covered ceramic bucket of milk along as a lunch.

They bused to the center of the city, where they caught a rural bus that took them north and west into the hills. How far they rode was difficult to gauge, but it took two or three hours. When they finally arrived, the bright full sun of mid-morning beat down on the dirt road, wooded hills, and poor fields around them.

The rest of the day involved a lot of walking and many conversations Plutarco could not understand. Most people spoke only Mixtec.

When they arrived at what Alberto identified as "his village," there was not much to be seen: fallow desolate fields lined by *maguey* plants and areas gouged by tractors or bulldozers. They walked to the site where Alberto's home had been. A bulldozer scar marked the spot. "I'm glad I didn't hide any money around here," Alberto commented. "I'd never find it now." They were at the site for a few minutes when an armed man on horseback showed up and ordered them away. He was gruff and wore a fancy straw hat tied back behind the neck.

"This is private property," he said. "No trespassing here."

Alberto behaved in a way Plutarco could scarcely have predicted. He took off his hat as the horseman arrived and held it in both hands in front of him, hanging his head as the man spoke. When he rode away, Alberto spat derisively after him. "That bastard probably has his wife and kids digging through the debris at all the houses. That's why he got here so fast. He feared we would get something. Let him dig here until his back breaks. I know how little gain is in it." He looked around as though disgusted. His lower lip, however, trembled as he gazed on the place of his birth. Plutarco was silent. They left the site in silence. Soon Alberto began to speak, reflecting once more on how lucky he'd been not to have sunk any money into the property.

They found, that afternoon, one of Alberto's uncles and a godfather. Both men were older, perhaps in their fifties; both were Indians who wore no shoes, spoke no Spanish and were drunk. Alberto was neither surprised nor particularly shaken in his purposes by their drunken state. He told Plutarco that in the countryside almost everyone grows *maguey* and makes *pulque*, which is a dietary mainstay. By mid-afternoon, he said, everyone is a little drunk.

Plutarco was so nervous that he got a little drunk himself. Alberto talked to the men a long time. Plutarco could not understand so much as a word. He was impressed, however, by the demeanor of the men. They were shy and affectionate with one another, giggling like girls at the slightest provocation. They seemed healthy, strong, and wiry, especially for men who are drunk every afternoon.

After a long, formal, affectionate parting, they left the men to their siestas and their *pulque*. They'd talked for a couple of hours. Alberto hadn't learned, however, as much as Plutarco might have thought.

A holding company of Mexican investors now owned the land, which they were going to lease to a "big outfit" known as Club Med. What would happen to the land no one seemed to know. Government officials, speaking through interpreters to the people being evicted, reminded them of their rights—guaranteed by the revolution—to work land in the public domain elsewhere. The people didn't understand and went away to live where they could.

Not too many people had been dislocated. There were, perhaps, a hundred people in the village, counting men who were elsewhere, but it had been a sad affair.

Alberto's uncle and godfather told him to forget the land. It was gone, and that was a fact of life. At least, they said, he'd not bought it, and there was, after all, other land to buy.

Alberto agreed that this was the practical view. "But I was born here," he told Plutarco.

Alberto had drunk more pulque than Plutarco. The men felt bloated in the afternoon heat. They walked a distance back toward Alberto's village, and they decided to rest for a while under a large cypress tree.

They lay under the tree and marvelled together at the world that continued to unfold in its characteristic fashion. The hills seemed wrapped in golden haze. To the tutored eye, this haze was a reminder of the drought that afflicted the area. In Plutarco's ignorance and Alberto's apathy, however, the golden haze was quite simply beautiful, as though the earth had been made an angel and been given a halo. In the blue sky above the golden rimmed hills, hawks soared.

From their vantage point beneath the tree, they could see a long way. The could see the small, jewel-like lake that had attracted Club Med. They could see what had been Alberto's village on a steep hillside nearby. They sat with their backs supported by a mammoth cypress, facing west into the sun. Before long the sun would set. Looking at the site of the village, Plutarco remarked that for a man like Alberto, with legs the same length, such a village was not appropriate. They laughed. They watched a deer walk onto the point of a hill just south of them and sun itself.

"It's said that a deer gave corn to humans," Alberto said. Plutarco, watching the graceful animal bask, did not reply directly. "That one there has not missed many meals," he laughed. "Perhaps that one kept the corn." They lay there and enjoyed themselves.

"This tree," Alberto eventually said, breaking a long silence, "was where the young girls came at this time of day to swing. It was here that I first spoke to Maria. It was so nice then. The girls would swing up and up. You would lose them in the sun. It was like they were soaring. The young men would come and push them. The boys would never swing. Once I came here in a rainstorm and swung by myself. I was crazy. There was lightning all around this old tree, but I didn't care. I wanted to know what it was like."

Alberto gazed into the depths of sky beyond the high branches of the tree. Plutarco could easily imagine the scene: beautiful, withdrawn Indian girls relieved for a time from the burden of servitude in the time between their sexual flowering and their first pregnancy. He'd seen girls of that age on the paths and roads, their heads bowed under the weight of some burden borne on their backs. There was grace in those bent, hustling forms, grace that would find ample expression in the act of swinging, stretching those bent limbs, arching those constrained pelvises toward heaven, open, ripe, and supple, swinging upwards as though to be mounted by the sun himself. He fell into a revery to match Alberto's. Visions of nubile maidens in braids and *huipils* danced about the men, gathering in demure, shy groups to whisper, as one girl after another took her turn. How easy it was, as well, to sense the male response. The bushes seemed full of shy, barefoot boys in handmade straw sombreros, watching the flight of their sisters, cousins, and sweethearts.

"How did you get up the courage to push the girls?" Plutarco asked.

Alberto laughed in response and then explained. "By piping. The boys made whistles from hollow reeds. We would hide in the bushes and make bird sounds. The girls would joke, saying, 'How ugly the birds sing today.' Then we would get braver. We would play little songs and sing them. These were songs that mocked women, like—

'My little cousin is restless tonight
Hear her petate as she tosses and turns
I have a tiny bird about me
Whose song will give her rest.'

"Finally we would have the courage to come into the open. We would stand over there, apart from the girls, and joke. Then we would sing a song, like this—

'How high Maria can fly
And higher yet she wants to go
If Alberto would lend a hand
What heights Maria might know.'

"The boy named in the song would then be teased by the others into giving the girl a push. It was a challenge. A challenge we welcomed, of course."

Regarding the tree, Alberto's face clouded over with sadness. "It is lucky," he said, "I sank no money in that land."

After that day, there was not much to be done. They returned to *El Arco Iris* and Serafina's house. Alberto spent several days more scouring the city for villagers or news. He found nothing. Hope seemed to evaporate. Plutarco let him be. "We'll stay as long as you need to," he said.

But it was futile. They all sensed it. Plutarco went each day with Serafina's grandson to the Oaxaca City *zocalo*, where the boy hawked tamales. He enjoyed himself and was company for the boy. He saw American tourists who assumed he was Mexican. He eavesdropped on their conversations. They were in another world, a different Mexico. They seemed foolish. The poor people enjoyed them. Club Med would soon open for them. Most of them seemed to feel honest affection for the Mexican people.

The two men left in the evening of the fifth day. Alberto was satisfied that the land situation was hopeless. He made sure that his family was situated. The proximity of old Serafina gave him a feeling of confidence that his wife would do okay. He gave Maria the money he'd saved from his work in the U.S. They spent the morning building a little enclosure next to Serafina's large pig pen. Just before they left, Maria put seven newly purchased piglets into the enclosure. She also showed off newly bought material and embroidery thread. She would sell textiles through Serafina. Alberto admonished her to take good care of the pigs and not to develop lavish tastes. Before they left, Maria smiled at the men and kissed their hands. A hint of a smile passed over Alberto's face, a shadow of the sentiment under the cypress tree.

"Don't let the kids run wild or get into fights," he said, and the men left. A perfunctory wave to Serafina was the only farewell they made. At the road, Alberto was hesitant—Plutarco could tell he wanted to stay. The bus arrived, however, and the men jumped aboard. "A man works like a dog here with no gain whatsoever," Alberto said, to no one in particular, as they found vacant seats and sat down. Plutarco was glad they were headed north. They'd done what they could do.

PAISAJE DE FOGON

Gustavo Sainz

LAS llantas se nos hicieron pedazos; una de ellas tiene veintisiete parches. En el arenal se podían freir huevos de lo caliente que estaba, y todos los hombres, menos el General Molina y yo, terminaron insolados.

Es la tercera vez que recorremos el desierto por tierra. Exploramos hasta una región agreste que derrite y empavorece con su calor de hornaza y su silencio casi absoluto: un erial, con gigantescas oquedades en forma de cráteres apagados y enormes dunas vírgenes que cubren todo el horizonte.

Molina iba manejando y juró haber visto a alguien que le hacía señas, pero al acercarnos comprobamos que sólo era una gobernadora mecida por el viento y no uno de los cuatro hombres desaparecidos. Total: regresamos cuando amainó un poco el calorón, por estar mal equipados para pasar la noche. Como quien dice: no hay que jugársela así nomás a lo tarugo.

HOY LA BÚSQUEDA duró más tiempo. Al Jefe ya se le echa de ver su miedo. Sabe que tiene toda la responsabilidad si la brigada muere, y contrató por fin los servicios de un avión Cessna piloteado por el gringo McGregor. Los acompañé en los primeros vuelos. El avión siguió la línea del ferrocarril hasta el kilómetro 132 y a partir de allí se internó por diferentes rumbos del desierto, pero no encontramos ni rastro de Bravo Menescal ni de ninguno de los otros. Observé al gordo del Jefe dándole instrucciones al Bolillo, como si él fuera aviador.

ENTRE OTRAS DISPOSICIONES igualmente pendejas, el Jefe ordena que el Departamento de compras adquiera cohetes de señales. Vaya momento de prevenir accidentes. ¿Estarán aún vivos? No puedo preguntármelo sin temblar.

EN SONOITA dicen que el Ingeniero Bravo Menescal días antes de su desaparición en el desierto, invitó a comer a sus amigos de más confianza. En la conversación de sobremesa recordó la leyenda esculpida en piedra en la fachada del Hotel Bárbara Worth, al otro lado de la frontera:

El desierto te espera abrasador
y fiero en su desolación
guardando sus tesoros
bajo el signo de la muerte
contra la llegada
de los poderosos y los fuertes

No sabía que el desierto realmente lo esperaba. Los jefes de la capital habían decidido localizar un nuevo trazo entre la Coconeta y Puerto Peñasco, del kilómetro 120 al 200, para satisfacer los deseos de ricos industriales de la zona que quieren explotar seriamente las salinas existentes muy cerca de la costa. En el momento de la convocatoria no fue muy bien la cosa y Bravo Menescal fue el único que pidió encargarse de la localización de esta vía....

Aquí creo que está la primera causa de la tragedia: Bravo Menescal tenía gran empeño en demostrar que su brigada realizaba trabajos que otros rehuían. Setenta o noventa kilómetros de trazo en el desierto eran nimiedades para sus hombres. Harían el trabajo en tres semanas: en ese lapso llegaría su esposa al campamento, y ambos celebrarían su primer año de casados en San Diego. Esto, claro está, si el Jefe les concedía el permiso o las vacaciones que aún no disfrutaba....

Aquí intuyo la segunda causa de la tragedia: a fecha fija, el Ingeniero Bravo Menescal iba a celebrar un acontecimiento importantísimo para su vida. Tenía pues que joderse y terminar el trazo en un término de diecinueve o veinte días....

Paradas, las máquinas de terracería esperaban línea. Esto obligaba a Bravo Menescal a reconocer perímetros de unos doce a catorce kilómetros y regresar. Acampaba en cualquier sitio, pues estaba acostumbrado a quedarse varios días en el desierto sin volver al campamento. Esta es quizá la tercer y más importante causa de la tragedia: su confianza.

El veinticinco de junio se celebró en Sonoita una fiesta pápaga. Los indios, en prolongada ebriedad desde el día de San Juan convirtieron las calles del poblado en pistas de carreras, desbocando y rayando los caballos. Sus atavíos de lujo, de géneros brillantes y tonos estridentes centelleaban por todos lados. Las bandas de música y los borrachos jodieron con tonaditas elementales y repetidas hasta el cansancio. Fue la última vez que vi al Ingeniero Bravo Menescal: repetía alegremente un estribillo.

SON LAS TRES DE LA MAÑANA y no tengo sueño. McGregor acaba de irse. Esta borracho y dice que no volará más si no le pagamos, que tiene mujer y cuatro hijos y necesita cobrar su salario y no perder su tiempo buscando fantasmas que juegan al escondite. Ignoro cómo el Jefe maneja el presupuesto.

LLUEVE, parece que por primera vez en todo el verano. La lluvia no alcanza el suelo, se evapora antes y las gotas que de casualidad llegan a tocar la arena producen un ruido chisqueante, igual al que se oye cuando alguien toca una plancha caliente con el dedo mojado....

El gordo del Jefe me ordenó leer a las brigadas los memorándums para que ellos sacaran conclusiones, y regañó al gringo que toda la noche estuvo armando pleito con una mujer que apodan La Jaiba....

EL SÁBADO VEINTISÉIS salimos de Sonoita rumbo a los campamentos en construcción. A los campamentos fijos El Doctor y El Roble, y al provisional en el kilómetro 132. Bravo Menescal manejaba la camioneta Ford 1947 con carrocería de madera, inventariada con el número once. Ese día el Jefe le ordenó repetidas veces que no se internara en el desierto más de unos quince o veinte kilómetros. Luego dijo algo que molestó a Bravo Menescal y éste arrancó su camioneta bruscamente, dejándolo con la palabra en la boca.

El lunes veintiocho Bravo Menescal y su brigada llegaron al campamento del kilómetro 132. Allí estaba el sobrestante de construcción de terracerías, General e Ingeniero Molina, un buen hombre, muy esforzado, amigo de Bravo Menescal y el primero en salir al desierto en su búsqueda....

El martes veintinueve partieron en la camioneta número once, el chofer, de quien sólo se conocen sus iniciales, GCM, los cadeneros, Heriberto López, Marco Antonio Burciaga y el Ingeniero Bravo Menescal. Llevaban dos cajas de madera con comida y cuatro bolsas llenas de agua.

Sólo sacaron un carro. Iban cerca y esperaban estar de regreso al día siguiente (¿para qué complicar el viaje cargando tantas cosas?). Sin embargo, Bravo Menescal y sus acompañantes sabían que iban a enfrentarse a un gran riesgo (en tierras inexploradas del desierto) por tratar de encontrar un paso entre los más peligrosos médanos. Al partir, según afirma el General Molina, le dijeron:

—Si no volvemos mañana por la noche salga a darse una vueltecita para buscarnos....

Y no regresaron.

EN ESTE MOMENTO el Jefe les niega permiso a los topógrafos para salir al desierto en busca de Bravo Menescal y sus acompañantes. Están en la habitación de al lado. Acaba de llegar un mensajero y dice que se derrumbaron por la lluvia más de 1,200 metros de vía, porque en la línea no hay obras de drenaje que eviten los deslaves; que en Sonoita está lloviendo desde hace dieciocho horas sin interrupción, por primera vez en siete años....

AHORA son las once de la noche y no hay nadie en el campamento: se llevaron a todos a las terracerías. De día cuidan mucho a los peones de la insolación y la deshidratación. No hay sombra dónde guarecerlos, aparte de las plataformas del tren, y les dan fuertes dósis de café negro y sal para rehidratarlos....

DIÁLOGO entre el Jefe y el contratista Torrijos, uno de sus protegidos:

—Este material no es de primera clase y no se sujeta a las especificaciones del reglamento. Es preciso que nos surtas los durmientes con las características establecidas por la West Coast Grinding....

—Mira, mira, mira.... ¿Desde cuándo me la haces de tanto pedo? Firma de recibido y acuérdate con quién estás hablando. ¿De cuándo a acá te me aprietas tanto?

ACABA DE REGRESAR el General Molina sin noticias. La búsqueda fue hasta el kilómetro 154. Dice que allí hay un volcán extinguido con sus faldas llenas de chaparrales y arbustos petrificados.

Otra brigada salió más tarde, muy norteada y sin saber qué zona rastrear....

ENTRE LOS MÉDANOS nacen lirios y azucenas silvestres, siempre en las inmediaciones de las llamadas tinajas, depósitos subterráneos de agua. Parece que estas plantas aprovechan la humedad del subsuelo y aspiran la del ambiente. A veces, tras una sucesión de lomos pardos de arena su descubre un oasis florido, y uno o dos metros más abajo hay agua dulce y fría. ¿Cómo es que Bravo Menescal y sus acompañantes no pasaron cerca de una de estas oquedades? Con Mc-Gregor creemos haberlas revisado todas. ¿Cómo diablos no dieron con un desprendimiento con su correspondiente tinaja de agua fresca?

DESPUÉS del niño ahogado tapan el pozo. Hoy se ordenó que cada diez kilómetros se establezcan puestos de aprovisionamiento y socorro. Las tiendas que protejan los depósitos serán de color rojo. Habrá en cada puesto altas astabanderas con paños de color amarillo, para orientar a los caminantes....

POR FIN: encontraron la camioneta....

Estaba abandonada frente a un banco de arena, un talud larguísimo imposible de rebasar con el vehículo. Sus ocupantes se bebieron hasta el agua del radiador y probablemente partieron hacia la costa en busca de agua.

Del campamento fijo El Doctor saldrán algunos automóviles con indios rastreadores pápagos. Un avión Bellanca de la Dirección de Ferrocarriles, piloteado por el capitán Arturo Salazar, también colaborará en la búsqueda.

La costa dista cuarenta y dos kilómetros del lugar. El Jefe dice que Bravo Menescal y sus hombres ya deben haberla alcanzado. No toma en cuenta que para avanzar un paso en las dunas de arena deben darse cinco o seis pasos en falso. Nunca antes había trabajado en el desierto.

ENVIAMOS al Bellanca cardillo con los espejos de los coches. Desde el aire es muy difícil seguir las brigadas que van por tierra. Los topógrafos afirman que las huellas de los desaparecidos no se localizan hacia la costa, sino que se internan en el desierto....

Las brigadas de rescate son seis, cada una con diez hombres, sin contar el avión que va arrojando agua, comida, llantas.

¡Cómo me acuerdo de Bravo Menescal! Era muy bueno para el cubilete. Yo no. Miles de veces lo vi arrojar al aire el vaso con dados y recuperarlo limpiamente, para arrojar los dados sobre la mesa. Cuando yo quise hacer lo mismo se me cayeron los dados: uno quedó atrás de la sinfonola, el otro se perdió y tuve que pagar veinticinco pesos.

LOS TROQUEROS descubrieron un remedio para evitar que los vehículos se atasquen en la arena y en los pozos de lodo y tierra acampechanada. Lo llaman Salvavidas del Desierto. Consiste en unas láminas de acero hechas con los estribos de los coches viejos que hay en el depósito de chatarra. Cada camión carga con varias láminas y las usan para, por tracción de las llantas, sacar el carro o camión del atascadero....

ENCONTRARON LOS CADÁVERES. Ayer en la noche vino el comisario de Sonoita y levantó el acta dando fe de los hechos. El chofer GCM estaba como kilómetro y medio antes que los cadeneros, como a doce kilómetros de nuestro campamento. Desde allí pueden verse las luces, las tiendas de campaña, los vagones de ferrocarril. Suponemos que su muerte fue muy desesperante. Cavó siete agujeros en la arena, enloquecido por encontrar agua. Su cadáver, paralizado, conservará para siempre su último gesto: la mano izquierda en la boca, los dientes clavados en los dedos....

Después, la brigada siguió hasta hallar a los cadeneros. Molina afirma que Burciaga murió trastornado del cerebro. Lo encontró abotagado y cerca de un pedazo de cholla verde, cactus que come el ganado y que en el cogollo a veces contiene agua....

El cadáver del Ingeniero Bravo Menescal estaba a varios kilómetros de allí. Murió contemplando algunas cartas de su esposa: éstas estaban semienterradas en la arena alrededor de él....

LOS PEONES tienen varias hipótesis, por ejemplo, ésta:

Los cuatro hombres se detuvieron en un lugar Equis del desierto y discutieron el rumbo a seguir. Bravo Menescal apenas podía caminar y allí lo dejaron. GCM le quitó los catalejos y el zaracof y se fue con los cadeneros rumbo al campamento del kilómetro 132 y la costa. Quizás Bravo Menescal se repuso un poco y trató de seguirlos, pero no supo qué rumbo tomar, insolado y débil. O rendido de cansancio, deshidratado, apenas y tuvo fuerzas para leer las cartas de su esposa, y luego las fue medio enterrando alrededor de él, en un rito romántico.

Cuatro kilómetros más adelante cayeron los cadeneros, y uno y medio más allá, el chofer....

HACE RATO llegaron los investigadores. Dicen que pueden probar que la camioneta de Bravo Menescal y los otros tiene perforado el tanque de gasolina; que se quedaron sin combustible cuando no lo esperaban, y no pudieron regresar por eso. Bravo Menescal, según ellos, murió el viernes dos, y sus acompañantes al día siguiente, el sábado tres....

EL JEFE incautó la brújula que utilizó la brigada de Bravo Menescal para el Museo de Ferrocarriles. Molina y los topógrafos dicen que estaba descompuesta y que fue la causa principal del desastre. Sugieren que escriba un informe para firmarlo todos.

El cuerpo de Bravo Menescal parecía casi carbonizado, la cabeza negra y la grasa del cuerpo saliéndosele por el calor. Según Molina, sobre la arena quedó un gran lamparón de grasa.

Los cadeneros Heriberto López y Marco Antonio Burciaga quedaron boca arriba, sin zapatos y sin camisas. Tenían los pies ampollados y el cuerpo lleno de manchas negras. López trató de amortiguar el calor construllendo una enramada de hediondilla; a manera de toldo puso su camisa y la de Burciaga. Tenía sus zapatos y su cartera como almohada.

El cadáver de GCM estaba completamente ennegrecido por los efectos del sol; sus miembros tiesos, con una consistencia semejante a madera balsa. Tenía consigo innumerables objetos personales de Bravo Menescal, aparte del zaracof y los binoculares, lo que permite extrañas interpretaciones. También tenía las cuatro bolsas de hule en las que llevaban el agua, vacías, desde luego....

DICTADO DEL JEFE:

"Se desató en mi contra la jauría. Un acontecimiento de estos es como un vomitivo para provocar náuseas a causa de la miseria moral de los hombres. Cierto que también es un reactivo para descubrir a los verdaderos amigos o a las personas de corazón bien puesto, aunque éstos sean los menos. Se presenta la ocasión de inculpar a alguien y los pequeños enemigos se frotan las manos, se me echan encima como perros: contratistas, ingenieros, aspirantes a ingenieros, peones despedidos del trabajo por flojos, borrachos e incumplidos, ambiciosos de toda laya y hasta fondistas y falluqueros que no pueden vender alcohol en los campamentos. Aquellos a los que no les gusta mi nombre, ni mi posición, y les soy antipático, han comenzado a ladrar, a culparme del lamentable accidente: me han creado un ambiente hostil...."

Etcétera.

Y termina su informe:

"Pero a pesar de los ladridos de la jauría, la verdad se impone."

¿Cuál verdad? ¿La de su burocratismo? ¿La de sus cómodos y rápidos viajes en avión y sus comilonas y borracheras en hoteles de primera, muy lejos de la aterradora realidad del desierto? Carajo: espero que se lo lleve la Chifosca....

EL JEFE sospecha que envíe a la Dirección un informe secreto en su contra. Dice La Jaiba que anoche andaba borrachísimo en el bule del Turco gritando que me iba a correr a mí y a todos.

Por otra parte hoy fue ampliamente felicitado por su actuación en el hallazgo de los cadáveres (él dice "descenlace de la tragedia"), cuando tal mérito les corresponde al sobrestante Molina y a los topógrafos que lo acompañaban.

Soplaba un viento de fogón....

REPLACEMENT

Tony Hillerman

HARJO'S consciousness had been drifting at the edge of sleep, just one small corner of his mind attending to the reality of the winter afternoon. Now the cawing of the crows snapped him fully awake. He shifted his back against the uneven stones of the wall and moved his cold right leg out where the sun would warm it. He had expected the crows to serve as his alarm, alerting him when the ammunition party blundering through the woods toward the town disturbed them. But these were the wrong crows, in the wrong place. They were down by the road. If the ammunition party was there it meant trouble. He glanced at Corporal Hinkle. Hinkle lay against the wall, knees pulled up against his stomach, helmet tilted over his face, snoring lightly.

A long way behind Harjo a machine gun fired, a terse pebble of sound dropped into the quiet afternoon. A ripple of snapping, falsetto echoes died away in the empty streets along the river. This sound had no relevance to Harjo's problem, which was whether to awaken Hinkle. He hated to do that. Hinkle was a worrier. Awake, he'd be thinking of tonight and talking about it. Of wading the river in the darkness. Of going among the houses across it. Speculating. Harjo had taught himself long ago to avoid that, just as he would avoid pulling off a scab, or putting weight on a sprained ankle. He would not think about tonight.

The crows settled again, still cawing. Nothing very frightening then. Hinkle's round face was placid in sleep. Let him rest. Harjo stretched. He thought about the crows, and of his brother who loved to stalk them with his .22 in the Washita River bottoms. He thought of summer in Pottawatomie County, of riding with his aunt in her Model A to the Pottawatomie Agency in Shawnee to see about something or other. He almost thought about going home. Only one crevasse of his mind attended the sounds he'd been hearing in the town behind him. It identified the rapid burst of fire as a German model 34. A minute later, it filed away the fact that the cork-from-the-bottle pop of the answering mortar came from the churchyard below—the B Company mortar site. It deduced from this that B Company had been prodded by the German machine gun and one of B's two remaining mortars had responded. The pop repeated itself, and repeated itself. Then silence. The three rounds required to complete the ritual. Not overdoing it—not enough to touch the nerve across the river that would arouse the 88s behind the town and thus begin a chain reaction of violence.

It was this part of his brain which, all through his pleasant daydreaming, remained aware that at 1 a.m. tonight B Company would cross the river. He would endure the raid. He dreaded it. It would be terrifying—but very likely not fatal to him. He would make no mistakes. It would eat replacements because replacements did stupid things. Such raids ate replacements, but it would not eat him, or Hinkle. Another wound perhaps. Perhaps even the million dollar wound for which every rifleman yearned. But even a broken arm would take him as far back as the clearing hospital at Saverne and would be good for a month. A bullet through a hip bone would be better. That was a stateside wound, if the break was bad enough.

The muscles beneath the swarthy skin of Harjo's cheeks hardened into a sequence of twitches. They made him seem to be smiling. He might have been. That part of his mind that analyzed the pattern of the sound told him that nothing had happened to alarm him. Someone, probably a rifleman in B's Second Platoon in the shattered houses along the river, had violated the protocol by which his battalion and a Panzer Grenadier unit shared this French town. It would have been a replacement. Always was. Someone not yet tuned to this, someone forgetful for a moment, perhaps stepping casually into a street, perhaps peering too long from an exposed window at the sunny afternoon, perhaps some other broken rule.

And a German, seeing this affront, had raised a surprised eyebrow, given this odd situation the automatic split second of deliberation which causes old soldiers not to die unnecessarily, weighed the knowledge that killing this offender slightly lessened his own chances to remain alive, balanced this against an index of other considerations, tightened the first finger of his right hand against the curved steel just long enough, but not long enough to insult the forward observer of the mortar with smoke or a muzzle flash, and then leaned away from the gun against his sandbagged basement wall to wait the inevitable reaction which, mathematically, might kill him but probably wouldn't.

Now the thumping reports of mortar shells had drifted up from across the river and faded away. Three: as exactly spaced as the pops which had launched them, completing the formula reaction to the action. Enough. Not too much. The bow met by the curtsy. This satisfied, the silence of the cold afternoon settled again over the town. No harm done.

In the cold woods across the fire break, the crows were noisy again. Protesting something. Harjo considered what he should do. Corporal Hinkle breathed gently, his leg twitching occasionally, like the leg of a dreaming dog. The ammunition party should be a mile west of the road, a mile west of the crows, twenty men loaded like mules with cases of grenades, mortar rounds and rifle ammunition. They should be coming through the deep woods out of sight of German observers and out of range of the German halftrack which prowled the ridge across the river. They would make visual contact with Hinkle and Harjo. By hand signal Hinkle would instruct them to wait for dark. When darkness came Hinkle and Harjo would bring them across the frozen field and into the cover of the buildings and take them to the Captain. They shouldn't be anywhere near the road. Nothing alive should be.

Well, Hinkle was the Corporal. And Hinkle was older, already twenty. He prodded Hinkle with his foot.

"Hink," he said. "Trouble."

Hinkle sat up.

"I think they got lost," Harjo said. "Stirring up the crows over by the road."

"Oh, shit," Hinkle said. He frowned up at the sun, then at his watch. "Too early," he said. "Way early."

The figure of a man emerged from the woods. He was on the road, walking briskly down the narrow old asphalt toward the outskirts of the town. It looked perfectly natural.

"Well, shit," Hinkle said. "Look at that." Hinkle's face was still round with baby fat—a mass of freckles. A puckered scar along his pudgy chin marked where a piece of shrapnel had hit him at Anzio. Hinkle ran his finger along the scar, staring out at the walking man. He cupped his hands into a megaphone. "Hey," he shouted. "Get—off—the—road."

"He can't hear you," Harjo said. The breeze was blowing out of the woods toward them. "Ain't no cover there anyway."

That was something Harjo remembered clearly about the road. It had deep ditches in the woods on both sides of the asphalt. But here where it crossed the field, where you needed them, the ditches were mere depressions. Nothing. B Company had come down it running. When was it? Two days ago? Three? Running. Spreading into the fields under the mortar fire. But their squad's replacements had sprawled into those shallow ditches, all four of them in a bunch, trying to hide with nothing to hide behind. The tanks had come out of the woods behind them, and the roof of the house against which Harjo now leaned had been burning. It had made a warm, bright flare of yellow through the falling sleet. But all this now seemed a long time ago. He remembered hearing Hinkle yelling at his replacements, cursing them. "Move. Move. Move. Move. God damn you, move!" Four helmets pressed against the frozen earth, safe from terror while the machine gun fire moved down the asphalt, kicking up frozen dirt when it missed their bodies. They had lain there, a neat line of four, all the day. By afternoon the sleet had turned to snow and made them four white humps. Harjo tried now to remember their faces. One face. Or a name. No faces came to him. Just a mass of shapes climbing off the replacement depot truck. The captain had put four of them in Hinkle's squad. No names. No faces.

The man walked steadily down the road, tilted slightly forward under a pack but somehow jaunty. Strolling 600 yards from the German rifle pits in the riverbank brush, less than a thousand yards from the stone sheds where the halftrack sometimes waited.

"Fresh meat," Hinkle said, squinting against the sunlight. "Silly son of a bitch." He cupped his hands again. "Hey," he screamed.

The man glanced toward them, raised a hand. Hinkle swept his hands downward, signalling him to get down. Instead, he angled off the asphalt toward them, still unhurried.

"Yeah," said Hinkle, satisfied with his judgement. "Right out of repo depo at Saverne. Too dumb to live."

The man walked steadily, swinging his arms. Whistling maybe. Harjo stared toward the river. If they used the halftrack to kill him, perhaps he would see the muzzle flashes. He was conscious that his jaw muscles were tight, opened his mouth and closed it.

"Maybe they're not going to shoot the simple bastard," Hinkle said.

Harjo could see now that the fresh green paint of the man's helmet bore a yellow bar. Second lieutenant. And then the lieutenant was behind a wall. Safe. Harjo wondered why they hadn't killed him.

"I'll bet he's for the second platoon," Hinkle said. "We're going to get him." He grinned. "The Sarge hasn't had a boss since Colmar and that one just lasted a week." He rubbed his matted head. "Wonder how he'll like having a boss again."

"We're going over the river tonight," Harjo said. "This guy will go, too. Sarge won't have to worry about it long."

Hinkle thought about it. "Yeah," he said, and shrugged. "You remember what happened to the last one? Smart aleck. Sort of skinny and he had that new kind of pack."

"It was a mortar," Harjo said. He wished Hinkle would stop it. The lieutenant's body had been bent backward in the ditch under the poplar trees with his shirttail out and snow on the lens of his glasses. What was the lieutenant's name. Robins? Thrasher? Jay? Something like that. Something that reminded him of a bird.

"They oughta take care of replacements when they first come up," Hinkle said. "Until they learn something."

Harjo couldn't remember the lieutenant's face either, or his voice. He couldn't remember any of them, hardly, anymore. Not the new ones. Some of those who joined them back in Italy he could still see and hear and put names to. But not those who came up in trucks from Marseilles, or the bunch they got from Dijon, or the new ones from Saverne they'd lost last week. Not any name at all.

The lieutenant re-emerged from behind the broken wall. Home free. The man was sweating. He dropped his pack beside the house where the snow was gone and leaned his carbine against the stones. It looked new. He held out his hand out to Hinkle. "Lieutenant Eberwine," he said. He shook hands with Harjo. The hand was hard, strong. Warm. "I'm looking for Company B."

"Headquarters is down there by the church," Hinkle said, pointing.

The lieutenant leaned against the wall. "Ah," he said, "It's a lovely day." He smiled at the world, taking in Harjo and Hinkle and the frozen field and the woods and even the town across the river. Harjo noted that his eyebrows were bushy and his eyes were sort of greenish and his cheekbones were high with the sunburned skin pulled tight over the bony ridge and the bridge of his nose had a bend from an old break and his mouth was sort of wide. It was a strong face and a happy face. Harjo looked again and then closed his eyes. He thought: bushy eyebrows, nose broken. But the face was gone.

"Lt. Eberwine," Harjo said, "What is your first name, sir?"

"John," he said. "John Eberwine." He looked surprised. Harjo took an envelope and pen from his shirt pocket. "How do you spell Eberwine?" he asked. He wrote it on the envelope as the lieutenant spelled it.

"I like to remember names," Harjo said.

Lt. Eberwine was smiling at him. Harjo looked away.

THE COMPLETE HISTORY OF NEW MEXICO

Kevin McIlvoy

A Short Story in Four Parts:
Mrs. Bettersen's Remarks
Charlemagne J. Belter's Complete History of New Mexico, 1965
Bus's Bus Route
Letter From A Ghost, 1984

Mr. Belter:

Your footnotes and bibliography are incorrect. Your outline is insufficient. Certain quoted passages are much too long.
MINUS 20 points

What is the meaning of your ridiculous illustration? Where are your assigned illustrations? The colored map of New Mexico is especially important.
MINUS 10 points

Did you use a dictionary? I don't think so. Historical places are not "found." They are "founded." Beaver are not "tramped." They are "trapped." The word is "omNiscient" not "omiscient".
MINUS 12 points

The Navajos held captive at Bosque Redondo were not tortured. The cattle boom did not end because the cattle had an uprising. New Mexico did become a state in 1912. Did you know these things were incorrect? Did you make up lies?
MINUS 55 points

Why did you never discuss the Jornada del Muerte?

I want to see your father and your stepmother immediately.

3 OF 100 POINTS = F

THE COMPLETE HISTORY OF NEW MEXICO

by Charlemagne J. Belter

Mrs. Dorothy Bettersen
Sixth Grade
November 27, 1965

MY OUTLINE

The Introduction
- A) The theme of Don Juan Onate
- B) Sandia Man and Folsom Man
- C) Our dads

I. Santa Fe Found
- A) Omiscient facts
  - 1) Mrs. Orofolo
  - 2) Bus
  - 3) Mr. Alvarezo
  - 4) Awful
- B) Indians
- C) Spaniards
  - 1) The Spaniard letter
  - 2) Santa Fe

II. Albuquerque Found
- A) Franciscans
  - 1) bells
  - 2) books
  - 3) ropes
- B) Pueblos rebell
- C) De Vargas Returns
- D) A Pueblo Nightmare
- E) Jornada Del Muerte

III. War With Mexico
- A) Colonizing
- B) A long voyage
  - 1) William Becknell
  - 2) The Santa Fe Trail
- C) Mr. Alvarezo's orchard
- D) Beaver Boom
- E) Some Texans try something
- F) More of Mr. Alvarezo
  My Illustration: Bus's Bus Route

IV. New Mexico Mined
- A) President Polk declares
- B) Mrs. Orofolo
  - 1) Chile field
  - 2) A tree in a fence
- C) Gadsen Purchase
- D) Beaver Hats
  - 1) Buffalo
  - 2) More about Pueblos
  - 3) Conquistador Women
- E) Mrs. Orofolo at her table
  - 1) The Seven Cities
  - 2) The Arizona Territory
  - 3) The Goodnight-Loving Trail
- F) Bosque Redondo
  - 1) Mines Boom
  - 2) Daniel decides
  - 3) Geronimo

The Conclusion
- A) Statehood
- B) Goodbyes
- C) We leave for Orla

THE INTRODUCTION

I am going to write about the state of New Mexico and put in some stuff from the encyclopedia. My theme is the Don Juan Onate trail and the Jornada Del Muerte. But I might write some other important things which, as it turns out, my stepmother got angry about and said she wouldn't type this until my Dad said, "Dammit, now it is history."

All of it was way before we moved here to Texas. It goes like this.

My dad and me moved from Arizona, which was 1962, to a town that's hardly a town. Hatch. It's close to nothing but it's on Highway 85 where one time, anyway, a lot happened on the Onate Trail. Sandia man and Folsom man were around. It was about 15,000 years before the highway was made, but they were good hunters so they did okay.

Daniel's dad was older but he was my dad's friend. Neither guy was married. They even both smoked cigarettes. We were nine, and we thought it was the neatest thing ever to know that. Man, oh man, almost all the same.

My dad was a Small Repairs Man, and his dad was a Writer which we thought was also neat because his dad used typewriters and my dad repaired them. It was funny sometimes too. Daniel always had a headful of new words.

I. SANTA FE FOUND

"Chum, I'm omiscient," Daniel said to me one afternoon on our bikes, "I'm plenty omiscient."

"So?" If you need to know, I got that name Chum because my name is Charlemagne which is goofy.

"So, I can know about anything, Chum."

And when I made him tell me like what, he said like he knew that old Mrs. Orofolo had a third arm growing out of her back and Bus the Greyhound bus driver was a top-secret double-FBIA agent and he knew a lot more like how Awful, Mr. Alvarezo's dog, had tatoos on his forelegs that said USMC and LSMFT.

It had to be true.

Mrs. Orofolo who I guess had been a Mrs. once but wasn't anymore really had a big lump on her back like a third shoulder. Bus was a guy who never said anything, not good morning or anything and nobody knew his name so he was named Bus after the Greyhound superbus he drove like a bat outa hell up and down the Highway. I never saw no tatoos on Awful but I never knew nobody who got close enough to look because, talk was, Awful killed other dogs and fed them to Mr. Alvarezo's pigs who were supposed to be big and blistery and maybe *could* of had tattoos too, you never knew.

The Anasazi had tattoos all over everywhere and they drew all kinds of weird things in the Chaco Canyon. Then the Pueblo Indians were around about 700 years ago. There was a lot of them in those days.

Then this guy from Spain came and gave them a big long letter they couldn't read if their life depended on it which it did.

> The end of it went like this. "Wherefore, as best you can, I entreat and require you to understand this well which I have told you, taking the time for it that is just you should, to comprehend and reflect, and that you recognize the Church as Mistress and Superior of the Universe, and the High Pontiff, called Papa, in its name, the Queen and King, our masters in their place as Lords, Superiors and Sovereigns of these islands and the main by virtue of these gifts, and you consent and give opportunity that these fathers and religious men, declare and preach to you as stated. If you shall do so you will do well in what you are held and obliged; and their Majesties, and I, in their royal name, will receive you with love and charity, relinguishing in freedom your women, children and estates, without service, that with them and yourselves you may do with perfect liberty all you wish and may deem well. You shall not be required to become Christians, except, when informed of the truth, you desire to be converted to our Holy Catholic Faith, as nearly all the inhabitants of the other islands have done, and when his Highness will confer on you numerous privileges and instruction, with many favors.
>
> "If you do not do this, and of malice you be dilatory, I protest to you, that, with the help of Our Lord, I will enter with force, making war upon you, from all directions, and in every manner that I may be able, when I will subject you to obedience to the Church and the yoke of their Majesties; and I will take the persons of yourselves, your wives and your children, to make slaves, sell and dispose of you, as their Majesties shall think fit, and I will take your goods, doing you all the evil and injury that I may be able; as to vassals who do not obey but reject their master, resist and deny him; and I declare to you that the deaths and damages that arise therefrom, will be your fault and not that of his Majesty, nor mine, nor of these cavaliers who came with me."[1]

"Daniel," I said, "how do you get omiscient?"

He had platter eyes and a burr haircut grew real fast over and behind his ears, so he was panda-faced all the time which I didn't much remember till I just now wrote it. He said how his dad said you can't get certified omiscient. It comes and goes. "It comes and goes," he said, and I didn't like the way he said it because he got a terrible kinda Indian Mask look on his face.

"Daniel?"

"Don't know, Chum. It only happens."

He was my real buddy and wouldn't keep it from me if he knew how to make me omiscient, so I said, "Don't it beat all get out?"

"Don't it?" We both watched an onion truck come over a hill on the highway and into town. If you ever smelled a fresh scab, that's what an onion truck smells like. It could be a good smell even.

"He's going to call me home," Daniel said.

Sure as heck, he did.

And then Coronado who was Spanish explored around. Pretty soon, he found Santa Fe, in 1610.

[1] Buckingham, Ed Smith. *The Relations of Alvar Nunez Cabeza* 1905, 1871 Barn's Co., New York. (61).

II. ALBUQUERQUE FOUND

The Franciscan preachers who liked to build churches built them everywhere they wanted. The Pueblo Indians, some of them anyway, didn't like the big churches or their loud bells or thick books or maybe they didn't like the look of those ropes around the Franciscan's middles.

My bed was way too low to the ground. If I dangled my arm over I could touch my elbow to the floor. Our house wasn't big or nothing. Our toilet was an outside job. So, I watched the Untouchables with Dad and because we didn't make popcorn we had a fight.

"It's bad for you to have it all the time," he said.

"Prove it," I said.

He called me a smartaleck and told me to shut my trap. So, I did. But I was hungry was the thing. Before bed, he made me some jelly on crackers and sat on the floor by my bed and kind of looked at himself. Then he said, "Chumbuddy, you know I was joshing about you shutting your trap."

I'm not the kind who lets a chance go by. "Another cracker?"

He broke it into four squares, put extra thick jelly on every one. "What do you say? Truce?"

I didn't tell him about the Pueblos going crazy and rebelling. I said, "I knew you weren't mad or nothing."

"Good." His jaw locked up, grinding some big thought between his teeth, I guess.

So, the Spanish Conquerors went away. It took them almost ten years to get up the guts to come back. Then, they came back mad. A *lot* of them. Their main guy was named De Vargas which is Spaniard for "From the Vargas."[2]

I could see him, after the lights were off, laying in his bed pretending he wasn't looking at me. That and the crackers must have gripped my guts because I had a nightmare.

I was in the back of the bus which was long as the long hall in school. And we were going maybe two, three hundred miles an hour and Mr. Alvarezo's pigs had the window seats but weren't looking out the windows. All their heads pointed one way, the wind whipping through their gums under their snouts making a noise like you never heard. Like hissing oil. Bus was pulling the handle to the bus door, sucking it open and closed. He wore a conquistador helmet. He was saying something to Daniel who was sitting way up at the front. Daniel was lit up every time the door opened, bus window green when it shut. His head shook no to Bus and his shoulders quivered kind of. And I called him. "Daniel. Hey!" But all the pigs' heads turned towards me and the wind through their stubby hairs made a crackling sound like little fires. "Hey," I said and didn't say it no more. But I thought, What's he making you do, Daniel? The door sucked open and Bus pulled the handle and sucked it closed, and I thought, No, Daniel. Daniel! Bus sucked it open. The whole long everything blew full of onion skins and they whirled and stormed and met in a million little seams. And there was Mr. Alvarezo in a long brown robe with a white rope around him. He took Daniel by the shoulders. He said, "Joe said. Joe said. Joe said." And I thought, Daniel! Hey! but the pigs' necks all creaked when they nodded up and down. "Joe said. Joe said. Joe said." Up and down. At the front of the bus, Mrs. Orofolo was staring right at me. The arm on her back was holding the driver's wheel. In her other two arms she was ringing a big silver bell and showing her gums which were pig's gums.

My dad woke me up. He looked at me funny but said, "Good morning," and didn't make no big deal about me shouting, "Joe said. Joe said," and all before I really came awake.

I guess to the rest of the old world it was no big deal. The Spanish conquered it all back, the whole state, which wasn't even a territory in those days. In fourteen years or so, the Pueblos were bored or sore or sick. They said, "Okay, already."

We ate oatmeal. I make my own toast most times. But he made me toast that time. He sat real far apart from me. "Is everything all right with Daniel?" he asked me.

"What do you mean?"

"Nothing."

It was 1706.

[2]Gonsalos, Lucy. *Spaniard Americans*, University New Mexico, Albuquerque. (12)

III. WAR WITH MEXICO

One morning Daniel said to me, "I'm adventuring. It's the first day." It was Sunday so not too many things had happened. They had found Albuquerque. They had built some villages, posts, graveyards and such.

"Adventure?" I said.

He looked like he was thinking about it. "A way down the road I'm going, lad."

"Lad?" I wondered what book he was reading. You never knew.

Daniel must have jumped out of bed right through his front door in one jump is all I can say, because every morning his face always had pillow wrinkles on it. His hair was half of it straight up and half of it, there in the front, smashed down which could make him look like a roadrunner because he had a quick neck and head.

"A long voyage, Chum, my lad. I'll take me one Miner Character."

"Me?"

"I'll be Major. You have to have a Miner and a Major."

It sounded good. "Me, then, I guess."

"A whole bunch of things have to happen to me, lad. I shall have to get sick or die. Or change a real lot. Maybe all of it."

I was catching on. "And I shall?"

"Be Miner." He pointed to the road. "It's an adventure," he said, because I guess he liked that word. But he knew it didn't explain nothing. "You *shall*"—there's a word makes your front teeth feel all noble—"you shall get me into trouble, Chum. You could get me out of it sometimes too."

That was in 1821 when William Becknell was tracking wagons over everyplace. He flattened a lot of cactus and stuff and had short legs in a picture of him and a big chest. It was the Santa Fe Trail. The Great Plains were "great"[3] is how people put it. Daniel said Mr. Alvarezo lived only "8 leagues off" and "was trapped by Sircomestands," which meant to me he was about as far away as 8 baseball fields and surrounded by pigs in armor, probably. We'd never been to his house because of Awful.

"We shouldn't," I said when we got to the high brick wall back by Mr. Alvarezo's garden.

"We SHALL," said Daniel. His mind was all made up. He said the word like it was in capitals and triple underlined.

I just loved that word. Could be talked into it just by that word, if you can believe it.

On the other side of the wall was the New World.

Mr. Alvarezo didn't have pigs. He had an orchard, a whole acre backyard of orchard with trees you never seen and some pecan, plum, peach, fig and apple trees and not one pig in sight.

Up the center of the orchard was a lane which had maybe 30 rose trees on either side and went straight to his backdoor. All the roses were pink.

I followed Daniel into the orchard. "Man, oh man."

"Wondrous," he said.

This History guy Castenada wrote it down: "The ground they were standing on trembled like a sheet of paper." Pedro was his first name.[4]

"Daniel, we could eat, huh?"

The idea didn't fit him right. He squirmed in it. "Your dad know Mr. Alvarezo?"

"No. Yours?"

"Nope."

We sat under a fat pecan and ate some plums, some overripe peaches too. That was early and lots of weird things were going on. Like pelts were invented and beavers were being tramped in the Rockies. It was a Boom. More women came West. "Have some more peaches," I said. The Texans wanted all of Mexico. They still do is my bet. In 1841 they tried to take it and it didn't work. "Here," I said.

"Couldn't."

"Plums are good, huh?"

"Shhh," Daniel said, and we flopped onto our stomachs quick because Mr. Alvarezo's back door had slammed. Awful must've been behind it. Over and over he barked three barks at a time like he was barking, Let me out! Let me out!

And it was Mr. Alvarezo alright. You could tell because he had greasy black long hair and a black greasy beard which didn't look like a beard much. It looked like a mess he'd got all over his face and neck eating black licorice. His black eyes were real small and far back inside his sockets with only a little white around them, like they were rocks blocking light out. He was skinnier than most of his trees.

Anybody could walk up that long row of trees and look like His Majesty The King of Spain. Mr. Alvarezo looked junky. He had a dirty cardboard box in his one hand and big scissors in the other. He set down the cardboard box at the rose tree near the wall. I was laying on top of my left arm and I wanted to move but he was real close.

Daniel had flopped down right next to me and I could smell his sweat and the fruit sap and rose scent all at once which smelled like bad news. When Mr. Alvarezo put down his box and scissors and started talking to the rose tree, I felt my heart jump where my pinned arm crossed it. And the arm was like a giant root I'd never be able to tear up quick enough to run.

Mr. Alvarezo bent a rose to him, then moved his hand down and rested his skinny, dark arm along the limb. He was saying things. Every other word was Therese and Therese, like how if you ever heard old Catholic priests say things, they say them over and over? You should meet my stepmother who is Catholic—and how.

He was saying, "Therese, Remarkable Child. Therese, The Holy Face. Therese, The Perfect Gift." And all the time he was close-eyed and creeping his greasy fingers through each petal of this one small pink rose. "Therese, Showering Faith. Therese, Burning with Zeal." My hand was buzzing some. I really needed to move. Mr. Alvarezo's hand kind of shivered on the rose. Daniel was breathing like he was not all right. I thought it couldn't go on but I didn't know about Catholics then like I do now.

Mr. Alvarezo moved his whole bony self more into the tree. He touched along the rosy edges of the petals in the center. "Therese, Inflamed Spirit. Therese, Passionate Mirror, Gentle Temple, Warm Fountain." He put his first two fingers deep inside the center of the rose. He touched the petals and his own fingers with his closed lips. He was softer and softer, saying things right into the rose real slow and some of it in Spaniard. I couldn't get any of it after that.

It was maybe noon. The tree shadows backed themselves back up into the trees. And Daniel looked like he was doing the same. All the dark shadows under his head went up into his face. He put his head down with his face smack into the ground.

It went on and on. Then Mr. Alvarezo stopped, stepped out of the tree, picked up his box and scissors. He clipped the rose and put it in the box. He clipped at least twenty more along the rows and he went inside. And then Awful got quiet.

"Daniel?" I rolled off my arm. I whispered, "Now?"

He turned my way. "He's taking them to Mrs. Orofolo," he said. The whole time I was counting roses and thinking about my arm, he was figuring that out. That was Daniel for you.

We went back over the brick wall. "Orofolo," Daniel said. "Oh ROW Fo Low" was the way he said it. So foreign-like you couldn't not follow him.

[3]Twitchwell, Ralph, *Encyclopedia Britannica* 1962, "New Mexico" (318).

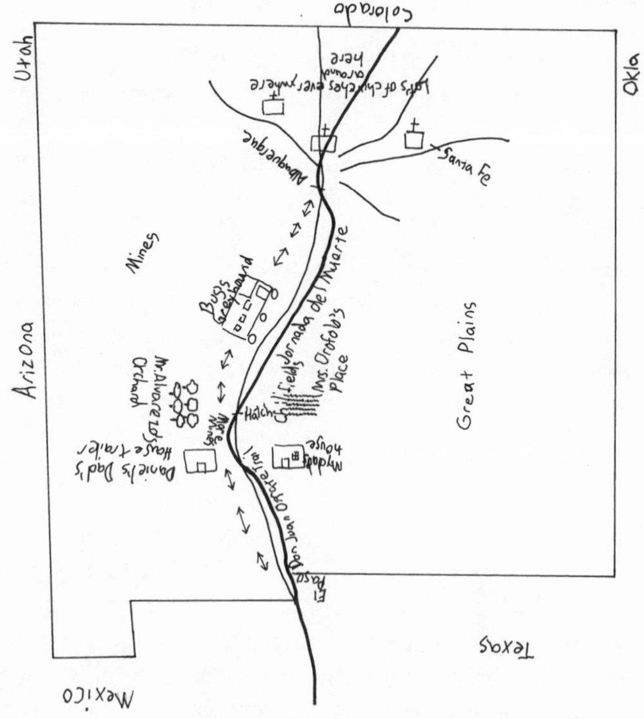

BUS'S BUS ROUTE

When I made this map I couldn't fit the 7-11 place which is in Hatch and which is where Bus parked to let people on and to give us stuff. He never talked except to Daniel who he talked secretly to. Daniel wouldn't tell me what it was. He said, "Bus said not to tell."

IV. NEW MEXICO MINED

The President in those days, which was the 1845s, was James K. Polk and he wanted a war on Mexico so he declared one. Daniel said, "It shall not be easy."

"No?"

The way it turned out, it wasn't one bit. We cut across the highway and belly-crawled a corner of a chile field. You don't feel chile juice on you all at once because you just don't. But then. Oh, man.

Mrs. Orofolo's place was one big room and an indoor john, and a tree bigger than either one. She had a garden growing and it was neat and weeded and muddy and rotty too like a facefull of noserun. Daniel said muddy shoes would make his dad mad.

"It ain't going to make my dad grin," I said real quiet.

"You don't know."

I didn't. Sometimes you couldn't take the time to sit and think Daniel over. Sometimes he was 15,000 years old. And I had a lot of questions I wished I asked. How come buffalos which there aren't many left except in zoos always got a look on their face like you just called on them in school? Did President Polk believe that stuff about the Seven Cities of Cibola? Did he just want a dead beaver hat like everybody else? What got into the Pueblos when they drew wings on snakes all over their jars? What was the whatever-it-was that Bus knew that Daniel told him that I didn't know? What about those Franciscan guys? How come they acted like they didn't know nothing about slavery and massacres and all? Why didn't somebody around 1706 invent the camera and take pictures? How come no Conquistador Women came over? Did they ever come over? Because you sure can't tell from the Encyclopedia.

Mrs. Orofolo had a tall white picket fence around her willow tree. A little rope-tie gate to it. And small purple flowers inside and not weed one. We crawled through the gate, into the circle of the must've-been-just-painted pickets. The tree was so big around you couldn't hardly fit yourself between it and the fence, especially not with your whole frontside chile-baking.

She came in the kitchen with the rose basket. Mr. Alvarezo left it off for her and went, I guess. She set the basket on the table and stepped back from it and took a big chestout whiff. It made her happy, you could tell, because a kind of pinkness just spread over her. If you could've seen it, I'll bet even her hump was the color of a baby's tongue.

Daniel gave me a look that said it was Some Adventure all right, wasn't it?

Mexico didn't fire a shot which means it's got to be the easiest war ever. First, the Mexicans gave up New Mexico, California, and Texas. Then there was some of New Mexico left so the U.S. got the southern part too by making a Gadsen Purchase. It was already 1853. I don't know what happened to President Polk because all of New Mexico is only 5 pages in the Encyclopedia and Bert Trujillo had the Peking to Probability Volume.

Mrs. Orofolo was sure happy anyway. She floated herself on to the only chair at her kitchen table. Scooted it back aways. Her hands crossed over her and each one unbuttoned the sleeves of her shirt. The hands went under the shirtsleeves and ran slow over her arms from elbows to wrists and back and over and under the way a praying mantis does to itself.

She unbuttoned her collar the way you'd do something if you were showing somebody. She was showing the roses, you'd have to figure. You know that little bowl where your chest stops and your necks starts going up? She touched that, and then she kind of measured off every part of her neck and front and back with her palms and her fingers. She was pink as new gum.

I was ready to go. Daniel was solider than the tree—which meant he wasn't going with me no matter how good of a Miner Character I was. With just the tips of her fingers she felt of her nose and traced over her jaw. She turned her hand down and passed her thumbnail over her lips like she was going to kiss her own thumbnail. But she didn't.

She bent her head and closed her eyes, which was the only time she wasn't looking at the roses. And you can only tell so much looking out a fence, but I guess she had a great big breath of herself because it wasn't like she could breathe anything else with her head like that.

And she cried. Quiet and private—except for us right there not looking at her longer, not looking at each other, just undoing that perfect little white gate and escaping like you always have to do in a real good adventure.

I made a lot of notecards about it. Pedro Castenada did too.

> "It seems to me that this happened to all or most of those who went on the expedition which, in the year of our Saviour, Jesus Christ, 1540, Francisco Vasquez led in search of the Seven Cities. Granted that they did not find the riches of which they had been told, they found a place in which to search for them and the beginning of a good country to settle in, so as to go on farther from there. Since they came back from the country which they conquered and abandoned, time has given them a chance to understand the direction and locality in which they were, and the borders of the good country they had in their hands, and their hearts weep for having lost so favorable an opportunity."[5]

On the shoulder of the highway, we slowed down. "Smarty," said Daniel. I thought, *Smarty*? because he never called me nothing but Chum, but the way he said it didn't make me mad or nothing, I guess. Just almost mad.

He stopped the way a state map will quit at the top. Colorado's up there but you don't see further than Durango.

"Go on," I said or "Come on, Daniel" or something like it. I wasn't sure if I wanted to hear what he didn't say. A lot was happening inside me. A lot was happening, period.

In four years half of New Mexico was made The Territory of Arizona and cattle drivers drove cattle up and down the Goodnight-Loving Trail like Bus in his Greyhound.

Navahos were chased out of Arizona and captivated at Bosque Redondo. Kit Carson did it. They were starved plenty and tortured some too. 1864 to 1868. There was a mine boom. Mines were everywhere you stepped.

"Smarty," Daniel said in his omiscient voice. "I'm not going home."

No lad stuff. No shall this or shall that.

I could've said, "Daniel, you got to go home. What do you mean 'I'm not going home?' What's with this Smarty stuff? Daniel, Captain, Buddy. Hey."

The fact of it is about as much time went by as you'd take to say such things, and then I said, "But I…."

"You go ahead there." Did I say he had a burr haircut? Who ever's got burr haircuts anymore? He really did have one. And when he meant something his whole head meant it.

That was 2 o'clock or so. I told him I could be around until supper if he was going to be around too.

"I'm not," he said. His voice was omiscient as all get out. A voice in a big, deep jar.

I patted his shoulders is all I did. His face got Zuni! He punched my arm mean and kept punching and said, "Don't...no...touch...no!"

So. I was going to punch him. I really was. Why not? But I said something my dad says. "Time wounds all heels."

He walked one way down the highway. I walked one way up it to home. That simple.

It was real, real simple.

After supper, I couldn't hold back and I busted out crying and my dad said, "About Daniel?"

"He ain't home even, I bet."

"Tell me all you know," Dad said. He repairs small things. He likes to have every little part laying on the table in front of him.

When I finished, he said, "Stay here."

Nine or ten o'clock I was still hearing Dad's voice and Daniel's dad's voice call, "Daniel. Daniel!" Over the cars on the highway even, you could hear it. It should've been the saddest thing you'd ever hear. But his name was the most beautiful sound, I thought. Beautiful. I was thinking it when I fell asleep at the kitchen table.

On the next day which was Monday, Daniel and I were back at school. "Found you," I said to him.

"Found me." Even Geronimo wasn't as sad when he said it.

All the cattle got mad after that. They shook their heads and said, "It's got to stop. Up and back. Up and back." Their hoofs were sore. They had a revolt which was dusty and bloody.

They won. And that was the end of a twenty years cattle boom. And after that some more happened.

"We're moving," said my dad a month later. "Orla."

It was out of the blue. "Orla."

"In Texas, Chum."

"But," I said. "Daniel."

"You'll have to say so long to Daniel."

[5]Howe, Andy. *Wild Land of Sun*, 1953 Albuquerque Wallace and Horn. (283).

THE CONCLUSION

And that's it complete. Nobody ever did make New Mexico a state which I know is hard to believe but a lot of things are, come to think of it.

Daniel's dad wouldn't let me say goodbye. My dad had come with me to their trailer. "Joe," Daniel's dad said, "you've got it all wrong."

My dad shook Daniel's hand. "Daniel," he said, "everybody knows. Police. Teachers. Everybody. It'll stop now."

"Joe," said Daniel's dad. "For Christ's sake, Joe."

Then my dad said, "Daniel. I can't take you with me. Listen, Daniel." But Daniel wouldn't listen. "It's the law, and I can't." He came down to his knees like he did when he hugged me sometimes. But Daniel wouldn't hug him. My dad kneeled there and didn't get up. It was quiet. And even Daniel's dad was dust blowing over dust which is a sound that's no sound. My dad said, "Chum doesn't know." Then he stood up.

I didn't know what it was I didn't know. Daniel was crying too hard to talk or I bet he would have explained, because I was his buddy and he wouldn't keep it from me if he knew how not to.

Then my stepmother is going to type it up and even put in some commas and quotations marks and such, if you got to know, which my dad says you do.

BIBLIOGRAPHY

Encyclopedia Brittanica, Ed Ralph Twitchwell, "New Mexico," 1962.

New Mexico Magazine, October, "Bosque Redondo," Dorothy Price, 1965.

National Geographic, April, "Mighty Lost Land," Clarence Boston, 1964.

The Relations of Alvar Nunuz Cabeza de Vaca," Ed Smith, Buckingham Barn's Co., 1905, 1871.

Spaniard Americans, Lucy Gonsalos, University of New Mexico Albuquerque, 1960.

Wild Land of Sun, Andy Howe Wallace and Horn, Albuquerque, 1953.

November 27, 1984

Dear Chum,

You will never read this letter. But it's still me—Daniel. Almost twenty years dead, Chum, and plenty omniscient. Remember it? My favorite game.

Now, this—this whole state—is all a page I have written myself across for twenty years. Here, on the latitude intersecting Redrock, Hurley, Hatch, Sunspot, and Hobbs. I'm low on the page without having once written what I must.

Well, then. Four things.

1) The Highway. The vans, busses, trucks: heavy doors closing. I listened to everything beneath me, heard signals in it. When we would walk south together on 85 I could close my eyes and tell you if the far away reverberation in the pavement was car or farm machinery. If it was Bus in his Greyhound, Mr. Alvarezo's pickup, the pads of Awful's paws, my dad's Volkswagen, your dad's Olds: I knew.

In June and July it all smelled of alfalfa, chile plants, and acacia, like a headful of dusty hair. The Rio Grande held to it like a tendon. Inhaled together, the asphalt and river silt were acrid as marrow.

For me, these things were urgent. You couldn't have known.

2) The land. Did we ever think it was unsettling—ever once—how the desert was the defining edge of almost every green field? I guess we never did, Chum. It always won, the desert always won, right, and why think about it? The tumbleweed would come when the onion, cotton, chile and alfalfa fields were fallow. Between us, we knew about the desert. What need to say it?

My dad's trailer was a true writer's place. Looking out our back window we saw a cottonwood break dividing field and desert. The trees made the sky a poised, serrated blade. I suppose a writer could look out that window at those keen edges and elementally varied colors and surfaces and could say to himself, Even Nature composes.

You never came into our trailer. I could never let you. See, I believed that what was happening there was something you knew. Had to know.

3) The site. The artifacts strewn everywhere, preserved even in my dad's cabinets and closets. I should have talked about them. Except. No answers in them. Certain clothes, certain cups that were not to be touched because they had been Marty's.

You didn't know my little sister. What was Marty? A jar full of photographs.

I should have said, "Come. Look." Except.

How did Marty, six years old, make the choice? Can a six year old deliberately plan her own suicide? Who believes?

Believe a mother abandoning a husband and two infant children. Believe her never once writing us. Believe a father promising us, over and over again, that she would.

Believe a father, almost three years after, calling his children home one day. "We're changing," he says. "We change ourselves every day before dinner."

He helps us take our clothes off. He takes off his. I watch what he makes Marty do. Every cell in me becomes an open eye. No single cell changes back.

After it, he helps her put on fresh clothes. He says, "Daniel and I will come out pretty soon." He shuts the door slowly. "Go, play," he says to Marty. I notice for the first time that the door is too small for the doorframe.

"Daniel. Daniel." His face touches my hair; he kisses my ears. "You love me?"

There is a stuffed chair. He bows me over the arm of it; his cool palms hold my head pinned as his stomach meets the small of my back. He asks me again if I love him.

Believe this, try to believe this: his voice was never so tender as when he injured me with himself and pushed my face into the chair to muffle my screams and said, "You love me? You love me."

He was never so gentle as when he cleaned me afterwards and made the hurting stop and bathed and dressed me. He had always ironed my clothing, pressing the handkerchiefs he bought me.

He always made us a splendid dessert after dinner and, if we asked, we could have more later.

He wrote in the evenings. He was often still writing when Marty and I fell asleep. I dreamed that he wrote it down. Each time.

4) The questions. Could anyone not have known?

And the coward Bus who had the whole route from Albuquerque to El Paso—each time—to think about what I had told him. Monday, Thursday, Sunday, 4 p.m. he would park his Greyhound at the 7-11 and meet us, remember? He gave us paperbacks and gloves and, once, eyeglasses, and, always, newspapers that passengers had left. And he would never say a single word but only offer a bent smile. You always took the horde and left the bus.

"Daniel," Bus would mumble, "wait a minute." He closed the folding door. We sat in the seats behind the driver's seat. "Are you okay, son? Have you told Chum?" he asked. "Don't tell people, son. I'm going to get you help." Believe this: he genuinely cared. He did nothing.

Did your father know all along? Our neighbors? Our teachers?

Who read them—who read all those questions configured on a stretch of highway where my sister Marty was crushed beneath a car?

I read them. I read them until I could see them from the moon, see them like God, sort and codify them, and compose one Godly answer.

I stood at the center of the highway, hoped for more darkness. Then, I simply pivoted, closing myself like a door against the dull eyes of the oncoming car.

The real truth is, I wanted to say, "Please, Chum. Help, please," even as my young bones knifed an indecipherable petroglyph into the asphalt.

It is only over now that I have written this. The dead, I think, are the best writers. Only the dying are their match.

Omnisciently,
Daniel

MOTHER DITCH

Patricia Clark Smith

DR. Markham looked a little skeptical when Catherine got to the part about the stoning, but she just went on with her story, careful not to sound overemotional.

"Anyway, my kids say this has happened several times, and then I saw it for myself, on Friday. There's got to be something we can do, don't you think?"

Markham sighed. She seemed to be skimming through the card file on her desk. Lipstick flaked lightly on the corners of her wide, bright mouth as she looked up at Catherine and smiled, meeting her eyes squarely. "Peer aggression, you know," she began. Catherine nodded. *Two white women, professionals together, except one of us has all the power, and she knows it, the old fart. And she's not going to do a damn thing,* Catherine thought.

"—it's just the other side of creative interaction; we merely have to channel it into healthier forms of competition. And it's usually a reversible phenomenon...." Markham hitched her chair forward. "And this I know from experience, Mrs. Krauss. One week it's one child; next week, he's the ringleader. Only last week Gilbert Martinez came to school wearing a Detroit Lions cap, and in this town they all root for the Broncos or the Cowboys or the Raiders, so it was him that day, even though he's so big for his age and manifests so many leadership qualities. They all ganged up and bloodied his nose and threw his hat in the dumpster. They're not savages, just terrible little *conservatives* about any deviation from the norm, and it's just a matter of sharing our wider values with them and helping the victimized child to be aware what in his or her behavior elicits the aggression…."

"This isn't like that," Catherine said. Her voice got thin, with trying to sound reasonable. Not like a sheltered graduate student mother new to the neighborhood, too full of ed-psyche courses, too easily shocked by real kids. Specifically, low-income Chicano kids. "Look, I know the kind of thing you're talking about, but this is different. It really is. This is vicious, and they don't take turns. Michael and Tracy say it's always these same two little boys. Playing keepaway with somebody's hat is one thing, but throwing *stones*…and…" She tried to convey what was, for her, the worst part. "It's always from a *distance*. As though none of them dare to get close to these two kids. Mike says they smell bad. But really, nobody tries to push them, or give them even a running punch, just that taunting, and rock throwing, and the two of them *stand* there holding hands and take it, and never say a word…." She broke off, "Doesn't that strike you as strange?"

Markham tapped her ball-point on the desk-top. "The only thing that strikes me as strange is that we've had no complaints from anyone, not even the regular bus-driver, and Mr. Sanchez is *most* observant. You say you don't know the family name? Or the residence?"

"No. No one seems to. But wouldn't they have to go to school here, at Los Avilas?"

Markham shook her head. "Not at all. They could have a parent living in a different district, or they could be at a private school…."

Catherine recalled sharply the loose, scruffy woolens bundled around the two boys even on that hot late-April Friday, their dull, matted hair, the circles under their eyes, eyes set in such pinched faces. They had deers' eyes, the two of them, eyes out of some Disney cartoon, much too big and limpid, and fringed with heavy lashes.

"I don't think…no, not a private school, anyway. They seemed so seedy. More than even…well, seedy." She had her own misgivings about most of the other children who straggled down the barrio road from the school bus stop. Michael and Tracy told her that a lot of *those* kids got to drink Coca Cola and grab handfuls of Frootloops right from the box for breakfast. Well, she believed it. But those children, however ill-clothed, cigarette-smoking, foul-mouthed they might be, still seemed so alive. Maybe they'd all be sniffing paint or pregnant in a few years time, but for now there was a flame inside them. She'd only glimpsed the other two little boys from a distance, that day she'd walked to the bus stop and come upon the other children—her own not included, thank God—stoning them. They must have edged off along the brushy path by the irrigation ditch while she was scattering their tormentors. But she remembered their terrible resigned sweetness as they held hands and looked around at the wide ring of frenzied, grinning children. They looked like photographs of children you saw in documentaries of earthquakes, war, famine. Not stunned, exactly, but children who know so much about evil they can only accept it, endure it, regard it calmly.

"You think they're brothers?" Markham asked.

"I'm guessing. But they were all bundled up just alike, the two of them, in these strange old heavy clothes. Jackets and wool pants way too big for them. I didn't hear them say anything to each other, but of course there was so much noise...."

(*Her own voice, O Christ, O Christ, stop it, her ragged breath.*)

"—and Michael said he thinks maybe they can't talk. And Mr. Sanchez probably didn't see anything because they never ride the bus. They just show up there by the ditch most afternoons, after he lets the other kids off."

Markham looked at the clock, edging toward four.

"Well, I'll ask around. They could be in some special program for the learning disabled at one of the magnet schools. Or visiting temporarily with relatives somewhere in the neighborhood. But of course you know the likeliest explanation."

Catherine stared at her.

"The best bet is that the parents are illegal aliens the authorities just haven't caught up with yet. That may be why the boys don't talk—they probably don't know English, and even their Spanish would sound strange here. Those people, you know, will do anything to stay this side of the border, even keep their children away from school and medical care, anything that might mean tipping off Immigration."

Catherine reddened, caught in the act of being the naive liberal. Of course: wetback kids. It made perfect sense. She hated Markham for being so smug and confident about what was undoubtedly true. Probably living in some shack deep in the bosque along the ditches, parents off working on one of the small farms farther south in the valley all day.

"Well, Mrs. Krauss, as long as you're here, let me ask about your own children," Markham said, a bit too brightly. "Even if you'd moved into a mostly Anglo school district up in the Heights, this year would be quite an adjustment for them, with your...the divorce, a move in the middle of the year, and all. And in these Valley schools in Albuquerque, the children can be so close knit, half of them cousins anyway...."

Catherine swallowed. "Fine. They're doing great, they really are. That's what both their teachers say. And some of the neighbor kids have been coming over after school. Michael and Tracy have even started picking up a little Spanish...."

Markham laughed lightly. "I can imagine which words."

"No, well, *sure*," Catherine said, "I guess it's just as well I don't know what all of it means myself, but I know they say other things too, like *cookie* and *come here* and...." *Stop it*, she told herself. *You're making it sound like talking to a dog.*

"No problems at all, then?" said Markham, fixing her with a counselor's eye: *you can tell me, I'll know if you're lying.*

"No. Well...." Damn it. She was a compulsive confessor in this sort of situation. "Just some bad dreams. The other kids were telling them some pretty hairy stories when we first moved in. About a woman, a ghost who's supposed to haunt the neighborhood and eat children, or something. I guess it really got to them. But I suppose they're at the age for that."

Markham nodded, sure of her turf now. "That's La Llorona. The wailing woman, you know? Well, no, probably not, you're fresh from the Midwest. You hear about her—it—in all the communities around here, though." She drew her mouth down. "The parents actually encourage the whole business, if you can believe that, to scare the children away from the irrigation ditches. There's a lot of versions, but usually she's supposed to have been a woman who killed her children back in the 1800's to spite her husband, and now she goes around crying and calling for them, along the ditches."

"The ditches?"

"Where she threw them, after she cut their throats or did whatever she did to them. The parents tell the children she's out looking for their bodies, or for other children to take their places. Well."

Markham seemed embarrassed at having told the story at all, as though her repeating it might give it some professional credence. "God knows there's enough real child abuse to deal with in this district. But we do get L.L. scares—that's what we call them—two or three times a year. Pants-wetting and hysterics in class, the whole gamut of regressive behavior. All the children from one neighborhood will troop in swearing they all heard her shrieking and sobbing outside the night before, when of course it must have been some domestic disturbance going on, and they'll set off the others...."

"What do you do to calm them down?" Catherine asked.

"Well, three years ago Miss Quintana had her fifth grade take time out from regular work to talk and write compositions and draw pictures. She was right out of the University, you know, and she thought getting it out, as she put it, might help. But of course the class was an emotional chaos, and Miss Quintana agrees now that it's better if we're all very firm about what's imagination and what's not, and stick to our schedules."

"I guess that must be the one, all right," Catherine said. "La Llorona, I mean, not Miss Quintana. The story that scared them."

Markham stood up. It was five after four. "Yes. Well. But it does sound as though your two are adjusting well, and as far as this other matter goes, unless those boys are enrolled here, I have no authority, as I'm sure you understand. *But*," she said, lowering her voice, "there's nothing to stop *you*, as a concerned neighbor, from contacting the police, and if they really *are* the children of aliens, I suspect you'd be doing them a double favor. As it is, they're probably not getting any education to speak of, much less their shots...."

Catherine stood too. "Thank you for your time," she said carefully.

Markham followed her into the hall. "Please feel free to come in and discuss anything with us, with me, any time," she called after Catherine.

MICHAEL AND TRACY were waiting for her on the playground. Michael scuffed the toes of his sneakers in the hard dirt beneath the swings, and Tracy, humming, floated a popsicle stick in a puddle left from last night's rain.

"Can we go home now?"

"What did she say, Mom? About those kids?"

How to begin? "Well, for one thing, she doesn't think they go to this school."

"Toldja," Michael said. Swing, scuff, swing, scuff.

"She thinks maybe their parents might be...visiting...from Mexico."

Michael hopped off the swing, and ran ahead of her, kicking up clods of mud with the thick toes of his K-mart sneakers.

"Do Mexicans smell funny and wear funny clothes like that?" he asked.

"*No*, it's just that…."

Tracy danced ahead, singsonging to herself in the way she often did. "I bet they don't have any mommy and daddy at all, I bet they just live in the woods, all by themselves, and when the dark night comes they don't have to take a bath, just lie down on the ground without any supper, and the wind blows the leaves all over them…."

Catherine felt herself shiver. "Quit it, Tracy. Come on to the car. Let's talk. You see, there's a lot of poor people in Mexico, and they come up here to New Mexico to work sometimes, even when they don't have permission from this country to do that, because the jobs are so much better here. The farmers here hire them even though they're not supposed to, because they don't have to pay them as much as they pay American workers."

She wondered if she should go on, try to make it all really clear. Better not, she thought, sliding behind the wheel of the Rabbit. If the rest of the kids got the idea that the police were after the boys' parents, it might make everything worse. Tracy and Mike didn't seem very interested anyway. Tracy was going on with her soft chant, "In the woods, in the night, and it is very *very* dark…"

Catherine knew one thing; she couldn't bring herself to call the police. She'd just have to be there, waiting at the bus stop, whenever she could, and try to see that the other kids left the boys alone.

BUT THE BOYS weren't at the bus stop the next two days. Catherine hoped their parents might have moved on, or else that the boys themselves had learned to stay clear of trouble.

The third day was Catherine's late day because of her afternoon seminar that didn't let out until four. On Thursdays, Mike wore the house key on a shoestring around his neck. She left a snack—raisins, granola, bananas, milk—in the fridge, and she had an arrangement with Mrs. Gonzales next door that the kids would go to her for anything they needed until she got home.

Catherine pulled the Rabbit into the driveway, feeling drained and depressed. Maybe trying to get her MA in Education was a mistake. She could be making decent money substitute-teaching full-time with her BA, right now. Chuck's support payments were coming in so grudgingly. Often they were late, and she bounced checks. She was always tired these days. Classes, her work-study job in the library, the children. Besides, the classes had begun to seem so abstract and repetitive, concerned not with real kids but with The Child. Catherine pictured The Child as looking like the Pillsbury Dough Boy without his chef's hat. This seminar on Educational Testing was the worst of all, nothing but stanines, norms, and curves. She had trouble balancing a checkbook; the numbers and boxes and symbols froze her. *Out of my depth*; the phrase kept resounding in her mind.

She sensed something wrong the minute she walked into the house. First the unmistakably strange silence, then a burst of suppressed nervous laughter, and Tracy's high excited half-whisper: "Please please hang up, Roberto!"

She could guess right away what was happening. She knew it from her own past; she had a sudden picture of herself hanging back, delighted and terrified, in her mother's neat kitchen in Minneapolis, while her bolder girlfriends crowded together in a small knot, giggling. Telephone games. Dialing numbers at random, asking, *Is your refrigerator running? Then you better go catch it*! Or breathing *fuck you* into the receiver and slamming it down.

She stepped quietly into the kitchen. The bright yellow telephone had been taken from its little wall niche and set on the floor. Three children, her own and Roberto, Mrs. Gonzales' boy from next door, squatted around it as though it were a camp fire. Roberto held the receiver out at arms' length so the others could hear. Faint noises came from the mouthpiece.

She snatched the receiver roughly from Roberto's hand, frantic to explain to the person on the line how sorry she was, how she could guarantee it would never happen again, and caught her breath. Someone on the other end was crying, a low, raggedly desperate sobbing, punctuated with gasped Spanish words: *Madre, Cristo, niños, Dios*.

Roberto started to edge out the kitchen door. Without thinking about it, her hand shot out. She grabbed his arm and held him fast. Good *God*, how long had these kids been at this? Long enough to drive some poor woman over the brink, calling and calling her, and saying who knew what?

"Look, I'm *so* sorry; please listen," she began, but the voice went on, a wrenched and wet keening. Catherine had never heard anyone cry like that, not in hospital emergency rooms, not herself when Chuck told her he was leaving her for Grace-Anne. She could not bear it, she thought, when abruptly, as though a switch had been flipped somewhere, the noise stopped. There was only the sound of someone breathing now, listening, and now Catherine's nerve failed, and she could not find her own voice. Almost involuntarily, her finger twitched down on the button, and there was only the long humming of the phone company's outer space.

She looked around furiously at the children. Tracy watched her wide-eyed, her thumb plugging her mouth securely. Roberto wailed, "You're *hurtin'* me," and she realized suddenly that she was gripping his arm very tightly indeed. She let go, moving fast at the same moment to block him off from the doorway with her whole body. *It's his fault*, she thought.

"Now tell me what's going on here!"

Roberto looked down at his feet. "We was just callin' her."

"Calling who? *Who?*"

"All the kids do it, Mom," Michael said in a reflex whine. But he looked as if he knew well this was no excuse, not in his unfair household where no one got to drink Coke for breakfast or got to stay up to watch *L.A. Law.*

"All the kids do *what*, Michael?"

"Call her. It's like you dare somebody to do it, and first Roberto dared me, and I did, and so now he's got to do it."

His voice was taking on a faint Spanish intonation, she noted irritably. "Tell me right now what this number is you've been calling!"

"It's just any old number," Roberto said. "If she's the one you want to call, sometimes you get her, that's all, and then we just listen to her. It don't work all the time. Just sometimes she answers, when she wants to, I guess. She didn't answer all winter."

Catherine stared down at the telephone, sitting very squat and yellow and normal on the linoleum, and then around at the three faces, her own children, the neighbor's child, all unknowable, this kitchen a stranger's room. First Michael and Tracy mentioning to her so casually about how there were two little boys all the kids threw rocks at every afternoon—they denied ever taking part, and she had believed them, but how could she be sure they themselves hadn't helped sometimes in the stoning? Now this, and these were her own, her babies, the same children who wept and pressed their faces to the rear window if they passed a dog, a rabbit flattened to a mat on the freeway. Her mind spun: they don't mean to be cruel, she told herself, but somewhere inside she knew she didn't really believe that. This story about dialing any old number was nonsense, of course. Some poor soul out there had a number some kid had once dialed by accident, and that number had proved so rewarding he'd passed it on to the others, and so now they all did it, dialed it, all the time. Maybe the woman on the other end was feebleminded, or crazed, or knew too little English to call the phone company and complain. Maybe she didn't even realize she could get her number changed, that she didn't have to pick up the receiver each time the phone rang, that she needn't listen to the voices on the other end, the voices of children saying things.

Roberto was rubbing his arm elaborately. "I'm gonna tell Mamma you hurt me!" She glanced at him. There were five dull red marks on his brown arm, just where the sleeve of his Spuds McKenzie T-shirt stopped.

"Roberto, I'm sorry I grabbed you hard"—*too hard, you little bastard, I admit it*—"but there's something we all have to get straight right now. It's *wrong*," and she paused for effect, "it's even *against the law* to do what you've been doing to that woman. She's probably very old, and alone, and she's terribly upset...."

"Oh, she's old, all right," Michael said, glad there was one thing he and his mother could agree on.

"—and you are making her suffer by calling her up and saying whatever things you say to her."

They all looked at her with true indignation. "Oh no, Mom," Tracy said, "we never say nothing to her, do we, huh, Mike? Because," she bounced excitedly, "because then she might *know* who *we* are, and she could find out where to come and get us!"

Michael was nodding, but stopped suddenly, and looked hard at his mother.

"But you talked to her, Mom, didn't you? Boy, you think she *heard* you?" He might have been asking if she thought that saucers might really land, one part fear, three parts anticipation.

She couldn't sleep that night until long after Mike and Tracy, tearfully, without television or stories, had gone to bed. The house was too quiet, except once, when Mike cried out loudly, defiantly in his sleep, "Come and get 'em!" Dreaming about selling something, she supposed dully. She tossed between anxiety and a fiercer anger than she'd yet felt at Chuck for leaving her. If that hadn't happened, none of the rest would be happening either. There would be someone warm and solid in bed to brush against as she tossed restlessly, someone to talk to about her classes, someone to take the kids aside and tell them in a deeper and surer voice than hers what was right and wrong. She wouldn't be trying to patch together a life of classes and children on too little time and money, or be stuck in a cheap rental in an alien town in an alien neighborhood, far from watered lawns and kept-up houses and well-ordered families who spoke English. And there was anger, too; she had to face it—anger at Mike and Tracy for making what was already hard harder for her. My God, she chided herself, they're only six and eight, and they haven't any father to speak of. But when she did sleep, she dreamed of them lost somewhere behind the house, alone in the bosque at night, with no one to help her find them. In the dream she scrabbled with underwater slowness along the trash-strewn path by the irrigation ditch, calling their names, scratched by the thorny branches of Russian olive, tamarisk. Always she had the sense they were somewhere just ahead of her in the darkness. Once Roberto stepped out from behind a cottonwood, rubbing his arm. The five marks glowed on his flesh, her own fingerprint whorls showing up as plainly as on a wanted poster. She told him again how sorry she was, begging him to help her find them, but he regarded her silently and stepped back into the shadows. She woke, shaken, at first light.

She got up then and made sure they were in their room, unhurt. Then she dressed quickly. It was only quarter to six, and cool, and when she stepped outside, the intricate crevices of the mountains to the east were plainly etched with mist in the first brightness. It was going to be better now. The dream upset her, but she knew it was good to face her anger and her fear. She would be better with Michael and Tracy. They were so vulnerable to all the world's harms, with only her to keep them safe.

She went back inside and started breakfast, deliberately making a little more noise than she needed to. She couldn't wait for them to get up, for things to start being better. When they drifted into the kitchen, tousled and flushed, yesterday gone, she hugged them hard, breathing in their warmth, their hair damp from their sleep, and the faint scent of Breck *No More Tears*.

"Juice and peanut butter toast and scrambled eggs," she said. "And don't take the bus this afternoon. I'll pick you up at school. There's a Disney movie we can go to, the late matinee, and eat at MacDonald's afterwards, OK?" She thought for a second how many tensions and lacks she'd made up to them this way, in a sudden shower of small pleasures, movies and hamburgers. Never mind.

AT THEIR PLASTIC TABLE in the clean brick MacDonald's, surrounded by other parents and children at other tables spread with little sacks and cups and containers, she thought about the movie. *Snow White*. She hadn't seen it in almost twenty years. She had forgotten how brutal early Disney could be, the wicked queen raging around with her pointed eyebrows and her swirling batwing cloak, the shadow of the huntsman and his knife falling across the kneeling girl, the still princess in her glass coffin. All the dwarfs bumbling into one another, all the mascara-lashed birds chirping harmony with Snow White—that was all frosting. The story was about an abused child, a motherless child; it was about death. She could remember herself as a child, trembling and crying at some of those cartoon features. She had even had to be carried out to the lobby, sobbing, in mild disgrace, when Bambi's mother died, and when Monstro the whale attacked Pinocchio's raft. But now her children and the other children in the theater watched calmly, even critically. It must be TV, Catherine thought; they were sanguine about anything they saw on a screen, expecting the Coyote to arise blackened from the explosion and skulk away while the Roadrunner beeped joyously. Once during the show, Tracy turned to her and stage-whispered, "Snow White just looks dead, but pretty soon she'll get up, I bet. They do that." And of course Snow White did.

After a few days, Roberto began coming over again in the afternoons. Catherine had spoken to his mother about the telephone business, and Mrs. Gonzales grimly said she'd make sure Roberto would not play any more tricks on poor old women. The two strange little boys continued to stay away from the bus stop. After awhile, Catherine no longer felt the need to be there to meet the children. She herself was patient with Michael and Tracy, careful not to betray her own weariness and worry over money or graduate school or loneliness.

Still, something new had entered their lives, some vague edge of mutual mistrust. She had learned and could not forget that her children were capable of a secret life, and she suspected they might take more pains to hide their secrets from now on. She told herself it was paranoid, but she found herself eavesdroppping more on their conversations, and making regular excuses to check on them when they were out of sight, even if they were only a few feet away in their room with the door wide open. She noticed any glances they exchanged in her presence. But they never alluded on their own to the two little boys, or to the telephone games.

ONE AFTERNOON, Catherine suddenly missed Tracy. She found her alone in the patchy back yard near the Russian olives, playing with a pair of stuffed toys the manufacturers had cutely named "Huggy-Pups." The plush dogs' paws were sewn with small strips of Velcro, and when they were new they could be made to fasten their arms lovingly around one another's necks. In time the bristle had lost its adhesiveness; when Tracy tried to make them hug, the pups' gangly arms flopped back passively to their sides. Tracy had lost all interest in them more than a year ago. But now Catherine came upon her daughter, her baby, with the pups beside her as she dug intently with a tablespoon in the loose earth by the spiney trees. Already she had managed a shallow trench; as Catherine watched silently, Tracy laid one of the dolls in the hole and began to throw fistfuls of soil on top of it. There was something terrible about the dirt sifting over the idiot stuffed-animal grin of the toy. Catherine stepped forward.

"Tracy!"

The little girl looked up.

"What are you doing to Huggy-pup?"

Tracy rocked back on her bare heels. "I'm gonna bury him good and deep. And his brother, too."

"But why, honey?" Catherine knelt beside her, brushing the crumbly dirt away from the matted plush.

"Cause his mommy doesn't love him and his brother, and they got dead. So it's better if he gets buried, instead of just hangs around."

Catherine picked up the dolls and led Tracy gently back into the house. She explained that a lot of poor children didn't have many toys; if Tracy were tired of the pups, they could give them to the Salvation Army to give to a little girl who wouldn't be getting many toys that Christmas.

"OK," Tracy agreed unenthusiastically. "But they'll still be dead."

"Toys aren't dead if somebody loves them, Tracy. You just mean you're tired of playing with them, that's all."

"Will you get tired of me and Mikey, Mommy? Will I get dead?"

"No! That is, we all die someday, but I don't stop loving you, even when I'm mad at you...." Catherine didn't know what question to address first.

"Some mommies get tired, though. And some kids get dead. Will you love me when I get dead?"

"Tracy, I won't get tired of you. And you *won't* die, that is, not for a long long time…." Oh God, she thought. She supposed it had to do with Chuck leaving them. Getting tired of them. She was afraid to say too much, not sure of what was mixed up in Tracy's head, not sure of what dark ditch-water she was skirting. Maybe, after her exams, she could get Tracy into some kind of free counseling, not that Markham person, but someone good, maybe somebody through the University. Still, didn't all kids do things like this, play graveyard, work out fears about death and abandonment through games? But the sight of Tracy consigning the grinning lop-armed toy to the shallow grave stayed with her. What was it, she suddenly remembered, Tracy'd said about the two kids at the bus stop, about them lying down in the woods at night, and the leaves blowing over them? Maybe it was a normal phase, but it sure as hell was a morbid one. Counseling, yes, just to talk to somebody, when I have time to arrange it, just a few more weeks, she thought, and once again she silently cursed Chuck, the deserter, the one who had grown tired of them all.

She hadn't been to the bus stop for weeks now, but that evening she asked Mike, trying to sound casual, "Those two little boys the other kids used to tease—they haven't shown up again, have they?"

Mike concentrated on pulling apart two stuck Leggos. "You never see 'em. But I guess they could just be staying back in the woods, playing by themselves."

"You think their parents might still be around, then?"

Still he did not look up at her. "Roberto says he thinks their mother's still around, for sure."

"But you haven't seen…."

He sighed impatiently. "I don't see anybody. And I don't talk to anybody anymore, ever, either. What's for lunch?"

She wanted to smack him for his flat insolence, but she let it go at that.

ON A WARM DAY IN MID-MAY, Catherine got home early, after the last of her exams, feeling numb and lightheaded. Michael and Tracy wouldn't be home for another three hours, and any misgivings she felt about her own situation were completely washed out in the pure flood of release she was experiencing. Summer school wouldn't start for weeks, and now there would be time to clean house and read what she wanted—time, maybe, to look into family counseling, but for right now, for this three-hour space, she could sit, just sit. Clouds were bunching up in the west; there might be an early thunderstorm by evening. Maybe—who knows?—maybe they didn't even *need* a counselor. After all, she'd gotten through a whole semester, alone, and she was handling it, handling it all by herself. She wished she could afford to call up Chuck and tell him that, laugh lightly into the phone and say, *Of course I'm fine, we're all fine, I'm growing in so many ways, I'm finding out so much about myself.*

She changed into cutoffs and a tee shirt. Then she got herself a Hamm's and sat on a kitchen chair on the front porch, her legs propped up on the spindly railing, trying not to go back over that last bitch of an exam in her mind. Let it go. She could almost feel the muscles at the back of her neck loosening, fibre by fibre. She slit her eyes against the sun and watched a breeze off the Rio Grande ruffle the shiny leaves of the cottonwood across the road.

She noticed, with a start, that the can of beer had gone warm in her hand. The angle of light was considerably lower. She must have dozed, for a moment anyway. She shook her head to clear it, about to get up to check the time, and then she saw them there, hand in hand in the road, standing just outside the gate of the low chainlink fence. Despite the warmth of the afternoon, they still wore the odd bulky woolen clothing she'd seen them wearing over a month ago. They waited quietly, stiller than any children she'd ever seen, staring at her with their impossibly big eyes.

She stood up, tucking her shirt back into her cutoffs. "Hi, there!" she called to them.

They smiled shyly at her then, still saying nothing. Her heart stirred. The other kids, her own and Roberto and the others, the stone-throwers, would be coming down the road soon. The best thing would be to keep the boys here for a while, at least until Michael and Tracy came home, and then walk them back up the road, maybe even drive them to their house, have a word with their parents, or whoever took care of them. She could scout out the situation. If she could get them to tell her where they lived, that is.

She headed slowly down the walk toward them, as cautiously as she'd approach deer, smiling, hoping not to frighten them off. They regarded her calmly, waiting. "You must be hot. It's so muggy this afternoon," she said. Again, they smiled at her, sweetly, waiting for whatever it was she planned to do to them. She lifted the latch of the gate. "Would you like to come visit, come in and drink some lemonade or something? My kids will be home from school pretty soon, and you could all play for a while, and then I could drive you home." She was sure they didn't understand a word she said. Their faces registered nothing. But her gesture of opening the gate and standing aside was unmistakable, and they followed her hesitantly into the yard. Now that she had them on the property, in her hands, why was she thinking of Hansel and Gretel at the gingerbread house? No one would hurt them here, not Michael and Tracy, certainly not her. But she thought of a younger cousin she'd detested. He was fat and stupid and picked his nose, and throughout her childhood her mother kept asking him over because she felt sorry for him. She remembered her anger when she was ordered to "be nice to Sammy," and all the small cruelties she and her friends had inflicted on him. He never did tell her mother on them, though.

"Come on and let's get lemonade," she said, using the teacher's "we" she herself hated; they followed her into the house, and stood in her kitchen watching her open the cardboard can, pour the water, crack the ice trays. Here in the warm house she was suddenly conscious of how right Mike had been. They *did* smell, poor babies, like meat gone bad in the summer, a cloying, sweetly sick smell. She thought fleetingly about lice. "*Stop it*, she told herself. *You've started this, and now you'll finish it.*

They took the sweating glasses from her mutely, but they didn't make a move to drink, even when she took a swig of her own, smiling encouragement. On top of the beer, with the thick smell of their flesh filling the room, the lemonade went down badly; she swallowed hard, and still they stood looking at her, Flintstone glasses in hand, like strange tools they could not guess the use for. Maybe they were retarded; they looked to be about six and eight, surely too old for that frozen shyness a younger child might show. *What now*? she asked herself, and then the screen door banged and Michael and Tracy and Roberto stood in the kitchen entryway, staring unbelievingly at this strange tableau in their own territory. "Bye," Roberto said, and he was gone.

She spoke quickly, before Michael or Tracy had a chance to, explaining that the boys had been walking by and were hot and thirsty, and they were all going to have some lemonade and play a little while and then pretty soon...the rest was lost in Michael's outburst: "You don't *play* with those kids!"

She moved protectively toward the boys. God, they stank. She knew she was being unfair to her own children, but damnit, they had to learn tolerance. Besides, now she could think of no course but the one she'd impulsively chosen when she'd first spotted them standing in the road. "*Michael*! Be polite or else go sit in the bathroom for an hour; you've got your choice." Tracy's thumb had gone into her mouth the minute she took in the sight in the kitchen, and her nose wrinkled at the undeniable smell. But now her face lit with—what? Interest? Curiosity? Challenge? Or perhaps just at the chance to show up Michael.

"It's OK, they can play with *me*," she said importantly. "Come on!" When she beckoned, the boys trailed after her obediently into the kids' room. Catherine could hear Tracy chattering away to them, or at them, more likely. On her last report, her teacher had noted she "tended to be an initiator of peer group interaction." These two might not speak English, but surely they could respond to Tracy's unselfconscious openness, to her toys.

Michael skulked after them, unwilling to be left out, despite the company his sister had traitorously chosen to keep. *Let them alone*, she told herself. *They'll work it out*.

A half-hour passed while she busied herself in the kitchen, straining to hear whether any fights might be breaking out. The storm was closer now, the sky much darker, and the wind had picked up. All right, that was surely long enough; it was time now, and now she even had a good excuse to drive the boys home, with the rain coming on.

In the children's room, Michael sat sullenly on his bed, pretending to read a comic book. The little boys sat on the floor, still mute, their untouched glasses of lemonade beside them. Tracy, always pleased to have an audience, however passive, seem to be putting on some kind of show for their benefit. Catherine was a little startled to see that two of the actors were the spurned Huggy-pups. And Tracy had produced still another toy, the Madame Alexandra Castilian doll Catherine's wealthy Lake Forest aunt had sent Tracy the Christmas before last, a señorita complete with lace mantilla and tiny eardrops and an elaborately flounced red satin dress. Tracy never played with her. If the Huggy-pups were too battered to please her any longer, the señorita's fanciness was apparently too intimidating; she had sat formally on Tracy's dresser for two years, an ornament, not a toy.

Now Tracy wielded the Spanish doll, making her stalk across the carpet, as best she could, and speaking for her in a cross voice. The two limp dogs lay sprawled at her feet. "Your daddy is gone, gone away," Tracy was saying, "and he is not coming back, ever, and I am sad!" She manipulated the Spanish doll's stiff leg, aiming an awkward but unmistakable kick at one of the grinning dogs. "Do you hear me, Luis? Do you hear me, Raimundo? Your daddy did something bad, and *you* are bad, *bad*, and now I will do something bad to you!"

The boys watched her, entranced, nodding slightly as if in agreement. Suddenly Tracy became aware of her mother's presence. She smiled brilliantly up at her. "We're playing, me and Luis and Raimundo, like you said. But Mikey won't play, just wants to read a dumb old comic. He doesn't *like* Luis and Raimundo. Not like we do," she added proudly, including herself and her mother in a club of two. *Those damned dogs* was all Catherine could think. But she smiled uneasily at all of them and sat on the floor beside the boys. Distracted by the abrupt halt of Tracy's performance, one of the boys, the bigger one, looked around the room. He spotted an old toy of Michael's lying nearby, a rough red-painted wooden pullcart Chuck had made, back when Michael was a baby. It galvanized him. "*Carreta. Carreta,*" he said in a husky whisper. His voice sounded unused. He looked at his brother, and reached out to clutch the cart in his lap. "*Carreta para los caballos, como...como....*"

Suddenly Michael jackknifed off the bed, and tore the cart roughly out of the boy's arms. "Don't touch any of *my* toys! You stink! You stink!" he shouted, and ran brokenly from the room toward the kitchen.

Catherine sat stunned. Tracy looked calmly at her mother, as if to say, *What can you expect from him?* "Mikey is just mean," she said. "Luis used to have a cart like that a long time ago I bet, didn't you, Luis?" She crawled across the floor and shoved the cart back toward him. "Before. A long long time ago. Here, you take it. Mikey don't play with it, anyway."

The boys sat sadly now with their arms around each other, looking at the cart. The younger one patted it gently. "*Carreta,*" he repeated, suddenly smiling, as if he just now remembered the word. Tears burned Catherine's eyes, tears for Michael, for herself, for these two lost ones. Convulsively she folded the two boys in her arms, cart and all, holding them close. The stench was terrible, but they turned their faces toward her breast, tentatively hugging her back. Their hands were icy and moist. She could feel them through the thinness of her shirt. She held them wordlessly for a moment, fighting her rising gorge, rocking them back and forth, sure she would not be able to bear the smell much longer. If she could only bathe them. She started to disengage herself from their embrace, and ran her hand soothingly around the little one's grimy neck. His flesh felt oddly soft—pulpy, almost, the way her ankles had in late pregnancy, but more so. Mushy. Her fingers discovered a thickness that ringed his neck. She pulled back a little on the collar of the woolen shirt he wore. It was stiff with dirt, and with some wetness that had partly dried, and then she saw the thick oozing scar that nearly encircled his delicate throat like a choker. Oh, God, she should have called the child abuse hotline a month ago. She stood up quickly. "I'll be right back," she said, and headed for the kitchen, for the telephone.

But Michael was there before her, clutching the phone with both hands, his face distorted with rage. "They're here! Come an' get 'em, you old bitch!" he shouted into the receiver, then slammed it down, glared at his mother, and burst into hard tears.

She bent to hug him, knowing she was supposed to. "Oh, Michael," she said. But she felt an edge of anger rising in her. She was so tired, so very tired. Why in hell couldn't the kids help at times like this, instead of making things worse? She stared past his head out the screen door, latched against the wind that was gusting harder now, the storm almost upon them. Before she called the hotline, she needed to try to find out their last names, where they lived, some name, anything. She picked up her son, almost too big to lift now, a burden, and carried him back to the playroom. Tracy sat there, clutching the two stuffed dogs, with the boys on either side of her.

She regarded Catherine coolly. "They're afraid, Luis and Raimundo. They say their mother's comin' for them. They say they gotta go now."

"But no, they can't…and it's going to rain *hard*…." She set Mike on his feet and hurried back toward the living room, thinking *sweaters*, *car keys*. The front door screen, unhooked from its latch, banged back and forth.

Tracy followed her, still clutching the Huggy-pups, with the boys in her wake. Michael trailed after. "I know what Mikey did," she said. "They know too. Mikey told their mother on them. Now she'll come to get them."

"Maybe she'll be good to them now," Michael mumbled.

"Hah!" Tracy replied.

Michael hung his head. "I was scared, Mom, honest. I didn't mean to…."

Tracy turned on them both. "Fraidy cat!" she spit out. "You don't like them, you never did, and Mommy doesn't either, not really!"

"Tracy. Of *course* I…." Catherine began.

"Just because they're *dead*," Tracy said scornfully, and buried her face in her armful of plush toys.

The wind tore at the screen door again and banged it, and then, in a lull between the gusts, Catherine suddenly became conscious of the other noise coming now from outside the darkened kitchen, the kitchen whose door gave on the weedy back yard and beyond that, the bosque, the woods lining the ditch where the wet leaves lay in drifts beneath thick tangles of thorny trees.

Hardly conscious of what she was doing, she negotiated the hallway, and froze before she stepped fully through the dark archway to the kitchen. For an instant, an eternity, for however long she stood there, there was time to remember that this door was latched, if only with a hook-and-eye, though back in the living room the front door still banged invitingly in the wind. There was time to realize that even if she should scream, and be heard, Mrs. Gonzales would certainly not be coming over tonight to see what might be amiss. There was time to hear what Tracy had just said, to hear what Tracy had in fact been telling her for weeks now. And there was plenty of time to print on her memory the sight of the arm in the red ruffled satin sleeve, soiled and ragged, as though torn by thorns, the thin hand with its long elegant nails raking the screen mechanically, up and down, the rasping sound of human nails against rusted mesh. There was time to register the voice, not keening now, but calling softly, an almost sexual crooning, *mihitos, mihitos*, an obscene coaxing. She could not make out the face in the darkness, but there was time to understand that the face would probably become visible in the next lightning flash, and she could well imagine that it might, at any minute, straining to see within, press itself so closely against the screen as to leave the imprint of the wire mesh on the soft flesh of its cheeks, nose, its red, open lips, as it strained and pleaded, asking for children to come out, or for someone, another woman, perhaps, a sympathetic woman, asking for someone who understood to issue an invitation to come inside.

Suddenly one of the long nails snagged horribly on the rough screening, and the voice outside broke off its hypnotic wheedling rhythm and shrieked, a long cry of rage. Then, from outside, Catherine could hear small soft sucking sounds. It was nursing its finger, comforting itself, telling itself *there, there*. Soon it would feel better. Everything would be all right. Soon, it would begin thinking about the next thing to do.

Catherine spun on her heel and stumbled back to the living room, back to the ones who had brought this upon her, to the living room where the screen door was blown wide in a fresh gust and the two others cowered beside Tracy, one of them still clutching the red cart for comfort as though he were a real child, looking up at her with the numb fear and blazing innocence a real child might show. That look gave her a second's pause, but then she remembered that they were clever cheaters, liars, the two of them, how in their trustful muteness they had pretended to be what they were not and gone and made a fool of her, like everyone else in her life, first Chuck, then Michael and Tracy, and now *them*, and she grabbed the stinking things by their pulpy arms and shoved them hard out the door, and latched that, and slammed the wooden door shut, too, driving the dead bolts home with shaking hands, shouting the whole while until her voice tore, "Get out! Get out! Get out!"

"NO!" Tracy screamed, "their *mother*...." and flailed against the locks, but she was not strong enough, and Catherine hauled her back, slapping her twice, so that Tracy's head snapped around hard both times, farther than it dimly seemed to Catherine a head perhaps should turn.

"No, you sneaking little bitch, let her!" she cried, shaking Tracy, and when Michael came running out of the playroom, all *please mom* and *no mom*, she grabbed him, too, in her free arm and collapsed with them both in a heap on the carpet, she breathing so hoarsely and them crying so brokenly that none of them could hear whatever might have been happening outside: two children, perhaps, being scolded by their mother for being disobedient, for being gone so long, for not coming even when she called and called and called.

Sometime that night Catherine fell asleep there on the carpet. She awoke at dawn, cold, alone, her throat aching. She found the children asleep together in Michael's bed, fully clothed, their arms about one another, like Hansel and Gretel in the forest. She had a sudden vision of the two sodden Huggy Pups lying in the rain, clinging to one another, with loose soil and wet leaves drifted over them, like a light blanket. A bruise bloomed darkly on Tracy's cheek.

While she waited for them to wake, she wandered blankly into the front yard. The mountains poked up flat and sullen against the sky. Mechanically she picked up the splintered pieces of red-painted wood scattered over the coarse grass, and carried them to the trash can out back.

MORE THAN A MONTH LATER, about eleven at night, the

phone rang. When Catherine answered, no one replied. But she could hear a soft, regular breathing on the line. It rang again, ten minutes later, and again she answered, because after all it might be Chuck, who would call, if he ever called, at this hour to save money; Chuck, who might even be calling to say he was sorry, to say that he needed them, and wanted them all back, and she could make him feel bad by telling him they were all in therapy now because of him, and then she could say yes, yes, we'll come. But still there was only silence, except for the breathing, heavier now, and hungrier, and she hung up.

At the fifth call, or perhaps the sixth, she snatched up the phone and began to cry in broken sobs into the receiver, harder than she'd yet cried in their regular Tuesday sessions of helpless humiliating tears in Dr. Markham's office, although by now both Catherine and the children had learned to call her Marjorie.

When the voice on the other end finally did begin to say something, it did not use words in any language Catherine herself spoke.

Still, she could tell just from the gentle voice how much the caller sympathized, and she knew she was hearing stories about how experiences like her own had been endured and overcome, and she felt so reassured to be speaking to a friend, a peer.

As she sat there crosslegged on her kitchen floor, talking and talking and sometimes listening into the bright yellow receiver, warm now itself from having been held so long against her own hot face, a wonderful thing happened, and she understood not only the tone of voice, but the words, and she knew what this new friend was saying: *yes, I understand*, and *now there are no barriers between us*, and *soon, now, soon, we can have a real visit.*

DOÑA REFUGIO AND HER COMADRE

Jim Sagel

HER comadre Sebastiana had been with her for years now. It seemed like years, at least. Doña Refugio didn't know exactly how long it had been because, from the moment the figure of Death had appeared at her door, Doña Refugio had quit ripping off the pages of the calendar. And the radio announcers, of course, never mentioned what year it was.

But that was just as well, for if someone would have told her the date, Doña Refugio might have been so shocked to know how long she had lasted with Death in the house that she would have died of pure fright.

Everyone else, naturally, couldn't see Death because they no longer believed in her. Even Doña Refugio's own daughter, Lydia, preferred to believe in priests and doctors rather than Death. That was why Lydia had gotten so angry when Doña Refugio had given all her possessions away to the neighbors.

"Death has come for me," Doña Refugio had told them.

The neighbors, believing the old woman had gone crazy, protested at first, but Doña Refugio was convinced she was going to die. "Keep it!" she told them, and eventually they did take everything that Doña Refugio indicated they should keep. Anyway, they figured that if they didn't get the things, somebody else would.

Doña Refugio had given her bed to Corrine because she knew her neighbor had more kids than beds. She had given her dishes to a nearby hippie who was a nice enough person even if she never combed her hair. Doña Refugio's comadre Felicia said that she believed all those hippies weren't really poor. They were just lazy and they certainly didn't deserve the foodstamps they received because they could work just like everybody else, but now that Death had arrived, Doña Refugio had quit judging people. She had given her wood-burning stove—the one her late husband had bought her fifty years ago at Montgomery Wards—to the same unkempt neighbor because the hippie was the only person in all the neighborhood who still cooked with wood instead of butane.

Doña Refugio had also filled seven large boxes with clothing she had planned to send to church for the poor, but Father José had refused to accept them. "I don't believe in poverty," he had told her.

So the boxes had remained in the kitchen where Doña Refugio had once had her table and chairs. It had been a good table too, but now that she was going to die, what did she want with it anyhow? She had given it away to Chencho, her comadre Felicia's son who was building a house near his mother's place and who was going to be needing furniture. Chencho had also taken Doña Refugio's chairs, refrigerator, hot water heater, washing machine, and livingroom couch, for he didn't believe in wasting money when it wasn't necessary.

But Doña Refugio's daughter! Well, she had gotten so angry at her, and for absolutely no reason. After all, Doña Refugio had given her first chance, but Lydia hadn't wanted to take anything.

"You're not going to die!" Lydia had scolded her mother like a naughty little girl. But, then, the poor thing couldn't see Death, even though she sat at the same table with her, while Death sipped coffee out of Doña Refugio's own cup.

So Doña Refugio had shared her few possessions with the neighbors because she knew she couldn't take all those things with her. But that was where Death had fooled her. She had simply stayed at Doña Refugio's house like an idle relative. At first Doña Refugio even suspected she might have died without realizing it. Maybe that's how death was—you simply remained right where you had always been, doing the same stupid things you had done when you were alive. But soon she realized that she couldn't be right in that belief because her daughter, after all, could still see her and talk to her.

And how she talked too—telling Doña Refugio that she had really lost her marbles, and maybe it would be better just to send her to the nut house in Las Vegas.

But poor Lydia couldn't see Death because she didn't believe in her, and so she refused to listen to her mother when Doña Refugio complained about the size of her bed. Now that Doña Refugio didn't even have a place to sleep, Lydia had been obligated to bring her mother to live with her. But when Doña Refugio had complained that her bed was too small for both her and Death, Lydia just couldn't take it anymore. She sent her mother to town to live with Clyde.

But that hadn't worked out either because Doña Refugio's oldest son lived in a trailer. Actually, Doña Refugio had been happy enough there, but not her comadre Sebastiana. Death claimed she just couldn't feel comfortable in a house that had wheels.

Anyway, there was a neighbor around there, the widower Tobias, who insisted on coming over to ask Doña Refugio for a date. He was ugly, with a large mole on his face and no teeth. What was worse, Clyde teased his mother, telling her that she had found a boyfriend, even though Doña Refugio always said, "God help me, but that man is uglier than Death!"

And so Doña Refugio told her son she would have to return to her old house because of that toothless widower. But when Clyde had refused to believe that reason, Doña Refugio had had to explain to him that her comadre Sebastiana couldn't stand the trailer anymore.

It was then that Lydia had informed her older brother that they had better send their mother to the State Hospital. But Clyde didn't believe the old lady had gone crazy. "It's just her age," he had told Lydia, and at last the two of them had collected enough money from the other brothers and sisters to buy their mother a bed, dishes, stove, refrigerator, and table and chairs so that she could move back to her empty house.

"But these aren't your things!" Lydia had told the old lady because she was afraid she might go nuts again and give everything away to the neighbors like before.

But Doña Refugio had no intention of giving away her things because now she had to take care of her comadre Sebastiana. It was a pity how skinny Death was. But Doña Refugio was trying to fatten up those bones a little. And, with time, Death had gained some weight with all the beans and chile Doña Refugio fed her, not to mention the wheat flour tortillas and the delicious chicken soup seasoned with mint.

And the two comadres entertained themselves quite well during the long nights, seated in the livingroom, talking about the dead relatives and compadres they both had known while they sipped on a cup of atole.

"Did you know that your compadre Salamón died?"

"Really? When?"

"Oh, about a half hour ago."

"You don't say! What did he die of?"

"Well, from drinking—what else?"

They'd go on talking like that while Doña Refugio crocheted a sweater for Death because another winter was about to come and she was sure to get cold in the New Mexican mountains. Doña Refugio had never been more content in her life because now she didn't need to call up her comadre Felicia for news about the people who had died, and she didn't have to bother Lydia anymore for the Sunday paper. No, Doña Refugio no longer had to search for the obituaries because now she had all the information right at home.

It appeared that Death was enjoying her visit too because she didn't seem to be in much of a hurry to leave. Doña Refugio made her feel so comfortable, and Death certainly had never encountered anyone who was more interested in her business.

Doña Refugio, for her part, still didn't understand why Death had decided to stay with her. But she certainly wasn't going to complain. It was better to share her home with Death in this world than to journey with her to the other one and, anyway, her comadre Sebastiana was really no trouble.

Well, there was one thing about Death. She'd stay in bed all day long. She claimed she was tired, fatigued from hassling with so many dead people. "The dead are so stubborn these days," Death complained to Doña Refugio all the time. "They don't cooperate like they used to. They don't want to accept me anymore, comadre."

That might have been true, but Doña Refugio knew there was another reason why Death was always so dead tired. She never slept at night.

Really. Every night was the same. Doña Refugio would go to bed at a reasonable hour, but Death would stay up, sitting in the livingroom, drinking coffee and listening to the radio. What was worse was that she only listened to one station, Radio KXRF, a religious station from Juárez. And while Doña Sebastiana listened to Reverend Santiaguito J. Samaniego, Doña Refugio would dream about the end of the world.

That, of course, was beginning to annoy Doña Refugio because during the day she found herself not wanting to talk about anything else but that same end of the world. The few neighbors who had come around now quit visiting her because they got tired of hearing so much about the final days. Doña Refugio even considered giving that radio away to

Ranger, the hippie's son. But she didn't have the courage to do so because Lydia had bought her that radio when she had moved back to her house. Anyway, she was now asking her daughter for another favor.

It had been awhile—who knows how long exactly, for Doña Refugio still hadn't removed a single leaf from her calendar—but, anyhow, it had been some time since Doña Refugio had asked her daughter to help her get a television. Of course the old lady understood what Lydia told her, that she had once had a good TV which she had given away to the boyfriend of her comadre Felicia's daughter. And Lydia reminded her that it had been the same color TV she herself had bought for her mother's birthday some years back.

Doña Refugio received her daughter's rage in silence, responding in a resigned tone: "I'm not asking you to buy me a new one. Any TV would be fine, even if it's old and used."

But her poor daughter. Since Death was invisible to her, she just couldn't comprehend why Doña Refugio had to have one of those idiot boxes.

Her plan was very simple. She would get her comadre Sebastiana interested in the soap operas that came out on TV all day long. Doña Refugio, you understand, had become very frightened. Death was listening to so much preaching about the end of the world that Doña Refugio was worried it might really happen. And, as everybody knows, the soap operas never end.

MY APPLES

Robert Granat

IT is Sunday, the seventh of May, just after noon. The sun is hot and clear. Everything about me seems sealed in silence, and the leaves in the orchard are so unnaturally still you would think the earth has ceased to breathe. The apple tree looks exactly as it did yesterday, but I have just come from examining it and know it is not the same.

It was a year ago last March that I rented the place. A dull cold day, and the cold did not sit still but roamed like a starving grey wolf through the orchard. The orchard was a wasteland, the trees stripped to gaunt black bonecages, the grass and garden dry, frozen and grey. As we talked, Sprouse and I, a strip of torn black roofing-paper kept flapping listlessly on the outhouse roof like the wing of a dying bird.

The house itself was cheaply made. The raw concrete plaster had cracked off in places, and the hollow-tile walls gaped meat-pink and ugly through the wounds. Obviously the house had not been lived in for a long time, and obviously the old man was eager to rent it. Twenty dollars a month was the price he gave me first. But after he had consulted his wife he went up to twenty-five.

"On account the apples, you know," he explained, caressing with his square callus of a hand the smooth and thighlike limb of the large tree we were standing beneath. "You gonna see, mister, these here's Mammoth Delicious, big fellers, best tree we got on the whole place. Good year give maybe twenty-five, thirty bushel, and you don't have to worry none 'bout selling 'em, truckers come over from Texas, pay two-fifty, three dollar a bushel...you gonna see, you gonna have a lotta apples offa this ol' tree."

An orchard of about two acres lay between Sprouse's house and the one I was thinking of renting. The apple tree in question stood directly behind the vacant house, alone and separate from the main body of the orchard. Apparently it had been planted before the others, for it looked almost twice as large. It was impossible for me, looking up into that skeleton of shivering black twigs, to visualize leaves, much less apples. But I knew I couldn't find anything better than this for twenty dollars a month, or even twenty-five, so I told Sprouse that OK, I'd take the place.

The old man shifted on his feet, rubbed his horny forefinger over his mouth and said, "Well, ah...the ol' lady, she tol' me, if you could maybe kinda, you know, leave a deposit on the place...." He obviously didn't like asking for money.

"Oh sure," I said, and wrote him out a check for a month's rent.

"Much obliged to you, sir." He snuffed loudly and poked the paper into the pocket of his blue chambray workshirt.

Sprouse was nearly seventy, I imagined, an unusually large man. In the rear he was perfectly flat and vertical; his pants sagged limply over what should have been his backside. But in the front he consisted of one gentle mound that swelled from his collarbone to his knees, as if a rolling hillock had been sliced from the prairie and stood up on end. Yet this great bulge spoke not of flabbiness but of power, like a unilaterally swollen biceps. As for his face, it was no more than a mounting for his nose, a large irregular formation in purple and red, filled with hollows and shining tubercles, a great hunk of burnt lava. He suffered from rhinophyma, I believe, an affliction which made me take him right off for an alcoholic, though I soon found out he never went beyond a nightly beer or so. Inlaid at the top of this multicolored nose was a pair of bright beady eyes, and the effect of it all was grotesquely appealing, a genuine homeliness, an enlarged humanity. I felt warmly toward the man from the very first.

"I thought of building a chicken coop over there and planting a vegetable garden between this tree and the ditch," I ventured.

"Sure, you jes go right ahead and do whatever you've a mind to. It's your place fer as long's you want it, boy. Gonna hire me a team in a couple or three weeks and I'll help you plow up your patch."

Sprouse spoke in the soft, phlegmatic accents of people who have lived their lives amid large expanses of land and time. An Okie or an

Arkie, I thought, something out of Steinbeck. So there actually were peasants left in this country, people who could be poor without an inferiority complex. This old man would do me more good than a hundred Dr. Sicklers.

"Thanks, Mr. Sprouse. To tell you the truth I'm a city boy myself. Never even had a garden."

"That's what I kinda figgered." From the shelter of his nose his little eyes sparkled out at me with the bright curiosity of a pair of forest rodents. "Course it ain't none of my affair, but I was sorta wonderin', how come a feller like you come 'way out here to New Mexico?"

How come? I guess I smiled, thinking how utterly meaningless "How come?" would be to this farmer. I remembered the way Bartlett's barbershop-tan face twitched, on one side only, as if being jerked by an invisible thread. I thought of the close, dead, female-secretary smell of the office, of the days I'd spent shopping for English flannel suiting of just the right grey and I could taste the revulsion, even here, two thousand miles away from it, the revulsion and the terror that always went with it. And I thought of Sickler sitting there in the same kind of grey flannel suit, of the smug modern look of his monthly "For Professional Services," of the weary way he fingered his bow tie as he listened to me, and the lewd way his lips undulated as he led me to understand that I was suffering from "a totally unreal conception of my environment."

"I came out here because my environment had a totally unreal conception of reality," I said, half-aloud, and stopped, realizing it all wasn't out of me yet.

"How's that?" Sprouse said. "'Scuse me, boy, didn't mean to be stickin' my big nose...." He paused, smiled, and touched his nose with his large hand.

"Oh no, Mr. Sprouse, not at all, I was just thinking...well, you see, I simply got fed up with living in the city, breathing in all that bad air and everything, and I knew it was now or never, so I bought a station-wagon, packed my family, and headed west. And just as soon as we hit the valley something told us 'This is it,' and here we are."

Sprouse turned his head aside, coughed and spat, squinting after the trajectory of spittle. "And so now you figure on bein' a farmer, eh?" He broke out into loud in-huffing laughter, and laid a heavy hand on my shoulder, as if to knight me into his affection. "Hey, hey, boy, you gonna learn a lot this summer."

I did. I learned a hell of a lot.

The following week my wife and I cleaned up the house, painted it, and moved in. I bought fifty chicks and a brooder and set to work building the chicken coop I had designed back in New York. It featured a horizontal door which opened onto a battery of nests, so that you could help yourself to the eggs as conveniently as to a sandwich in the Automat. When I demonstrated this to Sprouse he tapped his skull with his forefinger. "Smart feller," he said, "gonna have to tell the ol' lady 'bout that."

The old lady—I hadn't even gotten a glimpse of her yet. I saw Mrs. Sprouse for the first time on the day of the plowing.

The sun punctured the dawn air and woke me up, the sun and the sounds from the lower field, the shouts to the horses—"*Hey there!...Hey!...Ho!*—sharp and decisive as ax blows. I dressed quickly and went out to watch.

Overnight, it seemed, winter had fled. I stopped to examine my apple tree; its dry twigs had become tumescent, alive with grey velvet buds, its dull black limbs had taken on a ruddy glow. Here and there beads of sap caught the sun like clear jewels. In front of me an incredibly blue bird whirred to the ground, as if a chip had been nicked out of the sky, while over in the orchard a convention of mousy little birds was holding its squeaking disputations. I filled my lungs with the cold virginal air.

Down in the lower field the plow had already painted a long strip of faded ground a rich new brown. "Howdy boy!" Sprouse called out, raising his arm from the plow handle for a second and disclosing a sweat-stained underarm. "Morning, Mr. Sprouse." I stood there watching.

The superb black buttocks of the geldings, quivering with effort, frothy with perspiration, tails whipped like ensigns, heavy tufted hoofs lifting sprays of earth, flanks heaving like bellows, shoulders hard against the collars, heads down against the bit, nostrils steaming. The animal on the right snorted, raised its tail imperiously and made a magnificent, smoking contribution to the earth.

Behind them Sprouse was working just as hard, his arms hooped to the plow handles, his whole face the color of his nose, his voice roaring out commands to the slaves in front of him—"*Hey there!...Hup!...Ho!*—to the metallic grating of the plow blade, the jingling of chain, the slapping of leather, and the soft sound of the uprolling soil itself.

"Hey boy," he shouted when he came back from the far end of the field, "want to have a go at it?" He whoa-ed the horses, pulled an oversized orange bandana from his back pocket and patted his face with it.

"No, I...." But a moment later I was behind the plow, self-consciously gripping the warm wooden handles, shocked by the strong acrid stench of the horses. "*Hey-YUP!*" Sprouse yelled. The horses heaved forward. I had expected the idea was to push down, but no, the pull was to the right—no, to the left. The furrow began to carve out into the field and I struggled to guide it back. "Hold onto it, boy, hold onto it!" I wrestled with it. Suddenly the plow whipped violently downwards. My ankle twisted in the large loose clods and I was down on my face. "*Ho there!...Ho!*"

I heard Sprouse belly-laughing and saw the horses looking back at me over their rear ends—I swear with grins on their faces. I was about to laugh myself when I heard a voice I had never heard before.

"Here's yer water, Calvin." I looked up and saw an old woman setting down two buckets of water.

The first sight of her was a shock, for I had never in my life seen a living human being look so much like a Halloween witch. Grey, dry, brittle as a small dead tree, her trunk clothed in a washed-out print dress made from flour-sacking, her arms and legs stuck out scrawny and gnarled, webbed by a network of blue varicose veins which made them look rough and barkey. On her head a cloth of the same material, knotted down over hair the color and texture of Spanish moss. Resting on her sharp nose a pair of glasses so thick and grey I could not see the eyes behind them. Though I doubted she could see out of them, these lenses fixed on me briefly and piercingly as I stumbled hot-faced to my feet. And without a word more, the woman turned and plodded back toward her house.

"That your wife?" I asked Sprouse, wondering why he hadn't introduced us.

"That's the old lady." He bent over and sloshed water on his face, and when the horses had drunk, he took up the fallen plow.

He plowed all that day. By two he had finished his field, and after he had broken up the clods with a home-made harrow—a capsized bed of nails on which he rode over the earth like some burlesque Achilles—he came and turned over my garden patch in the upper field between the irrigation ditch and the big apple tree. I had to stand by like a fool, watching him exhaust himself engraving those acres of earth, incapable of helping him out.

"Oh, let me at least pay my share," I said when he had finished and was paying off the team's owner. Beside this marvelously dirty and sweat-stinking man, I felt ashamed of my cleanliness.

"Hell no, tha's OK, boy." He bounced his nose up and down with his thumb. "Tell you what, you come over and fix me one of them help-yourself egg drawers some time." He socked me good-naturedly on the shoulder and went waddling off home through the orchard.

Not five minutes later the sounds of an argument began to drift over from Sprouse's, alternating between the shrill screeching of his wife and the deep soft tones of the old man. Like a cacophonous sonata, it would die down for a moment and then a new movement would begin.

I had just settled down to reading the new book I had received that morning, *The Story of My Experiments with Truth* by Gandhi, when there was a timid tapping on the kitchen door. My wife opened it and there stood Sprouse. Shamefaced, head hanging, he entered and I closed my book.

"Say, I'm awful sorry to disturb you folks but—this ain't none of my idea but—well, you see, the ol' lady, she's all het up on account I didn't ask you nothin' fer the plowin'...maybe you wouldn't mind givin' a dollar or two...."

This request made me angry enough to keep silent. I took two dollars from my wallet and handed them to him, gruffly I suppose.

"Thank you kindly, boy." He stood still a moment, blinking his little eyes, hiding his nose with his big hand. He seemed to be trying to decide whether to say something more or just leave.

Finally he said, "You know, you gotta understand the ol' lady...kinda sick, if you know what I mean." He tapped his temple significantly. "Two years back had all her insides took out, all her female parts, you know, cost pretty near thousand dollars, still payin' on it...and top a that, why she's jes 'bout blind, you know, cain't see clear like you and me can...gotta understand."

I flushed with shame. My annoyance dissolved into warmth. "Oh, I'm sorry...I'm really stupid, I didn't realize...." I put my arm around his great solid shoulder. "Two dollars isn't enough; here, let me give you five."

"No, no, no, that's aplenty, boy, and 'scuse me folks."

I walked him halfway back through the orchard.

"Feels kinda like frost, don't it?" he said. "Sure hope it don't freeze."

"Pretty late in the season for that, isn't it?"

"No, damnedest thing, out here in New Mexico I seen it freeze late as last a May, wipe the fruit crop plumb out overnight."

"Is that right? Well, I wouldn't worry. I don't think it'll freeze tonight."

I was wrong; it did freeze. Thin white patches of frost lay on the ground when I went to rake the seedbed the next morning. But by noon it was hot. I was sweating, my back hurt, and five blisters had risen on each hand. "Hey boy, come take a look here," I heard Sprouse call as I walked up for lunch. He was over by one of the peach trees—there were a half dozen of them scattered through the orchard, some already almost in flower, the garish pink of dime-store bloomers. I went over to him.

"We was lucky," he said. He plucked one of the blossoms and crushed open the bulbous ovary. "See this part here; that's what turns into the fruit later on. See how it's a kinda greeny-yella color inside? Well now, if it a froze jes a mite harder last night, this here inside'd be black as tar, killed, and that'd be good-bye peaches. Might go have a look at that apple tree a yours, though I don't reckon it's hurt none."

The apple tree was all right, and that was the last cold night we had that spring.

During the next few weeks the place changed as astoundingly as a twelve-year-old girl. A flesh of new life covered all the skeletons, softened all the forms. Thousands of bright green geysers spurted up in Sprouse's cornfield. Vines of wild morning-glory scaled the outhouse and unwrapped their trumpet-shaped flowers fresh each morning, so vibrant a purple they could almost be heard. My apple tree was pink and then bride-white and for a week it sang with bees. And when its petals fell, hundreds of tiny green swellings remained. For the first time I realized I would actually have apples.

I saw very little of the Sprouses during the next few months. The orchard became a forest between us, and having to cultivate and irrigate their fields with no more than hand tools kept them busy morning and night. The old man came over once to look at the Toggenburg milk goat I had bought for my stomach. And though he gaffawed at first, when he saw the quantity and quality of the milk the little creature produced, he sobered into admiration and spoke of "gettin' me one of them." (He never did, however, nor did he ask me again to make him one of my automatic egg drawers.) And sometimes I met him at the ditch-gate or caught a glimpse of his wife in her wide witch's bonnet, crooked over her cabbages. I went over there very occasionally, to borrow a pick or pay my rent. Twice a man came to spray the trees, and after computing my small share of the cost, I paid it immediately. I gardened and thought and read Gandhi and felt my body growing lean and brown and my mind and my stomach healing. For the first time in my memory, time moved along at its aboriginal pace, silently and inexorably....

And then, in the middle of July, Dan arrived.

Were those shots? Was somebody shooting down in the lower field? Halfway down my cheek I stopped the razor and waited. Another shot. I heard my goat bawl out hysterically, her voice rising to an almost human scream. I rushed out of the house, soapy-faced, not knowing what to expect. Then I saw a man. He was standing on the embankment of the ditch that ran between the upper and lower fields and was firing a rifle into the pile where we threw cans and glass and other unburnable garbage, which wasn't far from the spot where I had built my goat-house. I could hear the animal pawing at the boards in panic.

"Hey there!" I shouted at him. "What're you doing?"

The man turned from the waist. He was young, younger than I, and naked except for his Levis. On his chest was a large tattoo, a nude red girl, it seemed, astride a flying blue eagle. He was well-muscled, Y-shaped. He squinted at me as I crossed over to him.

"What're you doing?" I said again.

"What's it look like?" His voice was high-pitched and his inflection provoking. He smelled very densely of a kind of "masculine cologne." *Seaspume*, the brand name is. I used it once myself.

"Does Mr. Sprouse know you're out here shooting?"

"Reckon he does...he's m'old man."

Old man?...Yes, now that I thought of it, Sprouse did say something once about having a son in the army. I remembered his name: Dan.

"Oh, you must be Dan," I said. Instinctively I disliked him, but I was determined to be civil and friendly. "I'm the fellow who's renting your father's place. My name is...." I stopped talking, because Dan had turned and was sighting at an empty bleach bottle that glittered around twenty-five yards away. My eyes fixed on the bottle. There was a sharp report and the bottle ceased to exist. Dan smiled, I shuddered, and from its pen the goat shrieked like a child.

"Listen, pal," I said, "don't you think you can find someplace else to shoot? You're scaring the life out of my goat."

"I ain't shooting at your damn goat." He didn't bother to look around but worked the bolt and took aim again. He had a small tattoo on his right wrist, the blue word MOTHER, surrounded by a sunburst of radiant red lines. Though his features didn't resemble either of his parents', in his whine and in the cast of his personality, I recognized Mrs. Sprouse's off-spring.

"OK," I said, thinking what an enormous amount of menace could be crammed into this expression. I brought the goat up to the upper field and kept her tethered to the pump until Dan had had his fill of shooting.

Fortunately, a few days later Dan found a better amusement. He acquired a red Chrysler convertible, which he used to tear in and out of his father's farm at all hours of the day and night, tires screeching and engine howling like a fire truck.

On the first of August I walked over to Sprouse's with my rent check, which I always paid exactly on time. It was a Sunday morning. There was a certain untraceable stillness about Sundays, as if some faintly vibrating motor had been shut off. In town the Catholic bell had just finished tolling nine o'clock mass. In fifteen minutes or so, the loud-speaker atop the Assembly of Calvary Mission would begin its Sunday broadcast—a record of militant hymns, which was becoming more scratched and fuzzy each week, though no less loud. Right now there was a valley of silence. Then I heard the banging of a hammer from Sprouse's and when I arrived I found him fixing the front gate, which hung off its hinges. "Mornin' boy," he said. "Want to hold this board here up a minute whilst I drive this nail? Dan come in late last night, tore the gate plumb off. I'm fixin' it up temporarily"—his little eyes twinkled—"temporarily fer good, that is."

After the nail was driven and the gate swung freely, Sprouse lowered his head and shook it gravely. "That Dan," he sighed. "Cost me too much money. You know how much the payments is on that car? Eighty-three dollars and sixty-seven cents ever' month."

"How can you afford it?"

"Afford it? I *don't* afford it. It's the ol' lady...only boy she got left, you know. Lost Calvin Junior in the war. Got blowed up in a airplane. Weren't nothin' left to even bury decent." Sprouse snuffled loudly through his great nose. "Now there was a fine boy, Calvin Junior, always talkin' bout how he was comin' home and farm; he's the one built that house you's stayin' in. Dan now, that's somethin' entirely different, lazier'n a twenty-year ol' dog...won't have nothin' to do with farmin'...been in the Army six years, you know, says he's goin' out and find him a job. But ain't gonna look fer no job, he don't look fer nothin' but havin' hisself a good time. And the old lady, she jes spoils him like a baby."

"Calvin!"

Speak of the devil. Hurtling from the house, as if blown out by a gust of wind, came the old woman. All dressed up in a black flowered dress, a black straw hat, a black patent-leather pocketbook.

"Don't be spendin' all mornin' gossipin', Calvin, and don't fergit you've a load of kindlin' to split afore dinner."

We watched her go off down the road, her body inclined forward as if riding a broom.

"Never misses a Sunday," Sprouse said, extracting his bandana and wiping his neck.

"How about you? Don't you ever go to church?" I asked.

"Who, me go to church? No, boy, not me. I don't have to pay no preacher to preach to me 'bout the Lord on Sunday mornin'. The Lord, He comes right here to my place, Sundays, weekdays, any ol' time He feels like." Sprouse bent down as if to disclose a secret. "You know where the Lord is, boy? Right inside here, that's where." He patted himself gently on his great mounded abdomen, as if to imply it was so large in order to provide the Lord with ample living quarters. "Sometimes like, when I'm havin' a fight with the old lady, right smack in the middle of it the Lord says to me, 'Listen here to me, Calvin, you be nice to her now, she's a ol' woman, and she's full a sufferin'. And if you keep on a-yellin' at her, ain't gonna do nobody no good, you jes gonna make her madder'n ever; so why don't you do somethin' real nice fer her, and you'll see, she gonna feel bad 'bout actin' so mean. Remember you ain't no chicken, neither, Calvin, pretty soon you gonna be curlin' up your toes, and you don't want to have to be totin' a sack a sins when you come a-knockin' on them pearly gates.'"

I stared at the man. *He was. I had to struggle to be*. How much of me was crammed inside my skull, how weak, how meager I was beside him, who *was*, in his back and in his heart. Yet I felt a pride in him, almost a father's pride.

"I don't think you need to go to church," I said.

He seemed suddenly ashamed. He lowered his eyes and looked at the ground over the bumpy topography of his nose. "Naw," he said, "the reason is, I cain't understand half what they's talkin 'bout."

"You understand more than they're talking about," I said.

He shook his head and was silent. But after a little while he said, "Say, one thing I been wonderin' 'bout, boy. How you make your money anyhow? You ain't no farmer; you got too much schoolin'."

"I'm starting to work for the County Welfare the first of September."

"Well, that's real nice. Gotta have brains fer somethin' like that. Feller like me, never could get nothin' through my thick haid."

Again silence congealed between us. *He was…I had to struggle to be.*

From a tree behind us a lark pierced the quiet with his fluty song, complex and formal as a theme of Bach. Before we could spot him he flew off, knocking an apple from the branch. We heard it swish through the leaves and strike the ground with a hollow sound, like the first heavy drops of a sun shower.

"Apples are almost ripe," I said, glad for a lighter subject.

"Yep, pretty soon now…them truckers'll be comin' 'round. What you figgerin' on doin' with all them apples a yours, boy?"

"I don't know," I laughed, "eat a lot of them."

Suddenly there was a harsh scratching sound, and the record from the Assembly of Calvary Mission imposed itself on the air. We listened. The woman who sang must have had a chest like an empty water tank. "*CHRI-I-IST THE ROY-Y-ALL MAA-AA-STER, LEE-EADS A-GAAINST THE FO-O-O-OE!*" she boomed through the static and the electronic hum. "*FOR-WAAARD IN-TO BAA-AA-TLE SEEEE HIS BAAAN-NER GO-O-O-O!*" The whole orchard seemed to shudder.

I didn't talk to Sprouse again for four weeks. Four weeks exactly, not until Sunday, the twenty-ninth of August, the day of the trouble.

Six-thirty in the morning, and outside a large motor was grinding up the Sunday stillness. Looking out, I saw an enormous black truck with built-up sides backing into the orchard. Dan stood signaling to the driver who hung out of the door. This was the first time I had seen Dan up this early, much less taking any part in the farm activities. Yet it was Dan who was in charge of the negotiations with the truckers. As he talked to them his mother stood at his side, saying nothing, but observing everything acutely through her thick lenses. Sprouse stayed a little behind, unusually subdued, as if waiting for orders.

"How many Johnnies you got?" The trucker was a man in a dirty white shirt, tall, but sallow and puffy-looking.

"'Bout thirty-five, forty trees," Dan's whine cut through the orchard. His shirt hung open as usual and I could just make out the blue eagle with its naked rider flying across his flesh.

"Give you dollar-fifty for the Jonathans."

"Dollar-fifty? You crazy, man? Them's three-inchers, worth two a bushel easy."

"Two a bushel for Johnnies? Dollar-fifty's what they's paying this year up and down the valley."

"Two's what we're askin'. If you don't want 'em, OK. Somebody else will."

"Give you dollar seventy-five. That's tops."

Dan turned to his mother. Her old head grimaced sourly but it nodded.

"OK, dollar seventy-five, only that's jes like they come...no pickin' 'em over," Dan said.

"Aw right, let's get at 'em, let's get all the Johnnies you got first."

Terms agreed on, work began. Armed with ladders and kitchen chairs, bushel baskets and lard buckets, they moved on the first tree. Just three of them: Sprouse, his wife, and the trucker's assistant. The two negotiators remained at the truck to load and tabulate the bushels and check on each other's lists. I saw the branches shake and heard the fruit ping in the tin buckets and I decided to help.

It took us the whole morning just to pick the Jonathans. It was boring work, yet it had that special exhilaration that almost always accompanies work done in community. Only Dan annoyed me, the way he stood there indolently by the tail gate of the truck, with his shirt gaping, his imbecilic tattoo, his drugstore sweetness. "Forty-seven," he said as I staggered up, sweating and straining under a bushel of his father's fruit. An arsenal of sarcastic remarks rose in my mind, but I fought down the temptation each time, and each time felt a kind of lift from having been able to restain my tongue.

Mrs. Sprouse was working harder than any of the men. She ascended to the tops of the trees, braced her skinny blue-mottled legs, and snatched at the apples like a large praying mantis. She did not pause for a moment, not even when the orchard was flooded with the voice of her church.

Sprouse himself remained strangely quiet. Once or twice I tried to banter with him, but he didn't rise to the bait. He seemed actually to have shrunken. Was it the old woman's presence that affected him like a kind of astringent?

After lunch the bickering began again, this time over the Delicious apples, this time raised a dollar. "Two-fifty a bushel...what you talkin' 'bout, man? Them's Mammoths, three bucks is cheap." "Aw right, I'll do you a favor: two seventy-five." "OK, two seventy-five, but that's jes like they come offa the tree, no cullin 'em fer worms or nothin'." "Aw right, but no rotten ones neither, none up off the ground."

The trucker nailed a wall of boards behind the Jonathans to keep them separated from the higher-priced Delicious, and we began to pick again.

A few minutes after we started a little accident occurred. I was climbing to a higher branch when the bucket in my hand knocked against something and half a dozen apples fell to the ground and bruised. Above me I heard a sharp gasp, as when a gas jet is opened. From high in the branches the face of Mrs. Sprouse glared down at me, lenses glittering, lips drawn back from a strip of teeth, perfectly even and white.

It was then I began to get angry. Nobody had even thanked me for my help, not even Sprouse. And more and more I became aware of the mercenary spirit that pervaded the whole operation. And these apples, what would happen to them? I listened to Dan and the trucker haggling over figures, over whether a bushel contained three apples too few or too many. These apples would be driven a couple of hundred miles to be haggled over again and sold at an enormous profit to somebody who wouldn't eat them but would sell them again at another enormous profit to housewives who bought them at last to eat.

The trucker's assistant passed me, beefy and red and trickling sweat. The old woman above me was picking as efficiently and joylessly as a machine, her glasses fixed fanatically in front of her, her grey dry hair sticking out like straw. Sprouse was working as inconspicuously as possible, his whole personality drained out of him. He didn't talk. Nobody talked. There were just the sounds of picking: the branches creaking, the leaves rustling, the fruit being torn loose and dropped into buckets, the apples rolling onto a bed of the truck. Suddenly I felt that I was taking part in a looting.

I climbed down from the tree, dropped the bucket, and walked home without a word to anybody. I felt the familiar unease, formless dissatisfaction, restlessness that I have learned preludes depression. I took out the New Testament and opened to Matthew.

"*...but I say to you, Love your enemies and pray for those who persecute you, so that you may be sons of your Father who is in heaven; for He makes His sun rise on the evil and on the good, and sends rain on the just and on the* *unjust. For if you love those who love you, what reward have you? Do not even the tax-collectors do the same?"*

I gazed at these words, these words of Christ that had quickened me once when I was emptied and lost. But now they stayed out there, ink on paper, words on a page. They seemed to have been said so long ago, to people so much simpler than we...I closed the book, lay down on the bed, and tried to nap.

At five-thirty I was sitting on the concrete back stoop with a pot of potatoes my wife had given me to peel for supper. To my left I heard the sounds of the pickers as they worked down the last row of the orchard, the one adjacent to my property. I looked at my tree. The sun sat like a great golden apple in the upper branches. The apples themselves hung everywhere, large and red as human hearts, and the lower branches almost bowed to the ground with the weight of them. Five seconds before anything happened I felt a small cold spurt of fear.

A skinny grey figure crossed the clearing and began to tear the apples from my tree.

"Hey! No!" I threw the potatoes aside and ran over to her. "Not that tree, Mrs. Sprouse, that's mine. I don't want to sell my apples." For some reason I really thought she had made a mistake.

Her grey head pivoted around at me with the quick noiseless movement of a reptile. Her lips drew back from her white, perfect, synthetic teeth. "Git outta here, you!" she hissed.

I am sure I would have seized her bodily and thrown her away from the tree had not Sprouse come lumbering up just then and grabbed her arm.

"No, Min, don't pick them apples...they's this gentleman's...I give him this tree when he took the place. Them apples belong to him, Min, leave 'em be."

The grey head whipped around to meet the new threat. "What you babblin' bout, you old fool! Turn me a-loose, d'y'hear!"

"No, Min, cain't pick 'em, they ain't ours, come on, we got a-plenty, come on back now." He dragged her gradually away; there was fear in his voice. Fear of what? Of her? Or of himself? Of snapping her in two with his unleashed arm? "Come on now, Min," he kept saying, "come on back now," while she shrieked at him.

"Turn me a-loose I say, turn me *a-loose*! They's *mine*! I'm the one planted that tree, think I'm gonna let him steal my apples, when I...."

"But I tell you I promised him that tree, Min, I...."

"You *fool*, Calvin, you damn old *fool*! You'd give away my whole orchard fer twenty-five dollars a month, you...."

But her rage was now too large for words, and it became a writhing, squalling struggle to escape that at last died down in squeaking, shoulder-twitching whimpers. Sprouse released her slowly. He lifted her scrawny claw and patted it between his big hands. "Come on now, Min, only three more trees to pick and we's through."

I don't know what I felt, standing there watching this—revulsion, indignation, embarrassment. Yet it all was washed with a genuine pity for this pathetic creature. "Oh let her have them," I felt like saying. I felt like saying, but I said nothing.

After supper, to calm down, I took a walk in the lower field.

The sunset was incredibly lovely that evening. All in a clear, frigid blue and a burning orange. High, high, seven miles above my head, coils of cirrus cloud glowed like hot wires beneath the ultramarine. A lone black bat reeled like a drunk over the flaming corn; a cricket chirped near my feet; a cicada buzzed once from a grove of cottonwoods; a pair of katydids clicked to each other across the cornfield, and when I leaped the ditch a frog gulped up at me. Coming home through the orchard I saw the intricate patterns of orange light dancing like fire in the high grass.

And I saw them picking my apples.

Two of them, the old woman and Dan, and picking fast. Behind them a stack of bushel baskets, a few already full of fruit. Sprouse was nowhere in sight. I stopped, my heart accelerated to wristwatch speed; a small pain began probing my stomach. I did not know what to say or what to do.

I did nothing. I strode past them without speaking, without looking, and when I went in the house I heard the screen door bang shut behind me.

My wife was in the kitchen.

"How long they been out there?"

"About fifteen minutes. But don't get into a fight with them, honey."

"I won't, I won't. But it's so damn *ugly*."

"It's horrible. But the best thing is to just ignore them; if you argue with them, it'll just make it worse."

"What happened to the old man?"

"I don't know; I think I saw him going to the bar."

"Those filthy...."

I knew I should stay in the house and I tried to, but it was impossible. I went out and sat down on the back stoop and watched them as they ravished my tree, like a pair of devils in the fading orange light. I felt exquisitely alive. The muscles in my shoulders were taut and my lips were quivering and my nails were drumming on the cement. My thoughts were clear too, and I closed my eyes to see them better.

The thing was to fight them, defeat them, make them ashamed—but not by violence, violence would only give them justification. This was a challenge. But what to do? What would Gandhi do with these two? "Hate the crime, but love the criminal," he said. Fight with truth. But how? Right here and now?

I opened my eyes and they were still there. I hated their guts. In abstract maybe I could love them; it was much easier in abstract. That was it. I had to keep from looking at them, keep them abstractions. I shouldn't try to prevent them by force from taking the apples, and yet I certainly couldn't let them get the idea I was afraid of them. Non-resistance from a coward—some farce! I didn't know what I was going to do, but the thoughts, the alliance, made me calmer and more confident.

"You may have my apples if they mean so much to you, Mrs. Sprouse." My voice sounded fine, steady, detached.

No answer. No reaction at all. They went on ripping the lovely red fruit from my tree.

"The apples on that tree belong to me, Mrs. Sprouse. I didn't ask for them. Your husband gave them to me. I paid to have them sprayed. If you really need them so badly you may have them. But please don't forget they're not yours and you are stealing them." My voice wasn't quite so steady, and on the last few words I heard it quaver.

It was Dan who answered. "Listen here, man," he whined, "we don't see it like that. You think you gonna git a house and a well and seventy bucks' worth apples fer what you pay rent, you crazy."

"I told you, I didn't ask for the apples, Dan, your father prom...."

"That don't have nothin' to do with it. This here's Ma's tree, see; she planted it and raised it herself. So why don't you jes go on inside and don't bother your head no more over these apples."

I didn't reply. I closed my eyes again, trying to quiet the mobilization that was going on inside me. Talking with these two was a waste of time. I had to act. Suddenly I sprang up, ran over to the tree, grabbed an empty basket and began to pick.

"Here, it's getting dark, let me help you." I didn't want the sarcasm but it was there.

Mother and child squinted at me suspiciously for a moment and that was all. I picked apples fiercely. I filled up the basket and another and then a third. But obviously my gesture wasn't having the slightest effect.

On them, that is—it was on me. I was getting hot. I felt indignation piling up in me like tinder on a pyre: *The poor ignorant...no, they're sly. The shameless trash, the sneaks, waiting till the old man was out of the way, the ugly...how can people act like this? How can they pollute themselves for a few lousy apples?...pollute themselves, pollute nature, pollute the whole human race! They're the kind that kill and lie and start wars, they're the kind that make the whole earth stink!*

I kept my eyes off them, but every time I breathed they came in through my nostrils, the dry, sour stench that was the old woman, the sickly synthetic sweet that was Dan. By now Christ and Gandhi were no longer around. Now I remembered Jehovah scourging them out of Eden, Moses smashing the tablets of God at the sight of them, Isaiah roaring doom on them in the first person Almighty. I stopped struggling with my anger.

I slammed the basket down, knocking out half the apples.

"God...."

I don't know what I meant to say—"God knows" or "God is watching this" or something like that. But I heard the old woman's hiss just then, loud and venomous, and at the same instant I saw Dan's sneer, his obscene, lip-lifted sneer.

"God *damn* both of you!" My fist hit Dan's face with a force I didn't know I possessed. He fell back, struck his head on the trunk of the tree and sat there sprawled on the ground, blinking at me, his mouth round. I stood over him, legs apart, arms fist-knobbed and shaking.

"Get up!" I yelled at him. "Get up!" I wanted him to get up. I wanted to hit him again. I wanted to split his head in two like an apple.

His finger was feeling his mouth for blood. MOTHER, his wrist said.

"And you keep out of this," I growled, turning on the old woman. I shook my fist in front of her glasses, feeling that one blow would reduce her to powder, as if she were made of paper ash.

Dan did not get up. His mother did not interfere. We remained there, a fixed and silent triangle, for I don't know how long. Then suddenly I lost interest in everything, in doing them injury, in apples, in justice, everything. I moved away from the tree slowly, careful not to turn my back on them, becoming aware of a slicing pain in my stomach.

I RAPPED ON THE KITCHEN DOOR SEVERAL TIMES. The house was dark. Dan had gone off in his Chrysler and his parents were in bed. Then I saw Sprouse stumbling toward the door, rubbing his eyes, tugging his pants up over his long underwear.

"Sorry to wake you up, but I just wanted to tell you I've decided to move just as soon as I can find another place." He heard my announcement in silence, his head bowed like a prisoner's head when he is hearing sentence. "Well, good night, boy," was all he said.

But the next morning he came to beg us to stay. "It's all my fault, boy." He spread his arms wide as if to offer himself. "I didn't explain to the ol' lady clear enough that I give you that tree…she didn't understand right…blame me, it's all my fault." He took some dirty bills from his back pocket and held them out. "Here, boy, let my pay you fer them apples, or you can take it off the rent if you want."

"And what about Dan?"

"Dan ain't gonna be here only till the end of the week. The feller's comin' today to take back the car and Dan's goin' back in the Army. Nobody gonna bother you no more, boy, you ain't gonna have no more trouble."

He was very large and very humble and his nose seemed purple with shame.

"It's not the apples that make me sore, Mr. Sprouse, it's the principle of the thing, the unfairness. When I see people acting like that, like animals, it makes me sick." I put my hand on my stomach. "You understand?"

"Sure, boy, sure, you perfectly right. But I promise you, you ain't gonna have no more trouble."

I smiled and shook my head. "No, I'm afraid a promise isn't enough, Mr. Sprouse. You promised me the last time, you remember. I don't mind staying. But if I do there'll have to be more than a promise. I mean it's going to have to be in writing, a legal agreement."

He looked at me strangely, his eyes suddenly cloudy, as if he'd never met me before. Then he said, "All right. Fair enough. You go ahead and fix up the papers and the ol' lady and me'll sign 'em."

I drew up two copies of a contract which showed a plan of the place with the location of the large apple tree outlined in red. On the bottom

I typed a statement to the effect that the fruit from this tree was to belong to me for as long as I paid rent on the house. The following afternoon we all drove down to the notary's office. I don't know how the old man argued his wife around to it, but she came and at the proper moment scrawled her signature.

The notary, who was also the lawyer, was a sharp-faced little man with a dingy, tan, double-breasted suit and shiny tan teeth. "You folks understand, now," he said as he crushed down on the papers with his little chromium-plated machine, "this is a lawful contract binding on both parties, and in case of violation you are liable to legal prosecution and that'll be four dollars please."

Sprouse dug out his billfold. "I'll pay, Mr...."

"No, no, let's do it right. We'll each pay half."

The lawyer-notary smiled after us. "And don't forget if any question arises, you folks be sure and come back now. I've handled a good many cases just like this one here."

All during the drive back Sprouse's little eyes blinked and he fingered the embossed notary's seal on the paper in his hand like a blind man reading Braille. But I am sure he could feel nothing through his thick-callused thumb.

Since that time I've noticed a change in my relationship with the old man. We talk as before; we are friendly; actually he seems to respect me more than he did. But the old easy familiarity is gone, as if a nerve had been cut. It's hard to put my finger on the difference. Maybe it's just that he has never again called me boy.

At any rate there was no more friction with the Sprouses all last winter. Nor will there be this summer either. We had an early spring this year, a succession of warm bud-enticing days. And then, last night, the sixth of May, the weather snapped viciously cold, like a baited trap. About nine o'clock I went out to examine the tree. It looked all right but it was too early to tell. At noon I went out again. I opened several dozen blossoms. The ovary of every one was black inside, ash black, as if each had been gutted by a tiny fire.

It was then that I became aware of the stillness in the orchard.

HOW HE WOULD HAVE DONE IT

Jim Thorpe

L.C. had always been a big man even among big men, but he had suddenly gotten bigger in such a way that his wife just had to worry. His neck swelled up over the collar of his shirt and it got so that it seemed he could hardly breathe when lying down in the bed at night. He wouldn't ever go to doctors on his own but she nagged him until he did and they said it might be his thyroid or maybe a tumor somewhere down besides it. They wanted him for tests.

If it hadn't been for this it wouldn't have been a bad year at all for them. Neither had been the least bit sick or beset with any kind of ailment, and the weather had stayed good until they had shipped all their cattle, all but for the six they had missed in gathering the month before. He would have trailed them out by now if it hadn't of been for this sickness. L.C. figured them as being the old cow with the twisted horn, dry again for her second year, the red bull, and the two white-faced cows they bought last spring, probably still with calves on them.

She knew enough to expect him to say how it wasn't right or wise to be asking those heifers to try and feed themselves and an overgrown calf and a little one inside too that was hardly half-made—that was of course having confidence that the red bull had done his summer's work. She knew enough too to know that there was no sense in keeping an old infertile heifer just to help wear out the grass.

Those kind of things she had learned about from L.C., from being married to this man who had tried to make their living from the husbandry of animals on lands that seemed poorly suited to it. They were all things that he had said, that she had had to listen to, but they had never been things that she had much of the doing with herself. She hadn't been born or raised to it but just had—at times and in piecemeal fashion—acquired it, not exactly half-heartedly but certainly without enthusiasm, knowing even as she "helped" him that it wasn't her proper domain or didn't even involve her rightful concerns in their division of life and its labors and that therefore she need not be terribly accomplished or proficient. Being tolerable, just being a body put in the right place that didn't do anything wrong, was good enough.

So even though she knew the long runs of fencing and the rough shapes of pastures, the approximate locations of gates, tanks and corrals, the startings of trails down through the rocks and the likely spots to find gaps in the wire, she had never had to contemplate these features and considerations all on her own, negotiate and navigate them and, in association with the habits and predilections of half-wild animals, produce and deliver a livelihood. There had always been L.C. to tell her and point her and send her, giving her the little cattle-bunches he had pulled out of inaccessible places for her to take care of and not lose, or take along a trail a little ways until he could get back and tell her what to do next.

But now it would have to be different. He was in no shape at all to go anywhere except to that hospital and they weren't going there until they had brought in the old cow and the two calves probably still on those heifers and got them to the sale. That meant that she was going to have to go out and do it on her own; there was no way around it.

SHE DIDN'T EVEN TELL HIM. She knew how he wouldn't let her go out and do it by herself without him, how his pride and all that he was couldn't ever let it happen, and yet he could hardly get off the couch where he had set himself because, at least, it wasn't a bed. He tried to breathe as easy as he could and not think of himself as lying in bed all day like the doctor told him.

She said that she was going to run on into Albuquerque and see what all was involved—just in case it didn't get better on its own, and even drove the car away from the house so that he'd think her gone, and when she went to saddle she made sure she was out of sight of the kitchen window even though she knew he most likely didn't have the strength to stand up and look.

It had been so long since she had caught and saddled a horse all by herself that she had to laugh because she thought how she had just about forgot how. She went for her "Buster," even as soft and slow as he probably would be from inactivity and lack of use because L.C.'s sorrel horse was of the kind that showed too much white around its eyes. She got the bridle reins over the neck to hold him easily enough and when he put his head low she put the bit in between his yellowed sets of teeth.

After she got him tied and brushed she found the pads and saddle so heavy and that place on his knobby back where they had to go so far up that she had to stop and catch her breath before going to cinch him. She didn't pull it tight enough because, once she had opened and closed the gate and led him up to the big log that L.C. had once set there for her, and had pulled herself about halfway up, the saddle went sideways on her, leaving her half-on and half-off, and she had to laugh, thinking of what L.C. would be saying, and she knowing how she could laugh because it was Buster—had it of been one of *his* horses, they probably would have been around the corral in the first of several wild circles, maybe even with her foot hung in the air and her head dragging the ground.

She got it right and got back on and then had to let Buster know how much she appreciated his gentleness by kicking and badgering him until he thought it OK to walk away and then OK to get out of sight. L.C.'s sorrel horse squealed after Buster and she had to wonder if L.C. was going to hear it, if he wasn't going to stumble up to look. She kept the sad shape of the barn between her and the house until she got to where the little hills would hide her.

SHE WENT FOR A LONG TIME without seeing anything, but that was to be expected. It was seldom, if ever, easy, simple or direct. It usually meant riding an hour or two before seeing anything at all, and then riding three or four before seeing enough to do something with. L.C., of course, always knew what to do. He would know where to look—he would even know where they were. He would feel the wind and the weather and look at the grass and the cloven tracks trailing through the dust and notice the clarity or cloudedness of water in the tanks and he would pronounce, with almost absolute certainty, where they would be and what the two of them would have to do to get at them.

Then they would ride, sometimes together but more often separate, she taking the trail and he scrambling up over a bunch of rocks so that he might come upon them at just the right spot, and she always asking him before he took off, "Well, L.C., how will I find them? I can hardly tell them apart from the bushes." And he, saying just before he disappeared, in his habitual high trot, "They'll be them that moves!"

Well, there was movement but it wasn't cows. There was enough of a wind sometimes to unsettle the landscape, bend and bow things before her in little mad rushes. There were flushings of rabbits, big jacks and cotton-tailed bunnies, surprised and startled, quivering in their hiding or dashing by in such panic that she would have been on a spooked horse if she hadn't been on Buster; and there were birds, little drab ones that just couldn't set still or dark solitary hunters, high and aloof.

On the ground were bits of bunchgrass, short and yellowed in infrequent clumps, snakeweed, rocks and rabbitbrush. It had the look of winter coming on to the hard and dry country that it was, tired and bare and just about wore out—she wondered how it was that L.C. had ever made it work, why it was that he had taken this place and not some other that might have had tall green meadows and wide muddy waters. It was maybe because he was such a hard man that he could only really be at home in such hard country.

She tried to take careful note of the grass, how much of it there still was and what kind of condition it was in, and the other plants and bushes too, things like cholla that could be eaten if they had to be and things like loco that had best not be eaten at all, because he would want to know; he would ask her and she would want to have something that she could tell him. She would have to *notice* like he did, and while she was looking for their few missing cattle she was also looking at all those minor signs and details that would together have their own cumulative significance.

She knew she wasn't far from one of the tanks when she saw that there was something on the ground on the other side of some bunched cedars. It had the unmistakable red-brown color and matted hairlines of a cow and she knew she had found one, bedded down, except that when she came up behind it, it didn't see her, it didn't get up and face her or get set to run off like a regular range cow would; it didn't get up at all and in a moment she saw why. There was a big hole eaten out of its back end, a large cavity that had once included the uterus and parts of the bowel, excavated about as far as a coyote or dog could reach in its head and lick the bony protrusions clean. The eyes too, the watchful, worrying, ambered eyes of a cow were just dry purple holes on a face stiffly turned toward the sky.

She didn't have any trouble in knowing which cow it was because of the S-curve made by its horns, one sweeping up above the head like it ought to and the other diving down and inwards until it looked like it was ready to start growing back into the head. She was happy to know that at least it wasn't one of their good producing mother cows but right away felt worried because she knew how he was going to ask of her not only what happened but how and why.

She looked over the scattering of dog-like tracks on the ground but there weren't any body marks that showed that coyotes or dogs had killed her. The birds had come after the coyotes and it had been too cold for snakes even if this cow was one that couldn't stand the swelling of a snake bite; there wasn't really anything poisonous in this pasture this time of year and there hadn't been any lions seen here in thirty. So besides having to tell L.C. when she got back that they had lost one that they should have got rid of already and now couldn't get any salvage out of at all, she was also going to have to tell him that she had no idea at all of the how or why of it.

That last part was probably going to be worse than the first part; he could probably stand knowing that they had lost one that wasn't worth much to them anyway but what he might not be able to stand would be the not knowing, the not knowing the unnamed thing out there that had compromised their existence by the value of one old infertile heifer, and, beyond that, the Great Indifference that caused things to happen to people without any thought to the lives and livelihoods that were being affected.

She knew that he would want to saddle up right away and go see for himself and that it would be all she could do to keep him from getting by her and through the door. And if he did somehow manage to get by her and through the door and down to the barn, and somehow again catch his horse and drag out his big heavy saddle, and then again throw that up and then his great enlarged body as well, that would probably be the last thing he'd ever do.

But she knew that was not likely to happen. She knew that he wasn't ever likely to get that far, past her maybe, maybe down to the barn and as far as his horse, but he was never going to lift his saddle, let alone his self. And that made her think that maybe it didn't matter anyhow, her worrying about it, that he wasn't ever going to run cattle again anyway, that they had maybe stayed here in this country longer than they should have. She decided that she'd allow herself to go no farther than the second dirt tank, thinking that if she were going to tell him anything at all she could tell him how she had covered the country that far without any sight or sign of cattle but she did notice the length of the grass and the condition of the fence. That would be enough because he wouldn't really expect too much else out of her.

Or she might instead tell him about going to Albuquerque, and if he really wanted to know about it, she could tell him what a big mix-up it was, how the doctors didn't have time to see her until she had to go and how, really, it had just been a trip wasted. But that would have meant lying to him, and she didn't like to lie.

When she dropped down on the trail to where the tank was at the head of the little canyon, she was just thinking of letting Buster take a little water and then giving him his head down the canyon trail. But then she saw how lucky she was. Down at the tank, taking water, were the two heifers and beside them—My goodness, she thought, they *are* fat and soggy—were their two big glossy calves. And it was just about right too, since they were between her and home and the only way for them to go if they got startled was down the canyon, right where she would want to take them. She chuckled. She was getting set up by luck for what L.C. usually needed all his smarts for!

They started easily enough, watching her at first from their distance and then only momentarily thinking of standing their ground as she and Buster tiptoed up toward them. They turned down the trail like they recognized it and didn't seem to mind being followed close behind like they were happy to be driven. She could only think of what L.C. was going to think of her—as long as she held on to them.

She didn't have any trouble at all until she got half-way down, right where the little spring came out of the ground amid a thick muddy stand of tamarisk. The cows stopped like they sensed something and Buster stopped too, ears pricked forward and nostrils in full dilation.

She didn't know what it was except that it was there—animals didn't lie. She had to be watchful that the cows wouldn't suddenly decide to turn on her and she wasn't sure if either she or her horse, singularly or together, would be able to hold them. It took her a minute before she finally saw what it was; L.C. would have known it right away, probably without even having to see it, but she, she was always the last to know.

It was their red bull, hid there in the bushes. Not even being able to see him clearly she remembered she had forgot how big he was: big, not just when compared to the others, but just in and of himself huge—big, powerful and just a mite dangerous. She remembered him from the time he got in a fight with one of their other bulls, how the two of them whirled about in such a violent fury and how she and Buster had been caught up in that frantic whirlwind and got pinned against the corral fence. Buster remembered it too, because he had ever since been skittish of a bull. It had been L.C. that had come in, barreling in between the two Goliaths on that big buckskin he had then and making to break up that fight like a teacher among rough and tumble schoolboys. It was the kind of reckless thing he'd do if he had to. And if he hadn't, she and Buster both might have been dragged under.

She was hoping that she could just leave Old Red there, there in the thickness of the bushes, because there wasn't really any need to bring him down now and turn him in to the house pastures; God only knew what mischief he might play with the fence down there anyway. If only she could get the cows and calves to ignore him and go on by; then she could tell L.C. when she got back how she had seen their bull.

The cows had lowered their heads into the bits of colorless grass that fringed around the spring area. One calf, standing set—playful and ready—was eyeing the bull while the other was watching the paired horse and human. Buster had relaxed just a bit because he had set himself to stand; it took a good kick to get him to move.

"Come on, girls!" she said, "Let's down below!" She pointed Buster toward the calf that was watching her; after a short stand it ran off towards its mother. The other trotted after and the cows started, taking steps with their heads still down in the grass, their legs scratching the dead brush.

She thought the best way to get by Old Red was to pretend that he just wasn't there. That way the bull would think he was hiding and Buster would think that she hadn't noticed, which would be fine, because Buster would just as soon not have anything to do with bulls.

It just about worked too. The cows and calves were by and seemed to be thinking once again to follow along the trail in slow but steady purpose. She and Buster had all but left him too, when all of a sudden he let out a bellow that was in the next instant followed by a crash as he hurled himself through his concealment, breaking branch and trampling brush, cracking and popping through in such a rush as to startle the cows and run Buster this time nearly into a tree.

By the time she recovered, pulling Buster in on the rein and pulling herself back up from where she had come behind the saddle, all she could see in front of her was the big muscled hind-end lumbering down away from her. Even though the rushing of blood throughout her body, and the need to get Buster to stand and wait half-way still, made such demands upon her senses, she already saw that something was wrong with that big brutish animal. It was in the way he walked, a dipping of his head and shoulder in the awkward progress of his monster's gait. He had gone and got lame.

Despite his defect, or perhaps because of it, there was a dreadful urgency in his walking. He put his head up in the air when he could, having to stop to do it. Resting at the same time, sniffing the air around his wet and runny nostrils, he whistled and blowed and bellowed after the cows that had run off away from him. He'd do that and then take a dozen or so steps and do it again, not quitting until he had finally gone far enough to see where they had stopped, heads lowered among the bits of grass, and then still not content until he had struggled up closer to where they were, and then still never content because they had already moved on.

THAT WAS THE WAY TO DO IT: if you had to bring a bull in it would most likely be easiest to bring it in with a small bunch of gentle heifers. That's how L.C. would have done it; he wouldn't have left a crippled bull in the pasture if he had the cows handy to bring him in with. So that's what she did. She didn't want to at first but after a while it was going fairly easy, and she was beginning to feel right proud of herself. Even if it wasn't such a great thing to have lost a cow and find that you've got a crippled bull, it was best to know about it so it wouldn't be around to surprise or disappoint you later.

She knew how L.C. wouldn't be inclined to get a vet out on the bull, that he'd either give it the winter to see if maybe he'd heal up or just go ahead and get rid of him altogether. In any case he'd want to see him and if she got him into the corral and got the gate shut good on him, L.C. probably could manage to get out to look at him. She was already thinking about it, thinking about what good it might do for him and how she could probably get him to agree to just a little stop at the hospital if they were going up that way anyway with the cattle.

She had them going along the fence now, just like L.C. would have, letting them go easy so that the bull wouldn't be inadvertently pushed through the fence; though as sore and hobbly and upset as he was, he probably had nothing on his mind but keeping up. The house and barn were easily in her sight though a little hard to see because the sun had got so low that she was nearly looking into it. It spread out in long straight shafts all over the landscape they had looked at and lived in every day for longer than she cared to remember, touching upon the mesa tops and throwing long shadows down the cliffs, making the interspersed plains look lush and verdant in a way they never ever had been or never ever could be, making the clumped cedars and piñon look like bunches of stock. The sun caught the side of the house roof direct for a second and glared distinctly at her like a large signal mirror.

There wasn't that much farther to go. She knew that all she would have to do now was get them through the gate and then she remembered it—*the gate*—dear God, she never thought to leave open the gate! What had she been thinking about when she left—or had she been thinking? Where was she supposed to put the cattle she had set out to gather when she had left—or had she never even supposed, or had the confidence to think, that she would have ever gathered them all by herself in the first place? And now that she had been out all day and come across them and brought them this far, how was she ever going to finish it if she had left the gate shut?

She could try riding out around them and then ahead to open it but what if they decided to turn back on her? Cattle had done that before, especially when going for a bunch of pens that to them usually meant a place where something unpleasant happened, a squeezing, spraying or dousing, being shoved about in close confinement. Their first memories of a place like this were of being roped and drug across the ground to a branding fire—they weren't just going to walk in. And this wasn't just because they may not be naturally disposed to go in, or because there wasn't any hay or feed or gentle cows in there already to bait them; it was because there could be no question of them going in at all if she didn't somehow get that gate open.

She knew what L.C. would say, how she got them all that ways and then lost them at the gate, but she wasn't seeing any way around it. She started out away from them once already, circling around so that she might sneak ahead and lope up to the corral, get off, open the gate, get on, lope on back and sneak around them and keep them going. But she only got as far as halfway around them before she saw how they had stopped, this time not with their heads lowered but with them turned, looking up toward the country they had just come from like they maybe had forgot something. By the time she got back behind them, one of the heifers had actually turned and started, with the bull behind her.

She didn't know what she was going to do except maybe take them as close as she could and figure something out, knowing that she was going to have to stay in the saddle and keep Buster going until she did. She wasn't going to give up on them now because she knew that L.C. wouldn't have.

And then finally, when she was real close, she had to look at it twice. The gate was open. All this time she had thought how she had closed it and now there it was—open. But there wasn't time to argue with herself because the bull, that dang bull she and Buster had fretted so much over, was bringing them all in, going in first like he just couldn't wait to stick his nose in the water trough and the others happy to follow because he had gone in first.

There still wasn't time for her to think about how she might be losing her mind or her memory or whatever because she had the gate to close and tie and poor tired Buster to put up. The sun had gone below the mesa and her hands were so cold that they hardly worked.

SHE COULD HARDLY help herself when she got into the house. "L.C.," she said, almost shouting so that he would be sure to hear her. "L.C.—you'll never guess what I did today." She wasn't going to tell him just now about the dead cow, or that their bull had got himself crippled. That could come later.

She found him where she had left him, on the couch, but instead of his pajamas he had on his clothes, his boots and belt and everything, and he had put his hat careful, crown down like he always did, on the floor. It was like he was asleep but his mouth was wide open.

"L.C.?" she said, not knowing if he was ever going to know now, not wanting to ask him again or step any closer because she didn't want to have to know any more right then.

HANG GLIDERS AND ONIONS

Ed Chavez

HE came running down the slope, the big fat guy, so fast he was bound to trip but he didn't, right to the edge of the cliff and jumped off. I put my sandwich down. Even though I was sure the fat guy knew what he was doing, my stomach moved because there was always the chance he wouldn't make it. But he did. He popped back up and sailed over us, his teeth showing through a tight grin, and the crowd of us went "Aaaaaaahhh!" That was the first time I ever saw a hang glider take off.

This was an unexpected bonus for rising seven hours earlier. There I was, snoozing, when Budgie came at O-dark-thirty in the morning and shook me awake. "The alarm went off, Daddy. We going?"

Now, a promise is a promise, I know, but it didn't make sense. Not then. "Mmmm...Good morning, Glory." The sleep was so sweet and I wanted to beg for five minutes more.

But enough of this laziness! Up! I dreamed I was already at the sink brushing my teeth when Budgie touched me again. "Dad?"

I rolled over and sat at the edge of my bed and rubbed the gumminess from my lips and my eyes. "Turn on the radio, Rooster."

"Some rock, Dad? News? Talk show?"

"No, Tenderfoot, make it middle of the road." I frowned longingly at my pillow. It had to be middle of the road or nothing at all. Any other noise would clang like a tin can in my head.

"Right, Dad," Budgie said and crooned, "K-JOY! K-K-J-Y!"

I flicked the lamp on and my wife immediately turned away from the light, mumbling an unmistakable protest. "A Summer Place" urged me on and I was soon enough gazing at my most unappealing morning self in the mirror. I skipped the shave, not because it was so early but because it was Saturday.

Blubbering through the cold water I thought of Steinbeck's description of how men the world over rise each morning yawning and hawking and letting gas and scratching and knew that in this man's case he is so right. I brushed my hair, what's left of it, on both sides.

A friend of mine is all the time urging me to buy a wig because he says it will make me feel better. "So, who feels bad?" I ask. "What you see is what you get."

But he doesn't stop. He likes to give me things like combs for Christmas, blowdryers for anniversaries, pomade for birthdays: thoughtful things like that. When I found a jar of Grecian Formula in his cabinet he tried to force some on me with the promise that just dyeing my hair will do me wonders. I had to patiently explain it would do no good to dye my hair because my hair died a long time ago.

He keeps telling me that I must have peaked early or something, otherwise, why should I be bald already? My fine friend says I'm prematurely bald, whatever that means. Now, I've never met a man who admits to being "maturely" bald (whatever that means). If we live long enough, I expect to hear him toast me for good health and a cure for my premature baldness on my eightieth birthday.

He's tireless. He has had me eat baked potato skins—which I happen to enjoy—and rub aloe vera juice in my scalp—which I find messy—and all kinds of eccentric remedies, none of which work. No harm. No luck either. But trying to grow back my hair gives him something to do.

I finished my sandwich of braunsweiger and raw onion and drained the last of my lemon-lime soda. "Want a plum, Pilgrim?" Budge shook his head no. I'd save the fruit for the walk down the trail. While Budgie finished the egg salad sandwich, we watched the last glider launch. All three were spectacular.

As we started down the La Luz Trail it seemed the white one was going to touch down at the Tanoan Country Club. We could see it floating over the golf course. The blue and the orange were idling high and wide apart over the city.

"Did you ever glide, Daddy?"

"Never. I used to want to, but not any more."

"Because of the way they have to take off?"

"No, Tiger. At least not until today. No, what scared me off is you never can tell what is going to happen."

"What could happen?"

"Well, a few years ago I read in the *Tribune* where a glider got lifted by an updraft and it took the pilot real high."

"How high, Daddy?"

"Too high. Twenty thousand feet maybe. I don't know. When they finally found him, the pilot was dead. He froze to death he went so high."

Budgie and I were walking down at a good clip now.

"I'd still like to try it sometime."

"Don't tell your mama, Macho."

The first part of the trail going down is the easiest because it's a gradual slope. It's the prettiest part, too, because of the bushes and all the wild blooms. The flowers attract honey bees.

"Remember when Aunt Marcie came up the tram and met us at the top?"

"How can you remember, Tadpole? You were only—what?—four years old?"

"Five. That was the summer I was going into kindergarten. But I remember lots of things from when I was three and four, too. Aunt Marcie brought up some sopaipillas stuffed with scrambled eggs and bacon."

"I remember she brought a can of chilled mandarin oranges, too."

"And some brownies."

"And chablis."

"We had a real picnic sitting there on the deck. Then she changed a dollar for ten dimes so we could look through the binoculars."

"You were too short to see through them by yourself so I had to hold you up. I got real tired holding you up."

"I know. I used all ten dimes."

"That's why I got so tired. And I had to piggyback you most of the way up and back down the trail. But keep growing strong, Pony; you might have to carry me some day."

"You still tease Aunt Marcie a lot."

"Poor Aunt Marcie. Sometimes I feel I shouldn't, but she's the one who laughs the loudest when I do."

"How come she got so scared on the trail?"

"It's the height. For some people, being up so high makes them panicky."

"She was OK at the top."

"That's because we had the rail around the deck."

"And on the tram?"

"Oh, Aunt Marcie loves that. She loves to fly. She takes airplanes all over the place. But here on the trail there's nothing to hold on to and that's what brought it on."

"She didn't know she as scared of heights till then?"

"I guess so."

"She kept hugging the wall and closing her eyes and poor Aunt Marcie finally tripped."

"That's when I took her back to the tram."

"Are you scared of anything, Dad?"

"I'm scared of lots of things, Casper."

"Like what?"

"Well, I don't like to be alone in the dark."

"Me neither. Do you think a doctor can fix you from being scared?"

"Sometimes they can. It seems they have phobia societies for everything."

"Phobias! That's what they're called. Did you every join a phobia society?"

"I thought about it once, but I also have a phobia about joining societies."

"That's funny, Dad."

"Well, Socrates, it's the truth."

We were on the hardest part of the trail now. We had to pass through a huge rock slide. It's about two miles of zig zagging, back and forth, back and forth through tons of boulders. I tried to imagine what caused the slide, what it was like, what creatures were buried underneath.

When we finally got out of those rocks and into the trees, we were walking around The Thumb. I can see The Thumb from my backyard and I like to gaze at it when I'm standing at the grill broiling burgers. The Thumb is just a straight up and down cliff all around.

Once I talked to some climbers who were scaling it for practice. They said they were readying themselves for a climb in the Alps and admitted the grade they were practicing on was probably more difficult than what they would encounter. A lot of climbers have had serious accidents practicing here. Some have been killed. I never learned how those climbers did in the Alps.

Budgie and I reached the midpoint of the trail and took a break.

We decided we were making good time but not nearly as fast as the joggers.

"Remember those joggers that passed us at the one-mile marker this morning, Dad?"

"Yeah, Inchworm. One of them looked twice my age."

"And he was pacing the other two."

"They already sounded tired at the marker."

"How long is the trail, Dad?"

"Eight miles."

"Those guys ran sixteen miles! Did you ever run sixteen miles?"

"Not at once. I used to be a good sprinter, though."

"What was your best distance?"

"The two-twenty and the four-forty. You have to have a real fast start to be good at the hundred. And the eight-eighty takes too much wind for a sprinter."

"You can lope it, can't you? Like the mile?"

"That kind of pacing I was not good at. You have to have good lungs and good speed, and you have to know how to pace yourself. I never got that kind of training. No, when I was young I just liked to run it all out at once. The two-twenty I could run well all the time. The four-forty when I was in shape."

We drank from the canteen and ate some plums. We talked about how the next time we would ride the ski lift behind the summit. And we talked about the hang gliders. We looked up and saw the orange one flying high over The Thumb. And then further north we found the blue one.

"How long have they been up, Dad?"

"Almost two hours."

"Look!"

Budgie found the white one. We thought for sure it had touched down at the Tanoan, but there it was, making a noiseless swoop in the west.

"It goes like a dove, Dad."

We finished the last of the plums and I shook the empty canteen. I had gotten so involved with the hang gliders at the top I forgot to refill the canteen. Well, it wasn't too far to the spring.

I craned for a better look down the valley when we heard the Brrr-rrrrp! It was a small green plane flying through the canyon. A Cessna. It was flying low enough for the passengers to get a good view of the Sandias. We waved as it passed. Budgie was sure they waved back. It kept on up the canyon and then it was gone. For awhile after we couldn't see it anymore we could still hear the echo of the Brrrp! Brrrr-rrrrrp! through the canyon.

"After I learn to hang glide I'm going to learn to fly a plane."

"That's up to you, Eagle."

I recalled when I was about Budgie's age a plane crashed in this mountain killing all the passengers. It took a long time to find it. A couple of years later—I think it was in a *True* magazine I read at the barber's—a reporter told how he was with the search party that found the plane and he described how you couldn't take a step in any direction without stepping on human flesh at the site. The teacher I had the year before was on that plane.

I didn't tell Budgie about that.

We were plenty thirsty when we got to the spring and even more so when we found it was dry. I hadn't checked it on the way up since we didn't want to lose time. Still, I had never known the spring to go dry.

I felt like a piece of jerky when I realized we still had three more miles to go in open country. No trees. No shade. The hottest, driest part of the trail. I shouldn't have let those hang gliders distract me at the top.

The onions from the sandwich were starting to act up. I love to eat onions but they cause me to phlegm. And the want of water only aggravated my condition. I should have known not to put those thick slices in my sandwich, but it's a passion.

Grandpa taught me to eat onions. I like to spread mayonaise on a tortilla like he did and then layer it with onion and roll it burrito fashion the way he taught me when we used to stay at the sheepcamp. He could eat an onion raw like an apple. He warned me, though, wives don't like it when you eat onions, so he was careful to eat them only when he stayed at the sheepcamp. I learned about the wife part soon enough, and appreciated more now what he meant when he said he liked onions but onions didn't like him.

I would have left the onion off my braunsweiger this morning but we didn't have any thawed green chile.

Budgie and I decided we would walk back to the campground without stopping. There was no climbing involved, the trail was well maintained, and our feet were not sore. We kept the pace steady but not brisk.

"Do you have any other phobias, Dad?"

"A bunch of them, Mouse; I've got all kinds of monsters inside me."

"What else makes you scared?"

"When I see you on the skateboard whizzing down to Eric's."

"That?"

"You could fall."

"I fall all the time."

"Yeah, and each time I get scared it's going to be bad. Remember the tooth you lost and the stitches in your lip?"

"I know—but you told me that's part of growing up. I'm more careful now. And I'm better. Not as good as Eric who can do a three-sixty, but I'm a lot better than I used to be."

"It still scares me."

"I didn't know that."

"Well, Snoopy, you asked."

Aunt Marcie likes to say children outgrow their parents but parents never outgrow their children. She tells me how upset Mom got when she found out I already knew how to swim when I was eleven years old, because there was no pool or lessons she had arranged for me. In later years I horrified her when I told her I used to play in the irrigation ditch all the time and sometimes in the Rio with the other guys while I was growing up. She warned me again about how I could have gotten polio playing in that muddy water. I never did tell her about the skydiving I did for recreation in the Air Force.

"If you and Mama never married each other, would I be here?"

"You mean *here* here? With me? On this trail? Right now?"

"All of that."

"I don't know, Starshine. Probably not. You probably wouldn't be anywhere. It took Mama and me to make you."

"Oh, I know how that happens. We had a movie in Health. I just wanted to know if I needed exactly you two to be me."

"You sure did. You couldn't have gotten here any other way. You're half Mama and half me. If we hadn't made you by getting married, then half of you would always be with her and the other half with me, and then maybe you'd be part of two other kids and you'd be so mixed up you wouldn't even be you. What do you think of that, Omelet?"

"Why did you marry Mama?"

"Because I had to be with her."

"Well, what's it like? Being married, I mean."

"It's a job, Mr. Koppel. We have to take care of each other and we have to take care of you."

"What about the romance part?"

"That's up to us, Paloma, but more than anything else, marriage is a job to be done."

Those last three miles took longer than I had thought. In the parking lot I opened both doors to the car and wound down all the windows to let the hot air spill out. I started the engine and turned on the air conditioner to blow out the hot air and pawed through the glove compartment. Sometimes I keep a pack of Doublemint in there. There was no gum.

Budgie called for me. He had made friends with some picnickers and they were willing to share their water with us. I sipped at a styrofoam cupful, and then gulped down a second. The water was very good.

I thanked the nice people and Budgie and I got into the car. I don't know how Budgie does it but he took their patronage in stride. Maybe he didn't recognize it. Still, I like to think he is astute enough to ignore it. We are told again and again not to treat the handicapped as if they are different, yet they fussed over Budgie in a way he had to notice. Oh, they didn't come right out and say it's too bad you only got one arm, kid, but the solicitude was there.

In our last visit to the clinic, the doctor said he'd have to do another biopsy on Budgie's good arm. Then we'd know if he'd have to operate on it. Maybe they could save it. Or maybe they'd have to remove it, too. Maybe nothing. I try not to think about it but until we've got this thing licked it's always right there silently staring me down.

I have always understood Budgie is not mine to own. One just cannot own another human being. What do we truly own anyway? I have known he is a gift from whatever Force or Law that determines such things. I need only to make him ready so he can go out and do the same thing. I accepted that before he ever came to be. Only, no one ever warned me about the joy of having a child. About the pride. The love. The temptation to possess. Yes, I know he has to leave me some time. But not now. Not like this. Not before my job is done.

How many more times will I have to massage his arm to pull the cramps? Go ahead, I tell him, scream if you must; it's OK to cry. Heck, I cry, too, but only when I'm alone. Not because I am ashamed of the tears. It is only because I cannot let him see my despair. I cannot kill his hope.

The sun was making it hard for me to see so I pulled the car to the side and fumbled for my handkerchief.

"You OK, Dad?"

"Fine, Grandpa," I sighed. "Just fine. It's just those darn onions again."

Budgie looked at me thoughtfully. "Onions sting my eyes only when I peel them."

I removed my glasses and pinched the bridge of my nose and squinched my eyes. "Well, see, Little Man, it's a funny thing with me. Onions just never learned to like me."

"Mmmmmmmm..."

Talking forces me to concentrate and to regain control. I blew hard into my handkerchief, wiped the dust off my lenses, and found I could focus a lot better.

Budgie pointed out the window with his steel arm. "Look, Dad."

I looked and found the hang gliders bobbing and arcing like curious butterflies somewhere between The Thumb and the Crest. "They're wonderful, Son."

My voice was steady once again and my vision clear. I was all right. I put the car in gear and eased onto the pavement.

"When I get home, Soldier, I'm going to have a tall glass of ice water...."

"I'm going to have two!"

"...and I'm going to pour some epsom salts into a tub of hot water and take a long soak...."

"And sleep!"

"...and sleep. Then I'm going to dry off and stretch out on the couch with the *Time* magazine...."

"And sleep!"

"OK for you, Mockingbird. And sleep. And maybe when it's time to eat I just might skip supper and go straight to bed...."

"And sleep!" we chimed together.

Budgie mechanically massaged his good arm with his steel claw and looked out the window again for the hang gliders. He marveled at their passing beauty and loved them for their impermanence. He told me they were there exactly as they were only for this once and here we were to enjoy them. He couldn't get over how they could sail like that for more than three hours without stopping for water or going to the bathroom even.

I liked it when he said they looked like colored stars in the sky.

BY LANTERN LIGHT

Keith Wilson

CLAY Rallison loved the evening. In late Fall, when the clouds came lightly and were illuminated by the setting sun, he liked to be in the barn with its strong smells of cows and horses, old wood. He would stand just inside the growing shadows cast by the barn's doors, watch the evening change. It never ceased to content him. After a few minutes, he would perform the ritual of lighting the coal-oil lantern, striking the match carefully, cupping the flame in his palm as he pushed the wire lever down, raising the glass shade and exposing the wick. He kept the wick trimmed and the flame ran its quick way into light the second he touched it with the match. Then he released the lever, letting the shade move down, and adjusted the knob exactly until the flame burned white and cool-looking, at just the right height.

On such an evening in 1933, he lighted the lantern, hung it up and turned to do the evening's chores. He pitched hay for both the horses and the two cows and was just settling down to milk the Holstein when he heard the noise of a car pulling up outside.

"Hey there, Clay? You home?"

Sam, he thought. His cousin. He hobbled out, his hip aching as much as it had those five years ago. He could still sense exactly where the fracture line had been; pain traced it like a sharp fingernail, reminding him intimately of just how it had felt.

"You comin' over to Aunt Jessie's party tonight?" Sam was almost an albino with his pale, nearly transparent hair, his light-colored staring eyes. His overalls were neatly pressed, almost new, his hands pink and soft. Sam's eyes blinked against the soft light of evening.

"Hadn't much planned on it."

"Got any coffee on the stove?"

"Guess so." Clay stifflegged it out into the yard, toward the house.

"You know, you ought to come. It ain't right to not have the whole family, on an evening like this, it being her seventieth birthday and all...."

"Until now, I hadn't been invited."

"Well, cousin, you are now."

Sure, Clay thought. One hour before it was to begin. Why? That was the question. He led Sam into the neat, clean kitchen of the small farmhouse. How many times had he seen his mother, Jessie's sister, standing there looking out the window, washing dishes mechanically. Now she was gone too, last winter, people said she died of grief. To Clay she was still there, the twilight on her face, a figure of his memory. He couldn't remember his father as well, and that often bothered him. His dad had been such a quiet man.

Clay poured coffee into a white china cup with blue flowers on it. "What kind of flowers are them, Clay?" he could hear his mother's thin voice asking. "I sure never seen no flowers like that round here!" It became a kind of repeated joke, but underneath lay the questions that plagued her, with her Midwest memories, as she lived out her life in the dry New Mexican valley with its trickle of water from the dam twenty miles to the north and west. Most of what grew was planted but the hollyhocks and daisies reseeded themselves without human care once they'd been planted. Clay himself didn't know what kind of flowers were on the cup, though he'd searched through the seed catalogs and his other books a couple of times looking for their pictures. "Artistic license," he said once and his mother sniffed her disdain for the only educated person the Rallison family had ever fostered.

"Hell, Clay," Sam said loudly as he stirred his third spoonful of sugar into the coffee, "Aunt Jessie asked for you special."

"You're going to kill yourself, eating that much sugar."

"Ain't done me no harm so far," Sam laughed and smacked his big belly with the palm of his hand. "All that's just for balance!"

"O.K. Why does she want me?"

"You're family, that's why." Sam stirred his coffee again. "Maybe some business," he said in a soft, thin voice, his eyes on his coffee cup.

"That half section of land?"

"Maybe."

"I told her and I told you that land isn't for sale."

"We know, we know. But what if a fellow was to just take a lease on that land—right in the family, mind you—maybe farm it on a share basis even?"

"That land's burned out. It'll blow away if it's not left to rest awhile."

"I guess they taught you that sort of stuff at the Aggie school."

"Yes, and they were right. Look at the prime land in this valley, or what used to be prime land. You can't hardly grow crops on most of it."

"Some folks say you never should've been sent away to that damned school."

"I wasn't sent. I paid my own way, worked for every penny and hitchhiked there to boot!" Hell, thought Clay wearily, they all know that story as well as I do. I bet Sam could tell it better. Words aren't of much use around here. They don't really get heard. "Where would you get the money to even lease my land?"

Sam's eyes went shifty, cunning. "Suppose you was to just loan it to us, say, till the crops come in? Pay you interest then!"

Clay started to say something but Sam continued, "Aunt Jessie, she says you owe it to the family, seeing what happened to Cindy and all."

They always bring Cindy up, Clay thought. Always. He saw her smiling blue eyes, the pale hair, then the blood trickled through her hair and bubbled out her mouth as she tried to speak to him. He held her on that lonely dirt road, his father dead in the wreckage of their old Ford pickup. When he tried to get up, the pain flashed through the shock and he'd been unable even to crawl for help. He passed out.

God damn me, I passed out. The doctor said it wouldn't have mattered. Cindy probably died in his arms. Her chest and head were shattered. Clay shook his head. "That's all water under the bridge."

"Sure, sure. That's what I say myself, but you know how Aunt Jessie takes on, Cindy being her daughter and all."

"I wasn't driving. The hearing established that."

"Lawyer words! To Aunt Jessie, you're the one killed her. Falling in love with your cousin like that...." Sam grinned.

"And she with me," Clay said. He felt his right fist clench. "I'm not coming, that's all there is to that."

"Aunt Jessie says she might have to sue, break that will your daddy left. It was your mother's land, our family land she inherited from her poppa. Aunt Jessie's poppa too, and my granddaddy."

"Mother willed it to me. I don't give a damn if she sues."

"Now just hold on a minute...."

"You better finish your coffee, Sam, and get on back home." Clay paused. "I heard in town that Aunt Jessie had a stroke, can't talk so well?"

"I suppose that's true," Sam replied cautiously.

"But she can do all this talking about land and wills and suing me?"

"I guess I better go. They'll be waiting. You sure you won't come on up?"

"No. Wish her happy birthday for me."

Sam shook his head, put his coffee cup down and walked slowly out of the kitchen door and into the yard. He stopped by his car and turned back to look at Clay. "You're going to be sorry about all this one day, Clay."

"I don't see how I could be any sorrier than I am."

"Aunt Jessie, she'll find ways!"

"Like I said, tell her happy birthday. Make up some story, you've always been good at that."

Sam heaved his heavy body up into the seat of the old Dodge and started the engine. He seemed to hesitate once more, then slammed the car into gear and drove off leaving a cloud of dust hanging in the evening air. It was growing darker, and heavy clouds were moving in from the north as Clay limped back to the barn. Shouldn't leave that lantern burning when I'm not in the barn. Just the same, the light from the open barn doors warmed his spirits. Doctor said the hip would never heal. Well, we'll just see. Every day he walked farther and farther and the pain was either lessening or he was getting used to it, accepting it, as he did the precious loneliness of the farm and its house. He wished often that he could always see Cindy's face in his mind the way it was before the accident, but her other, dying, face quickly imposed itself. His father's face always looked as if he were asleep.

He remembered so clearly. By the time he had come to, the bodies were gone and he himself was on a makeshift stretcher, a board lashed to his right leg. There were bandages up to his armpit. The doctor said a good surgeon, maybe in Houston, might be able to fix the leg, he didn't know. Clay thought of selling out, getting the operation and starting all over someplace else. Trouble was, who'd have enough money to pay him cash for the place? There wasn't much money anywhere. The valley pretty much lived on the barter system, even more now than in days before, what with the Depression.

"Tell you what, I'll swap you that lot of mine in town for that half section you got. Throw in the house on the lot for good measure," Lem Jones had said. That was the only kind of deal he would get. No money would change hands. And he would need money.

He finished milking the Holstein and the Guernsey. The sun was down, but crimson streaks still touched the crevasses in the black clouds. From where he stood by the barn door, he could see the unlighted windows of his house, almost see his reflection in the pale yellow glow of lamplight. Out there in the growing darkness was the dirt road, with the two white crosses near it.

That road led to Aunt Jessie's house. Right about now, all the surviving family would be sipping their iced teas or coffee and nibbling at pieces of birthday cake, trying to smile and cheer up the old lady who, Mrs. Peterson had told him, dribbled out of the side of her mouth and stared like a crazy person, or like a person crazed by what had happened to her body. Her face joined the face of her daughter Cindy and of his own sleeping father that Clay saw in the darkness. Beyond the arc of that gentle lantern light, he suddenly knew, the darkness continued on to the end of the world, to the end of forever and ever. All the places he would never visit with Cindy, the new faces he and she would never see, books he would never again read to his mother or talk to his father about lay out there in a silence much more terrible than the vanished stars or even his own dreams.

THE BEST LOOKING BOY

Nancy Gage

THE asphalt parking lot was spongy under the weight of the miners' boots, and they tracked into the cafe bits of black tar. Later, after the rush, Libby would scrape tar from the brown flecked linoleum with a putty knife.

The big kitchen fan slammed grease-clotted steam into the unmoving air outside, and the deep dishwater turned Libby's hands white and doughy. She plucked at her white cotton blouse with a soapy hand and blew down on her breasts. She scooped four mugs from the rinse water, a handle hooked on each finger of her right hand, and set them on the drain rack. She flicked the towel from the hook behind her and blotted her forehead with it.

"The health department's going to shut us down," her mother said, coming back behind the particle-board divider that separated the dishwashing cubicle from the rest of the cafe. She put a stack of dirty platters and mugs next to the sink and snatched the towel from Libby's hand. "I swear to God. Now get a clean one to wipe those mugs."

The waitress, Nita, stepped around the divider and picked up a stack of clean plates. "Rush is almost over."

"Good." Libby scraped the plates and put them into the wash water, ran cool water over the insides of her wrists. Sweat snarled her hair.

Now that school was out, the rhythms of the mines shaped her days. There was the morning rush from six to nine, while the shift changed. Then the cleanup while Goldie baked and made soups and stews. The noon rush, and then a break when she talked on the phone to her girlfriend who lived in town, or read movie magazines or tried new makeup and made wish-lists from *Seventeen* of the clothes she wanted to start school in, when real life began again in September. The shift changed from three to six, when they closed and washed the floors and scrubbed the grill with pumice stone and vinegar. The scent of the scorched vinegar stayed in her clothes and on her skin.

It was past 8:30 now; the dayshift was on. Across the flat dry plateau, men were descending into the earth in metal cages, and men just off graveyard were showering or sitting in the cafe having a slice of pie or an orange soda, a bag of barbecued potato chips or a bowl of chicken noodle soup to fuel them for the half-hour drive south to Grants. Outside, Libby's father was pumping gas into their cars. The jukebox played Jerry Lee Lewis. Heavy ceramic mugs made a dull clink on the formica counter.

Libby wiped her hands on her long white apron, marked with dishwater across the front and her sweat around the waist. She stepped around the partition and picked up the glass coffee pot, started down the counter, topping off the cups, one after another. The men lowered their cups from their mouths as she passed and held them out.

"How you doing, sweetheart?" said a miner who had three fingers on his right hand. The skin across the stumps of the fore and middle fingers was stretched and shiny. His eyes were set deep in their sockets, and when he smiled she could see tobacco stains on his teeth.

"Fine," she said, giving him a smile so he wouldn't think she was rude or stuck-up. He always said that to her, every day since she'd been working, a month now, almost, since school let out. She guessed he'd said it last summer too, but now it felt awkward to hear, like he was flirting. She looked down at his hands and passed by quickly.

The after-shift crowd was quiet. They played the jukebox and drank their strong black coffee, their thick muscled arms silent on the counter, their fingers slack. Some of them seemed almost asleep. The talk was quiet too. None of the loud teasing and heckling that went on with the guys headed toward the mines, hurrying to eat, yelling at her mother and Nita, shoveling eggs and potatoes into their mouths like the tons of ore they were on their way to move. They left more tips in the early morning, too, when the coins were lighter in their pockets, before they got all worn out and forgetful.

They heard the two-note whine of a siren. As it grew louder, the women and the miners and Libby came to attention, as though they were hearing a parade pressing forward, the first notes of the "Star-Spangled Banner." Libby had the momentary urge to clap her hand to her breast. The coffee sloshed in the pot, and she set it back on the burner, then turned to the big front window. She was aware of the sputter of bacon on the grill, Patsy Cline's voice from the jukebox by the door.

The siren mounted, pierced, and passed, and their heads pivoted as one, following the one red light spinning in the white air of morning.

Her mother stepped around the glass candy counter and rushed to the north window, a little skip-step, and the sash of her apron flew behind her. She leaned both hands on the pop cooler.

Libby went out the front door. Amid the parked cars stood three miners, watching to the north. Her father held the gas hose in one hand, watching. It was hard to see through the brightness of light pounding down from the sun and up from the parched earth. Far away, the ambulance turned left.

"Jackpile," her father said.

Libby went back inside the cafe. "Jackpile," she said just loud enough to be a public announcement. "It went to Jackpile."

Libby's mother stepped to the jukebox and bent from the waist like a ballerina, her arm arched in front of her, her leg off the floor behind her. She yanked the plug and "I Fall to Pieces" groaned dead.

"Hey," said a short squat guy halfway down the counter. "I played that."

Her mother turned around and looked at him. She jutted her jaw, blew upward at the hair hanging across her forehead. "How many plays you got coming?"

"Three more," he said. She crossed the room to the black rubber mat that ran behind the counter, hiked up her cook's apron, fished into the pocket of her jeans, came up with a quarter and slapped it onto the formica.

"Play 'em tomorrow," she said. The silence held for just a moment longer, and then the voices started again.

Libby heard Three-Fingers say, "My brother's day shift out to Jackpile."

"Lots of men on days at Jackpile," Nita said. "Could be anybody."

He nodded, but he looked toward that north window.

"We just had a bunch of guys headed to Jackpile. Those three at the end of the counter." Nita jerked her head, and Libby followed the motion and looked at the end stool, vacant now. The boy who was there before—not long before, an hour maybe—he'd left her a tip. Fourteen cents in pennies. He wore a black T-shirt and Levis. His hair spread back and away from his temples in shiny oiled wings, and the top curled forward in a twist. His name was Atencio. She had heard the other miners call him that.

"That Spanish kid," Libby said.

"That's right. Atencio. And the fellows he was with. They were teasing you, Lib."

"Everybody teases me." Libby slid her hand deep into her left pocket and touched the fourteen pennies. They had been under his napkin when she cleared the dishes away. Fourteen pennies laid out to spell "Hi." She had scooped them quickly into her left hand with a sweep of her right, and then trickled them into the tight pocket of her jeans. She had looked toward the door, and he'd been standing there, watching her. He winked before he slipped past the doorjamb and out into the parking lot.

It wasn't the first time she'd noticed him. He was different from the rest. Had her get the strawberry syrup for his shortstack and drank two Cokes, one after the other, to wash the pancakes down. "I like the sweet stuff," he'd said, and just his saying that had made her shy. "It's too hot to drink coffee anyway."

She'd gotten brave enough to talk to him, though he had to be four or five years older than she was. "Is it hot underground too?" she had asked him.

He shook his head and the curl bobbed. "Cold as a tomb," he said. "Until you get to working. Then you sweat, no matter."

She bit her lower lip and looked at the counter top, away from his eyes.

"Feels great going down in the cage," he said. "Like real air conditioning."

"I wish I could see it," she said. She wiped at the counter, looked at his fingers wrapped around the Coke bottle.

"I'd like to take you down," he had said. And she had looked him in the face then. He had those pale green eyes that some of the Spanish kids had.

She had wanted to call her girlfriend that very minute and tell her what he'd said, how he'd dropped his voice so that it was all just between them, not part of the teasing. To tell her how his eyes were the color of Coca-Cola glass and how they looked against the dark skin of his face. Tell how old he was, a miner, not a kid, not anyone from school. A man.

"Hey, Libby, got any more coffee over there?" She heard her name and turned from the empty stool, went around to the booths with the pot and refilled the empty cups.

The miners were beginning to go out now, on out to their cars and pickup trucks, out the straight hot State Road 509 into Grants. The cafe was getting quieter and quieter, and her mother stood at the cash register, taking their green tickets and their money, getting Milky Ways and Lifesavers out of the glass case for them. They took mints and toothpicks from the bowls next to the register.

Behind the partition Nita was scraping plates, and when Libby went back, she handed her the garbage pail. "This needs dumping," she said, so Libby took the handle and went through the kitchen, out the back door, across the hard-packed ground, past the trailer, across the gravel to the dump that the bulldozer had carved out of the whitened earth.

Three crows lifted from the dump and settled on the barbed wire fence just beyond, one on each post. She climbed the mounded dirt and upended the bucket on the other side, watched the bits of bread and egg, the coffee grounds and potato peels, eggshells and tin cans slide down.

Libby straightened and looked out over the tumbleweeds and grama grass toward Jackpile. An ore truck passed and the ground shook with the force of it. There was no other traffic. She could see clearly the orange headframe of Jackpile mine in the distance. Its triangular form was a tall silhouette against the blue sky above the flat earth. The tangle of forms at the base of the frame was cars and buildings and ore trucks and one ambulance. Behind her she heard the birds lift into the air and settle again on the garbage.

She started back toward the cafe to wash the bucket out with the hose when she saw the ambulance pull onto the highway. Back toward the cafe it traveled at a regular speed, maybe even slower than that. An awful misery in a slow-moving ambulance. No light, no siren. She stood and watched. He was dead. Whoever he was, he was dead. She wanted to cross herself, but she was not Catholic. Inside her there was a flutter.

Inside the cafe was almost silent. They sat waiting for someone to come, someone getting off late, someone who knew, someone to come and tell them. There were only her mother and Nita, her father, Goldie, and four miners. Sitting there, the miners looked like old men. The dirt in the creases around their eyes and mouths looked permanent. One had a face of white stubble. They sat, hands cradling their cups, not speaking.

Goldie was at the counter, her hands folded, elbows propped on the worn formica, a cigarette burning in a long holder. She worked her teeth the way that she did when she was concentrating, rolling pie crusts, or measuring out flour.

Nita was looking out down the south road, rocking on her long feet. Finally she looked around. "Might as well fill the sugars," she said and went back around behind the counter.

"Swede," Libby's father said to no one. He leaned around the doorway into the kitchen and got a broom, began to work the floor in short jerky strokes. "And Mike and Carl and Grubb. They're all at Jackpile."

"I think Swede's on swing shift," her mother said and lit a cigarette. She shook the match and dropped it in an ashtray. She blew the smoke from her nose. "Could be anybody."

A truck pulled off the road and they turned toward it. After a moment, Three-Fingers came through the door. He stood in the doorway. "Wasn't my brother," he said, almost ashamed to show his relief. "Was Jimmy Atencio."

"Ahh," her mother said. "Hell. That kid."

"That kid?" Libby turned toward the end stool.

"Just a boy," her father said.

"What happened?" asked one of the miners.

"Decapitated," Three-Fingers said. "I guess he leaned over, looking down the shaft, when the car came down above him. Took his head clean off." The three fingers sliced the air.

Goldie stood up. "Better get the pie crusts rolled," she said. Her ivory-colored cigarette holder hung from her lip.

"That kid?" Libby asked again.

"Yeah," Nita said. "That one that was teasing you this morning." She walked down the counter and took a sugar dispenser from each rack, slid them along in front of her. "That's the one. Just a damned teenager."

Libby looked at the counter where he had written a message in money. She thought of him, leaning out to feel the cool air rising from the dark shaft, thought of the scent of the wet earth, like rain, it must be. She could see him taking in the deep scent of underground water and cold air, his nostrils open, maybe a smile on his face. Maybe he had been thinking of her, thinking of taking her with him, down into the mine where it was cool.

And then the heavy wire cage cutting his head loose from his body, right at the neckline of the black T-shirt, the knit ribbing marking the place like a dotted line. His head tumbling over and over free and loose into the coolness and the dark, spinning slowly, she thought. And maybe he opened his pale green eyes, and maybe he had a last thought, and maybe it was of her.

Her hand slipped into her pocket, touched the fourteen cents. She squeezed the coins into her fist. Jimmy, his name was.

"Had a wife and a baby," Three-Fingers said. "That's what they say. Not too long out of high school."

"A baby," Nita said.

"A shame," her mother said.

"I just thought I'd stop and let you know," Three-Fingers said, "before I went on into town."

"Appreciate it," her father said.

"We were wondering," her mother said.

And Libby thought that she would call her girlfriend, and then she thought that she wouldn't, wouldn't tell anyone. What would she say anyway? And him with a wife and a baby. She wanted to cry for real now. A wife and a baby, a damned baby. They probably had to get married, she thought. He was too young to get married just because he wanted to. She tried to imagine his wife; maybe she didn't even know yet. Maybe she was hanging diapers on the clothesline or watching soap operas on TV. She tried to feel sorry for her, that Jimmy was dead. But he would have left her soon enough, if there had been time in his life. Already looking at other girls, winking and leaving notes. When he married that other girl, she thought, he had never even heard of me.

They were only at the end of June, and she would have seen him every day before his shift and after, and she would have been braver each time and dared herself to talk more. And he would have taken it slow. But he would have kept after her and pushed her until who knows? He would have filled her hot empty weeks. She turned to the south window and looked down the road that went straight until it disappeared long before it reached the town. Maybe she and Jimmy would have gone down that road together by the end of the summer, by September. Maybe they would have gone looking for something else. Suddenly she thought he was the best looking boy she had ever seen.

"Libby, honey, are you crying?" Nita asked.

Libby turned away, got the puttyknife from behind the pop cooler to scrape tar up from the floor.

"Honey, you're crying," Nita said, and Libby looked up to show them all that yes, she was.

But what she said was, "No. I didn't know him or nothing."

"Give it here, honey," Nita said, taking the knife from Libby. "Go on in the back. You can't do any kind of job now."

BANDIDO

Drummond Hadley

AT evening Santa Fe was driving his truck up the long hill from the canyon. He met a rough Mexican man who walked toward him down the hill. Santa Fe stopped the truck.

"*Dame tu jaqueta*, give me your jacket," said the man. "I am hungry. Do you have food?"

The forcefulness of the man's voice seemed unusual to Santa Fe, but he lay it to the man's having walked a long way with little to eat and nothing to look forward to but a lonely night on cold ground.

Santa Fe thought about the jacket he was wearing. It was down, only two years old with plenty of use left in it. But this rough man had a need for the coat more than his own. He took it off and gave it to the man.

"*No tiene algo de comer?*" the man asked again.

Finally Santa Fe was able to find some bread and a few tins behind the truck seat. He handed them to the man and told him of a nearby ranch where he could eat dinner. It was called the Puerta Blanca just across the Mexican borderline. The man grabbed at the bread and stuffed it into his mouth.

When he turned to leave, Santa Fe saw the grips of a large revolver sticking out of his hip pocket. "Ah," thought Santa Fe, "then I am nothing but a fool. He could have taken what he wanted and I have sent him to eat at the Puerta Blanca, home of the son of my old friend Porfirio."

Santa Fe was worried. He went to a neighboring ranch to borrow a gun. On the way back he met a narcotics agent tracking the man who said the gun Santa Fe had seen in the man's pocket had been stolen with a watch and a few other things—whatever someone could carry away over the long mesas and rocky canyons.

The narcotics agent could not go into Mexico. He asked Santa Fe to cross and lure the rough Mexican across the borderline into New Mexico so that the man would stand trial for the robbery.

"Who knows who that tired, spent man is," thought Santa Fe, "or what he has done or what has been done to him."

"I will try to bring back the gun," Santa Fe said, "but I will leave the man in Mexico."

Santa Fe stuffed the borrowed gun under his belt, pulled his shirt over it and walked through the borderline. In the darkness he came to the covered kitchen window of the Puerta Blanca. He could hear the voices inside. He knocked on the kitchen door.

"*Pásale*," said his friend's son. "*Toma café*."

In the yellow kerosene lamp light, Santa Fe sat down at the end of a cracked table near the wood-burning cook stove. Tortillas were being made. There was a pot of frijoles on the stove. At the other end of the table sat the man and the gun Santa Fe had come for.

The man began telling lies about the gun saying it had been in his family a long time. Santa Fe asked to look at it and got it in his hand. Then he told the man he knew the gun was stolen and that the law was waiting only one hundred yards away across the borderline.

"*Cambia tu vida*, change your life and go," Santa Fe said. There was silence. No one moved. The beans simmered in the pot on the stove.

"*Dios te bendiga*, God bless you," said the rough Mexican, and went out the door.

Santa Fe took the gun, said good-bye to his friend's son and went back across the border. He gave the gun to the waiting narcotics agent and went on his way.

Several days later he returned and found that the man he had allowed to go had crossed again into New Mexico and was breaking into isolated ranch houses. The man had also tried to steal a truck. He had shouted in the darkness that he had another gun and would kill. The ranchers began locking their doors and shooting at sounds and shadows in the brush.

"Ah," thought Santa Fe, "now I am twice a fool for having let the man go. I had better find him and take him to jail." Santa Fe picked up a seven-foot piece of swanson spot cord. He had been planning to use it to make a fine throat latch on a hackamore. He went again to the Puerta Blanca where a roundup was going on.

"*¿Qué húbole?* How is it going with you?" one of the vaqueros asked.

"*De veras*, truly," Santa Fe laughed, "I am looking for the *bandido*." No one had seen him. They laughed and parted.

One homesteader had shot at him. Santa Fe went to the homestead looking for sign. He found it, but the man would walk where his tracks could not show on the trails. If there was a pasture gate to open, he would leave no tracks at the gate. Still Santa Fe kept following. A knee that had been dislocated began to hurt.

Late afternoon Santa Fe stopped under the needles of an old cedar tree below the Valenci line camp. Ahead he could see smoke in the air from a fire. The line camp stood alone in the middle of the clearing. "Now the man is very close," thought Santa Fe.

He felt his throat tighten and the blood beating in his throat. He knew that if he walked from under the sheltering cedar limbs into the clearing anyone watching with a gun could easily kill him. He waited and listened among the still canyon cliffs for any sound that would tell where the man was.

Knowing no other way, with a lever-action twenty-two rifle in his right hand, he slowly began walking across the clearing. It seemed a long way. The afternoon shadows were beginning to come fast. Careless weed had grown since the last rain. A mourning dove flew from the edge of the clearing.

He came to the grey weathered line shack, placed his body against the outer wall and carefully peered in through a window. A bed was turned over, two chairs were broken, half-eaten food lay around the room, the cabinets had been rampaged. There was *mierda* on the floor. Smoke was coming from the ashes of the destroyed wood supply that Walter Ramsey had gathered to be ready for winter. Behind the corral leading east up the Valenci draw Santa Fe found the man's tracks.

He followed the prints in the arroyo sand past a black circle on the north side of the draw where the man had tried to set the rangeland grass on fire. There was too little grass and the fire had burnt out. "The man is crazy," thought Santa Fe, "but he is crazy as a fox."

Santa Fe kept following the tracks to a bend in the draw where the cliffs were steep and worn by water on either side and where, when the rains came, the water would flow down over the waterfall. In the middle of the arroyo, as though trapped by the shape of the earth itself, between cliffs on either side of him and the steep waterfall behind him, stood the man Santa Fe had come to find.

"You are hunting," the man said.

"Yes," said Santa Fe.

They began to walk along the arroyo together, the sound of their feet crunching in the stillness into the gray grains of the arroyo sand. Out of the corner of his eyes Santa Fe could see the man readying a rock from his pocket to throw at Santa Fe's head. Santa Fe felt calm. He thought, No more open clearings to walk across not knowing if a bullet waits, or when it will come with the hush of a hawk's wings cutting through the air.

"I will kill you, or take you to jail," he said to the man.

"*Mejor que me llevas a la cárcel.* Better that you take me to jail," the man answered.

Santa Fe told him to lie on the sand and that he would tie the man's hands together. The man would not. They stood looking into one another's eyes. Slowly with the thumb of his right hand Santa Fe began to draw the hammer of the rifle back. The slight click of the sear pin sounded loud in the stillness as the hammer lock dropped to the last notch on the sear ready to fire.

The man counted on the spring of a cat in his legs. Only one of them would have the chance to leave that arroyo as they looked into each other's eyes across the sand. The man heard the sear pin's sound, then slowly lay on the sand. His chance would come when the rifle had to be laid aside to wind the rope coils about his wrists. But waiting a moment too long in the stillness, he lost that chance when it came and Santa Fe drew the coils snug about his wrists.

They began walking together the long miles to where Santa Fe had left his four-wheel-drive truck. A sharp pain in Santa Fe's left knee like a knife, he knew if the man ran he would never catch him. They got into the front seat of the truck and drove along the four-wheel-drive trail.

Though he was driving, Santa Fe could see out of the corner of his eye the tops of the man's arms moving a little and he knew the hands were quietly straining to undo the knots that held his hands behind his back. Santa Fe knew that if the man freed himself, those hands could fly across the truck seat and be at Santa Fe's throat. "That is what I would do if I were this man," thought Santa Fe.

They came to a fence. Santa Fe got out to open the barbwire gate, then opened the passenger-side truck door to check the knots holding the man's hands. The man whirled in the seat, kicked Santa Fe in the chest to leap out of the high four-wheel-drive truck.

"*Yo creo que no estás bastante hombre para matarme*, I don't think you are man enough to kill me," he yelled. Santa Fe brought the rifle up sharp into the side of the man's head. Blood spurted onto the dashboard and the seat of the truck.

They went away together on the long road to town.

THE SCARS OF OLD SABERS

Gabriel Meléndez

I met a woman one certain summer, and while our acquaintance was neither fated nor long-lived, it provided a respite from ourselves and from the blur of rather uneventful days. And the woman was nice. She was a nice woman. Nice enough to invite me to her uncle's condominium. She obviously thought she was safe, thought I was pleasant enough, urbane enough, cultured enough, educated enough: knowing that, indeed, it had been such a long, long time since I had left the uninviting rude mud hovel which would-be newspaperman turned Rocky Mountain fur trapper, Rufus B. Sage, had disparagingly characterized in his 1846 account, "Degenerate Inhabitants of New Mexico," as the typical dwelling and condition of my forebears. My nice woman friend thought me attentive enough to meet her retired U.S. Army uncle, and I was...educated enough to find my way out of the tangle of the city and out to the ski, turned spring film festival, turned summer bluegrass, turned October fest, turned year-round California clique resort town. And so, on one perfectly turned summer afternoon we met to swim and sun at Uncle's extra-amenity condo pool. We swam till the sky darkened and the air chilled and pregnant summer clouds amassed and broke their water somewhere east of summer resort mountains and directly above us. I was politely asked to come up to Uncle's condo to wait out the downpour.

Uncle met us at the door of Uncle's neatly ordered condo. Uncle, Uncle was tall, lean, balding—willowing in his ripe years I would say—in his ripe retirement years. And Uncle, Uncle was pleasant enough. He offered a soft drink, offered his quiet and unassuming appraisal of the easy life in the prosperous afterglow of unselfish service to the country (Uncle was watching a P.G.A. Master's Golf Tourney on his Sony Trinitron), offered his placid reflections on enjoying the marvelous vistas of aspens, tall pines and shaved resort mountain ski runs. Uncle, at his niece's insistence, offered to tell us about his memorabilia.

Uncle's center table is from Pakistan, hand engraved and etched brass, etched brass and orangewood legs, to be sure. Uncle picked up the carved room panels in Indonesia, and the elephant, the fat one, Uncle's fat carved elephant is from Burma. Uncle offers more, but doesn't query into his guest's reactions. Uncle points to his Chinese screen drawings, delicate and somber in the shallow light of the rainy afternoon. "Uncle, didn't you get these in Hong Kong on your second tour of duty in the South China Sea?" Uncle offers an approving nod, and sweeps the room with a gesture of his hand. "Over there…no, the ivory carving…I bought it in Guam, but it's also Chinese…from the mainland, of course." Of course, Uncle, incredibly intricate, exquisite, yes, Uncle, absolutely exquisite in its detail. The highlights of Uncle's den and study have assumed their appropriate scale against Uncle's array of statuettes, ceramics, Persian rugs, English pipe racks and Spanish bota bags.

Appreciative Niece and unintrusive friend wait on Uncle to fill his pipe and offer more. Uncle offers a beer. Sure, why not? I'd love one, Uncle. (Old habits. The offer connects. Maybe old Uncle and I could hit it off after all.)

I'm not averse to musing over Uncle's momentos, his souvenirs of here and there, over and yonder. Who knows, there might be another beer in it for me, or a story in it for us all? Uncle draws on his pipe, steps away, and draws his hand across an ebonywood chest of drawers. We all muse at once.

"Uncle, can we see your leopard skin rug?"

"Sure, go ahead, I'll be right up in a minute."

A leopard skin rug, Uncle? Oh well, why not. I can't say I've ever been this close to anyone possessing a leopard he bagged himself somewhere in a Malaysian jungle. We move down the hallway and clamber up to Uncle's loft.

Upstairs in the loft, Uncle's loft that hangs above the kitchen and juts out a foot or so over Uncle's den and study, the gray light of the afternoon angles in through a west window and scuffs across the sleepy floor, to where, unavoidably strewn between Uncle's writing desk and king size bed is his trophy leopard: mouth agape, marble eyes, spiked teeth and hooked claws dangling from its tattered paw skin. Uncle arrives in time to switch on the light and revel in the heroics of his Borneo jaunt in '64: an organized harvesting expedition for U.S. Army *Coronels* or better.

What's this? I point to the half moon of a saber sheathed in brass and leather. Uncle pulls it from my hand before I've sensed its weight, its balance, its past tooled in steel. I would have run my thumb against its blade: a habit inherited from uncles who gutted deer and sheep with sharp-edged pocket knives. Uncle removes the saber from its sheath, holds it up to the light. The light has disturbed its moonless sleep. "It's an Indian Tulwaur, the same kind used by the Gurkhas."

"Who?"

"The Gurkha tribesmen of Nepal; the British used them in India. They were the crack units of their time."

The Tulwaur's blade has a nasty hook in its underside. Uncle runs his finger to the place where the hook turns in: "It's used like a seamstress's ripper, it'll rip a man's throat or abdomen wide open. Lunge in and rip upwards! You can probably see it's an instrument designed to kill, doesn't have much other purpose."

Probably, Uncle, designed to kill or to rest on old U.S. Army uncles' nightstands.

"Incidentally the Gurkhas held to the belief that once the saber was drawn it could not be sheathed until it had drawn blood....Sometimes they'd run the blade across their thumbs to appease tradition, you understand...."

Uncle replaces the blade. Americans can sheathe the Tulwaur with impunity, I assume; either that or maybe Uncle had the Gurkhas confused with the Samurai.

Uncle's loft is bedecked with other trinkets. Uncle attends to each but doesn't languish over these, his lesser possessions: departing whims from distant ports of call. Uncle pauses briefly and points to the Alpaca rug that serves as his bedspread. "Picked it up in Peru." Both Niece and I reach out to feel the feathery softness of the Andean highlands. Uncle turns slowly, reviewing the loft for things he might have omitted, then bangs his pipe against an onyx ashtray and lets his visitor's curiosity amble.

"And this, Uncle?"

Uncle hedges a bit, peers across his desk to the bookcase where Niece is standing. She points to the long blade of another saber resting parallel to its metal sheath. Uncle glances at me, lifts his head like a deer sensing the wind for predators. Uncle composes himself, assumes he is safe, or perhaps does not know enough to feel threatened. Uncle has operated on assumptions for years and has never entertained the need to concede anything. Uncle goes on to talk about the saber. "It's grandfather's saber…from the Indian Wars."

"Grandfather fought in India?"

"No, dear, from our Indian Wars…." Uncle slices a glance at me. "In the 1860s and 70s."

Uncle can't quite decide if I might be Indian. The high cheek bones, the arched nose, the, here, perfectly staged downcast eyes, confuse him, but he hasn't lost his confidence, since I haven't balked once or asked for more explanation than was offered. And should I balk? After all, these are Uncle's souvenirs, and he will have to live with them.

"Grandfather passed the sword on to Dad when Father graduated from the Point…Dad gave it to me just before he died. I suppose you'll end up with it, dear." Uncle thinks of his niece as his own daughter.

The saber's blade is extremely long, disproportionately long as compared to its concave steel hand guard and wooden handle. The long blade is dull, lead dull and covered with freckled rust stains that less pragmatic eyes might envision as the hallowed souls of dead warriors.

The rainstorm has now become a nearly imperceptible mist that arches a rainbow that can be seen through Uncle's west window, just above resort mountain chairlift. "Maybe we better run, Uncle, now that the rain has let up." We take careful steps down the narrow stairway and down the hallway to where we've left our jackets, my towel, and summer straw hat. We make our way back toward the door when the dimming of the condo lights and rumble of thunder announce a renewed downpour. "Better wait a couple more minutes," Uncle suggests. And, as we stand halfway down the hallway, the lights surge and beam steady again. Uncle is poised beside the wall covered with the paraphernalia that is his military record.

"I hadn't noticed this before, Uncle…."

"Just got it, dear, it's a letter of commendation from the President. I now have one signed by every president since Eisenhower." Uncle begins to index over the items on the wall, his cavalry hat, his braided insignias, his countless merit badges, his First Infantry Division patch, its motto stitched in gold: "The Big Red One." Uncle points to photographs of Uncle astride Stateside desk jobs and overseas assignment desks. Next to three wooden plaques—1st, 2nd, and 3rd tours of duty in Southeast Asia—a picture of Uncle and his staff at Da Nang. The pose is dated

January 3, 1970. "This is just before I finished my third tour of duty in Viet Nam," he explains. Just before Uncle was sent Stateside to wait out his last year and a half before retirement.

The downpour subsides quickly. Uncle ends his reminiscence and concludes on the note that life in retirement seclusion, beneath resort mountain shadows and in between summer rainstorms has been very, very good to him.

My nice woman friend and I dash out. We drive back to Salt Lake in separate cars. I drive unconcerned about and detached from Uncle's memories. I'm mindful only of the sunlight breaking through the clouds and the golden stretch of wet highway that swerves and races the canyon back into the city.

A couple of weeks later I'm surprised by a phone call inviting me to a barbecue with the nice woman and the nice woman's friends. She still thinks herself safe. Perhaps she still is.

The barbecue is standard fare. We eat, drink, talk superficially amongst ourselves. The nice woman's friends aren't quite as trusting; they're a bit suspicious, a bit reticent that anyone born in a rude mud hovel might enjoy the company of those weaned on prairie folklore, Midwest practicality, California pop culture or East Coast horn rimmed glasses, tweed sports coats, and Levis.

The long summer evening falls and rolls away with the hum of cars and headlights going west, and the nice woman has lit up the backyard with patio lights and music while the barbecue chatter lingers in the shadows of the warm evening, flaming itself aglow in the sweet, cool irridescence of freely imbibed drink.

The nice woman's step bounces with delight as she rounds her patio furniture circle of friends and speaks to each or speaks to all as the inner warmth of wine lulls her thoughts to words. "Did I tell you about my first trip to Albuquerque?" The nice woman giggles and giddily swings a chair out from the table to seat herself. "Well, let me tell you what happened. We got lost...." The nice woman holds her hand to her lips to quell her urge to laugh at her ineptitude at following road maps. "We got lost just out of...Oh, what's-it-called?"

The nice woman's friends offer help: "Moab." "Price." "Monticello."

"No, it's ship, ship, ship something or other...."

"Shiprock!"

"Shiprock, that's it....Anyway, we got lost just outside of Shiprock and ended up taking some back road through the Navajo reservation. I don't know how much longer it took us to get to Albuquerque, but it was hours more.…Anyway, we had to stop for gas and we had to use the bathroom a couple of times. But, get this, at every place we stopped the Indians wouldn't let us use the john."

"What?" An incredulous din rounds the table.

"…yah, well, they'd either say the bathroom was broken or that they didn't have one—and we could see the signs 'Men and Women'—so we'd ask: 'Well, what are the doors on the side for?' And they'd say, oh well, that they have a bathroom but it was broken or that they'd lost the key.…Can you believe it? At this one place, this old Navajo lady told us that they had a bathroom but somebody had stolen the seat. Wow, I couldn't believe it!"

The nice woman's friends are visibly concerned: "Why?" "Were they telling the truth?" "Was it 'cause you're Anglo?"

"I guess so," answers the nice woman.

"Maybe, maybe, just maybe it had something to do with the Navajos' forced march to Fort Sumner," I say.

"What?"

"The Navajos' forced march, you know, when they were rounded up by the U.S. Cavalry and made to leave their homeland in the Four Corners and marched down to a reservation at Fort Sumner down in southern New Mexico.…"

Obviously the indulgence in the wine has loosened my tongue. I have spurned the nice woman and her friends. I have retorted at such an inopportune moment, and the disparagement is of so little consequence. The nice woman's friends must think me crass. After all, what do bathrooms have to do with a forced march in another century? And two wrongs…? Especially such disproportionate ones…? What, after all, should I have to say about it? Haven't the years softened the rough edges, polished the gruff exterior and healed over scars that aren't even mine? Perhaps.

"Well," the nice woman says finally, "maybe, but I wouldn't do that to anyone and I wouldn't expect anyone to do that to me.…"

Perhaps, perhaps, I muse to myself as I leave the barbecue. After all, it isn't you that has those old sabers rattling around in your closet, and Albuquerque by way of the Navajo reservation is such a long, long way from your makeshift prairie sod house…and I, perhaps, have only run this pen across this page to appease tradition.

UNCLE MIKE

Ruben Salaz-Marquez

NICOLAS enjoyed school and his second grade teacher, Sister Albert, but on a Saturday morning he would wake up at the crack of dawn, pull on his clothes, and walk next door to his grandparent's house where Uncle Mike lived. During the summer Uncle Mike would already be sitting on the bench behind the house, soaking up the early sun as it smiled over the mountains. Recently Nicolás was having to awaken Uncle Mike, who was sleeping later these crisp September mornings.

"Uncle Mike, get up, it's me, Nico," said the boy as he knocked loudly on the back door which opened to Mike's room.

"*¿Eh, qué pasa?*" came from within.

"It's me, Nico. You want to play *tejas*?" asked the boy in Spanish. The door opened after a few minutes. Snow-haired Uncle Mike peeped through the slightly opened door and smiled broadly. He had put on his coveralls but not his shirt and his arms and shoulders looked very heavily muscled to young Nico. "You want to play *tejas*?" asked the boy again as he juggled the large washers in his hand.

Uncle Mike didn't say anything but he saw the washers and nodded. The grin didn't get any smaller, just stayed the same as the door closed. Nico went to the place in the back yard where the holes for the *tejas* had been dug. He cleaned out some sand from inside the holes, which were about seven feet apart, then carefully removed the dirt from around the entrance, taking special precaution not to damage the hard surface. The washers had to be able to slide easily into the hole so the area had to be free of sand, pebbles, and all other obstacles. When the job was finished

Nico took a few practice shots, first at one hole then the other. *Tejas* was Nico's favorite game and he had spent many hours practicing over the summer. Indeed, he had become fairly proficient for a boy his age. Last weekend he had even beaten his older brother once, though the brother had tripped him on purpose after the game. Nico had become upset but there was nothing he could do since his brother was older and stronger. Nico had never beaten his brother at marbles but at least he had beaten him once at *tejas*.

Nico was busy aiming and throwing the washers at one hole, going to pick them up, then shooting at the other side when Uncle Mike came out of the house. He hadn't washed his face, Nico noticed, because there was sleepy sand around his eyes. Uncle Mike still smiled broadly and his arms swung up and down enthusiastically. He was wearing a hat that was almost too big for his head. "*¿Eh?*" he said as he walked up to Nico.

"Hi, Uncle Mike. Watch this," said the boy as he threw the washer carefully. The metal disc almost went into the hole but not quite. "Doggone it," exclaimed Nico as he prepared to let the other washer fly. He stepped back and carefully took aim, trying to make good his second effort. The washer sailed gracefully through the air but missed. Nico sniffed, shook his head slightly, then walked to shoot from the other side. "Okay, you try it, Uncle Mike."

Uncle Mike pulled something out of his pocket. At first Nico thought it was another washer but then he noticed it was much shinier. The man sailed it through the air and the missile landed a foot beyond the hole in the ground.

"Aw come on Uncle Mike, you can do better than that," said Nico as he went to pick up the miss. It was then he saw it was a brand new silver dollar, shinier and heavier than his washers. "Hey, where'd you get this?!" asked Nico excitedly. He had never seen Uncle Mike with money before. "Is it yours?"

Mike just grinned and swung his arms up and down.

"Can I shoot it once, just once?" Uncle Mike nodded, or at least Nico thought he did, so he prepared a careful shot. First he rubbed the silver dollar between his two hands, then he felt the ridges all around the coin. He looked at the target and in a graceful swing tossed the dollar straight into the hole. "Wowie!" yelled Nico as he raced to the hole and pulled out the shiny silver. "Did you see that, Uncle Mike? Perfect!" The boy gave the coin to his competitor and said, "Okay, your turn. Betcha can't do it."

Uncle Mike threw the washers, one at a time, then Nico picked them up and returned them to him so he could shoot again. Out of more than two dozen shots, Nico offering instructions each time, Uncle Mike only made one. Nico became exasperated. "You might as well be blinded," said Nico and he pulled Uncle Mike's hat down over his eyes.

The sudden loss of sight caused Uncle Mike to panic. His arms agitated up and down and sideways. He seemed to be struggling to breathe, and he moved as if the jaws of a huge animal were around his midsection.

Nico was immediately aware that something was seriously wrong. "Okay, okay, don't...." said Nico as he tried to take the hat off, but one of Mike's arms caught him on the chest and knocked him to the ground. Nico picked himself up and wasn't quite sure what to do when Uncle Mike put both hands to the brim of the hat and jerked it up.

Nico didn't know whether to laugh or cry. Uncle Mike looked so serious. He had struggled so hard against a little old hat! And had Uncle Mike really struck him? He had never been dangerous before but now he wasn't even smiling, his jaw agitating nervously up and down. Uncle Mike's eyes seemed to be watery, as if he was going to cry. Then Nico observed something he had never seen before: Uncle Mike's head was small, too small for the rest of his body, and it was kinda pointed at the top, sorta.

Nico's discovery made him forget about being knocked down. It made him forget that he never should have teased Mike in the first place by pulling his hat down over his eyes. He probably wouldn't have thought of doing it if his older brother hadn't done it to him some days before. Nico's only reaction was to say, "Uncle Mike," and to feel his own head with his right hand. No, it wasn't pointed, just flat. "I'm sorry, Uncle Mike, I shouldn't have pulled your hat. I was only playing." Nico spoke in English and Mike didn't understand it. "*Perdóname,* Uncle Mike. *Nomás estaba jugando,*" he repeated in Spanish.

"*No hagas eso,*" said Uncle Mike. His jaw still working nervously he turned and walked back toward the house, entered his room, and shut the door behind him.

Nico just stood for a minute, not knowing what he should do; then he decided to clean the holes of sand and practice some more. He discovered he still had Uncle Mike's silver dollar so he used it. The shiny coin flew gracefully through the air and went into the hole several times. Half an hour went by as the boy continued to practice alone.

"Nico, you want to come have breakfast with us?"

The boy looked up and saw his Auntie Lucy standing at her back door. Their house was next to his grandparent's.

"What are you having?"

"Pancakes."

"Sure!"

"Dust yourself off first."

Nico did the best he could to shake and slap off the loose dirt he had gotten on his overalls; then he walked over to his aunt's house. He glanced at Uncle Mike's back room but the door was still tightly shut.

"How long have you been up, *Nicolasito*?" asked Auntie Lucy as she poured some batter on the hot griddle.

"Since the sun," Nico replied simply as he came up to the stove and watched the air bubbles form on the pancakes as they began to cook.

"Playing marbles?"

"No, *tejas*. With Uncle Mike." Suddenly Nico remembered about Uncle Mike. "Auntie...." he began uncertainly.

"What?" asked the woman as she continued to pour out batter, turn the hotcakes, test the temperature of the syrup, put on coffee, get milk from the refrigerator, and set a place for Nico.

"Auntie....why is Uncle Mike....kinda...."

The aunt stopped and looked at her nephew. For a moment she didn't know what to say, how honest to be, how much young Nico would understand. Then she continued getting breakfast and said, "Uncle Mike is probably the finest person you'll ever meet in your whole life."

"But...."

"Yes, he's different from most people, isn't he," continued Auntie Lucy, "but he's different mostly in good ways."

"How old is he, Auntie?"

"Oh, I'd say he's about sixty or seventy."

"Sixty! Gee, he's old. But he has big muscles. His head is funny, sorta."

"There, eat your pancakes. Here's your milk." The woman then fixed herself a plate. "I'm going to eat before the rest of the tribe gets up." She knew she had to make Nico understand about Uncle Mike, but how? "Always be good to Uncle Mike, Nico, because he's close to God." The boy looked puzzled. "Yes, he is special in the eyes of God because he has never done any harm to anyone. He has a place ready for him in Heaven. The rest of us have to work for it but Uncle Mike has already won it."

"How come?" asked Nico.

"Because he is the way he is."

The boy pondered this for a moment. "How did he get that way?"

"A famous writer once said that everyone is the way God made him," said Auntie Lucy. "God made Uncle Mike the way he is and he has always been good and gentle. When I was growing up he was the best babysitter you could ever hope to find. We all lived on the ranch then. If Uncle Mike was taking care of someone nothing could happen to him, even on horseback."

"How come he can't play *tejas* or marbles?" asked Nico.

"When you get older you don't do a lot of things you used to. I'm younger than Uncle Mike and I don't play marbles either, though I used to love it."

"Why does he chew so hard when he's not even eating?" asked Nico as he continued his breakfast.

"Don't talk with food in your mouth, *hijito*. I'm sure there's an explanation but I don't know it. I love Uncle Mike, just like you do. God made him that way and he made you the way you are and me the way I am. It's good that we are a family and can love each other even if we're not exactly alike."

"You know why I like Uncle Mike?" asked Nico.

"No, why?"

"Because he always has time to play and I can win him."

"Well, you have to be careful that he doesn't get too tired. He can't do all the things that you do."

Nico reflected a while then said, "I always beat him at *tejas* or marbles but he really doesn't try very hard, even when I give him another chance."

"Uncle Mike is like a saint and we can all learn from him if we want to," said Auntie Lucy. "I'm going to fix his breakfast tray. You want to take it to him?"

"Sure," replied Nico. *Like a saint*, thought the boy. He wondered if all saints had white hair and pointed heads. He felt his own head and wondered if its flatness and black hair would keep him away from sainthood. But maybe there was hope: the only other saints he had ever seen were the statues in the church and none of them looked like Uncle Mike.

"Here," said Auntie Lucy when the tray was ready, "take this to

Uncle Mike. Be careful with the coffee. It's very hot, don't spill it on yourself."

Nico took the tray and walked carefully out the door and across the yard, the tray grasped firmly in both hands. His shoulders were hunched slightly in an effort at protection as he walked. When he got to Uncle Mike's door he laid the tray on the outside bench and knocked.

"Uncle Mike, it's me."

"Eh?" came from within, then the door opened.

"*¿Estás listo pa' comer?*" asked Nico.

Uncle Mike smiled broadly. He was still wearing his hat. Nico picked up the tray, took it inside and laid it on Mike's table. The man sat down, smiled at Nico, and began to eat his pancakes and drink the steaming coffee. Nico sat down on the bed and looked at Uncle Mike, hard, then he thought of the statues in church. There was St. Michael and St....saint...the one with all the animals and birds. Ah well, he had a round head anyway, and bald in the middle. What was it with the heads of all these saints anyway? Maybe he could be a priest if they didn't mind his flat head and black hair.

Uncle Mike ate heartily, and noisily, thought Nico, especially when he slurped his coffee. The boy then reached into his pocket and pulled out Mike's silver dollar. Nico placed it carefully on the tray and Uncle Mike smiled as he took it and put the coin in his own pocket.

The boy put his arm around Uncle Mike and said, "You mustn't eat with your hat on." Gently he took the hat off the man's head and hung it on the coat rack in the corner. Uncle Mike watched the hat carefully as it left his head and journeyed to the rack. When he saw that it was safe he continued his breakfast.

"You like coffee?" asked Nico.

Uncle Mike seemed to nod.

"My daddy makes it every morning and I'm going to bring you a cup." The man smiled. Nico's eyes suddenly lit up. "St. Francis! St. Francis is the one with the baldy head! Do you know him, Uncle Mike?"

T.BOB IN THE YARD
(for P.G.M)

Robert Masterson

T.Bob felt good to have made it into the yard on his own. He had always liked to surprise himself with hidden strengths and knowledge and it began to look as if that afternoon was going to hold many opportunities for surprise. For instance, T.Bob had completely forgotten about shock and what he had learned about it in 4H first aid class until that very afternoon. It was true that he had a working definition of "shock" that had mostly been construed from medical shows on the television, but that wouldn't have helped him much. When he really needed it, though, all those facts from the green and grey Red Cross Manual had come back to him as clearly as if he held the book in his hand. He could see its illustrations and he began to think in its typeface. He had blocked off arterial bleeding (and thought "see Fig.11d"), had calmly constructed a makeshift tourniquet from materials readily at hand (baling wire with a corn cob for a winder), and had buttoned his jacket up to his neck for extra warmth before he passed out. From shock.

That seemed like—and had been—hours before, though, and T.Bob had awakened to crawl out of the barn's gloom into the yard. He pleasantly surprised himself with his ability to appreciate the fine day he lay in the middle of. The air was sharp and crisp, smelled sanitary and hygenic that late in October. There was little more than a hint of the bitter, plains driven chill approaching; the breeze that rattled yellow leaves was only the mild stepchild of the fierce cutters waiting for December. T.Bob felt smug that he could rise above his other woes to enjoy the rare autumn afternoon. He remained smug even as he fainted for the third time.

IT HAD BEEN an early summer day. They had been going out together since the Valentine's Dance and had stayed together after school let out. They had often come up to the Pools, an abandoned bath-house in the foothills, to be alone together.

They had finished the sandwiches that Colleen had made and were lying back close enough to almost touch. T.Bob had removed his shirt for the sun. Suddenly, and with strange decisiveness, Colleen had sat up and taken off her blouse and bra. She lay back down in a manner that clearly dared T.Bob to make a big deal out of her tits, to be immature and uncool. As if he hadn't spent nearly every Friday and Saturday night for months trying to establish some kind of position on the very frontier she so casually displayed unguarded. He felt her action might have been some kind of trick; he already knew that she had changed her tactics and had strategically maneuvered him into the defensive position. Her studied nonchalance forced him to accept her naked breasts in some new, nonerotic way. He had to sit up to hide his erection, an erection similar to the ones he had on occasion deliberately pressed against her thigh or stomach. He didn't know what to do with the one he had at the moment, though, and wished deeply for it to go away.

"Does this bother you?" she asked him.

"Nope. Does what bother me?" was all he could manage as a reply and, to prove it, turned to face her. Before he realized his error, she had clearly seen his eyes wobble wildly between her face and her breasts, between his intentions and his instincts. She blushed and rolled to grab her shirt, to cover her nakedness. He, it had been shamefully apparent, had made her feel embarrassed by her own body. His shallow, crude desire had spoiled her beauty.

T.Bob felt he had been taught a lesson and wondered if he was really ready for this kind of school.

THE SUN had obviously moved when T.Bob regained consciousness and the ground had begun to pick up some of its warmth. It was pleasant to listen to the noises (especially since the shredder was no longer running. Out of gas. Or jammed on something, thought T.Bob with just the right amount of grimness) and be warm. After a while, T.Bob decided to check his dressing. By squirming onto his side, he could bend and look and touch the feed sack he had wrapped around the place where his calf muscle had been. The bleeding had slowed down and the wad of burlap was only spongy rather than dripping with blood. "So far, so good," he grunted as he twisted the cob to tighten the wire of the tourniquet. T.Bob knew the leg was pretty much a goner and, even though he didn't like to resign himself to that, he knew the overall situation required him to pull in his priorites a little bit. If he wanted to save his ass, he knew he was going to have to give up the leg. What he could see of it that wasn't messed up was blue but he was certain that if he tried to restore circulation he would just be wasting blood needed elsewhere. It seemed typical of the kind of choices he had been making lately. A quick, sharp depression sapped most of the heat out of T.Bob and he choked back his tears and decided to rest where he was for a while. That kind of October day often reminded him of school because it was at this time of year that school had finally become real. The last blush of novelty had worn off entering a new grade, the crayons had begun to lose their factory points, the odor of mimeograph no longer intoxicated. The excitement of a new schedule with new classmates had dulled into another year's monotony and Christmas was far at the end of a darkening tunnel of days. It was the time of year when he and his friends had almost frantically prolonged their play, insisting there was enough light as they lost the ball in gathering blackness, attempting to stop the light from leaving. It was a season of vague dissatisfaction that was heightened because it ran so contrary to his elders' hopes and images of what childhood was, what childhood should be. T.Bob had often felt defective when Halloween appeared scant compensation, Thanksgiving arbitrary, and Christmas hysterical. He wondered if something was skewed in the holidays or inside himself. The feeling returned while he lay in the yard halfway between the barn and the back porch, losing his left leg and—perhaps— bleeding to death.

...AND REMEMBERING THE MAJOR SHIFT. Colleen was waiting for him when he got back from filling the propane bottles in town. She hadn't looked pleased to see him but she hadn't looked pleased to see him for many weeks. T.Bob just tried to keep out of her way without disappearing altogether. The fact that she was obviously waiting to see him seemed like some kind of good sign. He tried to play it cool even as he walked straight toward the porch without unloading the bottles but his heart couldn't help but visibly drop when she spoke.

"I've done a terrible thing," came out of Colleen's mouth in a rush and didn't stop until she'd said everything she'd planned out to say. "I know it's a terrible thing and I'm not asking you to forgive me for doing it but I am asking you to understand how such a thing could happen and that it's not completely all my fault. I'm asking you to understand and to move on and away from it together with me. I'm pregnant."

T.Bob's heart moved up a notch at her last words; it started beating again, and he waited for her to finish explaining why being pregnant was such a terrible thing.

"It ain't your baby, T.Bob."

That was the place where T.Bob's heart was finally devoured and he would always after think that the last words he ever spoke face-to-face to his wife had been hours before and about propane. He walked past Colleen into the kitchen but he didn't do anything once he was there.

"T.Bob?" she asked as if she hadn't been sure.

T.Bob gently pressed his head against the door of the refrigerator.

"T.Bob? Honey?" she tried again and that was all she tried. She went upstairs and T.Bob turned on the TV and got a beer from the refrigerator. Later, he sat down. After she had gone and after the whine of the El Camino's overloaded engine had faded away, T.Bob went to the screen door.

"That's okay, honey," he said. "I guess it really doesn't matter that much."

T.Bob had begun to feel that what had happened to him when his foot slipped into the shredder was almost inevitable, as if all the errors he had made and had been making were just pointing toward this particular disaster. It just didn't seem that unexpected when he reviewed the situation. Either this or something like it had begun to seem unavoidable. If he had said something when she was leaving, Colleen would not have gone and would have been in the house and would have heard him scream when the blades of the shredder had begun to rip away the flesh and into the bone of his leg. Of course, if he had said something and Colleen hadn't left, he wouldn't have been drinking at 7:45 in the morning and wouldn't have been drunk enough at 8:30 to let his leg slip into the shredder in the first place. Some pretty small things had really snowballed and he felt even dumber for not having said at least something if not the perfect thing instead of just listening to the noise of her leaving him.

He began to try to guess what she was doing at that particular moment and decided the odds weren't bad that she was thinking about him. If he could get into the house, he could get the phone and call her.

"You're kidding," he reminded himself. "You'll call the Sheriff's

Department and get an ambulance here pronto. Then you'll call Colleen."

T.BOB LAY IN THE LIVING ROOM and his feelings of accomplishment for having made it were diminished by the holes he saw there. There was the hole where the loveseat/dual recliner had been and the hole where the entertainment center had been and, he sheepishly remembered, the hole where the cordless phone had been. He had been thinking about getting another phone to go there, a regular phone that dialed and rang rather than the antennaed, beeping instrument Colleen had packed into the El Camino. He had tried to ignore the fact that she was handling their property in that manner and had done nothing to either hinder or help her. Nevertheless, she had managed to get away with quite a bit of stuff as other holes in the fixtures and furnishings of other rooms attested. T.Bob rolled onto his side and tried to think about the afternoon she'd packed up, about all the stuff she'd wrestled out into the yard all by herself. She'd come into the kitchen where he was watching the Albuquerque weather man and his vegetables. Colleen stood between him and the little B&W portable they had bought at WalMart for $59. She held the keys to the El Camino in her right hand and the keys to the Jimmy in her left hand. He tried to formulate an answer carefully but she didn't wait for him. The question on her face changed into a decision and she tossed the Jimmy's keys into his lap. She picked up the suitcase and the paper sack that were the last things to load up. T.Bob watched her leave and listened to her start to throw everything in the El Camino but that was about it.

Some of the things she had chosen to take surprised him (usually at the instant he realized that they were gone). He would be in the kitchen and realize that she had taken the can opener. He'd stand there for a while holding the can of tamales or creamed corn or whatever and try to figure out if she had done it to be mean or if she really did have some claim on an appliance like that. He'd be sitting on the toilet and realize that she had taken the blue plaster fishes that had hung beside the towel rack and wonder that she had felt such attachment to them. They seemed weird things to drag around.

He was no less surprised, though, by things she had left behind. He couldn't be 100% sure, but it seemed that she hadn't taken any shoes. He was sure she had been wearing sneakers when she left but the rest of them all appeared to still be in the closet. After he returned to the house from an errand, he would often check the closet first thing to see if she had been by to get some shoes. He wondered what she was wearing on her feet and found it hard to imagine her going to Payless to start her new life.

T.BOB SNAPPED BACK from his reverie and concentrated on the phone again. He felt guilty and lazy that he hadn't just gotten a nice black, plain, rotary dial kind of telephone. Instead, he had gotten into the habit of driving to Stuckey's to make his calls from the payphone. It was nine miles one way and, since most of his calls were to Colleen and—according to Colleen—"annoying," the drive kept him thinking about the importance of his calls before he made them. The lack of incoming calls had kept his hopes up and focused on seeing the El Camino pull up to the house because she hadn't been able to call and couldn't wait any longer to talk. She would want to talk about coming back if she drove all the way out to the house. When he called her, T.Bob always suggested that they meet someplace else, someplace closer to what he called her "town house." He'd kept asking and she'd kept refusing and after awhile she stopped waiting for him to ask and would just hang up.

Anyway, T.Bob reminded himself, he needed to figure out how he was going to get to Stuckey's. It seemed funny that getting to Stuckey's had become so important. He tried to imagine that all he really needed was a pecan log and rubber tomahawk. He was going to have to drag himself back out of the house, across the yard, and into the truck. Driving seemed to be about 50/50 with the leg dangling the way it was but he felt confident that, if he made it out to the truck, he would be able to figure something out. The only thing to worry about was getting the keys down from the counter. T.Bob wanted to get it over with as quickly as he could but it would be good practice for getting into the truck. He had to pull himself up with his arms, which he did, grab the keys with one hand, which he did, and try to break his fall with his other hand, which he really wasn't able to do. It was a comfort, though, to know that he had succeeded and wouldn't have to try again as he slipped back into unconsciousness.

...AND THERE HAD BEEN a winter night about a year and a half after they had graduated and he had gotten in from a late date with Colleen. It had been late because he'd worked late at the store with a load of new products; he'd missed the entire basketball game, and he'd had to drive around until he'd found her at the DQ. The DQ was where the adults hung out; the Rocket was for the high schoolers. He'd apologized, finished her fries, bought her some more, and taken her out to a hill. They looked at the lights of the town below them; she told him about the game, and she told him a little of the DQ gossip. A whole crew of their friends from school were adults, too, and were getting married, getting babies, and getting unhappy. It was disturbing for T.Bob and he often felt sad that things were turning out the way they were. It was strange to feel nostalgic when the high schoolers went by on their way to the Homecoming Dance and be looking foward to the Lion's Club Dance at the same time. They had moved into a different world and T.Bob wasn't sure if he'd gotten everything out of the last one. The new one wasn't what he had expected it to be at all and he wondered if he had really prepared himself for it. He squinted through the dashboard light and looked hard at Colleen. The soft glow from the radio looked good on her and he had begun to realize that she was the best thing that was going to happen to him, that she was the prettiest and the smartest and the best-to-be-around girl that was ever going to pay attention to him. That evening, after the date, T.Bob realized that he was planning on marrying her.

IT HAD BEEN A NICE, simple wedding and the reception had been at the Lion's Club. They spent their wedding night on the road and their honeymoon in Corpus Christi, Texas. They returned and lived in her friend's parents' trailer until they started renting the house where T.Bob woke up. He remembered about his leg but then saw the ring of keys in front of his nose and cheered up. He waited for his head to completely clear and, when it had, he moved around to get the keys, got them, and headed for the door. It was less painful now to drag his mangled leg behind him and that made it easier. He felt weaker, though, and his hands had a difficult time finding good purchase on the floor and that made it harder. The sun was hanging above the horizon and the kitchen and yard beyond seemed brighter, warmer, redder. T.Bob tumbled down the porch steps and twisted his leg underneath himself. The lack of pain saddened him and he thought about what it was going to be like with only one leg. He realized he was going to need a lot of taking care of and wondered who he was going to get to do it. He smiled and found it easier to pull himself along the dirt of the yard. T.Bob set his sights on the GMC parked at the top of the incline and started making tracks. In what seemed like no time, he had reached the truck and began to haul himself up to open the door. Things seemed to be getting easier all the time and the sunset was gorgeous. He got up into the cab, got the keys into the ignition, and thought about how he was going to jump start the truck. The battery had been dead for weeks ever since the night he had left the lights and the radio on, the night he had stumbled drunk into the house after coming back from Stuckey's and another thwarted, late night reconciliation attempt. It had seemed easiest to just park the truck on the incline. The sunset was looking good and T.Bob tried to remember other good sunsets he had seen but it seemed that sunsets might be one of the things he just couldn't remember that well. He could remember the color sweater Colleen had worn at the JV Sledding Party over five years ago (blue with a grey star pattern) and that she had worn a 14K pendant he had given her and that she had remembered to tuck the pendant into the sweater before she sat on the tobaggon behind him. He could remember that later the same evening she had asked him for the time. She had seemed so genuinely heartbroken when he told her how late it had gotten that his own heart had shifted in sympathy. T.Bob felt stupid that he could remember all that and not remember a single time he had watched the sun go down when he felt certain he must have seen it do that hundreds of times. He joggled the transmission into neutral, jammed down the clutch, shifted into second, and put his hand on the emergency brake. For a second, he couldn't remember which leg had gotten chewed up and then it didn't matter because things seemed to be going so well. He released the hand brake, let the truck build up some speed, and popped the clutch while he scrambled to hit the accelerator with something useful. The engine coughed into action, the radio he had again left on blasted a weather rundown from Santa Rosa, and T.Bob turned on the headlights for the drive over to Stuckey's.

EDNA'S PIE TOWN

Debra Hughes-Blanks

WHAT'S your favorite time of day?" Laverne asked.

I said, "It's sundown." I always get a little misty when the sun shoots streaks of pink into the evening sky. But I didn't think about that too long because I knew Laverne was leading me into something. Sure enough, the very next day she came by and as slick as could be pasted up enough paper to cover a roadside billboard. Now, layers of hot pink squeeze like cake icing between shades of orange, covering one whole wall in my cafe. She told me the names of all the colors. There's Magenta, Peach, Rusty Nail, and Sedona Sand. There's a man on a horse: his silhouette washed in pink. A cowboy hat shades his face, and I've wondered at times just what the man might look like. If he ever rode off my wall and stepped into my cafe, I might have the surprise of my life by laying eyes on the most handsome fellow ever in Pie Town. But for now, he rides through the colors toward the cactus with owls in their arms, where eyes peep out like shiny quarters.

Sometimes Laverne knows things I don't; I say it's blind inspiration, but I go along with her anyway. She gets me into things I'd never dream of or do on my own. The day I visited Laverne's Curios and Books when she was redecorating led me to my unexpected change.

"You should be happy, Laverne," I told her as she balanced herself, big hips, bosoms and all, on the ladder to paste a corner of paper over the last visible spot of the faded green-blue wall. "Now your customers won't mistake your store for a morgue," I said, looking at all four walls covered by yellow paper with streaks of royal blue, purple, and orange going every which way.

Laverne turned and pointed at me from her perch. A silver ring shaped like a snake coiled around her fat finger. That ring could give me the shivers when I looked at it. It came from a world I knew nothing about and sometimes made Laverne seem like some magical witch.

"You shouldn't talk, Edna," she said. "Your cafe isn't exactly gay Paree."

Laverne had the only place in town where a person could buy a book. She had romances, westerns, some cookbooks, and books on astrology, which I never messed with. She carried magazines, too. Her new decor wasn't just to bring in customers, I thought; there was something else at work. I figured she was cheering herself up and had just gotten tired of those old blue walls staring at her every day. That's why I gave her the OK to do my cafe; I was due for a little cheering.

When my steady customers first came in after the new paper was up, they said, "What are you doing, Edna—getting uptown on us?"

Stew, the local handyman, cocked his grey, burr head toward the cowboy. "Why I've never seen a pink cowboy. He sure is cute," he snorted. I would have kicked Stew in his cranky knee, but the counter was between me and him. A remark like Stew's could scare these men away. So I flipped an extra three silver dollar pancakes onto everybody's plates and prayed.

"Now fellas, a little bit of updating won't change my cooking," I told them. And sure enough it didn't. I didn't lose one customer. Now when they come in for breakfast, they sit on the stools at the counter, their backs turned to the pink cowboy as if he weren't even there. For me, I have my sunsets when I want.

I don't look like much, so I know my customers don't come in for something extra. A while ago I heard some kids passing my cafe, and they called it the "Turkey Lady's." It hurt at first because I had always prided myself on having shiny red hair and keeping myself neat as a pin and never dreamed I even resembled a turkey. Then just a few days ago I heard it again. These kids were screaming to each other from across the street saying, "Hey, do you want to go to the Turkey Lady's for a cinnamon bun?" "Have you seen her fag cowboy yet?"

I had never thought of my cowboy as having any type of manly weakness. When the kids came busting into my cafe, I looked at the cowboy's silhouettte and still couldn't see how they'd ever call him queer. But later that day, when I was washing up, I looked in the mirror. I patted at my hair pulled back in a bun. My blue eyes were magnified a bit too much behind my pink tinted glasses. My neck was scrawny. I did look a little birdlike, though I didn't like to think of myself in that way. I've always been lightweight, and now my chest caves in enough to make me look older than fifty. I blame it on bending over my grill for so many years.

I keep my cafe open mornings. I can't compete with the fellow down the road who sells pies at the truck stop. His daddy was the man who gave Pie Town its name by putting up signs with pictures of his pies along the highway on both sides of town. Truckers, ranchers, and travelers passing through flock over to the Red Chief Truck Stop for a piece of lemon meringue or apple pie. I even snuck over there once for a taste just to see. It's all show. The lemon pie was more meringue than lemon, too sweet for me. I won't fight big business, so I open my cafe at dawn and serve eggs sunny-side up with sausage patties and pancakes until noon. Then I close my doors.

Ten years ago, I had a girl working for me. We could have done real well together if she had stayed. She drops in now and then and sends me Christmas cards she paints herself. She went and married a young Indian man. The day she left—I surprised myself—I could have hugged her then and there, I would miss her so. But I kept my hands on my little bony hips and never let on. After she left, I moped around like an abandoned old dog. "Stop this," I'd tell myself when I'd find myself standing over the grill staring at nothing while an egg spattered and popped.

Antonia had a real way with the customers. She'd work fast and quiet the way people like. Even though I never said, I knew we could stay open afternoons with her help. One day after the breakfast crowd had left, Antonia was counting the money in the register. I had scraped all the leftover grease from the grill into a Folger's coffee can, put foil over the top, and shoved the can way back on the bottom shelf like I always do. When I stood up, I looked straight at Antonia. I felt a little dizzy from standing up so fast and I held onto the counter ledge. Her waist was willow thin and she had put in darts to take up some of the slack in her brown polyester smock. Her breasts curved out just enough. I felt my own breasts tingle. Antonia didn't even notice my stare, thank the Lord; she walked nearby, bent down where I kept the paper napkins, and reached for a pile to fill the napkin containers along the counter. As she bent down, her smock fell away from her chest enough to reveal a pale peach slip of a bra. I pounded way down low. I wanted to outline the slight rise of her round breasts with my fingertips. Thank God the phone rang just then, because I don't know what I would have done it if hadn't. I rushed to answer it.

While I was on the phone, Antonia took her purse and sweater and left. I hung up and the cafe was quiet. Just the ticking of the stove as it cooled broke the silence. I felt pretty rattled. My Lord, what had come over me? How could I ever want to kiss the flesh of another woman in the same way I had always dreamed of with a man?

Now all of this happened way before Laverne ever thought of painting a cowboy on my cafe wall. And when I think about it, Laverne was picking up on something back then that I couldn't admit. I bet she knew I was needing someone in the worst kind of way. It took some time for her thoughts to brew until she came up with my pink cowboy, who never leaves even if I stare my eyes out at him.

WHEN I GET TO THINKING ABOUT MY LIFE, it seems like I've always lived at the J-Bar-J Trailer Court. After Daddy died, Momma and her sister, Millie, and I sold our house in Socorro and moved out here. Daddy had bought some property, which one day we were going to ranch. But he died too soon. So Momma and Millie decided they'd still go along with the plan. I was thirteen when we moved here. At that time there was a filling station, grocery store, a First Baptist Church, and a few ranch houses anywhere from five to thirty miles away. The community didn't even have a name yet. One of the first things my mother said was that this place needed a cafe. We moved in with the preacher and stayed there until a man, saying he sold trailer houses, came through town: one of the hottest items in the housing market, as he put it. Before long we had moved into one, and so had two other families, and that was the start of the J-Bar-J.

It was next to the grocery store. We planted poplars and grass on the dusty flat desert land and, sure enough, everything grew. I guess Daddy had left Momma enough money to do almost anything she wanted, because in half a year her cafe was built, and someone put in a drugstore next door.

Momma's sister Millie couldn't stand living in a town so small it didn't have a name—everyone shared the same post office box number at the nearest post office in Datil, twenty-five miles away. So she left. Momma and I worked the cafe. Doing that took all of Momma's strength and, after a year, she never mentioned the land that brought us here. I liked it fine at the J-Bar-J and serving Momma's food at our cafe made me proud. As if blown by the howling winds, the land slipped out of our minds, the ranch house we would have built melted, soaked up by cactus and tufts of brush.

We never had a name for our cafe either. We never needed one. All of the ranch hands knew our good cooking. If a traveler stopped at the filling station and asked about a place to eat, he'd be given directions to our cafe. Even though the business was going well, something was wrong with Momma. I think she was tired of living without Daddy; the year I turned fifteen, she died, they say of a heart attack.

Though it about broke my heart to go back into that cafe where Momma's ladles, pots and pans, and aprons were, I did, and I ran the cafe by myself. Some of the neighbor ladies came in to help. I figured I'd ask them if I could hire any of their girls to help wait tables and clean. Two ranch girls about my age came to work the next week. I couldn't pay them much, but that was OK by them.

One day a man came to town and moved into our trailer court. Sweet smells of baking pies came out of his trailer windows. The next thing I knew his pies were for sale in the grocery store. Then he was building signs so big you could see them from one end of town to the other. He painted pictures of his pies on these signs, and soon enough he moved his pies to the Red Chief Truck Stop, where truckers would stop for homemade afternoon treats. I knew something was coming and had my name painted on the picture window on the front of my cafe. "Edna's" scrawled across the glass in bright blue paint.

Sooner than I would have liked, people nicknamed our community and the name stuck. My first tinge of jealousy rose in my throat. I was a citizen of Pie Town.

Then Antonia walked into the cafe and applied for a job. Her long brown hair was pulled back in a braid and freckles spotted her face where the sun had caught her.

"Have you ever waited tables?" I asked her.

"No," she shook her head.

"We'll give it a try for a week," I said and handed her a wash cloth. "You can start now."

Antonia fit right in. She was a smart girl. Sometimes, though, I'd catch her looking out the picture window with a stare that seemed to take her far away.

"When I get too much of pigs in a blanket, hash browns, and

sunny-side ups, that one on the cross keeps me going," I told her one day when I caught her dreaming. I tucked my grey strands of hair back under my net and pointed with a metal spatula dripping with grease to a painted wooden crucifix nailed to the wall behind the cash register.

While I spoke, Antonia turned from the window and looked at my spatula, then to the spot on the wall. Her whole face changed. Life seemed to burst into her cheeks and eyes. She had returned to my one-room cafe. She wiped off a table by the window where she stood.

"I have an Indian seed pot I dug up from our old ranch when I was a kid," she said. "I keep it with me wherever I go. Sometimes, at night, I sit in my room at Mr. Deaver's and stare at the fine lines that creep through my pot like a spider's web. My pot has a heart and there's one line that overpowers the rest. It snakes from the heart to the edge." Antonia stopped cleaning and looked at me. "I guess my pot keeps me going, too."

This was a new one for me. "Well, whatever works for a person...." I shrugged and turned back to cleaning the grill.

Antonia continued, "You know, that one line is as red as the clay on our ranch. When I look at the line, I remember how dust would billow behind us whenever we'd drive to the house on our road wide enough for one pick-up truck. I always liked it when Dad would pull up to the house and I'd run in before the red cloud could catch me."

The ranch she talked about was the Stapleton's now. It's where Antonia had been born and had lived until she was sixteen. The ranching business got tough for her mom and dad, she said. They sold it and moved to Fort Worth. After Antonia finished high school, she caught a Greyhound bus back to Pie Town. She rented a room at Mr. Deaver's Western Inn, one of our town's two motels, and got a job with me. She said someday she was going to buy back a piece of that land.

Though I never told her, I knew there was no way she'd do that with what I paid her. On payday I'd give her an envelope of seventy-five dollars cash that couldn't buy two feet of that red earth. I always felt bad about that girl not getting her home back.

One day, after work, I walked to Laverne's, a couple of stores down Main Street from my cafe. When I opened the door, the string of tiny brass bells tied to the inside knob tinkled. Laverne was sitting behind a wooden counter where she kept her money and orders and receipts. She sat, a fat lady with her hair pulled in a bun on top of her head, her cheeks ruddy, and wearing a smock made from striped beach towels.

To look at her, I would never have guessed that she and I would be friends. But we had stuck it out for years in Pie Town. We had been the first to come and among the longest to stay. Laverne always had great stories to tell about planets, horoscopes, and past loves, all of which I only half believed. I knew the expanse of the mesa surrounding Pie Town is what had pushed us together in the beginning and we just stayed friends, out of need, I suppose.

I admit I had looked forward to Laverne's newest discovery, Tarot cards. I'd never let anyone catch me even touching a deck, so I'd go to Laverne's when her store closed. We'd spend hours behind her wooden counter, sitting on stools with a board stretched from Laverne's knees to mine when she read the Tarot. One card appeared almost every time. When I asked Laverne about it, she said, "I've come to expect this one." She pointed to the card with a golden castle floating above clouds. "It pops up for me, too, and for everyone else, but not in the same card pattern as yours. You're looking for something, Edna, something you might not want to know about and I think it has to do with love.

Oh, those cards were right about love. I didn't want to be passed by, but there was no use in arguing. Who'd want to love me, a skinny old turkey lady? After that session, I lost interest in Tarot cards. That occult stuff can make a person crazy, I thought.

After the door had closed behind me and the bells stopped ringing, Laverne looked up from a book she was reading which she had bent until its back was completely broken.

"Hello, Edna," she said.

"Hi, Laverne. What's the news today?"

"The Dentons are having a cowboy funeral for Emmet, their hired hand. So he's going out on a wooden plank, pulled on a wagon. The whole Denton clan is going to ride alongside to the church."

The Dentons were among the three biggest families owning ranches spanning thousands and thousands of acres. The family had ranched the land before I had come here. Bob Denton, in his seventies now, took the ranch over from his dad. Bob started something big around here. Cowboy polo. Riders from around the county would compete in teams at the posse grounds. I remember seeing Emmet right along with Bob on the same team beating after a ball. Men and horses alike would leave the arena bloodied and mud spattered.

"I'm sorry to hear that about Emmet," I said to Laverne and glanced around the store. In the back sat a young woman. All I could see was the point of her nose peeking from the sweep of hair as she bent over a book. It took a while before I realized it was Antonia.

"What's she doing back there?" I asked Laverne. My voice sparked. I couldn't hide my jealousy. "Is she one of your new disciples?"

Laverne laughed. "I had nothing to do with it. She came in asking if she could just browse, and I said, 'Sure, Hon.'"

Antonia sat on the floor leaning against two cardboard boxes piled on top of each other in what Laverne had labeled the "Metaphysics" area. Antonia read as if everything in the book were new to her. I couldn't just go up and interrupt to say hello, so I bought a pack a *Doublemint* from Laverne and left.

I felt like some ninny getting all upset over seeing Antonia with Laverne. What was going on with me? Laverne was my good friend; what did I think she was going to do, steal Antonia from me? I was sick with myself for cherishing Antonia so, like something I had never had.

At work the next morning, I played cold; after all, I was the boss and Antonia was just my help. I couldn't let Antonia keep getting at me. She asked me if I had ever heard of reincarnation and energy that travels from person to person. I said, "A little, why?"

"I read about it yesterday and I swear my Indian seed pot is a message from someone. I remember the day I first held the pot after having carefully dug it out of the ground. When I held the piece of pottery, Edna, I knew I was connected to something bigger than I had ever imagined."

Antonia pulled a box of butter squares out of the refrigerator, then carried a flat of eggs over to the grill where I stood. "It's real strong," she said. I looked at her wondering what she meant. "The day I found the pot, my best friend was with me. We were digging side by side. The pot was my territory because I had uncovered it first and she dug next to me looking for another pot or just shards. When I lifted the tiny thing from the earth, a piece was missing. Kara tried to fit one of her shards into the hole. I've never been like this, but I pulled away from her and guarded my treasure, afraid she might break it."

She continued, "Edna, I felt crazy like our mutt dogs on the ranch, who would loll side by side in the sun outside our back door, then spring like wolves with lips curled and teeth snapping, ready to tear each other apart whenever a bone was pitched to them."

While Antonia talked, she had picked up a dish rag and held it crumpled between her fists, holding tight until her bones seemed close to breaking right through her skin at the knuckles. She watched me while I greased up the grill for the first customers and when I turned my head to look at her now and then to let her know I was listening, she looked at me but I don't think she saw me. She was gone again.

She finally zeroed in on the rag she was holding and threw it on the counter and walked to the cash register, where she cracked open rolls of quarters and dimes. "The feeling's real strong in me. I know it comes from more than the pot. It's the ranch. That land will never let go of its grip on me."

I used to have plans for my land. The day Antonia left, I almost let them out. I almost told her I owned land we could build a house on together, that she could move out of Mr. Deaver's. She and I would turn the acres into a place of our own. But I didn't know if Antonia would have cared for my land. Long ago people probably passed right over it looking for shelter and clay from which they could make cooking pots and vessels. Antonia's old ranch had that red clay. It makes the soil look as rich as can be, but a plow can never cut through it, it's so hard.

I didn't know how to tell her my plans. I was afraid that if I did, she might have laughed. A pretty girl would want nothing of an old bird like me even if I offered her the very thing that had driven her back to Pie Town in the first place.

I got to thinking about the land my daddy had bought. One day, after I closed the cafe I drove my Rambler to the land. It was farther west and on the other side of the highway from Antonia's old ranch. I pulled off of the highway onto the rutted road that I hadn't been on for a year. I'd come out every year just to look, to make sure those taxes were paying for something, even if it was dust and rolling hills of sage. Jack rabbits the size of small dogs tore in front of my car. I crossed two dried gullies and then climbed to a rise. I got out of the car and cupped my hands around my eyes to shield them from the low sun's glare. The land spread in front of me and went all the way to the far hills in the western horizon, the same way it did when I first came here. The earth was pale tan and spotted with sage and buffalo grass. The wind blew some of my hair loose from its bun. Then the wind blew with fury. To escape it, I tugged the car door open and shot into the front seat. Without my help, the door slammed closed. Even though gnarled or spiky plants grew out there, the whole place seemed dead. Like a ghost, a dust devil danced, weaving in half circles across the mesa and sending dried tumbleweed high in the air.

The sun hung above the horizon at an angle where it made the western sky shine white like a florescent light. I couldn't look straight ahead without squinting my eyes until they were almost closed. Just a few more minutes and the sun would be down; it would turn my land soft with a red and orange glow, I told myself. I took off my glasses and rubbed the sand out of my eyes, then readjusted my glasses on my nose. I looked in the rearview mirror to see if they were straight. My lenses were powdered with fine dust and my eyes stared out red and watery. Strands of hair stood up all over my head with static electricity. I pushed the mirror up so I couldn't see my reflection.

I cared about my looks. I don't know why because I had only been romanced by a man once in my life, and that was by Jess. He had been around Pie Town as long as I had. When he first came, he worked the Dodd ranch, east of town, then he took over at the Stapleton's. He once asked me to a dance at church, but I had nothing of him. He wasn't my type with his wind crusted hands and nails that never came quite clean. Except for my father, I had never loved a man. The right one might come along, I'd tell myself. But deep down when I was real honest with myself, I think I had lost hope.

I stayed until the sun was gone. No colors: no Sedona Sand or Rusty Nail streaming across the low sky, no cowboy either. I backed my car around. It rattled and bumped over dried ruts: probably tracks of some men out working cattle that had strayed. I thought that maybe I should fence this land. Keep people out.

Sometimes, Antonia drops by for coffee. "That's nice," she said when she first saw my sunset wallpaper. She looked at the pink cowboy, then back to her coffee cup. It's a cup that's made in England. My mother brought the set to Pie Town when we first moved here when I was a girl. I kept that china in a hutch in my trailer, but as soon as Antonia started visiting, I took some of those dishes to the cafe, just for us, when the doors were closed, when we could talk. I kept them up high in a box on top of the refrigerator. I would bring out squares of shortbread, which I ordered from a catalog that Laverne had at her store. The catalog's pages were filled with hams and pure maple syrup and sweets.

"You should hang out a shingle. Food and Comforting, it should say," Antonia told me.

She and her husband had lived in Socorro, in what Antonia described as a mustard yellow cinder block apartment. "I think we'll always be there," Antonia moaned one day. She said she had been promoted at the card shop where she worked. Instead of just painting within lines already drawn of yucca and women bending over bread in kiva ovens, she was designing her own scenes. Antonia bit into a piece of shortbread, its crumbs sticking to her thin curved top lip. "But that's not enough," she said.

"God, if I could just have my old ranch back."

"Are you still groaning over that?" I rattled my cup against the saucer. "Your parents sold it over fifteen years ago. Move on, girl," I said walking to the coffee machine for a pot of coffee for refills.

"Nothing else is good enough," Antonia said, looking me straight in the face.

"I guess that's what it all boils down to, doesn't it?" I said filling our cups, then placing the pot on the table, I sat down. I couldn't look at Antonia, so I took a piece of cookie and jabbed at it with my finger until crumbs scattered.

"It's sure easy to dream," I said.

We finished our coffee and looked out the window for awhile. I couldn't think of much to say and I guess Antonia felt the same. "Well, I'll be going," Antonia said. Then we stood, hugged each other so quickly we barely touched, and Antonia slipped out the door.

I turned away from the door and stared back into my cafe. There were times when I stayed inside after I had closed, especially after Antonia had been by and this was one. I flipped off the lights. Even then, the sun shone in enough to make the room glow. I walked to a counter stool and sat. As always, the cowboy heads his horse toward the place where the wallpaper stops. He's followed by a mangy dog with coyote eyes, so yellow they could turn into fury at the drop of a hat. Sometimes I'm riding behind the cowboy with my arms wrapped around his middle, but instead of feeling his warmth, I feel those coyote eyes burning through me, pushing me closer to the darkest corner of my world. I can get so scared my flesh crawls and I'm back again on my stool, where pinks and oranges swirl around me in the little space with only my name on it.

THE DEPUTY

Marc Simmons

EVERY boy growing up must worry sometime or another whether he's got the stuff in him to make a man. I guess I was no different in this way. With me, though, the fear may have run a little deeper, for the road was harder and mostly I had to look to myself for answers instead of to some older fellow who had been through it himself. I'm not complaining, mind you! Because I met rough going, I figure I'm stronger for it today. Besides, I got the right breaks when they really counted.

Most of what happened to me in those early years is not fixed too clearly in my memory. It all seems pretty shadowy and remote now—all, that is, except the events of the summer of 1899. I easily remember how with the first peep of sunup every morning, I'd saddle my Chico horse and, taking Dad's old .45, head for the dump a mile and a half south of town. That was the one thing that had real meaning for me then—going out in the crisp morning light by myself and blasting away at the litter of old bottles and cans.

Of course, my blasting didn't go on very long, being as I carried only half a dozen shells with me. I took a box a week as part of my wages from Mr. Pike but I'd make them last as long as I could by sticking in only one live one and the rest empties. Next I'd give the cylinder a good spin and that way I couldn't tell when that live shell would come around. So I aimed as if every shot would count. Old Pete Taylor used to come out to the dump some of those mornings and give me all kinds of good pointers about drawing and balance of the gun and such. But that was before he got himself killed, which really tore me up bad.

After my morning wake-up with the .45, I'd usually ride Chico around the few little arroyos, hoping to spot a stray cottontail. Then the two of us would go sit on the little rise that stood up like a round, treeless island right smack there in the middle of the San Augustine Plains. I called it Hamilton Island, naming it after myself, which I figured was all right. Nobody else seemed to notice it really. I guess because it wasn't much of an island as things go. But it sure was a keen place for spotting what was happening in the country roundabout.

Off to the north a few hops was our town of San Augustine Springs and way beyond that, the ragged edge of the Datil Mountains, marking the end of the plains up that way. The Magdalenas were around to the right where the sun had to climb over them every morning. They sheltered the new railhead at Magdalena town with its railroad and fancy stores and Saturday night wingdings that was pulling all the business off the plains and turning San Augustine Springs into a ghost. The Black Range which sloped on westward to the Mogollon Rim just about filled up the rest of the horizon and left us an' the big ranches sitting in a grassy bowl a hundred miles long and half again as wide. More'n once I'd heard cowmen around town allow that here was the best stretch of range in the whole New Mexico Territory.

A time or two I'd brought Penny Pike up to my island when the moon was riding high. You can't say I was really courtin' her for she insisted on treating me like a kid brother even though I was better'n a year older'n her. We'd just rest there on our horses and study the country turned silver under the moonglow and talk about things that really didn't mean too much. I couldn't blame Penny for the way she acted toward me 'cause I sure wasn't much when it came to muscles and good looks.

My father died before I was born and the only thing I had from him was the Colt .45 Peacemaker and the name of Bertram Hamilton. Everything else I guess I got from my mother, including a puny constitution. It was because she was ailing all the time that drove her to take a St. Louis doctor's advice and pack me up and light out for New Mexico. The dry air was a good tonic all right but she'd come too late for it to really take hold. I was just a sprout of twelve when they buried her in the churchyard at the end of Central Street.

Mr. and Mrs. Pike more or less took me in. I helped them out in their mercantile store which made up for my keep and caught odd jobs around town when I could. When I was sixteen Mr. Pike figured I was doing enough to draw a little salary to boot and that's how come I got the shells for Dad's old gun.

What led up to that first day of August 1899 really started with Pete Taylor. Old Pete was *alguacil* of San Augustine Springs. That meant he was the constable which was all the little one-horse towns down in the southern part of the Territory could afford in those days.

Whenever I had times off, I'd taken to loafing around the low adobe building that served as jail and office. Sometimes when I felt like it, I'd sweep the place good or haul the ashes out of the potbelly stove where Pete kept a sooty coffeepot working. Evenings the two of us would drag chairs outside and, tilted back against the mud wall, we'd watch the sun drop behind the Black Range and listen for the first oties to start barking and yowling. 'Bout then was when old Pete could be counted on to really open up with the windies. He'd talk on and on about how he'd been in all kinds of tight scrapes and gunfights in his young days back in the Kansas cowtowns. I naturally didn't believe all the guff he put out. I figured that if he had really been so all-fired great as he let on, then he wouldn't have ended up with this third-rate job of *alguacil* in our town. But then times was changing. Everybody said so. And anyway he was sure first-rate when it came to spinning a yarn, whether it had any truth to it or not.

But a certain happening the last week of June caused me to change my notions about Pete Taylor and his tales. It was getting on close to midafternoon. I'd finished up early helping Mr. Pike in the store and I was just hanging around out front soaking up some sun. Directly I saw this rider, all dusty, turn into Central Street from the Magdalena Road. He went on past, not paying any attention to me, and pulled up in front of Bud Tanner's Gold Dollar.

If I'd been anywhere else that day but the front porch of Pike's I'd have probably missed that fellow and he would've wet his whistle and been on his way to the border. But I was there, and I sure as heck recognized his face being I'd seen it before on a reward dodger tacked up in Pete's office. Soon as he disappeared through the batwings of Tanner's place, I sprinted for the jail to give Pete the word. Ten minutes later our *alguacil,* calm as you please, walked into the Gold Dollar and up to this fellow hunkered over the bar.

"Keep your hands where I can see 'em, Harlow." That was all Pete said, but you knew he meant it. Even so this Harlow would've jerked around but for the feel of cold steel prodding him in the back. I was watching from the door and saw the whole thing. So did Ollie Jackson, the telegraph operator, and Moon Buchanan, our blacksmith, and a bunch of others there at the time. In my hand I was still carrying the dodger we'd picked up listing this gent as a train robber and gunman out of the Dakotas. The look he gave me as Pete led him out sent a shiver down my back. I didn't breathe easy until the cell door clanked between us.

The big surprise for me though was the way the old man had acted. I began looking back at some of the stories he had told and seeing them in a new light. One thing was certain—when Pete got going, he was all business.

He took me aside then and let me know what was on his mind. "I'll have to take this fellow over to the U.S. Marshal in Magdalena tomorrow, Bert. If I push it we can be there before noon. Now, I figure I'm going to need my rest 'cause I'm not as spry as I used to be." I nodded and held my breath, suspecting what he was leading up to. "So suppose I just deputize you to sit up with this bird and make sure he doesn't fly the coop."

There was plenty around town with a head on their shoulders that would have been an easy match for this job, and it should've made me wonder why Pete'd pick a scrawny seventeen-year-old kid that was slow getting his full growth. Right then I was so stirred up at the chance he was offering me that I didn't stop to puzzle it out. I should have, I guess, and maybe I would have known then what I came to see later. Old Pete must have been a boy himself once, hard as that was to imagine. He had an inkling of what runs through a young button's mind and how much a little push or pat on the back could mean. Especially to one that's had to do his growing on his own.

I had had my heart set on cowboying and Pete knew it. Every time a rancher or foreman would hit town to pick up a few supplies he didn't feel like riding to Magdalena for, I'd brace him for a job. There was a lot of 'em my age and younger holding down a man's place out on the plains and beyond. I could start as a nighthawk or even cook's louse, I told them; I just wanted to be where the action was and get a chance to learn the tricks of the cow trade.

They'd look me over, maybe, seeing my bones that stuck out and red nose that was always peeling 'cause it wouldn't tan and then, most likely, they'd rub their jaws and peer off into space. But their answers were always the same. And while some of 'em tried to be polite about it, a good many got kinda gruff like I hadn't oughta' been wasting their time with such a loco proposition. Every stone wall I ran against took a little bit out of me. That's why Pete's wanting to make me his deputy really meant something.

With a badge pinned on my shirt-front I was about the proudest fellow on this side of the Rio Grande. *Alguacil de Asistencia* it read at the top and Deputy Constable below. In the Territory, everything was written in both languages that way.

I got very careful instructions on what to do that night, but anybody with half the eyes I had could've seen there really wasn't much to the job. Harlow was locked in tight as could be and wasn't going nowhere 'til morning. But I paid mighty close attention when Pete told me how to sit and hold the shotgun I was given and to keep the coal oil lamp turned up and not to doze and to raise a ruckus if any monkey business got started.

I know that was the longest night I ever passed. The later it got the more I tensed up, so once when a shutter banged I came about two feet out of the chair. The lamplight made little shadows dance on the wall and across the faces of the outlaws whose posters were tacked up there. Nothing but long snores rolled from the cell but that didn't stop me speculating on what I'd do if Harlow should suddenly come bustin'out of there. Just the thought of it set the butterflies to flopping in my stomach. I finally decided I'd probably freeze up and not even be able to pull the gun around in line. What had been gnawing at me for a long time finally came to the surface. I was yellow clear through. Maybe even it had gotten written across my face so that folks could tell by just looking. This kind of thinking really put me in a bad way so for the last few hours I just sat rigid, hardly daring to breathe.

I must have loosened up some with the first light of day because, when Pete showed up shortly before sunup, I was able to talk and joke with him almost natural. We stood out front for a time with the chill from the plains wrapped around us and searched the sky for any chunks of clouds that might be bringing rain. We hashed over the road to Magdalena and it was pretty plain that Pete was nervous about this job. Then he went off down to Buchanan's to borrow a horse for Harlow, and in another twenty minutes the pair of 'em was heading east out of town.

That was the last San Augustine Springs saw of its *alguacil* alive. We never did find out exactly how it happened. The posse that formed up afterward over in Magdalena read the sign and made a few educated guesses, as they say. Somehow Pete had let his guard down and given this Harlow his chance. The outlaw had taken both horses and Pete's gun and spurred south as fast as he could for the border. They brought the body back to our town and we all gathered for the hymns and prayers behind the barbwire that enclosed the churchyard. It didn't dawn on me 'til later that now I was the law in San Augustine Springs.

The first of August started out like most any other day for me. I left my little lean-to back of Pike's store early, saddled up Chico and headed for the dump with my Colt. I really wasn't any good with the thing but I kept at it mostly because I wanted an excuse to ride out every morning. Penny's father sure didn't approve of me wasting time or shells that way. But he never said much.

I got back in town a little after seven and sat around the office whittling on a cholla stick. Hadn't felt like doing much in the days since Pete had died, mainly on account of I was all confused inside. A lot had happened and I hadn't got it all sorted out in my mind yet. When I wasn't doing my regular work for Mr. Pike, I'd prowl around town "howdying" everybody and poking into corners as I'd always done, but all the same I knew things had changed. Fear was lurking right behind me like a shadow.

At first I'd been afraid Harlow would come back and try to get me for pointing him out. When that wore off there were other things I couldn't even name. Nights I'd lie in my bunk seeing all kinds of pictures in the dark and hearing noises flit around. I sure was wishing I had Pete to talk to.

I threw the cholla stick down and put my clasp knife back in my pocket. A hollow feeling down low told me it was getting close to breakfast. Across the street at the store, the front window shade went up. That was Penny's signal for me to come and get it, and I sure didn't waste any time.

I hustled through the store and back to where the Pikes had their living quarters. Penny was just taking the big coffeepot off the stove when I walked into the kitchen and she threw me a cheery smile. Mrs. Pike had been ailing for some time and kept mostly to her bed, leaving Penny to do all the cooking and house chores.

"Get the cups down, will you please, Bert?"

When Penny asked me to do some small thing like that for her, it sure as heck pleased me. She was holding a heavy white crock and was beginning to ladle batter onto a griddle in little puddles. I got a whiff of simmering hotcakes and of bacon popping in the deep skillet that set my mouth to watering.

I rattled around in the cupboard and pulled out three enameled cups. Then I plopped down in a chair at the heavy oak table and began to watch

Penny at the stove. Just the sight of her always managed to perk me up no matter how mopey I was. This morning she seemed as fresh as wild flowers when they first fill a mountain meadow in the spring. I figured she was about as perfect a gal as you could hope to find and the only thing that troubled me was that she couldn't take me serious. I knew in her eyes I was just a kid who had a lot of stretching to do before he reached manhood. This business of me being deputy showed that.

Ever since that morning Pete had ridden out with Harlow I'd kept to wearing my badge. Seemed like everyone around town knew how I come to get it in the first place and they didn't pay no more mind than if I'd been a ten-year-old sporting a play tin star. Nobody said out-and-out I wasn't deputy and I didn't go pushing it by boasting or anything like that. But it was mighty clear that if there was any lawing to do they weren't going to look at me. Lucky I was, too, that our wide-place-in-the-road was so quiet. The rowdy crowd stuck pretty much to Magdalena and the bigger towns over on the Rio Grande, like Socorro and Los Lunas. Just the same, I knew that trouble was bound to pop up sooner or later and no matter how much I dreaded it, I was going to be sucked in.

Penny didn't really chide me about the whole thing, but once she let on that her father thought I was something of a fool for pretending to take on a man's job. Allowed as how he was considering cutting me down to size with a serious talking to. I asked Penny if she looked at things the same way as him, and she got kind of embarrassed and hedged around until I knew how it was.

She set a tin plate full of her special hotcakes down in front of me and then heaped a mound of bacon on top. I sloshed a lot of syrup on and began to dig in while Penny poured herself a cup of coffee and sat down opposite me to wait for her father.

"You haven't forgotten that you're helping Dad unpack those new tools this morning?" she said.

"I know, I know," I answered kind of roughly. "I usually stick around and do my share of the work." Right quick I was sorry for the tone of voice I'd used because Penny got a little red and flushed and I could see the hurt.

"I didn't mean that, Bert. It's only that lately you've been. . . well. . . ."

I mumbled half an apology and stared hard at my plate. We didn't speak any more at breakfast and I hurried to get out of the kitchen and at those crates of tools.

In the front of the store I found a wrecking bar and really went tearing into things. Out of the wooden crates came shiny new axes and buck saws, posthole diggers, adzes and the like. 'Fore long Mr. Pike came shuffling up from the back and kinda grunted a good morning to me. He always acted gruff, but down under he was a decent enough sort of fellow. His mustache had a habit of wagging when he talked and he'd twitch his nose ever so often. Sometimes I'd catch myself watching these things and not paying any mind to what he was saying. He thought I was a mite deaf since I had to ask for repeats on directions now and again.

We worked for the better part of an hour: Mr. Pike jotting down in his ledger while I put stuff on display and hauled extras to shelves in the storeroom. Things was about done when Mrs. Monroe came jangling through the front door with her shopping basket on her arm. Her husband was our barber and undertaker. He kept saying he was fixing to pull stakes and move over to some of the new towns in Arizona where there was business enough to keep him and his family alive. But he hadn't got around to leaving yet and I'd about given up on him. Mr. Pike went padding up front to wait on his customer and left me to sweep up the splintered crates.

I really didn't mind working in the store too much. There was always a good smell like right then: red chile peppers hanging in *ristras* from the beams, saddle leather oiled and soaped, fresh ground coffee, cinnamon, grain and feed—all these jumbled in with the damp, earthy smell thrown out by the adobe walls. 'Course it was a far cry from the cowboying I wanted to be doing, but I learned to put that out of sight and not let it nag at me.

I was thinking about these things in general and Penny in particular, all the while pushing away at the broom, when I heard the jangling again. Ollie Jackson from the telegraph office was poking his bald head in the door.

"Trouble," he sang out. "Marlin boys shot up the Express office in Socorro. Heading this way. Everybody's meeting at Tanner's." Seeing the women, he added, "Tell your Bill, Mrs. Monroe." And with that he disappeared, slamming the door so the glass like to rattled out.

"Oh, mercy. What next?" Mrs. Monroe groaned, putting her hand up to her throat. Quick as a wink she bustled out, leaving her basket half-filled on the counter.

Mr. Pike came whipping out of his apron, barreling for Tanner's Gold Dollar. He just had time to holler at me over his shoulder, "Watch the store 'til I get back, Bert."

What ole Ollie had said sure hit me with a wallop. I just stood there for a time, getting numb all over. The Marlins were well-known in that part of the Territory, mostly for petty rustling and the fights they'd been in up and down the Rio Grande. Folks were always saying as how they'd cut loose some day and really bring the law down on 'em by startin' something big. And it looked like that prediction was coming true. There was the two Marlin brothers, Fitz and Henry, and usually a couple of hardcases tagging behind them that they passed off as cousins. Whatever they had stirred up over in Socorro was coming my way and it sent a little finger of cold running down my back.

"What's happened?" Penny asked, coming up from the back.

"Everybody's joining up at Tanner's. Some fellows held up the Express office in Socorro and headed out this way." I tried to keep my voice even and calm so as not to get her excited but I could see the worry start to creep across her face as I spoke.

"Oh, Bert! There won't be any trouble, will there?"

I didn't answer because my thoughts were jumping ahead. Whatever was being planned over across the street didn't include me, 'cause I sure hadn't heard anyone yelling for the deputy. Penny must've spotted the bitterness that came into my eyes because she paled a little and put her small hand on my wrist.

"You're not thinking of mixing in this, are you, Bert? Leave it to the men. They'll decide what's best. And besides, it's not your...."

I didn't wait for her to finish. I just tore loose and got out of there as quick as I could. I stood on the porch for a while and watched a few stragglers hurry toward the Gold Dollar. Kept fingering the badge sagging on my shirt-front and trying to figure out what I should do.

About then a rider turned off the road from the west and came jogging down Central Street. One look told me it was just another drifter—one of those lean, saddle-hardened cowhands that are a dime a dozen in the cattle country. His horse was a chestnut, short-coupled and muscled in the right places. The man himself wore faded jeans with dust beaten into them, the uniform of his trade. Only thing out of the ordinary was his black hat and the little shiny silver band around the crown. That headgear said he was from over in the Navajo country someplace. A hundred times in my imagination I'd seen myself as a cowhand like that—always on the move from place to place, following a hard life, doing a man's work.

The stranger pulled up in front of the Gold Dollar and eyed the place up and down. He stretched himself in the saddle, then climbed off and headed inside. Seeing him helped me make up my mind. If I was ever going to do any growing up, now was a good time to start.

The chestnut had been tied so he could lean his head over the hitchrail and dig into the water trough. I went over and rubbed his neck and at the same time studied the batwings leading into Tanner's. 'Fore long I puckered up courage and slipped inside.

They were all so busy yammering at one another that nobody even noticed me. I stuck close to the wall and kept quiet, trying to pick up the gist of their talk and get the situation straight. Ollie Jackson was the center of it all and he kept telling over and over the few details that had come in on the wire. Seems the Marlin crew had made a raid on the New Mexico Overland Express Office just after it opened that morning and shot up the place pretty bad. The clerk had put up a fight and got one of 'em while the other three lit out like the wind in our direction. The whole country was up in arms so it was figured they'd head for the wilderness down below the Black Range. But for a long run they would be needing supplies and stuff and, since Magdalena was too big for them to tackle, it was a pretty safe bet they'd try their hand in San Augustine Springs.

When everybody had this much straight they fell to arguing about what to do next. Ollie seen the attention was drifting away from him so he raised his voice a mite.

"Now the smart thing for us to do," he said, "is lay low until all this blows over. If they come in and we start trouble, this town'll be taken apart. Most of us have families and we don't want to see that happen. So what we do is close up everything and keep out of their way. Let them bust in if they have a mind to and take what they want. Like as not a posse is close behind and they won't get far."

"Now look here," interrupted Moon Buchanan, "are you saying we should just turn this town over to a pack of outlaws without putting up a fight?"

"That's right," Ollie came back at him. "If Pete was here, why then maybe we could think of doing something. But there's just too few of us to go up against a rough bunch like this."

When Moon looked like he was about to argue some more, Bill Monroe put his two bits' worth in:

"Ollie's got it right. He's talking sense. The first ones I'm thinking of are my wife and little Tommie. No use bringing grief on them. You don't have a family, Moon, so you can talk about standing up to the

Marlins, but not the rest of us."

Several others around the room nodded their heads and you could see they had made up their minds and was relieved. Bud Tanner cleared his throat from behind the bar and all eyes turned toward him. He was a big, even tempered fellow who seldom had much to say, but when he did open up, people had a habit of listening.

"'Pears to me," he said slowly, "that we want to preserve our property and look out for our women folks and the best way of doing that is to follow right along with what Ollie Jackson says. 'Course there's those who'd allow we're taking the coward's way out but then they're not here and in the same position as we are."

"That's right. These men are dangerous. If we make a show of force, only Bill Monroe's undertaking business is going to benefit," somebody chimed in.

That brought a few snickers but it was plain the whole bunch was uneasy. Now that things were settled, they were eager to go looking for their holes to crawl into and hibernate. But Tanner wasn't through.

"And how do you figure this, stranger?" he asked, turning to the man at the end of the bar.

Nobody had paid much attention to the cowboy when he first came in. He was kind've short and there was nothing particular about him to make you sit up and take notice, except maybe his black hat. But he'd been noticed now and the place got quiet waiting for him to answer. He leaned on the bar with his elbows and rolled a half-filled glass between his palms.

"I make it a general rule not to mix in other folk's affairs," he declared carefully, which is just about what you'd expect anyone to say. But then he added, "Unless, of course, I'm out to prove something."

"Well, it's all settled then," Ollie piped up, and you could tell he was pleased as pie about all his arranging.

"Not quite," came a voice from over against the wall. And it took 'em a minute or two to realize that it was me doing the talking. Every head had turned my way when I announced, "I'm still the deputy here and I say we put up a fight. If we don't, this town will be the laughingstock of the Territory."

I really meant it but I guess my voice didn't carry a ring of conviction. Instead of convincing anybody, I'd just made them angry. Ollie Jackson was the maddest. You could tell by his frown.

"Well, looka' here," he mocked. "The big man with the badge is going to throw his weight around and tell us how to run things. Now, kid, suppose you go climb off our backs and onto your hobby horse."

His words stung my ears like nothing else ever had, and all the resolve I'd worked up just seemed to ebb out of me. With everybody in the whole place staring, I shrank down to about an inch high. Mr. Pike came up to me then. He'd mostly kept quiet and let the others do the talking, but what I'd said put fire in his eyes.

"Bert, I thought I told you to stay in the store! Now is not the time for your brand of foolishness."

His voice was as stern as I'd ever heard it. I started to stammer something, but the words got snagged in my throat and all I could do was turn and walk out.

Without even thinking, I headed for the office where I could be alone. I'd really stuck my neck out but there was no turning back. I knew I was going to find out once and for all if I had what it took to wear that badge Pete gave me.

The late morning dragged into afternoon. I sat on the edge of the desk checking and rechecking my gun, its weight cold and strange in my hands. Through the window I kept an eye on what was happening. First off, a little crowd gathered to see Tommie Monroe mount his paint pony and get instructions from his father and a couple of others. Then they sent him off to the edge of town to keep a lookout on the plains to the east. After that folks started disappearing. Pretty soon you could see the shades come down and the shutters close, and in no time it was hard to tell the buildings with the people in them from those that had been deserted and boarded up for quite a spell. San Augustine Springs acted like it had suddenly turned over and died after a long sickness.

As the hours crawled by, my own worry began to wear me down. I went over again in my mind all that had happened until I finally settled on a single thought that kept hammering home. If I couldn't stand up to that saloon full of men, how in the world did I figure I could meet the Marlins head-on. Then every time I would come back to the knowledge that this maybe was my last chance to prove up and I'd better not throw it away. My best bet seemed to meet the outlaws in the street and then hope the others in town would back me when they seen I'd forced their hand. It was a crazy idea but the only one that would come to me.

A little after three, Tommie came pounding in on his pony shouting, "Somebody's coming. Somebody's coming." A few men ran into the street, and one got his horse to ride out and check. He was back in no time, all excited.

"It's them, all right. Three riders coming this way at a fast clip. Be here in less than ten minutes." This sent the ones in the street scurrying for cover.

I sucked in a long breath. At least the waiting was done. Walked out in the street and over to the edge of the boardwalk on the other side. The sun dipping behind the stores was just beginning to send a shadow creeping across the hard-packed sod. I took a long look up Central Street. After a couple of blocks, the east-west road crossed it and you couldn't see what was coming either way 'cause of the buildings squatting on the corners.

There was no denying it. I was plenty scared. A deathly silence had seeped into the town, making it seem more like a ghost than ever. A horse off somewhere whickered and I like to've jumped out of my skin. I began seeing how stupid this whole thing was. If nobody else cared about this town, why should I go trying to stop a bunch of rowdies from shooting it wide open? Maybe Mr. Pike had been right and this wasn't any of my business. Anyways, if I was to get gunned down, who was going to spill any tears? Not that crowd from the saloon. Ollie and the rest'd swagger around saying how they'd been right all along, then they'd show up at my funeral with long faces they didn't mean. When you got right down to bedrock, it was every fellow for himself in this world, which meant I was playing the part of a fool standing out here in the path of the Marlins.

My mind was really working fast 'cause I seen I still had time to get out of this mess. I knew folks was watching out from their windows, but most likely they were keeping their eyes glued up the street toward the Magdalena road and hadn't even spotted me. I'd just started to look for an alleyway to slip off into when I heard something behind me. My mind froze but I reckon the body moved by instinct because I whirled around, my right hand moving down toward the Colt.

It was that black-hatted drifter from the saloon. He was up in the shade leaning against an adobe wall with his thumbs hooked in his gunbelt. He studied me for a couple of seconds and then took a step out.

"Alrighty, deputy. Name yore play, I'll back you." That was all he said in a speech that was tight and purposeful.

I was so stunned that it took me a few moments to come to myself. Nobody had ever called me deputy before, and sure no man like him had ever spoken to me as his equal. Yet here it was, this cowboy offering to stand right beside me while I did the leading. The gratitude that swept over me brought a mist to my eyes and suddenly I heard myself talking in a calm and assured way that didn't seem to be a voice I knew at all.

"Much obliged, mister. But I'm the law here. It's my job. And like you said, this town ain't none of your affair."

"Have it your way," he replied, spitting out a little puff of air that was almost a gesture of relief. "I'm sure in no hurry to cash in my chips. Just wouldn't have felt right if I hadn't of offered, seeing the way things stood."

In that instant it dawned on me that he was as scared as I was, as everybody was. The trick, though, was not to let it buffalo you—to go ahead and do what had to be done. That was the little secret that every real man knew.

He nodded and moved back into the shadows and I was left alone there in the sun-splashed street. Started walking slowly up Central, feeling straight and tall for the first time in my life. Already you could hear the drumming of horses' hooves at the edge of town. I stopped after a ways with my eye riveted on that corner where they'd come. A dust-devil spun down the street, tugged at my clothes, then slammed into a wall, throwing little pebbles against a window pane. The pounding got louder and trickles of sweat slid down from my forehead and fogged up my eyes. But I stood rooted and I knew my voice would work and my right hand too, if it had to.

I had already started crouching when they busted around the corner—three blurs on horseback. My arm moved slightly toward the gun at my hip; my jaw went rigid.

Then all at once the voice of the drifter called out from somewhere to the left, "Ease up, deputy. It ain't them."

And it was true. I wiped the dust and sweat out of my eyes with the back of my hand and saw 'em clear. Three cowhands had reined up and were sitting easy and loose in their saddles, staring at me curious-like. People were already starting to empty out of their houses and stores and fill the street.

"Hey," Bud Tanner hollered. "It's Branch McAdams and a couple of his boys from the Circle M. What are you doing so far from home, Branch?"

"We just come from delivering a bunch of horses over on the Rio Puerco," said the rider in the lead. "What's going on here anyway?"

"We thought you all were the Marlin boys," volunteered Ollie Jackson.

"Haw, haw. That's a good one," roared this McAdams, slapping his thigh. "Not likely we'd be the Marlins. A posse of miners jumped them south of Magdalena just before noon. They're warming a jail cell right now. Reckon with all the excitement they haven't gotten around to flashing the word along yet."

All this time I'd been standing there alone wanting to run and hide or maybe go drown myself in the horse trough. That's how ashamed I was when I realized how ridiculous I must've looked. Better had they been the outlaws, then I'd most likely be dead now and out of my misery.

The crowd was all laughing and talking about what had happened and didn't even seem to notice me. Tanner went up to the three on horseback and said good-naturedly, "You boys climb down and come over to my place. We want to hear all about it. Refreshments on me, everybody." And a cheer went up as the whole crew began to surge toward the Gold Dollar.

The three cowboys, though, kept their horses right where they was. They were peering at me again and the older one out front had his face screwed up like he was pondering something mighty deep. Hot as the day was, I felt cold all over, knowing I'd come to a crossroad where all the choices seemed to dead end.

McAdams straightened in the saddle then and his eyes cleared like he'd reached out and got a' hold of some idea. The crowd had moved off, but he called after it. "I'll be right with you, fellows. Just as soon as I shake hands with your deputy there." That stopped 'em in their tracks.

"What's that you say, Branch?" somebody asked.

"I said, I want to meet the man who was fixing to stand off the Marlins all by his lonesome."

"Yea," echoed a cowhand behind him. "You can count me in on that."

I guess nobody could believe their ears, because I sure couldn't. The next thing I know those three men were on the ground and lining up to pump my hand.

"Anytime you need somebody to put in a good word for you, young fellow, just look me up at the Circle M," this McAdams says stoutly.

The other two followed him and one of them declared, "Mighty pleased to wring yore hand."

The blood had drained out of my face but I was grinning and giving back as strong a grip as I could muster. The rest was standing around gaping with their mouths hanging open and looking like they was seeing me for the first time. Pretty soon they all closed in and kinda sheepish-like was slapping me on the back and saying how proud the town was and all that. After a while, I pulled away and let them head for Tanner's again.

I'd caught sight of the drifter leading his chestnut out from where he'd been tied off the street. He was just starting to swing into the saddle when I caught up to him.

"Hold on a minute." And the cowboy stopped and turned. "I just wanted to thank you." We shook and I held onto his hand and repeated, "Thanks. Thanks a lot, mister."

He smiled and nodded. "Good luck to you, deputy." Then he was on his horse and pointing him up Central to the Magdalena road.

I remained there in the street until he was gone, feeling kind of washed-out, but happy that at last I knew my own mind. Across at Pike's, Penny was standing in the doorway. Walking over, I hooked a boot heel on the bottom step and said without even thinking, "There's one tired man here who sure could use a cup of coffee."

MEN ON THE MOON

Simon J. Ortiz

JOSELITA brought her father, Faustin, the TV on Father's Day. She brought it over after Sunday mass and she had her son hook up the antenna. She plugged the TV into the wall socket.

Faustin sat on a worn couch. He was covered with an old coat. He had worn that coat for twenty years.

It's ready. Turn it on and I'll adjust the antenna, Amarosho told his mother. The TV warmed up and then it flickered into dull light. It was snowing. Amarosho tuned it a bit. It snowed less and then a picture formed.

Look, Naishtiya, Joselita said. She touched her father's hand and pointed at the TV.

I'll turn the antenna a bit and you tell me when the picture is clear, Amarosho said. He climbed on the roof again.

After a while the picture turned clearer. It's better, his mother shouted. There was only the tiniest bit of snow falling.

That's about the best it can get I guess, Amarosho said. Maybe it'll clear up on the other channels. He turned the selector. It was clearer on another.

There were two men struggling with each other. Wrestling, Amarosho said. Do you want to watch wrestling? Two men are fighting, Nana. One of them is Apache Red. Chiseh tsah, he told his grandfather.

The old man stirred. He had been staring intently into the TV. He wondered why there was so much snow at first. Now there were two men fighting. One of them was Chiseh, an Apache, and the other was a Mericano. There were people shouting excitedly and clapping hands within the TV.

The two men backed away from each other once in a while and then they clenched. They wheeled mightily and suddenly one threw the other. The old man smiled. He wondered why they were fighting.

Something else showed on the TV screen. A bottle of wine was being poured. The old man liked the pouring sound and he moved his mouth. Someone was selling wine.

The two fighting men came back on the TV. They struggled with each other and after a while one of them didn't get up and then another person came and held up the hand of the Apache who was dancing around in a feathered headdress.

It's over, Amarosho announced. Apache Red won the fight, Nana.

The Chiseh won. Faustin watched the other one, a light-haired man who looked totally exhausted and angry with himself. He didn't like the Apache too much. He wanted them to fight again.

After a few moments something else appeared on the TV.

What is that? Faustin asked. There was an object with smoke coming from it. It was standing upright.

Men are going to the moon, Nana, his grandson said. It's Apollo. It's going to fly three men to the moon.

That thing is going to fly to the moon?

Yes, Nana.

What is it called again?

Apollo, a spaceship rocket, Joselita told her father.

The Apollo spaceship stood on the ground emitting clouds of something that looked like smoke.

A man was talking, telling about the plans for the flight, what would happen, that it was almost time. Faustin could not understand the man very well because he didn't know many words in Mericano.

He must be talking about that thing flying in the air? he said.

Yes. It's about ready to fly away to the moon.

Faustin remembered that the evening before he had looked at the sky and seen that the moon was almost in the middle phase. He wondered if it was important that the men get to the moon.

Are those men looking for something on the moon? he asked his grandson.

They're trying to find out what's on the moon, Nana, what kind of dirt and rocks there are, to see if there's any life on the moon. The men are looking for knowledge, Amarosho told him. Faustin wondered if the men had run out of places to look for knowledge on the earth. Do they know if they'll find knowledge? he asked.

They have some information already. They've gone before and come back. They're going again.

Did they bring any back?

They brought back some rocks.

Rocks. Faustin laughed quietly. The scientist men went to search for knowledge on the moon and they brought back rocks. He thought that perhaps Amarosho was joking with him. The grandson had gone to Indian School for a number of years and sometimes he would tell his grandfather some strange and funny things.

The old man was suspicious. They joked around a lot. Rocks—you sure that's all they brought back?

That's right, Nana, only rocks and some dirt and pictures they made of what it looks like on the moon.

The TV picture was filled with the rocket, close up now. Men were sitting and moving around by some machinery and the voice had become more urgent. The old man watched the activity in the picture intently but with a slight smile on his face.

Suddenly it became very quiet, and the voice was firm and commanding and curiously pleading. Ten, nine, eight, seven, six, five, four, three, two, liftoff. The white smoke became furious and a muted rumble shook through the TV. The rocket was trembling and the voice was trembling.

It was really happening, the old man marvelled. Somewhere inside of that cylinder with a point at its top and long slender wings were three men who were flying to the moon.

The rocket rose from the ground. There were enormous clouds of smoke and the picture shook. Even the old man became tense and he grasped the edge of the couch. The rocket spaceship rose and rose.

There's fire coming out of the rocket, Amarosho explained. That's what makes it go.

Fire. Faustin had wondered what made it fly. He'd seen pictures of other flying machines. They had long wings and someone had explained to him that there was machinery inside which spun metal blades which made them fly. He had wondered what made this thing fly. He hoped his grandson wasn't joking him.

After a while there was nothing but the sky. The rocket Apollo had disappeared. It hadn't taken very long and the voice from the TV wasn't excited anymore. In fact the voice was very calm and almost bored.

I have to go now, Naishtiya, Joselita told her father. I have things to do.

Me too, Amarosho said.

Wait, the old man said, wait. What shall I do with this thing? What is it you call it?

TV, his daughter said. You watch it. You turn it on and you watch it.

I mean how do you stop it? Does it stop like the radio, like the mahkina? It stops?

This way, Nana, Amarosho said and showed his grandfather. He turned the dial and the picture went away. He turned the dial again and the picture flickered on again. Were you afraid this one-eye would be looking at you all the time? Amarosho laughed and gently patted the old man's shoulder.

Faustin was relieved. Joselita and her son left. He watched the TV for a while. A lot of activity was going on, a lot of men were moving among machinery, and a couple of men were talking. And then it showed the rocket again.

He watched it rise and fly away again. It disappeared again. There was nothing but the sky. He turned the dial and the picture died away. He turned it on and the picture came on again. He turned it off. He went outside and to a fence a distance from his home. When he finished he studied the sky for a while.

THAT NIGHT HE DREAMED.

Flintwing Boy was watching a Skquuyuh mahkina come down a hill. The mahkina made a humming noise. It was walking. It shone in the sunlight. Flintwing Boy moved to a better position to see. The mahkina kept on moving. It was moving toward him.

The Skquuyuh mahkina drew closer. Its metal legs stepped upon trees and crushed growing flowers and grass. A deer bounded away frightened. Tshushki came running to Flintwing Boy.

Anaweh, he cried, trying to catch his breath.

The coyote was staring at the thing which was coming towards them. There was wild fear in his eyes.

What is that, Anaweh? What is that thing? he gasped.

It looks like a mahkina, but I've never seen one like it before. It must be some kind of Skquuyuh mahkina.

Where did it come from?

I'm not sure yet, Anaweh, Flintwing Boy said. When he saw that Tshushki was trembling with fear, he said gently, Sit down Anaweh. Rest yourself. We'll find out soon enough.

The Skquuyuh mahkina was undeterred. It walked over and through everything. It splashed through a stream of clear water. The water boiled and streaks of oil flowed downstream. It split a juniper tree in half with a terrible crash. It crushed a boulder into dust with a sound of heavy metal. Nothing stopped the Skquuyuh mahkina. It hummed.

Anaweh, Tshushki cried, what shall we do? What can we do?

Flintwing Boy reached into the bag at his side. He took out an object. It was a flint arrowhead. He took out some cornfood.

Come over here, Anaweh. Come over here. Be calm, he motioned to the frightened coyote. He touched the coyote in several places of his body with the arrowhead and put cornfood in the palm of his hand.

This way, Flintwing Boy said and closed Tshushki's fingers over the cornfood gently. And they faced east. Flintwing Boy said, We humble ourselves again. We look in your direction for guidance. We ask for your protection. We humble our poor bodies and spirits because only you are the power and the source and the knowledge. Help us then—that is all we ask.

They breathed on the cornfood and took in the breath of all directions and gave the cornfood unto the ground.

Now the ground trembled with the awesome power of the Skquuyuh mahkina. Its humming vibrated against everything. Flintwing Boy reached behind him and took several arrows from his quiver. He inspected them carefully and without any rush he fit one to his bowstring.

And now, Anaweh, you must go and tell everyone. Describe what you have seen. The people must talk among themselves and decide what it is about and what they will do. You must hurry but you must not alarm the people. Tell them I am here to meet it. I will give them my report when I find out.

Coyote turned and began to run. He stopped several yards away. Hahtrudzaimeh, he called. Like a man of courage, Anaweh, like a man.

The old man stirred in his sleep. A dog was barking. He awoke and got out of his bed and went outside. The moon was past the midpoint and it would be morning light in a few hours.

LATER, THE SPACESHIP REACHED THE MOON.

Amarosho was with his grandfather. They watched a replay of two men walking on the moon.

So that's the men on the moon, Faustin said.

Yes, Nana, that's it.

There were two men inside of heavy clothing and equipment. The TV picture showed a closeup of one of them and indeed there was a man's face inside of glass. The face moved its mouth and smiled and spoke but the voice seemed to be separate from the face.

It must be cold. They have heavy clothing on, Faustin said.

It's supposed to be very cold and very hot. They wear the clothes and other things for protection from the cold and heat, Amarosho said.

The men on the moon were moving slowly. One of them skipped and he floated alongside the other.

The old man wondered if they were underwater. They seem to be able to float, he said.

The information I have heard is that a man weighs less than he does on earth, much less, and he floats. There is no air either to breathe. Those boxes on their backs contain air for them to breathe, Amarosho told his grandfather.

He weighs less, the old man wondered, and there is no air except for the boxes on their backs. He looked at Amarosho but his grandson didn't seem to be joking with him.

The land on the moon looked very dry. It looked like it had not rained for a long, long time. There were no trees, no plants, no grass. Nothing but dirt and rocks, a desert.

Amarosho had told him that men on earth—the scientists—believed there was no life on the moon. Yet those men were trying to find knowledge on the moon. He wondered if perhaps they had special tools with which they could find knowledge even if they believed there was no life on the moon desert.

The mahkina sat on the desert. It didn't make a sound. Its metal feet were planted flat on the ground. It looked somewhat awkward. Faustin searched vainly around the mahkina but there didn't seem to be anything except the dry land on the TV. He couldn't figure out the mahkina. He wasn't sure whether it could move and could cause fear. He didn't want to ask his grandson that question.

After a while, one of the bulky men was digging in the ground. He carried a long thin hoe with which he scooped dirt and put it into a container. He did this for a while.

Is he going to bring the dirt back to earth too? Faustin asked.

I think he is, Nana, Amarosho said. Maybe he'll get some rocks too. Watch.

Indeed several minutes later the man lumbered over to a pile of rocks and gathered several handsize ones. He held them out proudly. They looked just like rocks from around anyplace. The voice from the TV seemed to be excited about the rocks.

They will study the rocks too for knowledge?

Yes, Nana.

What will they use the knowledge for?

They say they will use it to better mankind, Nana. I've heard that. And to learn more about the universe we live in. Also some of them say that the knowledge will be useful in finding out where everything began and how everything was made.

Faustin smiled at his grandson. He said, You are telling me the true facts, aren't you?

Why yes, Nana. That's what they say. I'm not just making it up, Amarosho said.

Well then—do they say why they need to know where everything began? Hasn't anyone ever told them?

I think other people have tried to tell them but they want to find out for themselves and also I think they claim they don't know enough and need to know more and for certain, Amarosho said.

The man in the bulky suit had a small pickaxe in his hand. He was striking at a boulder. The breathing of the man could clearly be heard. He seemed to be working very hard and was very tired.

Faustin had once watched a crew of Mericano drilling for water. They had brought a tall mahkina with a loud motor. The mahkina would raise a limb at its center to its very top and then drop it with a heavy and loud metal clang. The mahkina and its men sat at one spot for several days and finally they found water.

The water had bubbled out weakly, gray-looking and didn't look drinkable at all. And then they lowered the mahkina, put their equipment away and drove away. The water stopped flowing.

After a couple of days he went and checked out the place. There was nothing there except a pile of gray dirt and an indentation in the ground. The ground was already dry and there were dark spots of oil-soaked dirt.

He decided to tell Amarosho about the dream he had.

After the old man finished, Amarosho said, Old man, you're telling me the truth now? You know that you have become somewhat of a liar. He was teasing his grandfather.

Yes, Nana said. I have told you the truth as it occurred to me that night. Everything happened like that except that I might not have recalled everything about it.

That's some story, Nana, but it's a dream.

It's a dream but it's the truth, Faustin said.

I believe you Nana, his grandson said.

SOMETIME AFTER THAT the spacemen returned to earth. Amarosho informed his grandfather that they had splashed down in the ocean.

Are they all right? Faustin asked.

Yes, Amarosho said. They have devices to keep them safe.

Are they in their homes now?

No, I think they have to be someplace where they can't contaminate anything. If they brought back something from the moon that they weren't supposed to they won't pass it on to somebody else, Amarosho said.

What would that something be?

Something harmful, Nana.

In that dry desert land there might be something harmful? I didn't see any strange insects or trees or even cactus. What would that harmful thing be?

Disease which might harm people on earth, Amarosho said.

You said there was the belief by the men that there is no life on the moon. Is there life after all? Faustin asked.

There might be the tiniest bit of life.

Yes I see now. If they find even the tiniest bit of life then they will believe, he said.

Yes. Something like that.

Faustin figured it out now. The men had taken that trip to the moon to find even the tiniest bit of life and if they found even the tiniest bit they would believe that they had found knowledge. Yes that must be the way it was.

He remembered his dream clearly now. He was relieved.

When are those two men fighting again? Nana asked his grandson.

What two men?

Those two men who were fighting with each other that day those other men were flying to the moon.

Oh—those men. I don't know, Nana. Maybe next Sunday. You like them?

Yes. I think that the next time I'll be cheering for the Apache. He'll win again. He'll beat the Mericano again, Faustin said, laughing.

ALBA IN DIRECTED LIGHT

Terry Boren

AT the very limit of his sight, Mt. Taylor wavered: as tenuous as a fault in a pane of blue glass and as hypothetical as the mind of a walker. Abé could just make out the white chip of its snow-covered slopes above the junction of mesa and sky. Outside the reach of his vision, the orbital platform and its slowly reawakening hardware spiraled around the planet carrying optical and radio scopes, laser communications gear—and one pale-haired woman who would be making repairs to any intact equipment or curling in some weightless, fetal kind of sleep in her cramped quarters. At such a distance, Abelardo could not pinpoint her location.

Outside of his window, November and a dark border of tamarisks, thick and smokey along the Rio Grande, had forced the yellow leaves of the cottonwoods into high relief. Abelardo Klashin was finishing his weekly enchilada in a little bar near the Lovelace Facility and wondering if everything—like the adobe walls of the restaurant and its scattered patrons, like Craig Ping and so many others—was old or falling apart.

Abé had been expecting Craig Ping to meet him for dinner, and he was growing tired of waiting. He glanced down at his own large, scarred hands and then toward the exit hoping that Craig would show up for their appointment after all. Not likely, as Craig hadn't set foot out of the facility more than once or twice in the past year. Abé knew that someone on the staff was bound to notice Craig's condition soon and report it; he wanted to talk to him before that happened, not only because the little oncologist would be almost impossible to replace, but because Abelardo liked the man.

The ancient and ugly bartender, Ed Baca, grinned and brought out another bottle of red wine when Abé caught his attention. Ed was emaciated and bald, but his pitted, bluish skin was a remnant of adolescent acne rather than the usual plague or melanoma. Though the glitter of the antiquated med-chips on Ed's bald scalp identified him, like most of the elderly diners in the restaurant, as one of the facility's clients, he had to be the healthiest old man Abelardo knew. Ed had learned a few things in his nearly one hundred years; the old man squinted at Abé for a moment, then left the bottle and went back to the bar without comment.

Abé picked at his dinner and waited for Craig Ping, who would soon be too ill to work. It had been obvious that morning that Craig was much worse.

Abelardo had been checking routine blood-factor reads when he was paged to accept the incoming walker. Craig was on reception. Though he didn't want the responsibility for another walker—who would inevitably die—the page synopsis told Abé that Craig was unable to handle the walker by himself. He hurried through the white, uninhabited corridor to the emergency entrance.

Craig was hunched nervously among the few residents who had gathered around a lifter which supported what was left of the walker's unconscious body. Abé took the records packet from him as soon as he reached the little man's side. Beads of sweat glittered along Craig's upper lip.

"You'll take him, won't you Abé?" he said very quietly. Craig's hands were trembling as he tugged at the tight collar of his shirt; but when he noticed Abé watching them, he shoved them into the pockets of his lab coat as if hiding his hands would keep Abé from seeing that he was afraid. A lump of white, keloidal tissue stood out vividly against Craig's flushed throat. "I'm sorry Abé," he said, "but I've got to get back to the o-labs. I can't…you know."

Abé was disturbed by the changes in Craig over the last weeks. Though there always had been an almost child-like delicacy about him, Craig seemed to have wasted away to a dangerous extent. Black, swollen bags discolored the skin beneath his eyes, and his gaze kept shifting away.

Abelardo watched the little man hurry off—stiff-backed, holding firmly to the elbow of the old man who had brought in the walker. The group of residents began to lose interest in the motionless body of the walker and to drift back toward their own quarters. Few of them spoke.

The walker's cover-sheet gave his name as Michael Benvenuto, for all it mattered now; and the old man who had brought him in was the responsible party of record, his father. Benvenuto was fifty years old and had a record of hospitalizations that went back thirty years to his first signs of Walker's Virus. Some of the damage to his body was obvious—traces of various tumors and eruptive diseases, the castration, and the amputation of his right arm as the result of gangrene—but an even greater ruin was hidden by the desiccated husk of flesh and bone. Only the hysterical surge of progress in the biological sciences during the die-offs could have made it possible for Benvenuto to live as long as he had.

The lifter transported Benvenuto automatically to an antiseptic room in the facility's central tower. Before leaving the body to the care of the room's machines, Abelardo entered the walker's records at a console across from the bed and supervised the application of glassjacket which would seal Benvenuto's vulnerable body away from any contact with the environment. When he had finished, Abé paused wearily beside the bed; within his glossy covering of antibiotic jelly, Benvenuto looked like some glazed and withered fruit, blighted and twisted almost beyond recognizability as human. He was certainly dying; the next infection would probably do it.

Abé stood a moment absently combing his fingers through his own dark hair and watching the terrible old face, then turned back to the computer and called up the Lassen-holo of the old man's S.M.A. layers. Predictably, the holo revealed the characteristic heavy damage of Walker's virus. The Lassen display only confirmed that there was nothing left to do for Benvenuto.

Abelardo entered a memo asking Craig to meet him at the restaurant for dinner.

But Craig, of course, had not shown up. The piñon blaze in the corner fireplace lit the small restaurant; it picked out the med-chips in Ed Baca's scalp, the strings of bright red chile on the walls, and the wooden crucifix with its Christ staring from above the door like a spy for some government that no longer existed. Abé felt an urge to cut himself away from it all, as his grand had. He wondered how long it would be before he, too, stopped talking to anyone, as his great-grandfather had, before his heart simply dried up and stopped like the old man's. Abé couldn't even talk to his own wife; he obviously couldn't help Craig either.

Abelardo finished the last of his wine and then pushed his glass to the other side of the small table. It must have been hard for old Klashin, he thought. His great-grandfather had told him about the arrangements for Abé to marry Leona while the old man and he were lying back on a steep hillside watching their scrubby herd of goats dancing around in the stands of mountain oak. Abé had thought, then, that life must all be very easy for the old man: Klashin had been too old to contract Walker's during the die-offs and hadn't come down with any of the other plagues that followed in its wake. The two of them had kept goats and picked piñons in the fall when the aspens flared red in the cañons.

But the virus had taken the old man's whole world, and he must have remembered it all though he never spoke to the boy about it. He never talked much at all that Abé could remember. Instead, when Abelardo was five years old and Klashin nearly eighty, the old man had taken Abé and what was left of the boy's father to a cabin in the Manzano mountains and tried to forget what was going on in the rest of the world. "Manzanitos," the old man had called the mountains—the little apples. When Klashin had told Abé that he wanted him to marry and leave the mountains, Abé had wondered if his grand wanted him to die as his mother already had and his father would.

Abé didn't remember his mother's death from complications of the virus and cancer, though he sometimes thought that he could remember her voice or her scent; and he didn't remember his father, the old man's grandson, as anything but a walker. His father had seemed only nominally human to Abé—sexless, mutilated, and intermittently violent. But old Klashin had managed to keep the boy and his father alive, and Abelardo had loved the old man. Then his grand had taken Abelardo and the herd of spotted goats out of the mountains to sell off the goats and marry off the boy to the granddaughter of a woman Klashin had known years before at some university. Abé had never met either of them.

The girl's name was Leona, and his grand had called her a "coyote," meaning she was half anglo-something and half hispanic-something. They had married when Abelardo was thirteen and she was a leggy eleven year old with tanned skin and hair bleached white by the desert sun. He had thought of her as his own personal dose of cyanide, but had married her anyway because his grand told him to. He had not wanted her. Now, he wanted to see her again.

They had met last almost a year ago, on their twenty-second anniversary. She hadn't looked much older than twenty.

Abelardo pushed himself back from the table, shrugged into his coat, and said goodnight to Ed. He couldn't stand to be there any longer. He stepped from the garlic and firelight of the restaurant into the wind and stars of the mesa. The evening had turned cold, and he was slightly drunk. Orienting himself by the clean central shaft of the Lovelace Facility compound, he started home.

The tough, drought-adapted vegetation of the mesa stretched away from him: north, to the dead hulk of Albuquerque and south, to the enormous, familiar maze of the facility.

I wasn't fair to her, he thought.

She had walked over to his table, and his first thought had been that she looked as if she had never been sick a day in her life. He thought the same thing every time he saw her. She was tall and big-boned, though not as large as Abé. She wore her hair cut to a blond stubble, and her eyes were so dark they were almost black.

"Craig told me you would be here," she said. "Happy anniversary."

"Hello, Lea. How are things out at the Sands?" He knew that she was waiting for him to say something else, to make some crack. Maybe say something about her obsession with the old orbital platform.

"Everything's fine. Of course, we're working ourselves to death right now getting ready for the first run back up to the platform. How's Mrs. Baltzer?" She and Mrs. Baltzer, Abelardo's oldest contractor, had always liked each other; he wasn't sure why.

"She's fine. Asks about you all the time." Instead of saying any more and risking a fight, he turned her around by her shoulders and led her to the bar. She was a bit startled, but she smiled. He ordered a glass of wine for her and a shot of tequila for himself, and they settled in for the evening.

He watched her fine head silhouetted against the firelight as she drank with one foot up on the rail and an elbow on the bar; he found himself wishing that she didn't live out at the White Sands Array. He also wished, with some bitterness, that he knew more about what she had done with the last twenty years of her life.

"Why don't you come up to the facility for a few days, Lea?" he asked her. "Mrs. Baltzer would love to see you, and we could get to know each other a little better again." But he felt awkward and embarrassed: so many years had passed, and she had so little left for him.

"My God, that's the first time you've actually done the inviting. Do you realize that, Abé?" She took a long drink of the red wine and looked deliberately away from him. "I'm sorry, Abelardo. I would like to visit, but I have too much work to do. I told you all about that in my last holo. I wouldn't have to break my back like this if the facility would give us some technical support, or even a few people to help."

"Sure," he said.

Though she didn't bring up the subject again, both of them were quieter, distanced; and by the time they left the restaurant at dusk, Abé was depressed and a little drunk. But as he walked beside her toward the parking lot, she quietly put her arm around his waist. He stopped, and she leaned against him. Her clothes and hair smelled faintly of piñon smoke.

She explored his rooms as if they were full of alien artifacts which she had somehow never noticed during her arranged visits through the years. She handled the translucent chunks of obsidian, the purple-centered geode, the medical books, and then discovered the stack of plates beside the imager and slipped the top holo-plate into position. It was old and badly recorded, so the resolution was poor; but the little three-dimensional image caught in the flickering light was clearly a younger version of Leona. She watched for a moment, frowning, and then turned back to the stack of plates and shuffled through them quickly.

"You kept all of them. Why?"

On the holo-stage, a girl and a large black dog walked along the endless silvery line of a radio array. The girl looked over her shoulder, smiled, and waved into the camera. Her hair was the same color as the flat, endless expanse of gypsum which stretched out in front of her, white to the horizon.

Abelardo reached out to the imager and cut its power manually. He couldn't answer her question. She had sent him recordings many times, but he had answered only a few. He felt as if keeping her recordings had been unnatural, as if it were unhealthy to have kept them. He suddenly thought of Mrs. Baltzer's photograph of her long-dead husband and of the dusty paintings she collected, all old and inexplicable. When he realized that he was standing hunched-up with his hands tucked into his armpits, he made a conscious effort to relax. Leona was watching him questioningly.

"We've known each other a long time, Lea," he said. "You're my wife." The explanation seemed weak even to him, though he could think of nothing else to say. But she took even that small assertion with a smile. She was watching him—she always had—as if she were trying to see into his skull but didn't want to chase him off. As if he were some shy kid she didn't want to frighten. His face felt hot, but he was drawn toward her. She was all smiles; she held out her hand to him.

"Well," she said, grinning at him, "at least I won't have to follow you around like a puppy anymore." Her long fingers hopped over her shirt buttons, and his gaze dropped irresistibly from her lips to the hollow of her throat and the paler skin of her shoulder and breast.

Her face, her hands, and her arms were brown from years of exposure to the desert sun; but the tan ended in a wash of translucent, smooth flesh where clothes normally covered her skin. One blue vein slid through a delicately peach-colored areola. *She is a beautiful, healthy woman*, he told himself. He didn't flinch away from her, didn't say anything; but she must have read something in his face, perhaps only confusion, because her hand stopped on the last button of her shirt, and her face lost all of its animation.

"It's all right," he said quickly, and lightly touched her shoulder. "You are very beautiful." But it was no good, and he knew it: she had seen his face change, his shock at the plain fact of her body, and she was angry. She jerked the shirt closed. Her lips were compressed and bloodless.

"What do you want?" she said very quietly. "A goddamn cave? Some way you can make love by holo? Damn it, Abé, do you still think it's going to rub off on you, make you dirty? You're an educated man, not one of those castrated idiots with a religion and a sharp knife! Goddamn it! …Goddamn it, Abé."

The argument that followed was short, as always. Abelardo stood with his fists bunched and ended up shouting back at her: "So why are you still out at the Sands? Dedication? Don't kid yourself. There's nothing out there either; and even if you did pick up something at the array, whoever sent it would be long dead. Nothing lives that long, no intelligence and no civilization." He accused her of staying with the project only because the prospects of actually receiving any non-terrestrial signal were safely distant. "You wouldn't know what to do with someone who was alive and inconvenient." That he knew his words hurt her was almost enough to justify them.

"I tried with you for over fifteen years," she replied in a harsh flat voice. "My experience as your wife should make me an adept at dealing with corpses."

She slapped the back of her open hand into his crotch as she pushed by him in the doorway.

I wasn't fair to her, he thought.

The bitterness of their arguments had always surprised Abelardo; as he dragged his attention back to the present, the dirt road, the empty landscape, the lights of the facility, he could feel a hot flush on his face. He was glad of the twilight privacy of the desert.

The worst thing about it was that he knew he was wrong. Without the White Sands launches, there would have been no power satellite. And after the dieoffs, there would have been no power. It didn't really matter why the group at the array kept at it: the energy from the platform—as much as the string of medical facilities—had kept everything from falling apart during the dieoffs. Or it kept the technology from falling apart, anyway, he thought; the rest of human society didn't do so well. His mind circled back again to Craig Ping, the thin slumped shoulders, the haunted face.

Abé paused outside of the residence wing of the complex. Unlike the brightly lit intensive care and emergency units which occupied the central shaft of the building complex, the residence wing of Lovelace Facility was quiet and softly lit. In sharp contrast, the permanent care wing on the opposite side of the central tower was windowless and dark from the outside. Craig probably would be in his apartment. Abelardo ghosted into the residence wing; most of his clients on the floor would already be asleep.

On the way to his own rooms, Abé stopped briefly at the entrances to the apartments of Craig's three elderly contractors to check their stats. The monitors showed each to be alone, and Mrs. Bates and Mr. Salazar were asleep. Their stats were good with the exception of a slight irregularity in Mr. Salazar's t-levels, an indication of his chronic but controlled illness. Though Craig was increasingly unable to cope with stress, the records of his contractors made it obvious that he was not neglecting his duties; Craig had logged in to run all of their stats only about an hour earlier.

Abé made up his mind to go to bed and try to talk to Craig in the morning. He would not hunt the man down if he didn't want to be found. Abé had just reached his own door after checking the last of his personal contractors when Mrs. Baltzer's voice grated out of the quiet hall behind him. She must have been waiting for him to return.

"Mr. Ping said to inform you that he would be held up this evening," she said. Abelardo turned to meet her friendly smile. She was holding the door open to her gold and blue apartment. Warm light from the stained-glass lamp in her bedroom made a pool of color in the darkened hallway. "Won't you come in and have a glass of wine before you sleep?"

Though he felt as if he were moving through a fog of depression and fatigue, he could not refuse the old lady.

At one hundred and twenty-five, Mrs. Baltzer was the oldest of Abelardo's contractors. Her partial loss of hearing caused her more concern than any other symptom of her age because it made her speech difficult to understand at times: her voice was too loud, pitched strangely, and she chopped the endings off some words. At one time, she had told him, she had played piano and sung, but no longer even tried. Though Abelardo had replaced one of her kidneys a few years before, there was no way to repair the traumatic brain damage that had ended music for her. She often waited up for him at night and liked to read to him and serve him little sandwiches and candies.

Abé relaxed on her couch and sipped at his wine as she read to him, another horrible old story out of European antiquity, some fairytale about a daughter who had chopped off her hands to save her father's life. He drifted in the eddies of the story and hardly felt the tug of sleep pulling him down into its bright imagery until Mrs. Baltzer shook him gently awake. He had been dreaming that she was a little dog barking in the hall to get his attention.

"Go home and go to sleep," she said, frowning at him. "And leave Craig alone until he feels better." She walked him to her door and watched as he stumbled the few meters to his rooms, palmed the lock, and shuffled into the apartment.

He had first met her when he was fourteen, just a few days after he had come to the clinic for training.

"You are American?" she had asked him. "Don't you smoke? All the young American officers were always smoking. They would sit in the parlor, smoking, and I would play the piano."

He hadn't understood half of what she said; her world was as strange to him as her voice. "Tobacco? Do I smoke tobacco?" he had answered.

As Abelardo pulled off his shoes and fell into bed, he wondered what his life might have been like if he hadn't come to the clinic or known Mrs. Baltzer for twenty years. She was dignified and cultured, in a way he had known nowhere else. She kept books and paintings in her rooms and was as close as Abé had ever come to a link with that vanished world that she represented for him. She kept a picture next to her bed of herself with her husband who had died in some war long before the virus. Somehow, he had always had trouble associating the old lady he knew with the young one in the photo; but he had known so few young women. He didn't know Mrs. Baltzer's first name, even after living with her for twenty years.

Abelardo leaned forward on his bed and touched a finger to the holo imager on his night stand; a tiny figure shimmered to life on the receiver set into its surface. It was a recording of Leona, the last plate she had sent him more than a year before. She was singing something, but the volume was set too low for him to hear her voice. The light from the holo washed his bedroom in pale gold—like the gold of the light in the painting, the Byzantine Annunciation, that Mrs. Baltzer had given him as a present.

He knew that the painting must mean something to the old lady, so he kept it. But he wasn't sure that he understood why she wanted him to have it, and every time he looked at it he felt uneasy. He kept it half-hidden in a corner of his bedroom. It was a small, dark piece—beautiful, but as non-human as the face of a walker.

The painting depicted a small chamber, its murky gloom relieved only by the gilt wings of an angel, wings that were insectile and attenuated. The two figures standing in the dimness seemed to have fallen asleep though their eyes were wide open. A woman's image was frozen in a graceful accepting stance. She seemed surprised; her eyes were huge and expressionless. The angel knelt submissively at her feet and stared at her thin, elegant left hand. The delicate fingers touched one small breast. Her chin was too small, her mouth almost nonexistent, and her flesh was a greenish brown—discolored by oxidation.

As he watched her, pulled in by her face, her eyes, he saw the diseased flesh pulling away from her bones and falling like tears down the wall to the carpet.

Just before dawn, Abelardo found himself awake again and realized that he had slept. The low moaning which had seemed a part of his dreams resolved itself into the stifled sound of wind blowing across the mesa. He had forgotten to cancel the holo of Leona, and it lit the room in a faint golden flicker. The program was on hold, and Leona's face was caught in a close-up at the beginning of some expression; her head was bowed and she was frowning, considering some lyrical sorrow attendant to whatever ballad she was singing. Suppressing the impulse to remain half-asleep while he watched the holo, he rolled off of the bed and stood up. His head hurt, and he knew that he wouldn't be able to go back to sleep again. Abé stood for a moment in the dark room rubbing his temple, then dressed quickly and quietly.

The halls of the residence wing were empty, and the cold tiles licked the soles of his bare feet as he passed the apartments with their dim monitor screens and moved toward the central hospital complex. He could hear music filtering softly through the locked door of Craig's apartment, but there was no answer to his knock. He continued on toward intensive care, but as he stepped from the dark corridor into the glassed-in walkway between the wings he was stopped by the cold clear moonlight that filled the passage.

Although the wind rose and fell outside of the building, keening against the glass, the night was lucid and absolutely clear: a full moon hung just above the mesa to the west; tumbleweeds hurtled across the old lava flows; the stars were very sharp and bright in the dry night air. He had seen a few other nights like this one, but they were rare even on the desert. A chill slid up his back. His grand had taught him that such weather brought the flu and other, less pleasant visitations. The wind-driven grains of sand crackled against the building.

On another night like this—the landscape frosted over with wind and moonlight—his grand had told him that the moaning wind was the spirit of a grieving woman, angry and searching for her drowned sons.

But disease is not an aspect of the wind, he told himself as he watched tumbleweeds being driven against the compound's fences. As he no longer believed that Walker's virus was a plague brought by the wind or that its venereal aspect was a punishment for sin, he no longer believed in being haunted by the dead. Walker's was not, he knew, wind-carried as some viruses were; and it was not sent by God. But like a ghost, Walker's no longer really existed, at least in its virulent form. It had killed off its host. Walker's, quite simply, had been a spectacularly unsuccessful congruence of diseases—a "slow" virus that manifested years after exposure, hormonally triggered, quickly mutating, and in league with every other sickness in the world. It was only like the wind because it tore things apart, dropped them elsewhere, or swept them away entirely.

And analogies are not true likenesses, he told himself, though the comparison was certainly a bitter one. Benvenuto was dying of the non-existent disease in the Lovelace Facility clinic; Leona was somewhere trying to talk to the stars; and technology was all that had kept them all from blowing away completely—as his mother had blown away, as Leona's mother and father had blown away, as a whole generation and world had blown away.

Pretty soon I'll be as bad as Craig, he thought as he massaged his tense neck muscles, stiff from the fading headache. It was the arrival of the walker, he knew, that had made him so restless; and it was some comfort, though not enough, that there were so few walkers left. Abelardo pushed into the wider, brightly lit corridor of the clinic wing and announced himself at registration, then continued in the direction of the isolation ward accompanied and surrounded by the bird-sounds of hospital electronics.

Benvenuto's room was crammed with monitors and scented pungently by antibiotic glassjacket. Abelardo stood just inside the door while his eyes adjusted to the deeper night of the curtained space and then, careful not to jostle the dying man on the bed, he moved cautiously to the windows and pulled the drapes aside; the moon spread white light around the room. After seating himself at the terminal directly under the window, he ran through the same numbers that he knew he could have called up at the terminal in his own apartment.

Through the swaddling of his depression, Abé heard the rustle of fabric on fabric. He froze in place as the hair on the back of his neck rose to the sudden frisson of childhood fear the sound called up in him. *No*, he thought as he turned around to face the bed. But the old man hadn't stirred; Craig Ping leaned toward Abelardo across Benvenuto's body.

"His t-levels are way down," Craig said, avoiding Abelardo's eyes. "Lymphocytes are all within acceptable bounds otherwise." Craig's face was pale and serene.

"Yeah, sure, but I packed him full of antis and tumor specifics just this morning. His readings shouldn't be this low yet."

"Shouldn't? Sure they should be, Abé. Of course they should be; he's outlived most of them anyway…didn't have any immune response at all on his own." Craig stood and brushed one hand across Benvenuto's forehead. The blurry, imprecise gesture told Abé that Craig had sedated himself into semi-consciousness to be able to sit so calmly beside the walker in a dark room.

Craig looked at the old man a moment and then slid his thumb gently into the great pit in Benvenuto's face left by cancer and bone disintegration. Thin hair fell over Craig's eyes, hiding the little man's expression. "How long has he got, anyway? His old man wouldn't have brought him in if anything could have pumped up that corpse of an immune system one more time. Have you even identified every disease he's got? Shit, he's already dead anyway."

"The readouts say he is alive. Maybe you should stick to oncology, Craig."

"Sure he's alive. Alive as you or me. Only he'll never get up from that bed; and if he did, it would be because we've pumped him full enough of peptides and cerebral hormones to make his corpse—or any other corpse—walk around. You can't do anything about all the short-circuits in his brain, Abé. The lymphoma or something else we don't even know about yet is going to get him, soon."

Craig looked up again, across Benvenuto's body. His face was calm, his expression flattened by the sedatives. "I'm sorry I ran out on you this morning, too; but I just keep thinking he'll get up from there." Craig stood rubbing the old man's face until Abé reached across the bed and pushed him back into the chair.

"Don't worry about it," Abé told him quietly. "He'll never get up again, and I'm not going to pump him full of anything. It has all been done. Like you said, a time comes when there's nothing left to try."

Craig shifted uneasily; a muscle under his left eye was ticking. "But he is alive. He is still in there."

"Yeah, and a holo-plate without the reader is a useless chunk of glass. What does it matter, Craig? There's nerve damage, the SMA tissues are shot....He may be in there, but the reader is broken." Abelardo gestured toward the monitor and the little terminal with its undeniable figures. "I could call up complete records of the chemical and bio-electrical events in his head; I can prove that he isn't technically brain-dead and even digitalize the data that should make up the totality, the Self, of Michael Benvenuto; but it's all useless to us, and useless to him, too. How can we interpret the data? No two brains work the same way, Craig. We're each coded differently."

He wanted Craig to listen to him, to stop going back over the same facts and events with no satisfactory conclusions. But he knew that it was no use, and he knew what Craig's next question would be before he asked it.

"And my father," Craig said, avoiding Abé's eyes again, "was he still in there when he cut my throat?" It was the same question that Craig Ping, Abé's friend, had asked again and again.

"He was dying," Abe said, punching the words at Craig and leaning toward the smaller man. "He was sick, and he was crazy." He realized that he was shouting and forced himself to sit back and speak more reasonably. "I don't know. Hell, he had been dosed with everything your mother could think of sticking into him. He probably wasn't aware of what he was doing, but who can tell you for sure what was left inside? Most of them were violent in some stage. But he's dead now. How many times do you have to go over it?"

"It must be quite a few times in the last twenty years, I guess. Stupid isn't it? Neurotic." He looked down at his hands. "They won't let me see the kid any more, you know. I think they're afraid I'll hurt him. Life's filthy all over, as they say, huh?"

Craig was slumped motionlessly in his chair. Abé could think of no way to answer him. He felt like an idiot; but the truth was that Abé had no idea what it had been like for Craig to be caught in Albuquerque during the dieoffs, and he didn't want to have. He had seen enough as it was. But Craig had seemed fine until the birth of his son a few years ago. His disintegration had progressed steadily since. In the pale moonlight, Craig seemed thin and alien, like a strange insect, and Abé was suddenly repulsed by the man. Abé's throat tightened.

A few days after Mrs. Baltzer had shown him the Annunciation she had been scheduled for a routine medical interview. He was shining a small light into her nerveless ears when he accidently jogged her wig askew. Under the shiny headpiece was a gray web of her real hair; it was sparse and slightly damp. As he was staring at her, his breath moving the fine gray stuff, she turned around and looked straight into his eyes. Her high old cheekbones were prominent, and beneath the shine of moisturizer her skin was papery and wrinkled.

She hadn't said a word to him, just looked at him, but her face was like an arroyo where bones wash out of the banks after each rain. He hadn't been able to finish her examination because he couldn't force himself to touch her. He never knew what she had been thinking.

Later that evening, she had rustled cheerfully across the clinic hallway and stopped at his apartment. She spoke to him briefly in that loud barking voice about her friend Mrs. Bates, and about the weather, and then she invited him to her room for lunch. She was smiling and seemed happy, but she refused to let him talk for very long.

"I know you don't want to talk to an old woman who is deaf. I am sorry; please, will you have cakes?" After they had finished and she had read something German to him which he hadn't understood, she gave him the Annunciation and made him take it back to his rooms.

The little note taped to the back of the frame was only two lines long:

Remember me, wind, you one time smooth skin.
How many stars of space are like my son.

As the silence had extended in Benvenuto's room, Craig had pulled himself up from the chair. He was obviously hesitating, ready to run but wanting to explain himself. Abé 'spoke rapidly, trying to reach Craig and build some connection with him out of words.

"My grand brought me up in the Manzanos. It was beautiful up there," he whispered, as if only he were in the room. "I used to think that the old man was just mean, but sometimes I think that he really understood what was happening better than most of us did. He didn't talk much. There were only three of us. And my father didn't talk at all, of course; he was always just a little sicker, until one morning I couldn't find him."

Craig's face had turned toward him; the lump of scar tissue at the man's throat was startlingly white in the dim light.

"After I had looked for him most of the day, I asked grand what had happened to him, and the old man said that he'd packed my father with brain-actives that morning and he'd probably walked off of a cliff or something. I had found kid-goats all over those mountains, but I never did find him…I didn't look very hard though. I think I suspected what had happened. I knew he was dead, anyway.

"About a week after my father disappeared, the old man came into the milking shed with a burlap bag over his shoulder. He said he had a surprise for me. I had just finished milking, and the shed was warm and close; it smelled good, musty and sweet like goats and alfalfa.

"I knew he was up to something, so I asked him what was in the bag. He just kept grinning at me and said that I could either reach in and find out, or he'd leave the bag outside until morning and I could have it then.

"There were two bobcat kittens in the bag, and they tore the hell out of my hand and arm before I could haul the little bastards out. One of them bit all the way through my thumb."

Craig's eyes were very dark in the shadows away from the window. He looked as if he hadn't slept in days. Abé would have shown him the marks of the bobcat's teeth and claws, but Craig's attention was on his own past and his own scars.

"Grand had stopped smiling, though. I was bleeding all over the shed. He asked me if I didn't think it was pretty stupid of me to reach in the bag. I didn't answer.

"He was waiting for me by the fire when I came in. I just sat down and let him clean me up. He was a good medic, really.

"'Well,' he said—and he didn't look at me—'I guess you knew it was coming, Abé....There wasn't anything left of your father, you know. He was my grandson, too; so I put a hollow-point in his skull and buried him down in Fourth-of-July cañon. I'll show you where if you want me to.' I didn't want him to.

"That was right before my tenth birthday; we never talked about my father after that. Grand jerked me out of the mountains when I was thirteen. I never knew why. He said that I needed an education, that he'd taught me all he could. Maybe he had."

Craig had turned away. "Like I said, Abé, if you can work here, I'm glad you can stand it; but I'll be going back to the institute in Colorado, probably next week. So much for communciation. I was always better at research, anyway."

Abelardo felt a surge of anger at the research institute and its staff that avoided any human contact, with the outside or with its own members.

And he wanted to hit Craig. He was surprised at the anger he felt toward the man. "I guessed you'd be leaving," he said. "Maybe you should try it here a while longer." But Abé knew as he watched him that Craig would run again. There was something in the tightness about his eyes. Craig was afraid of hurting his son, but he was more dangerous to himself than to anyone else.

Craig reached for the door and spoke without turning to meet Abé's face. "You were going to ask me to get some more therapy, weren't you? Well, I don't want any. I doubt it would help anyway. I'll be much happier working in the labs, Abelardo." Craig pushed quickly into the hall, and the light struck at Abelardo's eyes.

He waited quietly by the window as his vision readjusted to the room, and then he waited simply as a companion to the old man who would never again walk into that brilliant corridor. After what seemed a long time, Abé glanced at the Lassen-display of Benvenuto's heavily damaged SMA and then at the old walker's ravaged face.

Benvenuto was unconscious, as he had been since he was registered. His breath was a barely-perceptible flutter, his body a ruin of mutilations and disease. The setting moon had smeared itself over the glassjacket; and Benvenuto looked to Abé as if he had been tortured, murdered, and then carefully preserved for viewing. There was, he thought, a great deal of truth to that image. Below the lyumphocyte and blood-comp readings on the screen, a red indicator had blinked on; the attendant display told Abé exactly how Benvenuto would finish dying.

The entire thing, the picture which encompassed the old man, the medical facility, Craig, and the ridiculous little indicator, seemed like an ugly joke scrawled in light. He began to laugh painfully, deep in his throat.

The surgical team would take the old man now, as if it were accomplishing something, and they would cut into his head to bypass the ballooning artery, signified by that red light, which without intervention would sweep the old man away as if he were a dried weed. If they managed to locate the aneurism in time, Benvenuto might live a few days or weeks longer, but certainly no more. If they did not locate it in time, the technicians and surgeons would simply stand and watch as the balloon exploded inside his head.

Benvenuto's death would be realized for them in the old man's blown pupils and the numbers on the monitor as it charted the progress of blood surging through delicate tissues. But from inside, Abé suddenly understood clearly, the stroke would come as a wave, a standing-wave which would carry Benvenuto's Self away in crests and billows of light. And if Self were indeed hologramatic, the holo that was the old man's mind would no longer have any use for its damaged reader.

Abé considered wedging the door closed. But as the first member of the emergency team maneuvered himself and his equipment into the tiny room, Abé reached out convulsively instead and ordered Benvenuto's complete records dumped into personal storage. He left his place at the terminal and got out of the way of death.

As he paused once again in the walkway between the clinic's wings, Abelardo could feel the deep cold of the high-desert night radiating through the glass. The wind had quieted, and—though the hour before sunrise on the desert was often of such an icy clarity that he could see the white skirts of Mt. Taylor almost seventy miles away—the western horizon was invisible, dark. He could barely make out the pale jumble of sage and wind-carried debris that was snagged on the clinic fences only twenty feet away. He looked briefly to the southwest, but no spark low on the horizon revealed the position of the orbital platform. He thought of his wife, up there talking to emptiness. He knew that he was very tired.

But Leona would not leave him alone. Her tiny, aureate figure continued in its soundless dance on the little holo-stage in his room. Abé stood just inside his apartment door watching her for a moment, then crossed to his terminal and sat down. He punched up Michael Benvenuto's records. Benvenuto had no surviving children, as Abé had none. The only man that Abé knew who had a son was Craig Ping, who could no longer stand to touch anyone.

Abé could smell the sharp fear-scent of his own sweat as he tied in to the facility's communications net and directed an up-link and fix on the orbital platform. He could not locate it by sight in the pre-dawn sky, but the facility always knew the platform's position.

With one touch, the communciations laser ceded to her the entire digitalized contents of Benvenuto's files. An exchange, he thought, the record of a mind for the record of a life.

She had once told him that before the dieoffs people had wanted to communicate with other beings from other stars, even to travel there themselves—or failing that to send their genetic material, like seed, out to other worlds.

She did not acknowledge receipt of the message, but her computer verified acceptance of his transmission.

This time, he thought, she wasn't going to answer him. In a burst of frustration, he typed an appendix to the file:

> *These records belonged to a man who hadn't spoken in thirty years. Maybe he was dead all that time. He is dead now, or might as well be, and these records are of no use to anyone. Relay them on to whatever you believe is out there. If we can't go, maybe he can. Michael Benvenuto will be in this data file to find again if a key to the code exists; and if there are only dead men out there, only creatures who can't listen or understand, then he'll be no worse off.*

Abelardo Klashin sat in the dark and watched the image of his wife that he had watched a hundred times before. She was singing; he could even remember the words of the song.

Again, her computer acknowledged receipt.

His attention returned to the holo, to her intense frowning face. Her body was taut and effort shouted from every line of her. The very eloquence of the little image almost robbed him of anything to say to her; but as the words of Leona's song came back into his mind, he typed the lyrics into the terminal and sent them back to her:

. . . shall her body never again
stream its light through the night for me?
—body whiter than snow,
it deceived my sight:
I thought that it might be
a ray of the moon's light;
then day came.

It was an old song, he knew, a very old song. Leona had made peace, somehow, with the pain and the beauty of the past. Outside of the planetary envelope, she might be awake now, working or exercising.

He thought about dead men as he turned back to the pale light of the holo. At least he had tried, perhaps she would know that.

A ray of the moon's light, he thought, and reached out to touch the holo's volume control.

A message indicator lit near his right hand as her voice filled the room.

ILIANA OF THE PLEASURE DREAMS

Rudolfo A. Anaya

ILIANA stirred in the summer night, then awakened from her dream. She moaned, a soft sigh, her soul returning from its dreams of pleasure. She opened her eyes, the night breeze stirred the curtains, the shadows created images on the bare adobe wall, an image of her dream which moved, then changed and was lost as the shadows moved away from dream into reality.

In the darkness of the night, smelling the sweet fragrance of the garden which wafted through the open door, lying quietly so as not to awaken Onofre her husband, she lay smiling and feeling the last wave of pleasure which had aroused her so pleasantly from her deep sleep. It was always like this, first the images, then the deep stirring which touched the depths in her, then the soft awakening, the coming to life.

In the summer Onofre liked to sleep with the doors and windows open, to feel the mountain coolness. Her aunts had never allowed Iliana to sleep in the moonlight. The light of the moon disturbs young girls, they had said.

Iliana smiled. Her aunts had given her a strict religious up-bringing, and they had taught her how to care for a home, but they had never mentioned dreams of pleasure. Perhaps they did not know of the pleasure which came from the images in her dreams, the images which at first were vague, shadows in a place she did not recognize, fragments of faces, whispers. The shadows came closer, there was a quickening to her pulse, a faster tempo to her breathing, then the dream became clear and she was running across a field of alfalfa to be held by the man who appeared in her dreams. The man pressed close to her, sought her lips, caressed her, whispered words of love, and she was carried away into the spinning dream of pleasure. She had never seen the man's face, but always when she awakened she was sure he was standing in the garden, just outside the door, waiting for her.

Yes, the dream was so real, the flood of pleasure so deep and true, she knew the man in the dream was there, and the shadows of the garden were the shadows of her dreams.

She rose slowly, pushing away the damp sheet which released the sweet odor of her body. Tonight the man had reached out, taken her in his arms and kissed her lightly. The pleasure of his caress consumed her and carried her into a realm of exhilaration. When she awakened she felt she was falling gently back to earth, and her soul came together again, to awaken.

She walked to the window quietly, so as not to awaken her husband. She had never told him of her private world of dreams, and even when she confessed her dreams to the priest at Manzano she could not tell him everything. The dreams were for her, a private message, a disturbing pleasure she did not know how to share. Perhaps with the man in the dream she could share her secret, share the terrible longing which filled her and which erupted only in her dreams.

She leaned against the door and felt the cool breeze caress her perspiring body. Was he there, in the shadows of the garden, waiting for her? She peered into the dark. The shadows the moon created were as familiar as those she saw in her dreams. She wanted to cry out to understand the dream, to share the pleasure, but there was no one there. Only the soft shrill of the night crickets filled the garden. The cry of the grios foretold rain, the clouds would rise over the mountain, the thunder would rumble in the distant sky, and the dry spell of early summer would be broken.

Iliana sighed. She thought of her aunts, Tia Amalia and Tia Andrea. Why had they not explained the dreams of pleasure? They were women who had never married, but they had said marriage would be good for her. All of the girls in the village married by eighteen and settled down to take care of their families. Onofre was a good man, a farmer, a hard worker, he did not drink, he was a devout Catholic. He would provide a home, they said, and she would raise his children.

The girls of the mountain valley said Onofre was handsome but very shy. He would have to wait many years and marry a widow, they said, and so they were surprised when Iliana married him. Iliana was the most beautiful girl in the valley. It was a marriage of convenience, the young women whispered to explain the match, and Iliana went to her marriage bed with no conception of what was expected of her. Onofre was gentle, but he did not kiss the nape of her neck or whisper the words of pleasure she heard in her dreams. She vaguely understood that the love of Onofre could be a thread to her secret dreams, but Onofre was abrupt, the thread snapped, the fire of her desire died.

She was unsure, hesitant, she grew timid. They ate in silence, they lived in silence. Like an animal that is careful of its master, she settled around the rhythms of his work day, being near when it was time to be close, staying in her distant world the rest of the time. He too felt the distance; he tried to speak but was afraid of his feelings. Sitting across the table from her he saw the beauty of her face, her hands, her throat and shoulders, and then he would look down, excuse himself, return to his work with which he tried to quench the desires he did not understand.

There is little pleasure on earth, the priest at the church said. We were not put on earth to take pleasure in our bodies. And so Onofre believed in his heart that a man should take pleasure in providing a home, in watching his fields grow, in the blessing of the summer rains which made the crops grow, in the increase of his flocks. Sex was the simple act of nature which he knew as a farmer. The animals came together, they reproduced, and the priest was right—it was not for pleasure. At night he felt the body of Iliana and the pleasure came to engulf him for a moment, to overwhelm him and suffocate him. Then as always the thread severed, the flame died.

Iliana waited at the window until the breeze cooled her skin and she shivered. In the shadows of the garden she felt a presence, and for a moment she saw again the images of her dream, the contours of her body, the purple of alfalfa blossoms. A satisfaction in the night, a sensuous pleasure welled up from a depth of soul she only knew in her dreams. She sighed. This was her secret.

How long had it been in her soul, this secret of pleasure? She had felt it even in the church at Manzano where she went to confession and mass. She had gone to the church to confess to the priest, and the cool earth fragrance of the dark church and the sweetness of the votive candles had almost overwhelmed her. "Help me," she whispered to the priest, desiring to cleanse her soul of her secret even as the darkness of the confessional whispered the images of her dream. "I have sinned," she cried, but she could not tell him of the pleasures of her dreams. The priest, knowing the young girls of the village tended to be overdramatic in the stories of their love life, mumbled something about her innocence, made the sign of the cross absolving her, and sent her to her small penance.

Iliana walked home in deep despair. Along the irrigation ditch the tall cottonwood trees reminded her of strong, virile men, their roots digging into the dark soul of the earth, their branches creating images of arms and legs against the clear sky. She ran, away from the road, away from the neighboring fields; over the pine mountain she ran until exhausted she clutched at a tree, leaned against the huge trunk; trembling she listened to the pounding of her heart. The vanilla smell of the pine was like the fragrance of the man in her dreams. She felt the rough bark, like the rough hands of Onofre at night. She closed her eyes and clutched at the tree, holding tight to keep from flying into the images of her dream which swept around her.

Iliana remembered her visit to the church as she returned to her bed, softly so as not to awaken Onofre. She lay quietly and pulled the sheet to her chin. She closed her eyes, but she could not sleep. She remembered the images at the church and felt again how she was overcome when she pressed close to the tree. It was the same tonight in her dream, the immense pleasure which filled her with a desire so pure she felt she was dying and returning to God. Why?

She thought of her aunts, spinsters whose only occupation was to care for the church at Manzano. They swept, they sewed the cloths for the altar, they brought the flowers for mass, they made sure the candles were ready. They had given their lives to God; they did not speak of pleasure. What would they think if they knew of the dreams that came to Iliana?

Release me, Iliana cried. Free me. Leave me to my work and to my husband. He is a good man, leave me to him. Iliana's tears wet the sheet, and it was not until the early morning that she could sleep again.

"We can go this afternoon," Onofre said as they ate.

"Oh, yes," Iliana nodded. She was eager to go to the church at Manzano. Just that morning her aunts had come to visit her. They were filled with excitement.

"An apparition has appeared on the wall of the church," Tia Amalia said.

"The face of Christ," Tia Andrea said, and both bowed their heads and made the sign of the cross.

That is what the people of the mountain valleys were saying, that at sunset the dying light and the cracks in the mud painted the face of Christ on the adobe wall of the church. A woman on the way to rosary had seen the image, and she ran to tell her comadre. Together they saw it, and their story spread like fire up and down the mountains. The following afternoon all the people of the village came and gathered in the light of dusk to see the face of Christ appear on the wall. Many claimed they saw the face; some said a man crippled by arthritis was cured and could walk when he saw the image.

"I see! I see!" the old man had shouted, and he stood and walked. The people believed they had experienced a miracle. "There!" each shouted in turn as the face of Christ appeared. The crown of thorns was clear, blood streamed down the sad and anguished face. The women fell to their knees. A miracle had come to the village of Manzano.

The priest came and took holy water and blessed the wall, and the old people understood that he had sanctified the miracle. The following evening people came from miles around, from the mountain villages and ranches they came to see the miracle. Those who saw the face of the savior cried aloud or whispered a private prayer; the women on their knees in the dust prayed rosary after rosary.

People from the nearby villages came; families came in their cars and trucks. The women came to pray, eager to see the image of Christ. Their men were more guarded; they stood away from the church wall and wondered if it was possible. The children played hide-and-seek as all waited for the precise moment of dusk when the image appeared.

The young men came in their customized cars and trucks, drinking beer, eager to look at the young women. Boys from the ranches around the village came on horseback, dressed in their Sunday shirts and just-pressed Levis; they came to show off their horsemanship to the delight of the girls. A fiesta atmosphere developed; the people were glad for the opportunity to gather.

The men met in clusters and talked politics and rain and cattle. Occasionally one would kick at the ground with his boot, then steal an uncomfortable glance at his wife. The women also gathered in groups, to talk about their children, school, marriages and deaths, but mostly to talk about the miracle which had come to their village and to listen to the old women who remembered a prior apparition when they were young. A young woman, they said, years ago, before cars came to the mountains, had seen the image of the Virgin Mary appear, on a wall, and the praying lasted until the image disappeared.

"One never knows which is the work of the devil or the work of God," an old woman said. "One can only pray."

A strange tension developed between the men and the women who went to see the miracle. It was the women who organized the rosaries and the novenas. It was the women who prayed, kneeling on the bare ground for hours, the raw earth numbing their knees and legs. It was they who prayed for the image to appear, their gaze fixed on the church wall, their prayers rising into the evening sky where the nighthawks flew as the sun set red in the west.

The priest grew concerned and tried to speak to the men, but they greeted him quietly, then looked down at the ground. They had no explanation to share. The priest turned to the women; they accepted him but did not need him. Finally he shut himself up in the church, to pray alone, unsure of the miracle, afraid of the tension in the air which had turned the people in a direction he did not understand. He could not understand the fervent prayer of the women, and he could not control it. The people of this valley in the Sangre de Cristo mountains, he had been warned, were different. Now he understood the warning. The image had come to the wall of the church and the people devoutly accepted it as a miracle. Why had he been sent to the church at Manzano? He belonged in the city, where the politics of the church were clear and understood. This transformation in his parishioners he did not understand. He opened the chest where he kept the altar wine and drank, wondering what it was he had seen in the lines and shadows when he looked at the wall. He couldn't remember, but he couldn't look again.

In the afternoon Onofre and Iliana drove over the ridge of the mountain to the church at Manzano. Onofre drove in silence, wondering what the visitation of the image meant. Iliana rode filled with a sense of excitement. Perhaps the image on the wall of the church was a sign for her. She would see her savior and he would absolve the pleasure dreams; all would be well.

Iliana smiled, closed her eyes and let herself drift as the rocking of the truck swayed her gently back and forth. Through the open window the aroma of the damp earth reached her nostrils. She smelled the pregnant, rich scent of the soil and the pine trees. She remembered the dapple horse she used to ride across the meadow from her Tia Amalia's house to her Tia Andrea's.

When they arrived at Manzano, Iliana opened her eyes and saw the crowd of people around the church. Cars and trucks lined the dirt road. Together Onofre and Iliana walked toward the group by the church.

Onofre felt awkward when he walked in public with his wife. She was a young and beautiful woman. He did not often think of her beauty, except when they were with other people. Then he saw her as others might see her, and he marveled at her beauty.

"It's the Spanish blood of her mother which gives her her beauty," her aunts were fond of saying.

Her oval face reminded Onofre of a saint he had seen once in a painting, perhaps at the cathedral at Santa Fe. Her face, the dark eyelashes, the dark line of the eyebrows, the green eyes. She was exquisite, a woman so beautifully formed that people paused to watch her. Onofre felt the eyes of the young men on his wife as they walked, and he tried to shake away the feeling of self-consciousness as he walked beside her. He knew the men admired the beauty of his wife, and he had been kidded about being married to an angel.

Iliana was aware of her beauty; it was something she felt in her soul. Everything she did was filled with a sensuous pleasure in which she took delight, and as they walked toward the church she took pleasure in feeling the gaze of the men on her. But she cast down her eyes and did not look at them, understanding that she should not bring shame to her husband.

Instead she looked at the children who played around the church; the gathering had become a fiesta. Someone had brought an ice machine to sell flavored ice. Another person had set up a stand to sell rosaries and other religious items, and a farmer was selling green chile and corn from the bed of his truck. There were people Iliana did not recognize, people from as far away as Taos and Española.

As Iliana and Onofre passed, friends and neighbors greeted them, but when the young bachelors of the village saw her a tension filled the air. Her beauty was known in the mountain villages, and at eighteen she was more beautiful than ever. All of the young men had at one time or another dreamed of her; now they looked at her in awe, for underneath her angelic beauty lay a sensuality which almost frightened them.

"Onofre must be treating her right," one young man whispered to his friend. "She is blossoming."

How lucky Onofre is, they thought. He so plain and simple, and yet she is his. God is not fair, they dared to think as they tipped their cowboy hats when she passed. All were young and virile men of the mountains, handsome from their Spanish and Indian blood, and all were filled with desire when they saw Iliana.

They called Onofre a lucky man, but the truth was that each one of them had had a chance to court Iliana. Each one of them had seen her at school; they saw her at church on Sundays, and each day they saw her beauty grow. They could not touch her, even in the games they played as children, they dared not touch her. When they grew into young manhood a few of them sought her out, but one glance from her eyes told them that Iliana was a young woman filled with mystery. They turned away, unwilling to challenge the sensuous mystery they felt in her presence. They turned away and married the simple girls of the village, those in whom there was no challenge, no mystery to frighten and test them.

Now, as Iliana passed them, she felt the admiration of the young men of the mountains. She smiled and wondered as she stole a glance at their handsome faces if one of them was the man who appeared in her dreams.

Her aunts were there; indeed, they had been there all day, waiting for the setting of the sun, waiting for the image of Christ to appear. They saw Iliana and drew her forward.

"We're pleased you arrived," they said. "Come, hija, it's almost time." They pulled her away from Onofre, and he sighed with relief and stepped back into the crowd of men.

The women parted as the two aunts drew Iliana forward so she could have a good view of the church wall. Already candles were lighted, a rosary was being prayed. The singing of the Hail Marys fell softly on their ears, and the sweet scent of paraffin filled the air. The women drew close together, prayed; the crowd grew quiet as the sun set. The cracks of the old plaster on the wall appeared thick and textured as the sun touched the horizon of the juniper-covered hills to the west. If the image appeared, it would be only for a few minutes, then it would dissolve into the grey of the evening.

Iliana waited. She prayed. Pressed between her aunts and the women, she felt their fragrances mix with the wax smell of the candles. So it had been at the church, the distinctive aroma of women comingling with the sanctity of God. The hush of the crowd reminded her of the hush of the church, and she remembered images and scenes. She remembered the pleasure that came with her first blood, the dapple horse she rode from the house of one aunt to the other...the field of alfalfa with purple blossoms and the buzzing of the honey bees, the taste of the thick, white paste at school, the tartness of the first bite of an apple, the fragrance of fresh bread baked in the horno behind her Tia Amalia's house, the day the enraged bull broke loose and tore down the horno until there was only a pile of dirt left, and the frightened women watching from their windows, cursing the bull, praying to God. She swayed back and forth on her knees, felt the roughness of the pebbles, heard the prayers of the women, felt the flood of disconnected images which dissolved into the smell of the mountain earth after a summer rain, the welcome smell of piñon wood burning in the fireplace and flavoring the air, the feeling of pleasure which these sights and sounds and memories wove into her soul....

She closed her eyes, and pressed her hands to her bosom to still the pounding of her heart, to stop the rush of heat which moved up from the earth to her knees and thighs. Around her she heard the women praying as if in a dream. Beads of sweat wet her upper lip as the images came to tease her; she licked at the sweat and tasted it.

Then the crowd grew still, the magic hour had come. "Look," one of the aunts whispered. Iliana opened her eyes and looked up at the lines and shadows on the wall.

"You see!" the other aunt said.

Iliana, in reverie, nodded, smiled. Yes, I see, she wanted to say aloud, her gaze fastened on the scene on the wall. She saw a figure, then two. Arms and legs in an image of love. Yes, it was the image of her dream. Iliana smiled and her body quivered with pleasure.

"Dear God," she cried, overwhelmed by the pleasure of the waves which rolled through her body. "Dear God," she cried, then Iliana fainted.

In her dream she walked on purple blossoms, and the sweet aroma rose like sweet wine and touched the clouds of summer. Red and mauve and the crimson of blood. In the darkness of the field the man waited by the dapple horse. The waves of pleasure dissipated, the thread broke before she reached the man.

Tia Amalia touched camphor to her nose and Tia Andrea patted her hand vigorously. Iliana awoke and saw the shadows of the women around her. Beyond the women Iliana caught a glimpse of the wall, dark now, the congealing of shadows and lines no longer held the secret she had seen.

"A miracle," her aunt whispered. "You saw the face of Christ! You are blessed!"

"Blessed be the Lord Jesus Christ," the chorus of the women responded.

"When you fainted you smiled like an angel," her aunt said. "We knew you had seen the miracle."

"Yes," Iliana whispered, "I have seen the face of God." She struggled to rise, to free herself from the press of the women. On their knees they prayed, in the darkness, and when she rose they looked up at her as if she was part of the miracle.

"Onofre," she cried. She pulled away from the cluster of women, away from the ring of candles which danced and snapped in the rising wind of night. What had become of Onofre?

Onofre, who in his quiet way had gazed at the wall, now stood waiting in the dark. He stood alone, confused, unsure, not understanding the strange messages of his blood. He had looked at the wall, but he had not prayed to see the image of Christ, he had prayed that Iliana would understand his dreams of the warm earth he worked daily. He had seen the men leave, taking away the exhausted children, the limp bodies of the boys and girls who moaned in their dreams as they were carted home. Chairs and blankets were brought for the women; they would pray all night. The men would return to work the following day.

The wind rose in the dark night, it moaned on the pines of the mountain, it cried as it swept around the church and snapped at the candle light, creating shadows on the church wall. The women huddled in prayer. Iliana stumbled in the dark, wondering why she had seen the image of pleasure on the wall and not the face of Christ. Was it the devil tempting her? Or had the image on the wall been the answer she sought?

"Onofre!" she cried in the dark. The cold wind made her shiver. She found the truck, but Onofre was not there. In the dark she crossed the road, drawn by the dark, purple scent of alfalfa. She ran across the field, stumbling forward, feeling the weakness in the pit of her stomach give way to an inner resolution she had to follow. "Onofre!" she cried, feeling as if she had awakened from a dream into another dream, but this dream was one she could live in and understand.

In the middle of the field she saw the image of the man, the man who stood in the dark holding the neck of a horse, the dapple horse of her dreams. Heart pounding she ran into the arms of Onofre. She felt his strong arms hold her, and she allowed herself to be held, to feel the strength of his body, his muscles hardened by work, his silence instilled by the mountains.

"I did not see the face of Christ," Iliana confessed.

"Nor I," Onofre said.

"What then?" Iliana asked.

"A dream," Onofre said, unsure of what she meant, sure of his answer.

"Have I done wrong by dreaming?" Iliana asked.

Onofre shook his head. "I remember the old people saying: Life is a dream...."

"And dreams are dreams," Iliana finished. "There is a meaning in my dreams, but I don't understand it. Do you understand your dreams, Onofre?"

"No," he smiled, the first time in a long time he had smiled at his young wife. Holding her in the dark in the middle of the field, the desire he felt was new, it was a desire rising from the trembling earth, through his legs into his thighs and sex and into the pounding of his heart.

"Sometimes at night I awaken and go to the open door," he said. "I look at the beauty of the night. I look at you lying so peaceful in the bed. You make soft sounds of contentment. I wish I could be the one who draws those sounds from you. Then you awaken, and I step into the shadows, so I won't frighten you. I watch as you go to the door to look at the garden. I know you have awakened from a beautiful dream because you are alive with beauty. At those times, you are all the beauty on earth."

"We need to share our dreams," Iliana said. Onofre nodded. They looked at each other and understood the secret of dreams was better shared.

"It is time to go home," Iliana said.

Yes, it was time to go home, to sleep, to unravel dreams. Arm in arm they walked across the field of alfalfa, walking together with much pleasure, stirring the purple blossoms of the night.

NOTES ON CONTRIBUTORS

RUDOLFO A. ANAYA was born in the llano of eastern New Mexico and grew up in Santa Rosa. His books include the New Mexican trilogy of novels—*Bless Me Ultima*, *Heart of Aztlan*, and *Tortuga*; *The Silence of the Llano*, a collection of short fiction; and *A Chicano in China* which documents his impressions during a 1984 tour through China. In 1987 he edited *Voces: An Anthology of Nuevo Mexicano Writers*, a Southwest best seller now published by the University of New Mexico Press; in 1984, with Simon Ortiz, he co-edited *Ceremony of Brotherhood*, a commemoration of the Pueblo Revolt. Rudy takes time from his writing to do editing because he is committed to celebrating the writers of his state and his region. "We have a wealth of talent in the Southwest," he says, "and a public eager to read us." He teaches creative writing at the University of New Mexico in Albuquerque where he is also editor of the *Blue Mesa Review*.

TERRY BOREN is a native New Mexican (as were her parents and grandparents) of debatable ethnicity and random, though determined, education. She has had publications in poetry and non-fiction, but after attending the Clarion Science Fiction Writers workshop in 1981, her talents have been directed toward science fiction. Her story, "Sliding Rock," was included in the anthology *A Very Large Array: New Mexico Science Fiction and Fantasy* published by the University of New Mexico Press. Of "Alba in Directed Light," she writes: "It explores healing in a world where disease is the rule, communication in a time when isolation is the rule, and New Mexico when the land has moved beyond the experience of itself." Though a lover of green chile, she is now tasting moose and seal for the first time in Fairbanks, Alaska, where she lives with her husband, Jim Ruppert, and her son, Spenser.

EDUARDO CHAVEZ is a native of Albuquerque who graduated from St. Michael College in Santa Fe. While in the USAF, he was a news reporter broadcasting first from AFN Orleans in France, then from SMN Torrejon in Spain where he met his wife. They have three children. He currently works for the Social Security Administration. His fiction has been anthologized in *Voces: An Anthology of Nuevo Mexicano Writers* and in *Atole Azul*, and he is a published poet. He is presently two-thirds of the way through a trilogy which deals with New Mexico culture, land grants, and history.

MAX EVANS (1924) was born in Ropes, Texas, and went to work on a ranch south of Santa Fe just before his 12th birthday. Soon he owned his own ranch in Union County, New Mexico. After serving with the combat infantry in France and Germany during World War II, he moved to Taos to pursue a career as a professional artist. Just when his art career had become very successful, he decided writing was what he really wanted to do. His novels include *The Rounders* (which was produced as a movie starring Henry Fonda and Glenn Ford), *The Hi*

Lo Country; *Super Bull*; *Bobby Jack Smith, You Dirty Coward*; and *Xavier's Folly*. He also acted and performed stunts in, as well as writing a book about, *The Ballad of Cable Hogue*, a film directed by Sam Peckinpah. He was the recent recipient of the Western Writers of America Golden Spur Award for the best short fiction of 1988, *The Orange County Cowboys*.

NANCY GAGE (1947) was born in Kansas, but lived in Colorado and Utah until she came to Grants, New Mexico, at the age of seven. Her father was a geologist, and his work in looking for uranium took his family all around the Four Corners area. In 1958, they settled in Ambrosia Lake 25 miles north of Grants where her parents opened up a cafe/gas station. She moved to Albuquerque in 1966 to attend the University of New Mexico. Her plays have been produced in Albuquerque by the Vortex Theatre and the Second Story Arts Center; by the Actors Theatre of Louisville, Kentucky; and in New York City by the Thirteenth Street Theater. Her short fiction has appeared in *StoryQuarterly* and *Cosmopolitan*. "Death Row Wedding" will be published in *New Mexico Plays* to be published by UNM Press.

ROBERT GRANAT was born in Havana, Cuba, graduated from Yale, is married, and has six kids. He spent 38 years of subsistence living and farming in the villages of Northern New Mexico and moved to Las Cruces in 1988. He has had two novels published, *The Important Thing* and *Regenesis*. Chapters from a new, as yet unpublished book, have been published in *Parabola*, *New Realities*, *Tributaries*, *The Roll*, and *Studia Mystica*. His stories have appeared in *New Mexico Quarterly*, *Story*, *New American Review*, and *Short Story International*. "My Apples," the oldest story in this collection, won the O'Henry Award in 1956; and it has been translated for publication in the Netherlands, Italy, and Argentina.

DRUMMOND HADLEY (1938) was born in Missouri. He received a B.A. and M.A. from the University of Arizona in Tucson. He studied with the Black Mountain Poets in 1963 in Vancouver, B.C., and in 1964 in Berkeley. He is the author of three books of poetry: *The Webbing*, *Strands of Rawhide*, and *The Spirit by the Deep Well Tank*. He has worked as a cowboy on ranches in Arizona, New Mexico, and Old Mexico; and he now ranches near the Mexican border with his lady "Slim" on a commercial cattle ranch which he has owned and operated since 1972.

TONY HILLERMAN (1925) was born in Sacred Heart, Oklahoma—a village which grew around schools established by the Benedictines and Sisters of Mercy to educate Potawatomie Indians. His father ran the crossroads general store and a farm. Hillerman got his grade school education attending St. Mary's Academy, a boarding school for Indian girls. He writes that it "was a great place for a farm boy to learn how it felt to be a minority problem. I was twice lacking—being neither a Potawatomie nor a girl." United Press made him its New Mexico news manager in 1952; he later became editor for *The New Mexican* in Santa Fe. "In Santa Fe," he says, "Navajos, Apaches, and Pueblo Indians were all around. Indians had been my childhood friends. I made friends again and I wanted to write about them." He is best known for his mystery novels involving Navajo Tribal police—books which have won him the Edgar Allen Poe award of the Mystery Writers of America, *Le Gran Prix de Litterature Policiere* in France, and a unique "Friend of the Navajos" award from the Navajo Tribe.

DEBRA HUGHES-BLANKS is a native of New Mexico and lives in Corrales with her two sons and husband. She teaches "A Writer's Workshop," a creative writing program for adults now in its fourth year. She has been a correspondent for *USA Today* and staff writer for *The Albuquerque Tribune*. Her essays and articles have appeared in national publications. Her book in progress is a collection of short stories entitled *Liquid Silver* in which "Edna's Pie Town" appears.

TIM MACCURDY is the pen name of Raymond R. MacCurdy, a professor emeritus of Spanish at the University of New Mexico. Born in Oklahoma, he grew up in San Antonio, where he acquired an abiding affection for Hispanic culture, cuisine, and people. During World War II he served as an intelligence officer in India and China. After receiving his Ph.D. in Romance Languages from the University of North Carolina, he joined in 1949 the faculty of the University of New Mexico. In 1980, a year before his retirement, he began writing fiction. "The Day It Rained Blood" was his first published short story. He is the author of an historical novel, *Caesar of Santa Fe*, which has not yet been published.

ROBERT MASTERSON has lived in New Mexico since childhood with occasional residency in Colorado, Florida, and the People's Republic of China. His work has appeared in *La Confluencia*, *Conceptions Southwest*, *Century*, and *Tyounyi*. He works at the University of New Mexico and is the managing editor of *American Literary Realism*, *American Poetry*, *Shakespeare Studies*, and *Blue Mesa Review*.

KEVIN McILVOY lives in Las Cruces, New Mexico, with his wife Margee and sons, Paddy and Colin. He teaches writing at New Mexico State University where he is editor of *Puerto Del Sol* magazine. His novel, *The Fifth Station*, was published by Algonquin Books of Chapel Hill; Collier Books will publish the paperback in 1989. "The Complete History of New Mexico," which received the 1987 Indiana Review Fiction Prize, is the title story from a collection of New Mexico stories.

GABRIEL MELÉNDEZ is a native of Northern New Mexico. He is a writer, scholar, and teacher. He has published articles on Chicano literature and culture and on the contemporary Mexican novel. His work, he writes, "issues from a concern for restoring the sense of place and originality of Indo-hispano culture and values in the Southwest." His poetry and fiction have appeared in *Writers' Forum*, *Palabra Nueva*, *Voces: An Anthology of Nuevo Mexicano Writers*, and other anthologies. He is currently engaged in an ongoing oral history project on New Mexico and is preparing a manuscript of short fiction for publication. He lives and teaches in the Bay Area.

JOHN NICHOLS (1940) was born in Berkeley, California. He lived all over the United States growing up; but in 1969 he moved to Taos, New Mexico, where he has lived, in the same house, ever since. His novels include *The Sterile Cuckoo* (1965), *The Wizard of Loneliness* (1966), *The Milagro Beanfield War* (1974), *The Magic Journey* (1978), *The Nirvana Blues* (1981), and *American Blood* (1987). His non-fiction work includes *If Mountains Die (1979)*, *The Last Beautiful Days of Autumn* (1982), *On the Mesa* (1986), and *A Fragile Beauty* (1987). Since 1980 he has also worked on a number of screen projects, two of which were actually produced: *Missing*, directed by Costa-Gavras, and *The Milagro Beanfield War*, directed by Robert Redford.

SIMON J. ORTIZ is from Acoma Pueblo. He is the author of numerous books of poetry and stories among which are *Going for the Rain*, *A Good Journey*, *Howbah Indians*, *The People Shall Continue*, *Fight Back*, *From Sand Creek*, and *Fightin'*. He co-edited *Ceremony of Brotherhood* and *Califa*, and he was a newspaper editor of *Americans Before Columbus* and *Rough Rock News*. When asked in an interview why he writes, he replied: "Because Indians always tell a story.…Your children will not survive unless you tell something about them—how they were born, how they came to this certain place, how they continued."

JIM SAGEL was born and raised in northern Colorado. He came to New Mexico in 1969, marrying native Españolan Teresa Archuleta and settling into the river valley where he has been ever since. He taught himself Spanish and began writing bilingual poetry. His poetry collections include: *Hablando de Brujas (y la gente de antes)*, *Foreplay and French Fries*, *Small Bones/Little Eyes*, and *Los Cumpleaños de doña Agueda*. His first book of short stories in Spanish, *Tunomás Honey*, won the 1981 Premio Casa de las Américas in Havana, Cuba. His most recent collection of stories is *Sabelotod Entiendelonada* from Bilingual Press. He has recently completed a bilingual play based on "Doña Refugio and her Comadre" which appears here.

GUSTAVO SAINZ was born in Mexico. He served for ten years as professor and chairman at the Department of Journalism and Communication Sciences, Autonomous National University of Mexico. He has taught at the University of Texas, San Antonio, and the University of Wisconsin in Madison. He is now teaching at the University of New Mexico in Albuquerque. He has received grants from a number of foundations, including Ford, Guggenheim, Tinker, and the Center for Inter-American Relations. Among his works are: *La princesa del palacio de hierro*, for which he won the Premio Xavier Villaurrutia; *Gazapo*; *Obsesivos días circulares*; *Compadre Lobo*; *Fantasmas aztecas*; *Paseo en Trapecio*; and *A la salud de La Serpiente*.

RUBEN SALAZ-MARQUEZ is an author, teacher, and inventor who was born and raised in New Mexico. His writings reflect his bilingual and multicultural traditions which, he says, are "genuine New Mexican gifts." His favorite work is his trilogy *I am Tecumseh!*, but he has written essays for *USA Today*, dramas including *Embassy Hostage* produced in Albuquerque, and popular history like *Cosmic: the La Raza Sketchbook*. "Uncle Mike" is from his short story collection *Heartland: Stories of the Southwest.*

LISA SANDLIN came to live in Santa Fe after her graduation from Rice University in Houston in 1974, but her great grandparents had come to New Mexico much earlier, around 1912, in a mule-drawn wagon. In Santa Fe she studied Spanish dance with the wonderful teachers there. "Flamenco," she writes, "is rooted both in discipline and abandon; it is an astonishing art form, full of life's sorrow and grace. The source of each dance is a distinct rhythm which may not be transgressed, but within this rhythm infinite variation is possible." The story "Crease" evolved from her fascination with the point at which student becomes dancer, when the years of technique find expression. Her story "Crease" was awarded first in *Emrys Journal's* 1988 Fiction Competition, and the Jeanne Charpiot Goodheart Prize, 1989, for Best of Issue in *Shenandoah*. She is now at work on a novel, *Jimmy's Eye*, set in New Mexico.

MARC SIMMONS is a professional historian who rarely writes fiction. His writing, lectures, and research focus on the Indian and Hispanic heritages of New Mexico. He has taught at UNM, at St. John's College, and at Colorado College. He is a member of the Western Writers of America and the Author's Guild, and he is currently president of the Santa Fe Trail Association. His writings include more than one hundred articles in scholarly and popular journals; a weekly history column appearing in several New Mexico newspapers and the *El Paso Times*; and contributions to the *Encyclopedia Americana*, the Smithsonian Institute's *Handbook of North American Indians*, and the National Geographic Society's volume *Trails West*. His book *Albuquerque*, A *Narrative History* received the Golden Spur Award by the Western Writers of America for the best non-fiction book on the West, 1983; and *Murder on the Santa Fe Trail* received the 1986 C.L. Sonnichsen Book Award.

PATRICIA CLARK SMITH grew up in Maine. She received her Ph.D. from Yale University and taught at Luther College in Decorah, Iowa, before moving further west. In 1971 she moved to Albuquerque with her two sons, Joshua and Caleb, where she teaches literature and creative writing at the University of New Mexico. Her book of poems, *Talking to the Land*, was published by Blue Moon Press, and her poems have appeared in various magazines and anthologies including *Blue Moon News*, *South Dakota Review*, *La Confluencia*, *Voices from the Rio Grande*, and *Southwest: A Contemporary Anthology*.

MICHAEL THOMAS (1946) was born in Raton, New Mexico. "As I grew up," he says, "the railroad declined and everything in the state seemed to go military." His family moved to Alamogordo where he was surrounded by the many voices of New Mexico and "the bizarre culture of a post-WWII rocket-town." He followed his fascination with the profusion/confusion of cultures into the study of anthropology at UNM and the University of Washington where he received his Ph.D. He now teaches at UNM where he directs a culture study program in Michoacan, Mexico. His novel, *Crosswinds*, is a funny, sometimes painful, look at cultural tensions in southeastern New Mexico. "The Swing" is taken from *Mexico Makes Americans Fall Down*, a work in progress.

JIM THORPE (1953) was born in southern California, but grew up from an early age in Santa Fe, where his family runs a well known resort hotel north of that city. He has worked in various capacities at his family's resort, including nearly ten years as wrangler and trail-guide. He is married and has two children. Of his story in this anthology, he says: "For a couple of years we winter-pastured sixteen horses from the resort at a small place on the high broad plans east of the Sandias. It belonged to an old man and his wife. The old man was big—huge—and there was no doubting he ran the show. Going into the second year he got sick; a large growth appeared on his neck and it got to where he couldn't leave the house. It was a hard winter with a lot of snow, high winds and drifts. Besides taking care of him, the old woman had been out there every day, beating a path through the drifts to check on the horses, carrying an axe along to chop through the ice in the watertanks. He passed away in the fall; she pastured our horses one more winter, then sold the place and moved into town. About a year or two later when I had the urge to write I thought of these folks. I thought I could give their kind of people, their kind of lives, a better conclusion than what they got."

SABINE R. ULIBARRÍ (1919) was born and raised in Tierra Amarilla, New Mexico. He received his B.A. and M.A. from the University of New Mexico and his Ph.D. from UCLA. He is the Chairman of the Department of Modern and Classical Languages at UNM, where he has been teaching since 1950. His collections of bilingual stories include *Tierra Amarilla*, *Cuentos de Nuevo Mexico*, *Le Fregua sin fuego*, *Mi abuela fumaba puros*, *Primeros encuentros*, and *El condor*. He received the New Mexico Governor's Award for Excellence and Achievement in Literature in 1987.

KEITH WILSON (1927) was born in Clovis, New Mexico. He graduated from the U.S. Naval Academy and the University of New Mexico. In 1987 he retired as Professor of Creative Writing from New Mexico State in Las Cruces, where he still resides with his wife Heloise. A poet and short story writer, he has received many honors and awards including a National Endowment Writing Fellowship (1974), a Senior Fulbright-Hays Fellowship (1974), a D.H. Lawrence Fellowship (1972), and the New Mexico Governor's Award for Excellence in the Arts (1988). His many books of poems include *Sketches for a New Mexico Hill Town*, *Graves Registry and Other Poems*, *Midwatch*, *While Dancing Feet Shatter the Earth*, and *Lion's Gate, Selected Poems 1963-88*. His poems have been translated into Spanish, Polish, Japanese, Romanian, Hungarian, German, and Indonesian.

(Acknowledgements continued)

"Doña Refugio and Her Comadres" by Jim Sagel was originally printed in his collection *Sabelotodo Entiendelonada and Other Stories*. Copyright © 1988 by Bilingual Press/Editorial Bilingüe, Arizona State University, Tempe, AZ, and is reprinted with their permission.

"Paisaje de Fogon" by Gustavo Sainz. Copyright © 1989 by Gustavo Sainz and is printed with his permission.

"Uncle Mike" by Rubén Salaz-Marquez was originally published in *Southland, Stories of the Southwest* from Blue Feather Press in 1978. Copyright © 1978 by Rubén Marquez-Salaz and is printed with his permission.

"Crease" by Lisa Sandlin appeared in *Shenandoah, the Washington and Lee Review* (Volume 38, Number 4, 1988). Copyright © 1988 by Washington and Lee University and is reprinted with permission from the editor.

"The Deputy" by Marc Simmons was first published in *Far West Magazine*, October 1978. Copyright © 1978 by Marc Simmons and is reprinted with his permission.

"Mother Ditch" by Patricia Clark Smith. Copyright © 1989 by Patricia Clark Smith and is printed with her permission.

"The Swing" by Michael A. Thomas. Copyright © 1989 by Michael A. Thomas and is printed with his permission.

"How He Would Have Done It" by Jim Thorpe. Copyright © 1989 by Jim Thorpe and is printed with his permission.

"Witches or Tomfooleries?" by Sabine Ulibarrí appeared in his collection *My Grandmother Smoked Cigars* from Quinta Sol Publications in 1977. Copyright © 1971 by Sabine Ulibarrí and is reprinted with his permission.

"By Lantern Light" by Keith Wilson. Copyright © 1989 by Keith Wilson and is printed with his permission.

El Paso • Texas